ENDLESS SKY

An Island in the Universe Trilogy: Book 1

Greg Remy

ISBN: 0692986774
ISBN 13: 9780692986776
Library of Congress Control Number: 2017917932
Greg Remy, Albuquerque, NM

DEDICATION

To you.
Thank you.

TABLE OF CONTENTS

Chapter 1	Loomings	1
Chapter 2	A Proper Introduction	13
Chapter 3	The Aviatrix	16
Chapter 4	Smooth Seas and Soothsayers	24
Chapter 5	A Lesson on Quantum Entanglement	44
Chapter 6	To Infinity and Beyond	50
Chapter 7	Majora's Mask	60
Chapter 8	From Eggs to Onions	71
Chapter 9	Signs Point to a Mild, Yet Abrupt Spring	78
Chapter 10	Two Eyes, One Nose, and a Forked Tongue	86
Chapter 11	A Funny Thing Happened on the Way to Troy's Banner	88
Chapter 12	Some People Just Have Too Much Time on Their Hands	94
Chapter 13	The 13th Day	99
Chapter 14	A Bear on the Moon	103
Chapter 15	Cheers, My Friend!	108
Chapter 16	The Riotous Dr. Earl Saknussemm	116
Chapter 17	Manifest Discrepancy	121
Chapter 18	Doors	135
Chapter 19	Don't Expect Compliments from a Serpent	145
Chapter 20	The Witching Hour	148
Chapter 21	Good Thing No Little Ones Are Present	155

Chapter 22   Requiem for a Doctor   159
Chapter 23   The Fury and the Anthropos   162
Chapter 24   Let's Try That Again   170
Chapter 25   Kratos Snubbed   173
Chapter 26   The Storm of the Century   184
Chapter 27   Profundity at its Simplest   186
Chapter 28   Let History Make Its Own Judgments   196
Chapter 29   A Sparkler in Time   200
Chapter 30   Syzygy   207
Chapter 31   After All, We're Only Ordinary Humans   227
Chapter 32   An Absolute Resolution   235
Chapter 33   Who Watches the Watcher?   241
Chapter 34   Kappa Ignites   251
Chapter 35   Verve, Nerve, and Adventure   264
Chapter 36   A Somewhat Good Man Goes to War   272
Chapter 37   Out of the Frying Death Ray into the Sun   277
Chapter 38   I'm a Fan of the Doppler Effect   287
Chapter 39   Cold War   298
Chapter 40   Scuttle!   309
Chapter 41   To the End   315
Chapter 42   The Photon, the Glitch, and the Cosmos   319
Chapter 43   Blood from a Stone   330
Chapter 44   Divided   340
Chapter 45   The Only Real Prison is Fear   346
Chapter 46   The Torpor Torpedo   363
Chapter 47   Rise   373
Chapter 48   Interlude to a Showdown   379
Chapter 49   In the Thick of It   381
Chapter 50   The Watchers   385
Chapter 51   The Age of Enlightenment v2.0   393
Chapter 52   Endless Sky   397
Chapter 53   Epilogue: The Imperial Bower   399

About the Author   407

CHAPTER 1

LOOMINGS

She peered out the cockpit window; nothing in particular to be seen, but still on course. She threw her arms around the backside of the chair, stretched, and exhaled; her breath lightly fogging up the lower corner of the window.

"Humph," Zoe murmured to herself. Boredom had all but become her. She looked down at the control panel. With great accuracy, she speedily typed away on the touch screen, autonomously paging through folders and opening the music player she so often used.

"Turn music uuuup," she said to herself, cranking the projection dial near max. Music came blaring out from all around the tiny ship. She leaned back in her chair, relaxing and closed her eyes, feeling the beat thumping away at her innermost core.

The bantam craft rocketed on in the black yonder. Along the backdrop, millions of stars created paths along every vector, mimicking her directionless journey.

⊫+ +⊨

A beeping suddenly started, signifying an anomaly found by the gamut-tracking sensors. Zoe immediately bent down, looking at the screen. Typing away with flying fingers, she identified the source's location, about .75 floating-parsecs away portside and changed course to intercept.

At moderate speeds, it would take several hours to reach the source. Zoe set the ship to auto-pilot while busying herself with programming knick-knacks, however soon dozed off. Sometime later she awoke suddenly to a blaring countdown alarm and jerked her face up from the control panel. In a flash of thought she figured she had accidentally initiated the ship's self-destruct sequence. She quickly turned it off and yawned. Turning up her bass-infused music, she went back to coding once more.

Nearly an hour later, Zoe came in proximity of the location, signaled by a long tone from the ship's computer. She looked out and examined the empty environment through the cockpit window, shaped as an acute triangle coming down to a long point just below the horizontal.

"There!" She spotted a ship slightly off her port bow. Zoe stared at it for a few minutes, both herself and her craft silent. It was floating with a slight spin seeming abandoned and set adrift. "Odd," she thought. She corrected her course while initiating thermal scanners with agile finger movements. As the unprocessed numeric information came flooding back, in forms of compounding polynomial loops and infinitesimal tensor strings, she visually scanned the rapidly flickering pages, analyzing the raw data, and concluded the ship's engines were working. For whatever reason, the vessel was in a prolonged abeyance, aimlessly floating along. Moments later, the information collected by her ship's computer was compiled. On the main screen, results showed what she had already concluded: the interstellar drive, capable of speeds around .06 floating-parsecs/ year, was functioning normally and had been set in a recursive mode. Thermal scans had also determined the cabin was still pressurized but temperature levels neared 10 degrees Celsius.

Zoe visually inspected the derelict ship as she neared it. She recognized it as a transport vessel, smiling as she thought of how they were often called 'semis,' as a throwback to the days when transporting goods was accomplished by such vehicles. There it drifted among the stars. She slowly curved her ship around the floating vessel. It was several times the size of her ship, having a large cargo bay as its thorax surrounded on either side by over-sized engines; a vehicle plump with power and ungainly in gait. On its side it bore the logo of IQS Express, a common ship-building freight company. She promptly recalled their motto, used in every advertising campaign as far back as she could remember: "Neither snow, nor rain, nor supernova will stay us from swift completion."

As Zoe's ship moved to the semi's front, she peered into the head of the semi. All was dark in the cockpit, with no pilot to be seen, an abandoned carrier ship in outer-space. "Odd," she thought again. Zoe knew it was standard for the pilot's door of a semi to be on the starboard bow, which is, as she came about, exactly as she had expected to find it. "At least that's there" she said aloud.

Approaching the hatch with nimble maneuvers of her tiny craft, Zoe brought her ship next to the entryway, preparing to board the semi. She stabilized her position to be in unison with the drifting ship's trajectory. With her fingers on the virtual haptics keyboard and flipping unlabeled switches all around her, Zoe instructed her ship to extend its vacuum seal to connect the two ships' hatches.

The vacuum seal adit extended several meters to the opposing ship's hatch, suctioning around its edges, and establishing a concatenation for Zoe to delve into the unexplored mine. She leapt out of her captain's seat, grabbed a wrench, and opened her hatch. Though her ship had a faux gravitational field, it did not extend through to the vacuum seal and as Zoe left the confines of her ship, into the cylindrical connection, she became weightless. Pushing herself from her hatch, she gracefully and silently floated to the abandoned ship's entryway. During her approach, Zoe examined the hatch and upon reaching it, turned and kicked against it, flying weightlessly back to her ship.

She came back momentarily with a grin on her face and a larger wrench in hand. She had noticed the metallic locking mechanism was not standard; it was larger than she had anticipated. Resting the lower jaw of the wrench's mouth under the rounded handle and with her feet on the semi's hatch, she gripped the lock and forced it upwards. As it stiffened, she quickly twisted left in a precise manner and the lock popped off. It floated away, and Zoe scrambled to open the hatch.

Upon easing through the half-opened door, her leading leg became weighted once more and Zoe tripped over herself. She grumbled and stood up. The gravitational field was obviously still present within the semi. She jumped to test its might; it felt slightly less than the standardized Earth-1. Zoe began to shiver as the frigid air began working its way through her skin; it sure felt colder than 10 degrees. Looking around, she could see little through the darkness, but definitely did not perceive any signs of life. She reached in her shirt and produced a small, flat, rectangular card. Upon touching one side of it, the screen turned on and with a few finger gestures, the device came alive. A bright light shone in a singular direction from its top edge. She stuck the lightcard to her wrist. Holding her arm out, she illuminated her surroundings and continued on, quickly passing through the semi's small vestibule, noticing it still contained all its hung jump-suits, and exiting through its only doorway, arriving at the cockpit. She shined her light over the dashboard but touched nothing. It seemed the ship's computer was hibernating though still active, hence the gravitational stabilizers, air pumps and thrusters continuing to be online.

Zoe moved past the cockpit to the cabin in the back. Nothing abnormal was seen, just the usual space trucker's untidy living quarters containing a bed, commissary, and bathroom. She backed up and went through the cockpit's left doorway, opening it up to a corridor. Leaking mechanical lines salivated along the hallway's ceiling while tarnished metal walls gorged on what little light there was, rejecting all external radiance from lack of portholes. Halfway down was a hatchway, undoubtedly leading to the cargo bay. Zoe could see a second hatch, at the far end, to which she surmised must be to the engine room.

Coming up to the cargo bay hatch, she stopped and examined it with her light. The metallic door was without a handle or window, though at its center was a small touch-screen, inferring an electronic lock. She leaned her shoulder on the door and tested it with her weight, but it remained secure. "Humph," she mumbled and continued on.

The engine room's hatch was open, and she could feel warm air flowing out from it. Crossing the hatchway, she entered into a cramped room of wires and piping, all chaotically hung about, as if it were a maze for unsuspecting fuel and additives to navigate and be thusly rewarded for completion by annihilation to near pure energy.

Narrow walkways led around various ancillary components strung up by the very cables utilizing them, half of which lacked thermal and electrical insulation. She walked around evaluating the engine; various upgrades could be seen, but ineptly installed and obviously of second hand parts from speeder vessels. It seemed the engine was hacked for extra speed, though these enhancements would undoubtedly not be authorized by any transport agency. To her pleasure, as she continued further into the engine room the warmer it became.

Her wrist rounded a corner, guiding her steps, when suddenly a scream was heard. Zoe jumped back and tripped once again over herself, landing on the unforgiving metallic floor. She quickly stood up and went into a combat stance, mentally trying to locate her wrench but realizing she had left it on the ground where she had first fallen. A man scrambled around the corner in the opposite direction she had come so close to pass. He looked as shocked as her and put both hands up.

His initial scared expression soon began to dissipate. It was evident he now was making new assumptions about the stranger in his vessel. Zoe stood, with fists raised ready for battle; though she knew her presence was limited, as she was in good shape being in her 20s, though of small stature. Through the diffuse illumination, reflected from the ceiling by the light she wore on her wrist, she could see him first fixate for a moment on her hair, jet-black with hues of blue in it, and move downwards, pausing again with the smidge of a smirk at her half-shirt, emblazoned with her favorite comic character and his accompanying catchphrase, "Bazzinga!" Again, his eyes tended downwards, to her black shorts and then to her pale legs, doubtlessly catching the glare of the light, and finally grounding at her cobalt sneakers.

"I am Zoe," she said emphatically, with fists still raised.

"Ahem." The man cleared his throat and gutturally responded. "I am Captain Henry, pilot for this heap-of-rubbish."

Though staying mentally combat ready, she lowered her fists and shined her lightcard on the Captain. He covered his eyes with his hand as the bright light passed over his face. He was perhaps in his early 40s, with an unkempt beard, unkempt flannel shirt dyed in oil stains, and exceedingly unkempt overall. She surmised her evaluation that this hermit-looking man was probably as he said he was, the captain of this ship.

"Unkempt," She muttered to herself.

"Pardon?" He asked.

"Captain Henry," she started, ignoring his question, "why are you flying in such a nonlinear trajectory? Surely you have shipments to be delivered, things to do, people to see?"

"Aye," replied the captain throatily. "Do ya mind lowering the light Miss Zoe?"

"Oh! Sorry." She quickly lowered her wrist light to the floor; the diffuse light now barely allowed each to perceive the other.

"Follow me," he said and stepped past her, leaving the engine room. Zoe caught a whiff of a long unwashed man. She followed him as he slowly walked through the hallway. He began, "I have been sleeping in the engine room. The heat there keeps me warm; confound this ship!" He stopped and kicked the wall. Zoe smirked, how often she had done the same on her ship. He was a captain indeed. He continued walking, with Zoe following close behind using her light to illuminate their way.

"You see, about three weeks ago I was struck by a damn meteorite, two in fact! Let me show ya." They entered the cockpit and he pointed in the direction of the ship's port beam from the main window. Zoe pressed her face against it to get the best possible view of the portside hull. "Right above the external LOX tank," he said.

"Ah! Wow." Zoe spotted it; she hadn't noticed the damage during the initial overpass of her vessel. Directly above the main oxidizer chamber, two small identically circular perforations could be seen, creating burnt holes straight through the thruster's supply line. From the charred dust around the impact site Zoe gathered they were high velocity impacts.

"Took out my primary fuel lines, now all I can do is hobble in reverse. Heh. I tried some repairs, but I don't have the tooling for this. So here I remain, adrift. I set all systems to hibernate to conserve energy." As he leaned back to sit in the captain's chair, Zoe could see the ungainly shape of his body fitting perfectly into its grooves. He huffed and crossed his arms tightly across his chest. "I have sent out a Smart Beacon to go fetch some help." Zoe coolly leaned against his computer dashboard as he continued, "by the time I saw those rocks coming towards me it was too late."

Zoe interrupted further dialog from the captain. "But why didn't your proximity sensors go off?"

"I do not know. They seem to be performing normally, as with all other systems on this ship, except for my engine...," he trailed off with aggravation in his voice.

Zoe cleared her throat and put on her serious facade. "Redundant systems are required on all transport vessels and if there was a technical glitch, your diagnostic aid, located here," she pointed with a svelte finger above the captain toward a black hexahedron module, "would have identified the problem." Zoe was suspecting the captain was leaving certain details out.

"True. Ah, this ship." He paused, evidently reminiscing the annoyances associated with his vessel, though, through a slight positive curl of the lip, a certain pride shined through, doubtless from the powerful feeling of respect towards it. Zoe was all too familiar with this paradoxical emotion. "And truth be told, I am one lucky bastard; they lit up the side of my ship like the surface of Eta Carinae. I'm thinking they contained magnesium. If they had hit here I'd still be smoldering." He half smirked and then solemnly added, "probably dead." The captain cleared his throat a few times and relaxed, sinking deeper in his seat.

Zoe slowly inhaled, evaluating all she had heard and witnessed: she had never seen such strange meteor impacts; the speed modifications to the engine; and all the other oddities associated with this transport vessel. The compilation of these mysteries gave the situation a vague aspect and she did not like the feeling. Zoe exhaled.

"Okay Captain Henry, just what do you have stowed away here?"

The captain looked suddenly stunned and dissimulated, "ah the usual—Vanadium construction plates, and some other construction supplies."

"Uh-huh," Zoe retorted flatly. It was the captain's turn to take in a deep breath. He again looked her up and down and then stared out beyond the cockpit. She knew, based on the apparent verisimilitude of her rebellious persona and the silent sanctity of outer-space, he would see little danger in telling her. She leaned in to hear the truth.

"I'm transporting space moonshine." He turned and closely scrutinized Zoe.

"Space moonshine? That's illegal in all quadrants of the galaxy, captain," she responded matter-of-factly. "And this isn't an IQS vessel, is it?" Henry shook his head no. "Hmmm." Zoe paused, then quickly straightened up and ran back to the engine room.

Once there, she began investigating conduits and cables, rapping on pipes with her knuckles and poking her head through interstices of engine parts to get better views of various components. The captain had followed her.

"What are you doing Miss Zoe?"

Not saying a word, she turned and brushed past him, rushing back to her ship, and returning with handfuls of mechanic's tools. She dropped them on the floor, keeping the largest of the bunch, an oversized, pneumatic hammer, firmly in her grip. Zoe darted around a corner, led by her lightcard, and began pounding away on the engine.

"What are you doing?!" the captain cried out.

"Head wrench please," she responded, holding out her hand from around the corner, the beam from her wrist illuminating the pile of tools at Captain Henry's feet.

Stunned, he unwittingly complied and handed her the wrench. More banging was heard; the captain never leaned around the corner, evidently afraid to see what damage the re-fractory girl was causing among his ship.

Zoe became a blur, moving with celerity around the captain in his engine room, removing various pipes, welding others, constantly running back to her ship and returning with more tools. The semi pilot stood helplessly watching, constantly asking if there was anything he could do. The best he received was a "hand me this" or "hold that."

During one of the return trips from her ship, Zoe had accessed the instrument panel in the semi's cockpit and began running programs synced from her ship. As she continued to tinker away in the engine room, an assortment lights and buzzing sounds came from his cockpit. Zoe had with her a small accompanying computer, which she constantly typed away on between clanging of the engine. After an hour of dashing around and ignoring the captain's many pleas to discontinue her assault on his ship, she stopped and declared, "All done!"

"What?!" exclaimed the captain, his wide eyes communicating through them the unsurety of anything that happened within the last hour. Zoe smiled. He looked as if he should lay down and reawaken later, recounting all this as a wild dream.

"I have rerouted all aft-thruster major and minor systems, allowing you full control of forward flight." She smiled and brought up her side computer. With a flick of her wrist and a few finger gestures she remotely turned on all the lights in the semi. "Though it may not fly as fast as it once had, it should get you to a close port, no problem!" Zoe slowly stretched out her entire body, creating a wave of crackling joints from toes to neck. "Just make sure to get a new lock on your outer hatch, your current one seems to be... malfunctioning."

She piled her work tools together and began walking back to her ship with both hands full. The captain did likewise, following her with the remaining tools, still with the look of astonishment upon him. She could read his expression: This small woman, this lone space girl, had just claimed to have fixed his transport vessel. Upon entering her ship, Captain Henry dropped the tools where she pointed and hastened back to his vessel, returning momentarily with armfuls of moonshine jars.

"Miss Zoe, please accept this gift for fixing my ship."

Zoe had just finished putting away her tools and turned towards him. She looked down at his arms holding the illegal alcohol and smiled. "It would be my honor Captain Henry."

The two exchanged their goodbyes. Zoe retracted the vacuum seal and both vessels set off in opposite directions. While Zoe was resetting her course, as before meeting the bootleg captain of the stars, she examined her main screen to see what her ship's progressive scanners had found of the two impacts sites on the semi. Shapes and potential velocities were computed, revealing the damage was generated by two small cylindrical-like objects of great speed. The twin meteors had penetrated entirely through the semi and left in their wake near-perfect circular wounds. Simulations determined the objects each measured just under a meter in both height and diameter and each had retained its exact dimensions during the entire encounter. She had never seen such a phenomenon before, thus knowing all she could for now, archived away the information.

⚔

Zoe set sail, her ship throttled to maximum, the thrusters burning bright and becoming one with the stars. She settled in her captain's chair, in much the same way the semi captain had in his and all captains in their respective chairs—that singular comfort in the entirety of the infinite void, among the nameless and uncharted, containing countless mysticisms and mysteries, in which humankind was apt to contemplate the beyond. These contemplations drove the captains of old Earth-1 to circumnavigate the waters of the world until it unhanded every mystery and wheezed out every last adventure, and so once more they had embarked, taking to the skies to fulfill that deepest desire on which they sailed.

CHAPTER 2

A PROPER INTRODUCTION

W elcome to the Milky Way Galaxy—an expanse stretching over 35,000 floating-parsecs, comprised of a Spiral-Bc galaxy, containing within its galactic disk more than 730 billion nebulas, stars, planets, exo-planets, and home to the Homo-sapian-neosapian species. Congruent to Earth-1 time, the year is currently 4243 and had you been standing on its northern hemisphere, you would have found yourself in the warmth of May. Though now long abandoned, the original home of mankind has been left as a shrine, with a single museum on its lone, lonely moon.

It has been approximately 2,000 years since the human race successfully took to the stars, colonizing first the nearest hospitable systems, and soon dappling all four quadrants of the Milky Way. Each newly discovered lush environment notching away at the memory of Earth-1, replacing in its stead, the planets, moons, and space habitations providing greater extravagances and marvels than anything it could have provided.

As an effect of these new fertile romping grounds, the human race has begun to evolve with the peculiarities of each uniquely inhabited locale. Take for example, the elongated and quaint peoples of the Vardo System, living on its two largest planets and many retrograde moons. Their tall stature, defined after generations of living within the region, has been attributed to the light compositions of their spherical worlds. Even their central star contains more helium than usual. Or, consider the ever-angry citizens of the planet Urghag, revolving around their equally scornful red sun of Cantank.

Voyages and trade between planets and systems are common and as such, disputes do arise. Though these conflicts are not common, they are the one perpetual part of humans which will never be ameliorated by evolutionary means. Ergo, diplomacy is prevalent throughout the galaxy, allowing open commerce and travel for any and all. Space-liner vessels brilliantly zip from sector to sector and upon the whole, humanity has whittled out its beloved but forgotten Earth-1 from the nothingness of space.

To travel amongst the stars, to awaken under the warmth of Sirius, to eat lunch under the moons of Jupiter, and finally, to rest among the nebulas of Orion, requires transportation capable of superluminal flight, and it is so. Though the fastest of these crafts are often massive and generally utilized by the galactic peace-keeping Copper Force, some are of smaller sizes, expensive indeed, and generally reserved for dignitaries throughout the galaxy.

Zoe's small craft was not of this status, yet among ships of its single-manned, lightweight-interstellar class, it was the most innovative, and in particular, the fastest. Directly after purchase from a junk lot, the dilapidated vessel was completely gutted and pieced, by Zoe herself. It was then reassembled, once more exclusively by Zoe, into a craft capable of speeds nearing .511 floating-parsecs per hour, as achieved solely by her. During that daring test flight, she had nearly decorticated the ship's exterior from its own framework and vibrated all but the 'Terminate' button from her cockpit dashboard. It was in those final moments of existence when Zoe mightily threw her hand down upon it, engaged the automated shut-off, and saved both her craft and herself from certain doom.

It was Zoe's masterpiece, hers to fly through the stars, to outrun every supernova blast, to scrutinize every dark corner of every moon, and to sail amongst the radioactive and the ultra-heated. Everything, from the ship's onboard scanners to its hybrid landing roller-pad, had been fabricated and installed by Zoe. The ship housed little: a central chamber containing storage compartments within every capable space, a cramped cockpit for one, narrow sleeping quarters—though rarely used as Zoe preferred the cockpit, a meager lavatory and a commissary containing less than minimal necessities. This was all more than enough to suit her needs. It contained no cooking equipment or large stores for water; as such, Zoe dined on self-warming nutrient packets and remained hydrated from the external filtering system, which autonomously collected water from space dust as she flew. The ship's inner hull was composed of a deep-space rated titanium alloy. The outer was of a single piece, cast from a special plasma-poured mixture which Zoe had concocted herself. The ship gleamed effervescently, a star by its own might, a comet of its own course. It was hers, to dream in at every waking moment of the unknown just beyond sight.

CHAPTER 3
THE AVIATRIX

Three soft tones awakened Zoe. She lazily stretched while yawning and looked down at her control panel. She pulled up the ship's monitoring and diagnostic systems; not even the slightest abnormality to be found onboard or anywhere within the region. Zoe yawned once more and rubbed her eyes. She laid back in her captain's chair, staring out of the fused silica window; the same scene seen for weeks now. The emptiness of space antithetically felt confining.

"Screw this," said Zoe aloud and leapt out of her chair.

She made her way to the ship's central chamber and began rummaging through drawers, tossing tools and equipment over her shoulders until she found what she was looking for.

"Ah, bingo!" she happily exclaimed.

Zoe held up a jar of moonshine as if it was holy in essence, reflecting the effulgence of the heavens above, though in her case, from the recessed plasma lighting overhead. She unscrewed the cap and sniffed the alcohol; her body shuddered from the overwhelming vapors.

Next, she pulled out a handheld, cylindrical device with a glass door on its top and dials along its side. Zoe headed back to the cockpit and loaded the complimentary program. She then fastidiously trickled a few drops from the jar into the toroidal spectral analyzer and closed its lid. After a moment of whirring around, the results were displayed on the projection screen. Zoe smiled; the composition was perfect.

Zoe headed back to the central chamber and continued rummaging through more compartments. A short while later, buried underneath a hodgepodge of components, she emerged like a beast from the swamp, grasping a stannic riveter, sonic welder, and scraps of electronics, with rolls of wires wrapped around her. She climbed out and crawled above the metallic mire towards the cockpit. Thanks to much experience traversing such homebrewed environments, she shortly reached the cabin and laid down the materials, soon after rigging up something new with the grin of a mad scientist on her face.

As witnessed by the ever-silent and ever-watchful eye of space, blinding lights shot out from the cockpit window at random intervals while the small craft sporadically tilted and swayed. Inside, Zoe was tinkering away, opening up control panels to link thick gauge wires, welding components, tweaking program routines, and every so often taking a swig of moonshine. She had on her favorite welding goggles, her hair was tied back, and she remained for hours deeply involved in her work.

Finally, with a short, accomplished huff and a long sigh, she drooped to the ground and draped her body across the mounds of components and equipment. She relaxed there for a few minutes and then stood up, once more approving of her work, excited and ready to begin the experiment. Zoe took her station at the helm and prompted several programs.

"Pchh. Prepped for launch. Over.

You are cleared for launch V'Ger 6.

Engaging clearance sequence. Confirm go.

Go confirmed. Ten. Nine. Eight. Seven. Six." Zoe typed a command on her virtual keyboard. "Five. Four. Three." The dashboard lit up from the initial program autonomously sequencing the oncoming protocols. "Two. One." Her ship grumbled and shook for a moment. "Pchh. We have liftoff."

Zoe clambered out of her chair and peered through the cockpit window. Below, a hatch had opened out into the void of space and a metallic hexahedron propelled out, via a gaseous jet, and stopped several meters in front of her ship, tethered by long electric cords. Zoe leaned over her control panel and typed in further commands. Two ingresses on opposite, horizontal sides of the box began to slowly open, marked by escaping greenish smoke. Then, upon the termination of this movement, a tube laggardly extended out from each opening. Zoe watched with great anticipation. Each tube reached its maximum length and then split apart, blossoming into a parabolic dish, and pointing away from one another. Zoe looked over at the empty jar on the dashboard, feeling slight remorse and then regarded the experimental cube in space, filled with that nose-painting liquid and amalgamated with the innards of a sonic welder. *I do hope this works*, she thought.

Floating in vacuity, the module began emitting ethanol-based electromagnetic resonances from each dish, transmitting invisible radiation through space. Data streamed across Zoe's main screen to which she rubbed her hands together. "Good. Good." She let loose a maniacal laugh and then smiled, amused by her own antics. She checked over the running programs. Satisfied, Zoe initiated a subroutine and stared out. The box began to vibrate as the power input increased, continuing to do so for a minute and soon easing as the flow stabilized. She leaned forward in anticipation, arched over the control console, and then started the second subroutine.

Lights throughout her ship flickered and the module outside shook once more from the enormous amount of power surging into it from her craft. Her virtual monitors suddenly became flooded with information deluging from the module. Zoe scanned over the data and noted the synchronous effects of the two emanations, nodding in approval. *The next phase may yet prove a taaad more difficult.*

Zoe took in a deep breath. Holding the oxygen in her lungs, she entered in the third subroutine and tightly pressed a cupped hand over her mouth and nose. The accustomed lighting in the ship was suddenly snuffed out and replaced by red flashing lights and emergency horns. Zoe could feel the air suddenly get very cold and the air pressure reduce. Outside, she could still see the module, which was vibrating spasmodically but maintaining its construction. As it began to successfully intake the dynamism put forth into it, to which it was then outputting through the dishes, all systems inside Zoe's ship ere long returned to normal. The recessed lights returned, and Zoe took in several luxurious breaths. The module outside seemed calm now and completely rigid in space as if tied taught by the fabric of the universe.

Zoe stared with veneration. Emanating from either dish, in so singly a path, a mesmerizing, thin, azure line, extended out as far as she could see in either direction. She slapped the console with the good nature of achievement and began evaluating the flow of data.

With a crack of her knuckles, she initiated the fourth subroutine and began following the computer with quick finger movements. The beams from the dishes began to pulse. Zoe was busy typing away, ever so slightly tuning the parameters of the device. As resonance nodes became higher, the visible pulses increased in intensity; diffuse white and light blues hues oscillated through space with perfect sine curves.

A doubled tone announced the beams had reached their predetermined lengths in space, each nearly a hundred million kilometers long. Zoe initiated the feedback loop. The ship's computer was working hard, continuously calibrating the pulsed beacons with the aid of Zoe's hand whilst compiling information and delivering the infinitesimal analyses. Zoe was in the zone, sitting comfortably in her seat while modifying a dozen programs at once. Her eyes remained fixed to the screen, save for a few moments to ensure there was no catastrophic malfunction of the floating box.

With third or fourth finger movements of each keystroke, she was preparing the next and last stage of the experiment. *Well, there's no time like the present. Either this will be epic… or maybe it will fizzle.* Zoe took in a deep breath and pressed the Enter button on her projection keyboard, initiating the final subroutine. She sat completely stationary in anticipation, staring at the module. Nothing happened. She furled her eyebrows and hit the enter key again. This time, massive shocks instantly reverberated throughout the ship, nearly tossing her from her seat. She was quick to regain her balance and looked out at the module and then down at her computer display. The wild steed soon abated, and she loosened the grip on her arm rests. Immense pulsing beams of cerise and white were spewing forth from either side of experimental box. The entire module was glowing a dull red. With each second, the beams enlarged, soon matching the diameter of her ship. Lights within her spaceship flickered sporadically from the growing feedback of energy. Zoe worked fervently to adjust the input signal's resonance in order to reduce attenuation from unwanted frequencies that kept cropping up. Suddenly, three blue markers appeared on her display. She opened her mouth in near unbelief for a second and looked out to the module.

"It worked," she whispered in awe. Zoe stood from her seat and watched with amazement.

The light emanating from the two dishes were becoming homogeneous, like two long cylinders of light. Zoe knew what was happening. Along each's axis, at the atomic-level, particles flowing through the beams were being rearranged, flowing in a compounding resonance sequence. Despite the zettajoules of pure deadly energy being shot out just a few meters from her, it was quite a beautiful sight. Next, as hypothesized, the two beams of opposing polarities began to curve upwards, slowly becoming to a single loop, by much the same way cathode rays bend under the influence of applied voltage. Zoe watched as the two massive plasma beams slowly arced upwards and toward each other on a truly fantastic scale. The loop had not yet completed, but it was evident the diameter would be of solar system-scale.

Suddenly, red lights flashed all over her display and sirens blared throughout the ship. Zoe sprang into action, instantly in her seat with hands poised above the virtual keyboard. The loosely interacting plasma jets were becoming unstable as each licked at the other with the energy of a hundred thousand nuclear weapons. The computer could not anticipate and compensate frequencies quick enough. A giant ark of wild blue energy split out from the loop and struck her ship. This time, Zoe was thrown from her seat. Just as quickly, she was up and typing into the console to steady the experiment. Despite her efforts, more arks ripped away wildly into space.

"Come on, come on."

She typed away furiously. Her concentration was broken by a large red square with bold red text suddenly overlaying her work. At this, Zoe leapt out of her chair and dove towards a circular control on the left side of the cockpit. Just before her outreached arm could slam the emergency stop button, one side of the experimental module exploded. Incalculable heat and energy erupted from it; the shockwave sent Zoe to the hatchway of the cockpit. The hard landing knocked her unconscious.

⊶⊷

All space in the vicinity had been instantly boiled by the energetic expulsion, leaving an enflamed fog from the microcosm of over-stimulated sub-particles throughout the entire region. Within the lone ship, discharges branched over the electronics and the internal power went out. Outside, as quickly as the cataclysmic event has begun, it passed, and the smoke began to wane as icy licks from the tongue of the macrocosm tasted and then proceeded to swallow all it could with insatiable entropic appetite.

⊶⊷

A single slow beeping started up. Zoe let out a cough as self-awareness slowly came back to her. She groaned and remained lying down. Slowly, she opened her eyes and winced as she propped herself up. She looked at her arm. It was already evident a large bruise was forming from elbow to wrist. Zoe groaned again and stood up with only the light of the reddened cosmos to guide her steps. She looked about; everything around the ship was in complete disarray, more so now than when starting the experiment. She slowly walked over to her chair and eased in it, letting her muscles go completely limp. With a languid arm, she reached up and flipped a switch, disabling the alarm. She then flipped several more switches to begin the ship's rebooting process. Zoe returned to her wilting position and stared out of the window. There was a dissipating red mist overhanging all she could see. Zoe watched it until it had nearly completely dissipated and only a few thin lines remained, though were rapidly drifting away. The dead, broken module was also slowly drifting away, taking with it, its own umbilical cord. Zoe sighed and decided to rest her eyes for the next several minutes while her ship auto-compiled its diagnostic efforts.

A soft beeping began several minutes later, signifying the internal scan was complete. Zoe stretched her neck, reviewed the results, and began the manual process of restoring the main controls. Soon after, the display was up and running and she was quietly reading through the massive report of ship errors. Included in in this list were scores of propulsion fuses which had been completely vaporized and the voltaic limiter was damaged beyond repair and would require replacement.

The mood in the spacecraft was quite somber; both Zoe and the ship continuously grumbled from aches and both were slow in their functions. Zoe was finally able to return the lighting in the ship, though the extensive damage disallowed the return of all computational and drive systems to their previous states. To her relief, the data from the experiment was not corrupt, but she was in no mood to try the experiment again anytime soon.

After several hours of programming work-arounds and error checking, Zoe plotted out a course to the nearest port which would have the components she required. With course in-laid, she began the fourteen-hour journey at idling speed, currently the maximum available from her craft. The ship huffed and puffed along, shambling on towards its repair salvation.

CHAPTER 4

SMOOTH SEAS AND SOOTHSAYERS

Amid the glorious white-speckled backdrop of the cosmos, an untethered buoy tranquilly bobbed along ethereal waves shaped as a bulbous ring encircling the base of an enormous tower with a white beacon atop its long thin apex. Churning deep within, a ballast the size of a mountain allowed for static positioning, yet also for a slow stable rotation around its axis of symmetry. This deep-space outpost served as a relay for the many different peoples on many different journeys, all converging hence for food, rest, supplies, and, of course, a bit of entertainment. Lights emitted from the station's various apertures gave the overall appearance of space, as if it were indeed a natural piece of the tranquilized universe; however, just on the opposite side of this metallic facade, its interior was in full clamorous commotion.

Within the glossy white-walled hallways, tumultuous seas of people ebbed and flowed about commissaries, shops, inns, and connecting flights. The masses swelled toward the steep cliffs of gambling rooms and washed out and away from the shores of hapless peddlers. Navigation through the maze of corridors, without the sun or moon as a guide, was possible via projected signs every so often, though as was the paradoxical problem with signage of ages past—a highway's numerical value always becomes zero when multiplied by infinity.

⊫⊣ ⊢⊩

Zoe was among the flowing crowd, keeping up with the general pace so as to remain untrampled by apathetic waves of travelers. Whilst in this deluge, she observed the people around her, making a game unto herself by trying to deduce from where they had originated and where they might be headed. It was her especial pastime, to espy the details of one's attire, mannerisms, and the sometimes-minute physiological changes evident from one Sector to another. She took note of a taller man directly in front of her dressed in black. From the backside of his head, topped by top-hat, she presumed he was from the Svire Sector, owing to his hairline reaching below his neckline. She had never yet met a Svirian, but it would be nearly impossible to say due to the known fact that a traveling school of fish cares little for conversation. She glanced to her left. Scrunched against her was a squabbled man with the unmistakable persona of a common salesman, even more common onboard midway space stations. Zoe took note of his relaxed gait and never-ending smile, pushed further out by the whiskers of his moustache. Strewn across his shoulders and broad belly were the goods of his trade—knock-off Etherian Necklaces, 'wooden' goblets, and infinity scarves with flittering projection tips like digital firecrackers. Pushed against her right side was a long-nosed woman; Zoe assumed she was probably a hoi polloi making her way to the next bus stop from a previous layover. What an eclectic mix of characters within these chambers! Zoe relished in the identities of humankind. She strode on.

The nature of the sea, however tranquil within the moment, may become discordant and unbridled in the next. Zoe was accustomed to this chaotic flow. For her it was a normal, rational fluid. She navigated far into its waters, commanding her way through the flowing masses and respecting them just the same. She came to a larger ventricle where multiple hallways converged. Shops and stalls were on both sides of her. She looked through their windows but saw nothing of particular interest. Positioned immediately outside the shops, people were braving the tides to sell their trinkets and faux goods with shouts and brazen, flailing arms.

From here, the masses dumped into a larger section of the station. Zoe's progress slowed from to the increased crowds. She suddenly smelled something fantastic and lifted her nose. Looking ahead, she spotted an oncoming group of commissaries. One canteen stood out from the rest with a large neon sign above its entrance reading. "The Scalawag" with blinking lights surrounded its entryway. Zoe steered hard to her right in order not to over-shoot the pub. She smiled as she passed through its entrance, pleased with her sailing skills.

The pub was very casual, minimalist artwork was framed on every wall and the furniture and fixtures were very plain, all accented by only a single strip of blue. Zoe walked up to the bar and hopped up on a stool, sending it into a spin which was ceased as she planted her two hands on the counter. She ended up directly facing the bartender.

"Hey there," Zoe said.

He lazily eyed her, revealing a longstanding boredom of his job. His voice was even more so lethargic.

"What can I get you?"

"Ah, let's see..." she looked behind him at the wall full of drink options. "Oh, how 'bout a Carnegie Cosmo?"

He made no affirmative gesture and turned to create the concoction. Zoe tapped on the counter with her fingernails, happily anticipating her purple liquor drink. She looked over to her left, a couple was sitting next to her, absorbed in each others presence. She swiveled to her right, the next several seats were empty, and an overweight man was sitting on the end, paying no mind to anything else in the galaxy but his glass pitcher. With an articulated 'whoosh' sound effect, Zoe spun back around just as the bartender set her drink on the counter.

"Yay!"

She paid for it and took a great cheek-withering swallow from the pink straw. She winced, puckered her lips and her eyes began to squint, the right one twitching with dramatic effect. The bartender noticed but did not indulge her antics and went on servicing other customers. She took another wild gulp.

"Ah, brain freeze. Brain freeze." Zoe's hand shook about her head, as if shooing off brain freeze gremlins. She cleared her throat and as the feeling faded she relaxed in her seat. "Ah, that's the stuff." She swiveled around to see what the rest of the bar's inhabitants were up to.

The many tables and lounge seats were occupied with people conversing, some smiling, some laughing, and some involved in brow furrowing discussions. Great bay windows gave a view of space along the entire far side of the bar. The stars outside boldly flaunted their bright-sides, beckoning to be gazed at, though in vein, for the pub-goers were far too enthralled with earthly affairs.

Zoe's gaze settled on an old man sitting alone at a table and staring at a game of Weltraumschach set up in front of him. It consisted of a triple-tiered pyramid of checkered boards, many tiles of which were set with various game pieces.

"Hmmm," Zoe mumbled and took up her drink to join the lonesome gentleman.

"Hi there! Wanna play? Or are you waiting for someone?" The old man snapped out of his trance, and Zoe then realized he had been in a game against himself. He looked up at Zoe and then settled back down into his game. His face was stolid; free of emotion, though chained by age. The many deep wrinkles on his forehead and cheeks drooped low, giving the appearance he was melting away. "Mister?"

He coughed and then spoke stoically, "Ah the pestilence of youth—always superlative, always..." He muttered on lowly and revved back "...endemic ignorance spanning further than I care to quantize." He shot a look at Zoe, though it lost puncture through the creases of his skin.

"Please, let's play!"

"Miss," he said slowly and patronizingly, "I don't care to play you. Now, go." The old man went back to staring at the board, fully disregarding her presence.

"Please mister! Come on."

He looked up at her, an aggravated expression now coming through layers of skin. Zoe smiled back from ear to ear.

"You, miss, are a simpleton, a saturnine girl."

Zoe whipped back, "Then you, sir, are most certainly jupiter-nine! One game. Then I won't bother you anymore. Promise." The old man huffed, making much the same sounds Zoe's ship had on the way to port.

"Hmmph. Well, satisfactory. The last iota of intelligence has seeped from this lot long ago."

"Game on!" chirped Zoe as she happily sat down across from him. She took a sip of her drink at set it on the table beside the triple tiered playing field. "Roll for reds?" she asked. "What? Hmmph. The coloration will make no alteration to the outcome." Zoe began to place her pieces in their respective side-line positions on the bottom grid.

The old man had been ready for centuries. Zoe took another sip of her bright-purple concoction which brought about another indignant look from her competitor.

"Please, begin," he said calmly and motioned amicably with his hand, though his eyes remained narrow.

As Zoe looked at the game boards in deep thought with a look of uncertainty swelling across her face. The old man's eyes continued to become little beads. She slowly picked up a piece, formed like a cone intertwined by several circlets and an iron cap, and moved it several spaces forward on the first checkered level.

"Amateur! Hmmph. There's no rational purpose to that position. You, you are wasting my time. Do you even..."

She cut him off, "Your turn mister." He looked over at her, his face sharpening into a sterner expression, though suddenly turned to surprise once met with the giant smile Zoe was boring down on him. He focused back on the board, moving a white piece from his side near the center of the top tier. Zoe cocked her head to the side and picked up her next piece, placing it next to the first cone.

"What is this!" the old man lashed out. In response, Zoe took a large gulp of her drink, leaving bright purple all over her lips, annoying the old man further. "Hmmph." He moved his second piece to the center stage of the middle level.

The two went back and forth, setting their pieces in starting positions—the man in a strategic and fortified array around the board, Zoe in a chaotic mix all on the bottom tier. The wrinkles on the old man's brow had eased; he had no doubt concluded this game would be over soon and he would teach a lesson to the "wasted youth."

⤙⊹⊹⤚

"That's what I said, everything went dead for a moment before going buck wild. The baro-sensors, the motor relays, the—"

"But not the air locks, or the door seals, or anything that would actually hurt you, eh Erik?"

"Bah. I'm tellin' you how it was. Ya, all essential systems were fine. Ya, I'm fine, thank you very much."

"Ah. I don't care you loaf, just would have been pissed if you hadn't made it for a drink." There was the sound of glass pitchers clinking. "I bet the boss wasn't too happy."

"Ah screw him! Look George, it wasn't right—," Erik interrupted himself with a large burp, "—it was a haul of Kapteyn and hex-plutonium generators. Meaning-"

"Meaning you were wrapped up from the generators, nothing in, nothing out. I've done a couple loads. Just admit it, you buzzed off for a day to get a cut-rate lap dance. Or maybe it was to see Caroline? Eh?"

"Oh no. Don't you mention her. Argh. I get goosebumps thinking about that gal."

"Everyone wants to blame them sensor ghosts. But I know. So, come on Erik, tell me."

"Bah. They are all full of shit." There was another loud burp. "Sensor ghosts! George, you son of a gun. I shoulda written that in my report." There was another clink of glasses.

⊱✦⊰

"Begin," said the old man as the last piece took its proper place. Zoe snapped back to reality, having been distracted by the conversation going on somewhere behind her.

"Yes sir!" she said enthusiastically and moved a small cylindrical piece with a gear on top from the bottom to middle level, replacing one of his pieces and now centered in a sea of white enemies.

"Bold," he said smugly, "but you're vulnerable under a multiplicity of conditions."

He moved a midsection piece down to the base where it assumed the place of one of her pawns. Zoe quickly moved her lone red invader to an empty spot on the top level and sat back satisfied in her chair. The old man moved two pieces down, creating a triangular system, a move Zoe recognized was to protect his exposed pieces and at the same time allow them to retain offensive capabilities. She took her time and moved a single piece from the bottom to the outer edge on top. Over the course of the next several turns, the old man moved his pieces about, creating complex defensive positions with interwoven attack positions, capable of removing Zoe's pieces from a variety of vantage points. He exercised this capability and proceeded to work his way through her pieces, while chasing around the board that relentless pirate of Zoe's—her iron-capped king.

Fifteen minutes into the game came the first announcement of "check," but it did not come from the old man. To his unmistakable astonishment, Zoe had executed a quadruple vault by a three-level multifaceted coordination from separated groups of her pieces, slipping past his defensive efforts and coming within striking distance of his king. The wrinkles upon his brow furled foreword greater than the hurricanes of Arcanis.

"Argh!" He coughed and cooled himself. "Hmmph." He moved his king to a new fortified position and redoubled his defensives. Zoe tingled with an excited anxiousness at the thought that the old man may just pop, and confetti would come showering out. Now that would be something.

The game continued. The old man's graveyard was now quickly filling up while Zoe suffered minimal losses. Another "check" soon came from Zoe. Her opponent was turning quite sour. He was forced into further defensive positions, suffering substantial losses over the next several rounds. He waived down a waitress and ordered a stiff drink.

"You. Hmmph. Do you know how long I have been playing this game little lady?"

"Long enough to get your butt kicked?" she smiled and winked.

His face turned a bitter shade and he puffed up his withered chest. "I have been playing Weltraumschach for over 75 years now, since I was a little lad. Never have I…" He seemed to be at a loss for words and Zoe did not respond, she simply moved a piece up one level and over by several tiles.

"Checkmate, mister."

"Argh!" The old man suddenly seemed to have lost all interest in the game. "Leave." He waived her off and finished his drink in one large gulp. Zoe shook her shoulders and got up with her drink. She wanted to smirk and gloat with the few smart rejoinders she had prepped, but the blow to the old man's ego was a bit more than she had anticipated. Perhaps confetti in a pub was not for the best. Instead, she turned toward the two voices she had overheard earlier and spotted the two men talking near the window. With drink in hand, she decided joined them.

"Hi there," Zoe said with a smile. Two bloated semi-drivers, both with gruff beards, paused their conversation and looked over at her, startled.

"Why hellor' miss," said the obviously drunker of the two— Mr. Erik, Zoe presumed.

"Hello, I'm Zoe. Please excuse me, I overhead you two talking about sensor ghosts?"

"Hello, ma'am," said the other man, "I'm George. This is my buddy Erik." He patted his companion heartily on the back.

"Pleased to meet you," Zoe shook both their hands.

"Now look Miss Zoe," said George, "there ain't nothing to sensor ghosts. We truckers just like using that trick to annoy our superiors." The two men smiled.

"But I overheard your semi went down and began to perform erratically."

"That's true. And I swear to it." Erik eyed George. "There was something odd going ons' out there." George sighed. "Like I was sayin' to George, I was haulin' hex generators for a new fleet in the Fratough Sector. I was outfitted with a Faraday enclosure 'round my ship." He let out a hiccup. "Nothing outside could effec' my ship. Yet something was triggering all my systems. I swear it."

"Hmmm," she said, taking a sip of alcohol.

"I had thought my ship had suffer'ered some electronics meltdown or somethin'. So, I rushed and started opening up panelin' just to find its all fine. I ran diagnostics and got greem, een, green lights on all systems. I always run my rig smooth, top off everythin' before I leave for a haul."

"Interesting," said Zoe.

Erik took another drink as did Zoe. "And so there I was, in dead space at a full stop with my ship lighting up like I was throwing a disco party. Lasted just minute or so, but took hours to get everythin' up 'n runnin' again."

Zoe leaned against the glass and looked out at the stars.

"You're drunk, Erik. Everyone loves a good story."

"Damnit George, I swear it!"

"Ya? Then let me see your flight logs." At this, Erik's stance settled back. "Well?"

"Alright. I'm not ready to give those up to prove to ya anythin'."

"And why is that? Caroli—"

"Don't you finish that sentence George!"

"Ya. well hey," said George, "I got to get running, these shipments aren't going to deliver themselves."

"Too true George," said Erik. The two friends shook hands and George gave Erik a slap on the shoulder. "Next week then?"

"Aye sir," responded Erik.

"Take care. It was nice meeting you—eh Zoe?"

She smiled. "You too. Safe journeys." George gave her a strong handshake and went about his way. Zoe turned to Erik who was taking a giant swing, emptying about half of his pitcher. "So, care to tell me more about these sensor ghosts? It's the first time I've ever heard of such a thing."

His eyes lit up. "So, there I was, in the Margo Sector—," he hiccupped once more, "—about three days off deliverin' my shipment when suddenly my semi gets a mind of its own. I mean EVO systems screamin' murder and baro-sensors reading in the red. The engine went completely offline. All hazard lights went up around the ship and I was freakin' out. I looked out, and nothing."

"Nothing?"

The pair sat in silence for a moment, taking in their drinks.

"Well," perked up Zoe, quickly sputtered out from raw thought, "what if a natural phenomenon, not yet discovered, capable of distorting electronics through a shielded ship giving false readings, unnoticeable by lack of quantum fluctuation, but has the ability to carry narrow band current it in order to..." she trailed off seeing Erik shrug his shoulders.

"I don't know 'bout all that Miss Zoe. Now look, I don't wanna go upsetting anybody. Like George said, it's just something us trucker use to annoy our bosses. I means, all I means is—"

"I understand," she said. "Say, what were you hauling again?"

"Kapteyn and hex-plutonium generators."

"Those hex-plutonium generators; hot stuff. I definitely understand why you were shielded. Cheap and fast propulsion systems meant for interstellar crafts. Man, I hope it's not common to ship them around in semis; doesn't seem safe. Did you know they burn endothermically by precipitating atoms toward their ground-state, meaning that if one got a bit too excited in your cargo, it would pretty much make a hole straight through the space you were in." She laughed, and he did too.

He clinked his glass to hers. "See, that's what I'm sayin'. That's why I was a bit late. Phew! The things they got us haulin'." He took a large drink and let out a belch. Zoe reciprocated and let out one of her own.

"Hey, do you mind if I get the coordinates of that event from you?"

He was a drunk, and perhaps a liar. But maybe there was some fun to be had—a resonant node from some wireless power relay he had come across perchance; or maybe an electromagnetic sink in the area had interfered with his ship; or even more tantalizing, an undiscovered mini-black hole. Anyhow, there would be no loss in looking.

"Sure, no probleeem." He clumsily fumbled in his trouser pocket and produced a small brick computer with a push-button interface. Zoe reached in the top of her shirt and took out her lightcard.

"Here, download to this," she said. He keyed into his device and held it up to hers, syncing to it. His device beeped.

"There ya go Miss Zoe."

"Thanks Erik! Well, I need to be off now. You know how it is." He held out his glass and Zoe clinked it. They both took one final swig and set their empty glasses on the window ceil next to George's. Erik nodded and slow danced with himself to the barkeep. Zoe smiled, replacing the lightcard in her shirt and left the pub in spirits to resume the business of fixing her ship.

⊶⊰⊹⊱⊷

"All hail the coming dawn!" came a screechy yell as Zoe exited the bar. Zoe jerked in surprise to her left and saw a man backed against the wall near the pub as flowing crowds abrasively brushed against him. He was in a mix of rags both black and white, thrown over him until all skin was covered, except for his face, marked by a scraggily eye patch. She paused for a moment, staring at him, but quickly resumed her pace as not to be singled out by him. Unfortunately, she was luckless. "You, missy!" he shouted as she passed him, "The eye is always watching ye! Hee-Hee!" Zoe was rapidly washed away by the river of people, leaving the vagabond behind her.

She maneuvered towards the repair section of the station, though progress was slow, as it was apparent a tide was coming in. After zig-zagging through many corridors, Zoe came upon distinct shouts breaking through the ever-present tumult of commercial space station noise. She porpoised several times above the sea of faces to get a glance of the hubbub. There was definitely some sort of angry raucous ahead. People were crowded off to the left side, encircling something, or someone.

Zoe approached the gathering and became one with it, trying to see through the mob, like a deer through a thicket at what might be a predator or friend. The shouting was all directed toward the epicenter of the group. She strained to look above and between people, leaning on shoulders and trying to pry past people. Her small stature made this quite the task. Suddenly there were approving cheers from the heart of the matter. A clear yell followed.

"Fuck you clone!"

A clone? Zoe thought to herself. She worked her way further through, no longer apologizing as she squeezed in between bystanders. Then she saw him. Huddled against the corner of the floor and wall in plain clothes with stains and tears. His face was buried low under his arms, but she could see each swarthy arm had the distinct markings of his designation. The same insignia was again repeated on each hand and on every finger. Markings of property. The crowd shifted, and she lost her view, so she used the shoulders from two men just in front of her to try and see over everyone.

Mental prostheses and direct mind-to-machine communications were banned in the late 2600s, unless prescribed by doctor for severe mental retardation, seizures, and such. Genetic manipulation and gene grooming were banned even earlier than that, again unless prescribed for severe deficiencies. Yet, human cloning had been allowed to persist for centuries. Zoe's thoughts continued; she knew why. The humanoid form eases the transfer of knowledge and is able to utilize tooling built upon millennia of know-how. The human mind is apt at quickly learning new tasks and has the creativity to problem solve any work-related obstacles. Lastly, cloning meant no abnormalities; every single one is exactly the same, trained exactly the same, and expected to act and react exactly the same. Altogether, clones were better workers than any machine could ever be. That was why they were still mass produced throughout the galaxy and, Zoe thought to herself, probably half of the infrastructure of the galaxy was owed to them.

Zoe got a good look at the clone on the ground. He was now looking at his antagonists, bearing the verbal onslaught. He looked to be about her age, and had matted black hair which needed a good trimming. Zoe could see his neck and cheek had also been branded. He shot a quick look around at the crowd and Zoe's heart skipped a beat. His eyes. Even his eyes—on the side of his pupils—had been imprinted. She couldn't look away, even though the entire situation really began to really annoy her. Those eyes.

The clone attempted to stand up but was pushed down again, ended up back in the same sitting position looking up at his perpetrators. "Stay down like the dog you are, clone!" said the man whom had pushed him. Many snickered and jeered at the subhuman. He stood up once more. A particularly large man in front balled a fist and landed a blow square in his jaw, sending him right back to the floor. The clone held his face in pain and turned his face away from the crowd. Another man, feeling the rush of the pack, broadened his shoulders and spit on the clone. This was followed by more jeers and a few woops from the crowd. The clone remained on the ground with his eyes fixed to the floor. He no longer attempted to get up; instead he remained unmoving and defeated. Without further persistence from the clone, the blood moon in the hallway sunk low and the tide washed out, leaving behind just a few flapping fish, who were soon after joining their companions in the safety of deeper waters. Zoe had remained silent in the foreground, waiting for the crowd to fully dissipate. She stepped up to the clone and squatted down to be at eye level with him.

"Hi," she said.

He didn't look up, as if he dared not to, and continued staring motionlessly at her feet. She waited, hoping for some sort of response. "Okay then." Zoe stood up and turned to walk away but stopped mid spin. She knelt back down and grabbed his arms, lifting him up. Even though he offered little resistance in standing, he kept his gaze to the floor. "I'm Zoe." Still no response. "Come with me." She took his arm, first gently pulling him, and then dragging him down the corridor along with the masses. The subjugated clone unwillingly did as he was forced to do. The two soon came to a snack outlet with several stalls. "Let's get some Dippin' Dots. It's the ice cream of the future ya know." She gave a warm smile. "Do you like vanilla or forpegi?" He remained a statue; an obedient dog. Zoe turned to the snack attendant. "Vanilla and forpegi. Large please." Zoe produced a card to pay from a small pocket on her shorts and took the two cones from the attendant. "Here ya go." Holding one cone in each hand, she offered both to the clone who made no motion to accept the snack. "Here," she said again in a harsher tone. He gave a quick upward glance, just quick enough to survey the cones and he carefully took the vanilla. The clone slowly nipped at it, never once looking at Zoe. She leaned against the white wall, pulling on the collar of the clone for him to do the same. She licked at her cone.

"So, I hear you're a clone?" She looked over at him but received no response. Zoe brought her face close to his and spoke up louder as the noise of the hallway seemed to surge. "You. A clone. A clone of whom may I ask?"

He stopped eating and finally looked at her. His green-blue eyes shimmered magnificently. They again caught Zoe off guard and she paused consuming her cone, wholly transfixed by them. It was as if they contained all the wonder and majesty of the entire universe. His broad face was squared at the jaw and rounded on top with proportional cheekbones and light red lips. She remarked he was not a traditional clone; all work clones she had ever come across had dull dark brown eyes, broad facial features; overall, very droll facades.

In an unhurried, yet intelligent voice, he said, "I am a clone of humans." She realized she was still dumbly staring at him and shook it off.

"I can see you're human. A clone of which human in particular?"

He sighed. "I am mix of all mankind."

Zoe's mind twinkled. The clone seemed to lose interest in the frozen treat and slumped his shoulders. "I stand before you, a one-off experiment."

"Fascinating!" she blurted out. The clone did not smile. He seemed to take in her words as mocking. His labeled eyes sagged away from her and to the floor once more. "Hey. Hey." She tenderly pulled up his chin so their eyes met. "How's the ice-cream?"

"It is good. Thank you, ma'am."

"No need to thank! So, what are you doing out here?"

He took a big bite, swallowed, and solemnly replied, "Just traveling." He began to look back down but she preemptively pulled his face back up and gave him a tender smile.

"Do you like to travel?" she asked.

"Yes." Zoe saw then just a hint of some deep-grained excitement. She motioned for him to go on. "I stow away where I can, but it has been... difficult."

"I can imagine," she responded. "Clones are nearly never seen outside their work facilities, much less so in outer-space. I can't recall a single time I have seen a clone outside its designed work site..." she trailed off, once more becoming lost in his dazzling eyes. "You're one in a million," she whispered, more to herself than him. "Well, I'll tell you what. Are you familiar with blank tool systems?" He gave an affirmative nod. "And are you here on your own?"

"Yes," he said.

"And are you in the habit of pilfering and killing?"

He stared with immediate shock. "No! Never. I would never—"

"Then come along! You and I have exploring to do!" Zoe began to march off.

"Wai—," he started.

She paused suddenly and spun around. She could see he was suddenly very uneasy. "Right, what is your name?"

She anticipated a numerical designation, but he quickly responded, "My name is Darious."

"Darious. I like it!" She looped her arm with his, and this time, without resistance, he headed off with her into the crowd. He was keen to keep his head down and Zoe soon realized what hardship he must have endured out here. Whenever someone looked beyond their route and saw Darious, nasty expressions followed, sometimes with pointing and directed obscenities. Sure clones were considered lowly, but she had never thought this low.

"Not very popular are ya?" she said, giving him a broad smile as he momentarily looked up at her.

They finally reached the machine shops. Zoe kept Darious in arm's reach which enabled her to quickly pull him out confrontations—which there were a few. They popped in and out of multitudinous shops, checking through various stores' stocks. Zoe's purchases were loaded onto Darious' arms which soon became a pile taller than he could see through. He clumsily followed her as she guided him by the sound of her voice.

"Let's see, one last thing."

They searched through several more depots before coming to a shop which had what Zoe required. She pulled a palm-sized quadrature modulator off a shelf.

"Bingo!"

She strutted over to the store's counter for payment, happy the last of her shopping was now over. The attendant was an ogre of a man. His bulging belly was scarcely covered by an oil-stained shirt. Greasy hair streaked down his face by which a large wart-covered nose stuck out, giving him the appearance of some sort of space troll. He snorted loudly and swallowed the mucus. Zoe put the limiter on the counter with a muted expression. He scratched at his arm and looked at them with a sneer.

"What's this? Get out of here."

"Eh?" Zoe responded.

"Go on," he said in a harsh gruff voice. "Get out." He waved Zoe and Darious away. Zoe was puzzled, and it showed on her face. The mechanic turned much sterner and leaned forward, banging his open palms on the counter. Both Zoe and Darious jumped. Several people outside heard and look inward. "We don't want your kind around!" Zoe looked back at Darious and realized what was going on. The space troll was fuming and pointed a floppy arm at Darious. "Get Lost!" Darious was paralyzed and instinctively looked down at the ground.

"Okay, okay. We'll go," said Zoe as she threw a bill on the counter and picked up the limiter. She turned with Darious and they both quickly left the shop as the man barked at them.

"Ruf! Ruf! Get lost!"

People were now pointing at Darious. Most had contorted faces when seeing him as if something rotten had pervaded their nostrils.

"I think our business is done here Darious. It's time to go."

"Yes," he replied.

On their way back to Zoe's ship, they passed by a large bowed-out out viewing room. Above its arched entrance, holographic monitors projected galactic news headlines, departure and arrival flights, and the current space weather. The room, shaped by a semicircle floor and great curved bay window, allowed for an unobstructed view of outer-space. It remained dark and desolate, backlit only by soft blue lights, allowing the viewer a non-polluted view of the cosmos. Zoe and Darious both slowed, drawn in by prodigious view. The adventurer and the archetype entered in with quiet reverence and both stood as close to the glass as they could. Zoe put her purchases on the floor and took Darious' heap from him, setting them too on the ground. They stood silently next to each other; the bustle of the hallway was drowned out by the grand view of the infinite of infinites.

Bright specks from hundreds of thousands of stars were visible, ranging from soft whites to deep reds. Sliding into view, a silent asteroid drifted by, oblique with shades of browns and grey, on a journey that could easily last a billion years. Just beyond the glass and in-between every pastel sun was blackness, both ever-present and never changing, the absolute essence of the universe.

The pair remained completely absorbed for some time, each enthralled within their own thoughts. Zoe herself imagined moonlit nights illuminating Martian canyons, sudden bursts from prismatic nebulas as newborn stars ignited, proto-planets undergoing metamorphosis from world-wide volcanic eruptions, and the awesome power of stars at the end of their life-cycles igniting for one final fireworks show. Zoe's eyes dazzled with an affinity for the infinity to which she was an inhabitant of, upon an island of its great sea. Darious turned to her, and Zoe saw within his eyes that same shimmer she felt within her own soul.

CHAPTER 5

A LESSON ON QUANTUM ENTANGLEMENT

The pair disembarked from the space station and idled in nearby space. Zoe was quickly able to replace the broken parts and cleared a space in the cockpit behind her captain's station, installing a seat, monitor, and controls.

"Taa-daa!" Zoe said as she lifted her hands from Darious' eyes. He stared at the setup for a moment and then back to her. She motioned for him to sit. "It will be nice having some help around here."

His expression showed puzzlement. "Is this for me?" he asked.

"Yes sir. You're part of the crew now."

"I... thank you."

She ushered him into the seat.

"Go ahead. Give it a whirl."

Darious fumbled with the control panel, managing to turn on the projection controls after a short bit and the screen appeared with a brilliant wave of colors.

"Alright then," said Zoe as she assumed the captain's chair. "To infinity, and beyond!" She punched in the ignition sequence and the idling engines roared with eagerness. The ship leapt forward, pushing both Zoe and Darious back into their seats before the gravitational system caught up. Zoe heard commotion behind her. "Sorry about that. I'll warn ya next time." She turned to see Darious regaining his seat with his controls in disarray.

The ship flew at great speeds out and away from the space station, leaving behind the sojourn slog and pursuing the road less traveled. Zoe's craft was soaring along superbly; in addition to the repairs, she had found and installed a little gamma amplifier allowing her to tweak the pinch point of gamma flow from the engines and gaining just a bit more oomph.

"Course plotted in. Looks like..." Zoe brought up a side screen. "about two weeks until our destination."

"Ma'am, where are we headed?"

Zoe got up from her controls and sat on the floor next to Darious, looking up at him. "So, what do you like to do for fun?"

"I am sorry. I do not know, ma'am."

"Please, no need for formalities."

"I am sorry."

"Or apologizing."

"I am—" Darious somewhat froze up and shrunk his shoulders like a child in trouble.

Zoe knew she was going to have to take it slow with him. "Well," she said, "how about this: I know it may take some time, but how about you become familiar with the ship? I have plenty of reading material on it. Meanwhile, I've got a bit of coding I wanna catch up on. If you have any questions don't hesitate to ask." She leaned over and typed into Darious' projection console, bringing up schematics of her craft along some thruster mechanics. He leaned forward and began taking in the information in silence. She watched him for a bit and then got up and went back in her seat, opening many screens, the first of which was her music player. The subwoofers in the cabin sent low vibrations through the tips of her fingers and the melodies harmonized her mind to her task.

The two weeks of travel went by quickly, and though Zoe had tried several times to break down those walls of Darious, they turned out to be sturdier than stone and much taller too. On one day she had even made her version of green chili stew and told him about its old Earth-1 origin, to which he seemed interested, but continued to retain his formalities and timidity.

"So, tell me about your family. Got any sisters or brothers?" Zoe asked on the last day of their voyage.

Darious was reading a mathematics tensor book in the central room. He had quickly worked his way through the calculus material she had given him and was consuming this book at an amazing pace. She told him he could take notes within the pages, but he insisted on separating his notes as not to discredit the book in any way. Darious paused his reading and set the book down. Zoe took an excited seat next to him seeing that just maybe, that wall was finally coming down.

He took in a breath. "You," he said, "were born of nature and grown by nurture. I was borne of machines and matured by them."

"I see," she said, "Ah, you test tube babies." She smirked but it faded as the face staring back at her remained joyless.

"Though I could not speak nor see until I was past puberty, I do remember my benefactor once visiting me. At the time, I knew not what his words meant, but I kept them." Darious' voice went low, and he spoke in a serious manner. "'You are corporeal embodiment of the quintessential human; the single resonance node from hundreds of trillions intersecting waves.' He then took up my limp hands like this." Darius lifted his hands together, palm upwards, and continued, "With your hands you will hold the dreams of your species." Darious then put his hands to his eyes. "Through your eyes, you will witness the captivation and imagination from every single Plank frame." He then pointed to his tongue. "Your tongue will speak with the hopes of all and hold in confidence the secrets of all." Darious then stood up and brought up each leg in turn as if someone was lifting them. "Finally, your two feet will guide you." Darious sat back down with a sigh. "And that was it." Zoe was in awe. "After my vision had developed, I saw these markings all over my body. It is law for clones to have such identifiers." He stroked each arm. "They exist on every appendage, every organ and bone."

With eyes wide Zoe said, "But nevertheless, your benefactor—I mean, wow."

Darious looked down and shook his head. "He died shortly after telling me those things. That was it. I learned later I was simply an experiment of his. I was created from a synthesis of genetic coding from all mankind; a blending of all sapiens. When he died, I was thrown out, later to be found and sent to work in the mines on Escobar-3. But really I—"

"Ha! You got out, you sly dog, didn't you?" Zoe was beaming. Darious nodded nervously and fiddled with his hands. "Ah Darious, one in a million." He smiled. That was the first time Zoe saw him smile. "So, you've been traveling around, eh?"

"Yes," he replied, "for about 7 years now. It has been—"

"Awesome, right? I know!" Darious looked slightly defeated. "I know, I know, sometimes it's bullshit. But I saw it in your eyes, you like what's out there." Zoe pointed past the cockpit, out to space.

Exhilaration momentarily passed over his face. "Oh yes." He paused. "Zoe, if I may ask—"

"Ask away."

"Have you ever been to the center of the Milky Way?"

"Aww nothing there but a big hole. What you really ought to see, if you haven't, are the Floating Gardens of Cabernet."

"Oh yes! But beware of the carrion flowers; reeks worse than death!" They laughed together. "Cabernet has been one of the few places my hitchhiking has allowed me to visit."

"Can I ask you something Darious?"

"Yes, Zoe."

"So, you got out and went exploring, but what about an education? I can see you're no dum-dum."

"I suppose I have been built with certain cognitive abilities."

"Well, I've got a little stockpile of reading material back from my college days and more I've picked up through the years, as you may have no undoubtedly noticed. It's all yours to learn from, if you're interested that is."

"Oh, thank you Zoe!"

"Speaking of which, you had better get brushed up on ionic thrust injectors because next on my to-do list is to recalibrate the one I have."

Darious beamed with pleasure. "Yes, ma'am!"

A beeping from the cockpit announced the ship had arrived at its destination.

"Ahh ya."

Zoe stood up and went to her captain's chair. Darious followed and peered over her shoulder out at empty space. She typed at a maddening pace, flipping screen after screen as she initiated a multitude tests. She spoke as her fingers rattled over the console.

"Background radiation. Normal. Cosmic dust. Normal." She scrolled through more screens. "Normal. Normal. Zero value. Normal. Hmm."

"What is it you are looking for?" asked Darious.

Zoe continued whipping through more screens and then reached up, flipping switches and checking back at the monitor. "Nope. Normal. Zero. Normal." Her typing slowed. "Nope. Nada." She sat back in her chair and tapped on her chin. "Well, I guess he was full of shit." Darious was about to say something but Zoe cut in, "Well, that was lame."

"What—," Darious began, but then seemed to stop himself, before trying again with a timid confidence. "What was the purpose of this mission?"

"Eh. Don't worry about it. What do you want to do now?"

He looked at her blankly.

"How 'bout lunch?" She asked.

Zoe left and quickly returned with two silver pouches, handing one to Darious. She tore off a corner of hers with her teeth and began sucking at the sweet substance.

After they finished their Vita-Pals, Zoe went to work recalibrating the sensors with Darious acting as her assistant. She chatted him up as they worked, explaining the finer points of space flight. Zoe even got a few more smiles from him. The pair spent the next few days modifying the thrust injectors while talking about topics ranging from quantum creation theories to the best toppings for scrambled eggs. They were bonding resplendently, like two electrons, forged on opposite ends of the galaxy and quantumly entangled so that their two separate realities had become indistinguishable.

CHAPTER 6
TO INFINITY AND BEYOND

After several weeks of roaming the galaxy, Darious asked Zoe about family. He elaborated on his curiosities of the family-dynamic and had even inserted a well-placed joke about his zygote infancy. He had wondered aloud if it was worth seeking out a family. Though Zoe had grown quite close with him, she wavered at these questions. Her uncomfortableness went noticed and after Darious apologized many times, Zoe thought he had abandoned the topic entirely.

Several days after this incident, Darious suddenly asked, "Can I meet your family?"

The question caught Zoe off guard, as they had just been talking about possible upgrades to the aft thrusters. "My family? Why, um, well…" She twisted her lips in thought. Looking over at him, she could see a hint of anxiety in his sparkling eyes. She couldn't resist. "Well, why not! It's been a while since I've seen 'em." She smiled, and he reciprocated with a larger grin. Zoe spun around in her chair and typed in a set of coordinates. "One family reunion coming right up." With that, she pressed the virtual 'Enter' button, to which it turned the ship about and fired thrusters near max.

"Behold!" said Zoe, six days later. She could hear him fumble with a book and drop it on the floor. "Did I startle you?" she chortled as he joined her in the cockpit. Darious halted as his eyes touched the view beyond the cockpit.

They were approaching a massive behemoth of a planet, comprised of genial colors from vast deserts and oceans with small spots of verdant greens. By a true show of harmony on this colossal scale, at either side of the world, two enormous satellites— each easily the size of Earth-1—were in orbit exactly opposite each other, appearing to be so perfect in their symmetric positioning that they looked to be painted amongst the stars. Zoe smiled when she saw Darious' awestruck expression.

As they neared, mountains became evident, waters of varying depth changed by tones of blue, and evidence of civilization appeared all throughout continental habitable zones. Along the planet's edge, the atmosphere blended in such fantastic hues, it seemed as if the whole planet was enshrouded in a divine halo.

"Amazing," said Darious as he continued to observe the passive giant. Neither he nor could Zoe hide their feelings of admiration. Zoe whole-heartedly smiled in view of her great-uncle's home world.

The ship came down through the thick atmosphere and landed in a desert region. Darious remained glued to the window, even after Zoe had left the cockpit to prepare a small backpack.

"Are you coming, compadre?"

He snapped out of his daze and joined her. The pair exited the craft through its rear gangway. Zoe shaded her eyes from the brilliant sun and saw Darious looking around with his eyes wide open. Through watery vision, he took it all in. Zoe chuckled; he was just a tad excited. She had parked her ship next to a dirt roadway and looked around at the barren land surrounding them. For kilometers in all directions, the desiccated desert saturated the terrain. Overhead the sun bore down, and the two ever-present moons bulged from either horizon. Just up the road a short way was a line of homes. Zoe led the way, whilst probing her memory for the facade of the house.

A hot wind sent up gusts every so often and lone tumbleweeds wandered by. The temperature could rival the hottest on Earth-1 and the first beads of sweat soon formed upon Zoe's brow. Just as Darious parted his lips and the first syllable from some word was about to escape, Zoe announced, "Ah! Here we are!" and stopped at a rusted metal gate leading to a two-story, white-washed house. Desert shrubs covered the fenced-in lot and the angled roof was full of patchwork. It had a dilapidated by homely look just as Zoe remembered. Next to the house was a separate, well-maintained barnyard that had been refashioned as a mechanical shop.

Zoe took the steps up the porch by twos and rang the doorbell three times. At first there were no sounds, but then stirring and wooden floorboards creaking toward them could be heard. Zoe also heard a young voice within and smiled. The paint-chipped door opened, giving way to a tall, slender man of many years, although his steadfast movements evidenced much capability and strength. His rugged face creased inward as he surveyed the two individuals at his door. Suddenly his expression lightened up and his wrinkles were muscled back into broad smile. "Zoe? Ah, Zoe!" Just then, a little girl peeked from between his legs, shuttering with excitement.

"Zoe!" she exclaimed and ran out, hugging Zoe's legs.

"Hi there Renee!" Zoe bent down and hugged the girl.

"Zoe!" she gasped with excitement, "Grampa!" She turned toward the man behind her and back at Zoe. "Grampa told me all about you! I can't believe you're here!" She was wiggling from joy. "Your hair is so beautiful!"

Zoe laughed. "Why thank you."

Next her great-uncle came in for a hug. "Haven't seen you in a long time missy."

"Well, I was in the neighborhood, so thought it'd be nice to stop by."

"Indeed, it is." He hugged her once more and Zoe held on tight for a moment longer. He put a hand on each shoulder, surveying her and then looked over at Darious. "So, who is this artistic gentleman?"

"This is my friend, Darious. Darious, this is my great uncle, Sampson Thorgood."

"A pleasure sir." Darious simultaneously bent over, held out his hand, and bent a leg backwards, evidencing several greeting customs at once. Sampson shook his hand.

"Please, come inside. Today is a hot one."

Zoe picked up Renee and the four went in the house.

Iced-tea was served and they all sat around comfortable, yet worn, fabric chairs. Sampson told them that his shop was well busy; he had fixed up Apollo Adelric's hover cargo system the other day and was reworking the townsfolk's engines for better fuel economy. If Zoe had time, she should see his current project—a fully automated personal jetpack that was fueled by starch. Zoe's young cousin constantly interjected, saying her grandpapa was the best there was, and 'oh Zoe look at this,' and 'Zoe can I brush your hair?' Zoe was happy to oblige.

Zoe spoke of her recent adventures, which she talked up, though noting that as of late, there hadn't been much, and truth be told, there hadn't ever been any real adventure. They ate an early dinner consisting of potatoes and baked chicken, topped with country herbs and spices. Darious looked on with a keen curiosity as the family spoke and thanked Mr. Thorgood for the delicious meal every time his name was mentioned.

As the afternoon faded, Darious was guided to the couch and obliged to relax, to which he did not contest, and he spent the next hour digesting the six chicken thighs he had devoured while reading a farming book Sampson had given to him. Renee was on the floor playing with plastic bricks. Zoe and her great uncle went outside and sat on the backyard porch with a view of kilometers of uninterrupted desert.

Zoe was silent for some time, staring out to the horizon; her eyes followed a dust devil in the distance. The sand from it would get kicked up, do several twirls, and settle again only to be picked up again as the gust perked up. She relaxed and placed her head on Sampson's shoulder. He began to softly stroke her hair, just as she remembered from long ago when she was a little girl.

"Zoe," Sampson began. Somewhere, at some moment undefined, the air had turned cooler and a somber mood had fallen upon the porch. "What happens when you pass through an event horizon and finally, after eons, reach that singularity?" Zoe didn't respond, but continued to look out at the oncoming sunset. "What happens when all of time is done?" He paused and then continued on, "to whom do we even ask such questions? Antecedently, why do we even ask such questions?" A little smile crept along Zoe's lips and she sat up looking into his eyes. "If we are not here to ask such questions, then I propose, we are pointless creatures. Nettle fish. Mindless all-consumers." Sampson whisked a few hairs from her face with his fingers. "Thus, I propose to you, that indeed those who do question, who must do the exploring, are necessary for the endurance of the species and for the forward development of it. You cannot plant a seed on a road; you must till on open lands. The same is true for thought." He paused once more and surveyed the landscape. "Though, I do suppose, without roads, bags of seed do become quite burdensome." A soft smile showed through his wrinkles.

Zoe remembered wholly; he somehow always knew, as if he could sense any hint of self-diminution, even without words, and fix everything. He was a mechanic for the soul.

Her great uncle let out a short cough and cleared his throat. "I feel an old expression would do at this moment: an arduous task, one which requires sweat, sacrifice, and long hours of work, simply indicates the treasure at its end is that much greater. Zoe," He looked squarely at her with his old eyes, as if could see through to her deepest core. "I believe in you. You will find what you're looking for, simply because you are looking for it. Nobody today ever gets that far. The fact that you are currently unsure of yourself is a sure sign your path is unpaved. The unknowns you yearn for, both out there," he paused surveying the land and then back at her, "and within yourself, are what make you that singularity. To men like me, the universe is chaos; to you, it's harmony." He kissed gently her on the forehead. "On this infinite plane, you are the only paradox I have ever witnessed—you are unique."

Zoe let loose a giddy smile. "Keep going." She chuckled, and he smiled broadly. "Thank you," she said.

Just as she stood up to go in and see how Darious was getting along, Renee came out to the porch. The sun was now setting and the clouds on the horizon produced glows that rivaled the most transcendental nebulas. Sampson motioned for her to sit in his lap.

Once she had settled he pointed out to the desert and asked, "Look out; what do you see?"

"Umm." Renee looked out to where his finger was directing. "I see a cactus."

"No, past the cacti, what do you see?"

"I see some bushes. Sand. Oh look, a dust devil!"

"And past that?"

"I see... hills past that." She looked up at him, though his eyes remained fixed to the end of the world. She looked back out. "The horizon. Clouds!" she answered excitedly.

"And past that?" he continued.

"Past that?"

"Yes."

"Umm. Past that...I suppose..." she paused, her face blank.

Zoe bent down to be at eye level with the little girl and looked out with her. "Past that is space."

"Space!" The girl blurted, her voice assured. She turned to her grandfather, "but space isn't anything. I learned that in school grandpa."

He responded, "Space is not just the empty distance between destinations, it is all of this—all the planets, moons, and stars, you and I, everything; an endless sky." His definition seemed to be lost on Renee.

"Well all, the sun has gone down, and the moons are always up," said Zoe as she took Renee by the hand, "I think it's just about bedtime."

Next morning, Sampson Thorgood served a heaping pile of waffles and eggs, which earned more praise from Darious as he ate with cheeks packed full. They all sat around the wooden kitchen table, Renee wagging in her seat while she ate and Zoe deciding to join in with her antics, elevating the laughter in the room until Zoe recalled another memory from her childhood.

"Sampson, do you remember, ah what was it called, Lake Semp-or-eel?"

"Lake Semporal. Yes." Zoe's eyes lit up. "Ah. A good summer destination indeed. A good place relax for a bit. It's in Regole, just shy of the 85th parallel."

Darious swallowed another large morsel. "Lake Semporal?"

"You'll like it. Come on! We're burning daylight!" Zoe quickly stood up and tucked in her chair.

Her great uncle stood up too. "No leaving before I get a hug." Zoe wrapped her arms around him and then smothered Renee.

"Bye Renee, see you soon okay. You keep an eye out on this one." Zoe thumbed towards Sampson.

Renee responded with a dutiful look. "I will! Bye Zoe, I love you!"

"You too." And with that Zoe was already at the doorway motioning for Darious.

"You had better go if you want to keep up with her," said Sampson to Darious who was still at the table and had paused mid-chew. He swallowed and stood up, backing in his chair. Sampson held out his hand. "It was a pleasure."

"Thank you, sir," said Darious.

Zoe skipped all the way back to her ship with Darious in tow. "Come on slow-poke!"

The pair boarded the craft and were on their way, a quarter turn around the planet and soon parked at a small lake shaped like a figure-eight. The park was a bit dismal and the heat of the day was sweltering. They were the only people for kilometers. Zoe deboarded with a couple towels and Darious carried two white folding lounge-chairs.

"Set them there, as close to the water as you can." As soon as he had, Zoe plopped down on one and stretched out. "Darious, there are some very specific, serious laws at this lake. Numero uno: take a seat, lean back, and relax." He complied. "Now, take a deep breath in. Like me." Zoe filled her lungs "and exhale, slowly." She blew out the air and could hear the same from Darious. "Now smell!" She picked up her nose and again inhaled. "Ahh." She reclined further. Soft splashes of water nipped at her bare feet and the hot wind that had circumnavigated the planet brushed across her face. After a short while she could feel the onset of that other-worldly feeling when dreams begin to connect to reality and wandering thoughts expand like ripples on the water's surface.

Zoe came to around noon as her stomach began to rumble. She realized Darious was snoring. Smiling, she tapped him on the shoulder and softly spoke, "Hey, do ya want some food? I'mma run to the ship and grab some stuff."

He turned over and faced her with sleepy eyes. "No thank you."

Zoe soon returned with a single silver pouch and ripped into it. Laying back, she scanned the surface of the lake. Nothing had changed. The small population of the planet allowed for the preservation of the whole for ages and little beaches like this one remained more or less untouched. Though it was nice and calming, she couldn't imagine spending more than a couple day's repose here. It was after all, quite a dull place. Zoe snickered. Dull. She lazily eyed the rolling waves in the distance and tracked their nodes from side to side. They could continue indefinitely, lurching forward to fill the lower energy state in front while being urged onward from behind. At the core of pseudo-forces, like the Coriolis Effect, were the real ones—oscillations, motion from harmonics. Zoe followed the waves for so long she soon felt the same bobbing motion within herself. In her musings she imagined herself as a crest just as a watery trough came along, a node in perfect harmony with its antinode. What would happen? Negation; nothingness.

Zoe sat straight up; her entire mind had suddenly ignited. "I can't believe I missed it!"

Darious tilted his head and stared at her.

"Wha—," he began.

"Darious!" her eyes were sparkling "Before I met you at the space port, I was having a conversation with a semi driver about sensor ghosts he had experienced in deep space."

"Sensor gho—," Darious began, but was shut down by Zoe continuing her excited thought.

"His ship had errored for a minute, even though he'd been completely shielded in a faraday cage, and all commercial fleets utilize redundant systems. That's where we were a few weeks ago. I obtained the coordinates from him and checked it out for myself."

Darious was now fully awake and sat up. "But I thought you did not find any abnormalities, Zoe."

"You're right. But in fact, we did miss something. Something so big we were staring right at it and couldn't see it for what it was." Darious looked like a blank slate. "We must go to the IRC Majora Station!"

"What was there that we missed?" he asked.

"No, no Darious, aren't you listening? It's what wasn't there! That's what we're going to find!" The slate crumbled but Zoe paid it no mind; she was still completely jolted. "Darious, I can't believe we missed it!" She quickly packed up her things and began running back to the ship with Darious picking up the chairs and everything else as fast as he could to ensure he kept up with her.

CHAPTER 7
MAJORA'S MASK

Darious was just finishing to strap himself in as the thrusters roared to life and the ship began its explosive ascent. Zoe was at the helm; her gaze set beyond the limits of the atmosphere to a destination beyond the limits of sight. Darious' voice shook as the ship tore through the turbulent ionosphere of the planet.

"Zoe, where are we travvveling to?"

She turned toward him and was about to answer but laughed as she saw him belted sideways to his seat.

"Darious, we are headed to the IRC." She giggled and turned back.

The ship evened out as it reached space. Zoe leaned over her console, bringing up several virtual screens of coding. Meanwhile, Darious worked to release himself and then joined her at her side.

"Zoe, what is the IRC?"

"A sub-ionic research station."

"Oh. What is that?"

She continued typing. "A place where people study radiation from the universe."

"Oh. And—"

Zoe interjected, "Hold on, and hold onto to something Skipper. I'm going to initiate the turbo drive." She pressed her finger to a button with a lightning face. Darious stumbled backwards a few steps until the sudden acceleration evened out. Without looking from her screens, she asked "Are ya still alive back there?"

"Yes. Zoe, we need to work on your warnings."

"Ya ya. Can you go to the central room? Directly to your left, open the third drawer up from the floor." Her fingers continued programming. "Look for a rectangular black box with lots of small circles on one side."

Moments later Darious came back with said item. She quickly glanced at it. "Yup, that's it. Okay, now smash it on the floor."

"What?"

"Lift it high and fling it to the ground." She made a motion with one hand while the other continued pelting the keyboard.

Darious perplexedly looked at the box and proceeded to break it on the ground, flinching as debris went flying. The enclosure burst apart, exposing electronics and wiring. Zoe, without missing a beat of her programming sonnet, instructed him to locate a specific circuit board with two long green wires. Then she had him open a panel on the lower left-side of the cockpit.

"Okay, so we gotta rewire the azimuthal elevators. I noticed they were a bit shaky on the last landing and though we can't feel it now, they're causing a bit of vibration to the hull. Nothing to worry about, just an inefficiency we can edit out."

Zoe told Darious to pull out the free ends of all the blue wire loops from within the panel and remove the insulation from each. In total Darious had counted out 245 thin-gauge wires. He was to connect each one to an open port on the electronic control board; it didn't matter which—the computer would sort them all out. As for the two green wires, Zoe was going insert them into the main control panel as soon as he was done and then the elevators could be balanced.

Darious went to work, meticulously hand welding all the wire connections by Zoe's guidance. At first, he clumsily fumbled along, but soon he was into the groove. Before Zoe knew it, he had announced he was on wire #115. She paused her computing and looked over at the human epitome, hunched over in the corner of her cockpit, methodically and carefully working away.

"Darious."

"Yes Zoe?" He didn't look up, as his concentration was still very much on his task.

She paused a moment, mouthing a few inaudible words before settling on the one that would do and softly spoke. "Thanks." Her mellifluous meaning expanded within herself and a soft smile lifted her lips, warming her cheeks.

"No problem," Darious quickly responded, not seeing the blossoming rose behind him. It budded for a few more moments before a gale of corporeality blew off its petals—a beeping began from the center console. Zoe whipped around and checked on several computer systems.

"The ship is prepped for full input, I just gotta finish these last sequences."

"Okay, Captain. I should be completed soon. By the way, I recently read that Polyflex tubing can sustain much more deteriorative wear. Perhaps later we could phase out these connectors with some." She peered over her shoulder for one more quick glance, smiled, and continued her computational onslaught.

The following day, after the azimuthal controls had been corrected, the ship reached its destination, the IRC Majora Station. Zoe explained to Darious it was funded by the local universities and originally tasked—hundreds of years ago—with studying the sights and sounds from the earliest recordable universal history, but now its main focus was to annotate universal constants out to n-th places.

As they neared the research center, its massive size had an obvious effect on Darious as he stared with eyes wide open. The Majora Station was composed of giant bulbous sections connected by long corridors, like a science fair project of geodesic marshmallows and toothpicks, with enormous satellite dishes protruding from several sections. Zoe snickered as she told Darious its bright white exterior was exactly what they should expect to see on its inside—white walls and white lab coats. She continued, "Yup, the nerdiness level in there is so high that it's seeping out through the seams." Darious remarked that he hadn't known intellect was a leaky physical substance. Zoe assured him it was.

The pair docked and as they were exiting the craft, Zoe stopped Darious and looked in his starlit eyes. "Darious, any tall tales I weave, just sew them with me, k?" He nodded in the affirmative. She took his hand. "Come on raggedy man!" and tugged him down the ramp.

They signed in at a computer interface and made their way past the first white bubble, through its only connecting corridor to a similarly-shaped, albeit larger, white lounge area with chairs. Zoe espied a console on the wall. She walked over to it and began navigating through the station's computer while Darious looked around. Zoe read through a list. "Uh huh. Uh huh. Uh huh." One eye flickered and she took in a longer breath, "uh huuh." Darious came next to her. "It seems we are in luck. The Margo Sector was scanned at the time of the incident. Now we gotta find someone who will let us see the data." Zoe keyed in the location of the student labs. "Alright, let's go."

Several marshmallow rooms later, they reached the laboratory section and Zoe paused at a lab marked by the Greek letter 'Phi' with two transparent sliding doors underneath it. Looking inward, Zoe saw a single person, seeming to be in his mid-20s, tinkering with some electronic tubes. There were instruments and gadgets on tables and on the floor, and a large clear tank at the center of the room. Zoe stepped up to the doors, which opened horizontally at her presence. The individual looked up from his work, his body freezing as he saw her, his young moustache forming an "M" as he mouthed his surprise. He adjusted his glasses and put the pen he was using into his pallid lab coat.

"Hello!" said Zoe cheerfully.

He stumbled over his words for a moment. "He-hello."

Zoe confidently strolled toward him. "I'm Zoe. And this," she motioned behind her, "is Darious."

His lip curled slightly downward upon seeing Darious. Zoe noted that for being so young, societal ego apparently had a strong grasp on him already. He was probably one of those reclusive types, not taking in what college was supposed to teach one about an open mind before being too compacted by roles and responsibilities. "I," said Zoe, cutting into whatever thoughts he might be having, "am looking for someone to help us, to help me."

His eyes lingered on her for a moment. "What is it-can I do for you?" he said, his voice slightly squeaking.

"But before you do, do tell me about this experiment you're running!" She walked over to the clear tank and ran her finger along its riveted edges.

"Please, please don't touch it. It's very sensitive."

She tapped the glass. "Seems to be filled with de-ionized water. Let me guess, you're running trials on subatomic particle vector potentials during their flight through this," she tapped on the glass again, "aqueous medium." He looked momentarily stunned. Zoe held out her hand. "We are from the university; just here to check a couple things. This lab seems to be in tip top order."

At this the student seemed to relax a bit. "Pleased to meet you," he said as he shook her hand. Darious offered his but it was ignored. "I'm John Echelon. Professor Hollik is my advisor."

"Very good. So please, tell us more about your experiment."

"Yes, ma'am." He spun a ceiling-mounted computer screen around and brought up several line charts. "Through the water solution, utilizing simulation quantum energy potentials, I am setting and tracking electron movement possibilities. What's so very interesting about this is the likelihood that each particle during its swim is in fact not swimming at all, nor even in the reservoir!" Zoe looked impressed and nodded her approval. "It is truly fascinating work." He expanded the charts. "During parallel accelerated runs through 100,000 years' time, completed within nine months, thanks to the hyper-span infinitesimal string computational methods I'm utilizing; it's what my dissertation is on, I found fourteen instances of tracked electrons beyond this room, even though they were wholly contained within the reservoir." That ego again showed through in his tone. "My experiment is good to the thirteenth decimal; only four off from the current standard model." *Oh, how so very boring.*

"Oh, wow! Very good sir," Zoe said sounding captivated.

"Yes," he replied self-assured.

"However, for the moment allow us to have you stray from your experiment. Could you aid us with the hollo-plotter? It's different from the one we have, and I don't want to risk interfering with another's work."

"Yes, ma'am. No problem whatsoever." Zoe noticed a slight reddening of his cheeks.

"By all means, lead the way, John."

He was careful to swing around Zoe, though brushed up against Darious somewhat aggressively. Zoe turned back and gave Darious a sympathetic look. They followed the student through a maze of corridors and bulbous laboratories until they reached a set of silver double-doors. John typed into the control panel and the doors slid into the walls, revealing a spherical room with the floor stretching along its center line, elevated from the true ground like a tongue with railings. As the three stepped in, diffused illumination lit the short pathway to a large control panel at its center. John turned on the console with a flick of his wrist and the entire room lit up with astronomical grandeur. The surrounding sphere became transparent, yielding an unobstructed, digital view of outer-space. Even as Zoe looked behind them, the doors they had come through had vanished and for all appearances they were now floating amongst the stars. Darious turned around several times in awe.

"Okay," said John, "What in particular can I retrieve for you?"

Zoe focused back on him. "Margo Sector. 24-28-853. Timestamp: 3270975. Give or take."

As John typed, the stars around them flew backwards, disappearing beyond the group's periphery. Zoe saw Darious stumble a moment on the unmoving floor and chuckled. The trio zoomed through floating-parsecs in mere moments with entire solar systems flying by. The computer animation began to slow, and they soon stopped. Then the space surrounding them rotated, lining up the bright ring of the Milky Way with their horizontal axis.

"Perfect," said Zoe. "Now, please display all ion trails from twelve hours before to twelve hours after."

"Resolution?" asked John.

"Umm. Let's start at 10 meters. That would show vehicle traffic, correct?"

"Yes, ma'am." As he typed into the console, the view of 3D space did not change. "So, what is this for anyhow?" John asked.

Zoe ignored his question. "I don't see anything. Let's try lowering the resolution." The panorama remained the same. "Lower the resolution."

"I did. We are at 1 centimeter, the minimum before the image will start to become fuzzy from qua—"

"What?" said Zoe, perturbation stirring her voice.

"We are at 1 centi—"

"Yes. Yes. Okay let's broaden our scope then. Zoom to a single cubic floating-parsec." The stars around them quickly closed in and more pushed into view. "Where is the ion trail? Are you sure your plotter is tuned?"

"Yes, ma'am." John pulled up a projection screen which floated just above them, showing calibration logs, all with green checkmarks next to them.

"Zoom out. 10 floating-parsecs." The view of the cosmos once more scoped out, now presenting a vast collection of stars. Darious heaved and swallowed, putting a hand on the railing. A wavy band of pink became observable at this scale leading diagonally across the room. "There we go," said Zoe. "Sooo..." She followed it along its winding path through the stars and then pointed above them. "There." There was a small blip in the otherwise unbroken string. "What is that?"

"It appears to be the ion trail from a small cargo ship," said John.

"Indeed. It's a semi's ion trail," said Zoe. "But look, there is a piece missing."

John rescoped the 3D screen so that just the tip of either pink line was visible on either side of them and they were standing within its gap. "That is where we started. 24-28-853. Correct?"

"Yes. But..." She paused in thought. "So, we are being shown that a semi was rambling along here." She pointed to the pink line at their right side. "Went somewhere." She gestured at the blank space right in front of them. "And then reappeared over there." She exaggeratingly tossed her arm to their left to where the line continued on.

"Yeah," said John. "That is really... odd. Who knows."

"Who knows! Oh, come on! Look. Do this: same zoom as we currently are, but put us at nanometer resolution."

"But the rendering will suffer—"

"John, now." He did so, revealing a pixilated mesh of pink dots and lines all around them, except for the same perfect sphere carved out from the centered location. "Isn't it obvious that this spot has been edited out?" said Zoe flatly. John turned around and stared at her with a peeved look on his face.

"Edited? I beg your pardon?"

She sighed and pulled out her lightcard, setting it on the control panel. *Azimuthal elevators are one thing, but this is on a whole other level.*

"Please download the information to this."

John typed in a command and blue swirls on the panel emanated around the lightcard. In a few seconds they were replaced by a crisp green circle, signifying the sync was complete. "Okay John, please bring up the lights; we need to move on." Zoe was already leaving the room with Darious trailing her as the doorway once more reappeared. At the end of the hallway, she sat on a metal bench and Darious took a seat next to her. She thought back to Semporal beach. *Nothingness.*

"Zoe," began Darious, as if reading her thoughts, "this is what you had suspected at the lake, is it not?"

She looked over at him. "While we were at those spatial coordinates, I had scanned everything around us inside and out. Nothing. Not even any evidence a transport vessel had recently been through there. Ya, I figured something was up."

John came up a moment later. "Well, ma'am, is there anything else I can do for you?"

She looked up at him and smiled. "Would you happen to have a singlet vectorizor in the microwave-band?"

He thought for a moment. "Yes. There should be one or two in Storage Six with the other microwave instruments. Follow the hallway to the left and take your fist right at the next juncture. Then follow it straight to its end."

"Thank you, John."

"Anything else I can do for you?"

"No. I do appreciate your help. Keep up the good work."

When he had left, Zoe stood up and looped Darious' arm around hers. She smiled at him. "Let's go pick up the vectorizor and we'll be on our way."

Upon reaching Storage Six, Zoe at first thought the door was locked; she couldn't even find a service panel. "Ugh. It's not like anyone's going to steal anything." She pulled out her light-card and after typing a few commands into it, she held it up next to the door. "Ah, it has a magnetic lock. Probably to keep out those hooligans." She pushed hard and it simply opened with a loud pop. Shrugging to Darious, Zoe entered in, returning with a bronze device having multiple ports on either of its two long ends. "You never know when you're going to need one of these." She smiled to him and the two made their way back to the ship.

Darious seemed to be more at ease once the gangway had retracted and they had both resumed their respective chairs. Zoe brought up the data from the lightcard on her main monitor. "Do you think they would be upset if they knew I had uploaded their entire main frame?" She shot Darious a smart look and turned back to her monitor. "Naa."

She flipped through several screens. "Erik's flightpath has indeed been edited out of existence." She swiveled to Darious. "Now the question is, who would do that?"

"I suppose a good follow-up question, for Mr. Erik, is why?" said Darious.

"Right," agreed Zoe.

"But can you even 'edit' out an ion trail?"

"Sure can," said Zoe, continuing to scroll through the compiled information from the IRC. "However, it takes a real effort and real power. Imagine a controlled burn of open information from all around the galaxy, and not just, that but from under the noses of public institutions and so on. Covert military operations used to do it when the technology first became available. Then corporations used to do to hide exports for tax reasons. I have seen edited ion trails, but this one is really a brute. Brute and blunt. Seems someone has a tad of arrogance about them, supposing that no one was going to have a look into it." She added rhetorically, "And who would? So, a semi, among a million other semis, malfunctioned and lost a day. No one was hurt. No one but the driver saw anything. There is really nothing to do. And I bet anyone who sees that little missing blip will just assume it's a glitch. But we know that Erik's time-location stamp matches up. Galactic coincidence? I think not." She paused in thought. "What is going on here?"

Zoe looked at Darious, at those tattooed eyes, and could feel her own being etched. She sat in silence for a few minutes, continuously matching up her fingers and pulling them apart like a zipper. A thought entered her mind and excitation followed. "Darious, I believe I remember Erik mumbling something about filing a report. I assume it has been deleted like the semi's ion trail. However, it may give us a clue as to the why and the who did this."

Zoe did a quick search and found all semi-drivers in the region were employed by the shipping company, Millennium Co. Luckily, their local headquarters was only a couple of floating-parsecs away.

"Well, well. Let's see what the Millennium has to offer," said Zoe with a half-cocked, surely grin, and the ship blasted onwards to its target.

CHAPTER 8
FROM EGGS TO ONIONS

Zoe had looked up more information on Millennium Co. and decided to give them a call. "Darious, hang around, but don't say anything." He nodded. Zoe initiated the call and two thin microphones raised from either side of the captain's console encircled by a ring of neon-blue. The speakers around the cabin crackled momentarily as the call connected.

"Good day," came a woman's nasally voice, "Welcome to the new Millennium, Sub 6. How may I direct your call?"

Zoe smiled at Darious who was hanging overtop her chair. "Hello, ma'am, this is Martha Wagner. I have a friend who uses your services. Through him, I had the recent pleasure to meet one of your drivers, a Mr. Erik..." Zoe quickly pulled up his information. "Mr. Erik W. Cavendish. He did such a fantastic job; I wish to hire him for shipments to a new business I'm heading up." There was a momentary pause on the other end.

"Yes Mrs. Wagner, we can help you with that. We are always pleased to hear positive feedback from our drivers. One moment please." There was a brief pause. "You said Mr. Erik Cavendish?"

"Yes," said Zoe.

"Oh, our apologies, ma'am, Mr. Cavendish is no longer with the company. May I suggest another driver for your needs? We carry a substa—"

"Erik is no longer with the company?"

"I'm sorry, ma'am."

"Why is that?"

"One moment please," said the secretary.

"Darious," Zoe whispered under her breath, "it's never easy, is it?" Darious nodded in agreement.

"Ma'am?" the voice crepitated over the speakers in the cabin.

"Yes?" said Zoe.

"Mr. Erik Cavendish was let go eight weeks ago. I do apologize for the inconvenience."

Zoe didn't skip a beat, "May I ask why he was let go? He was such a very good driver."

"I'm sorry, ma'am."

Zoe strengthened her voice and added a dash of incredulity. "Miss, I am a woman of little patience. I request to know why Erik was fired. You can be sure I will be following up with your superiors." There was another pause from the other end.

"Ma'am, it shows on my records that Mr. Cavendish was let go for inebriation during a delivery."

Zoe turned to Darious with a wince and whispered, "Well, that I might believe." Then Zoe snapped back to the microphones.

"Wait, let go eight weeks ago? I saw him on a delivery just a few weeks ago."

"I'm sorry, ma'am. Mr.—"

"It was a delivery in your region and he didn't seem like he was bootlegging."

"Bootlegging? Ma'am, I—"

"Millennium Co. is the only delivery service in the area, am I correct?" asked Zoe.

"Yes, ma'am, Millennium has established itself as the premier delivery service for the nearest forty sectors and is..." Zoe muted the microphone and spoke over the woman.

"Darious, Erik sure seemed to be on a run for Millennium. He had mentioned logging, and the cargo he was hauling was within their line of business. And considering they have the monopoly here..."

"More of this 'editing' perhaps?"

"I do think so," replied Zoe, unmuting the microphones and cutting into the sectary's continued diatribe. "Excuse me, do you have the forwarding information for Erik?"

She paused, and Zoe could hear distinct annoyance through the phone line. "I'm sorry, ma'am. I'm not seeing anything here."

"I expected as much. Well, thanks. Have a good day." Zoe hung up the line before the secretary could respond.

"Oh Darious, it's going to be one of those days."

"It is odd, is it not?" he asked, standing next to her. "It seems unusual for a business to carry on this way."

"Oh, trust me, it's not. But it feels more than your run-of-the-mill company corruption. I dunno Darious, I have an odd feeling about all this. Shall we continue further drown the rabbit hole?" Darious looked a bit puzzled. Zoe tried again, "Shall we explore this mystery further?" At this, Darious displayed a bit of nervous excitement.

"By all means Miss," he quickly cleared his throat, "Zoe." He smiled bashfully.

"Okay Mister Darious, get to your station. We have a bit of... investigative computing to do." Zoe stretched out her arms and cracked her fingers while Darious prepped himself at his virtual console.

First up was general research regarding Millennium Co. They found it had greatly expanded its shipping influence in the last ten years after being acquired by the corporate giant, Pantheon Industries. That struck a cord with Zoe; she had heard of Pantheon—it had its porky finger in most everything. Now that was certainly one black hole to be avoided. Before being gulped down, Millennium had thrived on a smaller scale as the company 'Two Guys and a Semi' but it was their more recent history Zoe was interested in.

"Darious, can you search for any and all information on Millennium's driver stats, hiring and firing rates, etcetera? That is, if they have such information public."

"Certainly captain."

Zoe herself was absorbed in research on Pantheon Industries. The black hole had begun to consume her. The conglomerate had existed for centuries and had subsidiaries out the wazoo, including subsidiaries within sub-subsidiaries. The corporate headquarters occupied an entire planet. Now that was logistics. The further Zoe looked, the more she realized, Pantheon, in some form or another, was indeed everywhere: shipping companies, metal-work companies, and even printing companies. As her head began to whirl, she paused and decided to oversee Darious' progress over his shoulder.

"I have not been able to find any pertinent information," he said.

"I'm not surprised they don't have it available, but it was worth a shot. We may have to go a bit deeper. Come and sit next to me." She resumed her seat and diminished all prior research, bringing up a clean screen. "Millennium Co." Its home screen popped up with a graphic of a burley man shaking hands with a businesswoman and several descriptive lines below them. Zoe brought up a second window, overlaying the first with developer coding. She navigated though it with the same swiftness by which she piloted her ship. Upon a third window, she began her own coding which drew feedback from the website. "A little peep is all we need. No need to open a backdoor, just a little peeeep through the keyhole."

She waited a minute and then was signaled that 63 of the 10,000 attempts by her computer were successful. Several more screens appeared, and Zoe picked out a singular one, navigating through its many titles and subfolders. She homed in on the company logs at the date of Erik's bamboozling booze occurrence.

Upon opening it, she sighed. "Of course," she said. Darious looked in closer. "See there," Zoe said pointing.

"Ah, yes. The gap between hours 13:00 and 16:00."

"It's all gone. And there should at least be the user-access information automatically generated here." She pointed to a lower left-hand string of text "But it's also been blanked out. Looking at these data chunks, this sure looks to be an outside job." Zoe poked around a few more files, but no further pertinent information presented itself. She closed up the search, piece by piece, in the reverse order of her inward navigation, backing out and fully restoring each data block to its initial position. All traces of her peek-a-boo game would be nullified. She closed the last window with triumph and then looked over at Darious, "Well, considering how the Majora Station was wiped and now this, it sure looks like someone up high is pulling the strings." She pulled at imaginary whiskers on her face. "I'm tempted to look into Pantheon Industries, but oh man, that could be a bad idea."

"Repercussions?"

"Pretty bad I imagine. Consider a corporation with multiplicities of quintillions of dollars, capable of who knows what—for sure able to bend diplomatic wills and wield the CF as its personal lap-dog. And as for the CF—you certainly don't want to be on their bad side."

Zoe turned to the view of outer-space, staring at the grand magnificence just outside her window. The Milky Way shone brilliantly. "Ah screw it; just a peek." She began the same computational procedure, but after thirty minutes and 4,815,162,342 attempts by her computer, no backdoors could be pried open. Zoe was soon enthralled in all sorts of work-arounds while Darious silently watched. After another half hour of furious typing and negative alerts, inspiration struck. "Aha! I just remembered another way." Fifteen minutes passed in unspoken data-crunching fervor. "Damn. Okay, we're going to need all the computing power we got." She laid her lightcard on the table which her projection console encircled with blue rings, integrating the device's computing capabilities with its own. "Have any electronics on you?" she asked Darious.

"No, sorry."

Zoe continued typing and soon another alert went off. She instantly wiped all windows clean and yanked the lightcard from the console. She sighed. "Well, the information seems to be stored locally. Makes sense I suppose." Zoe drummed her fingers on the armrest. "We can try to pick it up from somewhere local, upload the information tied to their internal servers. I bet one of their larger subsidiaries would have access."

"I have concerns," said Darious, "but Zoe, I agreed to join you down the hole for lagomorphs." He nodded courteously to her, stood up and resumed his own seat.

"No worries. We will be quick."

Zoe compiled a short list of major Pantheon extensions nearby them. "Bingo. They have a wholly-owned industrial zone not too far off. Skipper, change course! We've got some huntin' to do!" She shot the coordinates over to Darious' console.

"Aye captain!" he affirmed, with a hint of excited zeal in his voice.

Zoe observed him as he carefully input the new destination into the ship's computer, just as she had shown him, and approved of his work. The ship made an elegant sweep toward its new objective, powered on by its meteoric rockets.

Zoe looked out at the stars. *That was a dirty hack,* she thought. *And nothing to show for it. What was it about the cat? Curiosity killed the cat.* Well, that was until Schrödinger came along. So maybe they had a chance. That was the funny thing about the fundamental laws of physics—it basically boiled down to luck.

CHAPTER 9

SIGNS POINT TO A MILD, YET ABRUPT SPRING

"That is a small planet we are headed toward. Is it some sort of free-roaming dwarf?" asked Darious as the ship neared the yellowed spheroid. "There are no stars in vicinity and it is certainly not part of any solar system."

"Sort of," Zoe replied, "It's been artificially grown. One of dozens in this sector. It's more of a factory than a planet. Notice the exhaust at the southern pole?"

"Yes! I do see it! Is it a factory in its entirety? Massive."

Black plumes puffed from planet's bottom, dissipating as they reached the edge of the atmosphere. Darious leaned in, squinting his eyes, so Zoe brought up a window that mimicked their view and zoomed in at the base of the plumes, revealing monstrous smoke stacks.

"Alright," said Zoe "I'm inputting landing coordinates now. See that the craft lands safely. I've gotta prepare some things." She went to the ship's main cabin and began shuffling through compartments as Darious took control of the helm. She prepared a small sack with supplies and soon reentered the cockpit. Leaning over the captain's chair, she put a hand on Darious' shoulder. "What's the damage capt'n?" she said playfully. Darious turned to her with an expression searching of hers, and she smirked, prompting a blank expression from him. He turned and refocused on his task.

Down went the craft. The thick miasma of the planet whipped at the heat dissipaters on the bow of the ship, making for a slightly rocky descent as the ship worked its best to disperse the energy. Darious was constantly adjusting a plethora of landing parameters, though despite his best efforts, Zoe had to put both arms around the captain's seat. Through syrupy clouds of pollution, the ground slowly became perceivable. Grays from building tops sketched into view and spotted citrines and browns were strewn throughout the landscape to the horizon. The mock planetoid looked sickly. It coughed a deep black cough from its deepest bowels and its skin was flecked with some sporelating pathosis; it was forsaken—alone to suffer its corruptible disease away from its natural, healthy kin. Up came the ground warnings.

"Okay Darious, steady," said Zoe. With a slight nod, though not taking his eyes from the controls, Darioius continued typing, priming all systems for landing. The craft took several drops as uncorrected turbulence overtook the dampeners. Zoe increased her grip on the chair. "Easy now." The ship was descending sluggishly, with its underside nearly parallel to the ground and its landing thrusters firing spasmodically as Darious maintained a rough balance. Not the way Zoe would have done it, but to each his own. She was accustomed to coming in like a lion, and going out, well, also like a lion.

Zoe could see sweat forming on Darious' forehead. "You have this. Oh, look, just over there."

The virtual monitor had marked the landing station which was soon visible through the cockpit window. Several ships were at the port, some were landing, others taking off, and a few seemed to have been docked for quite a while. *Overall,* noted Zoe, *not an overly busy day.* It was a fine day for a new pilot to land an interstellar spacecraft. The computer indicated the particular landing pad which the control tower had designated for Zoe's ship.

With a loud thud, and a low bending of its alloyed knees, the ship came to its final resting position. Pressure exhaust motors initialized, signifying a successful, albeit hard, landing. Zoe patted Darious on the back. "Not bad! Come on, let's get the low-down on what's up."

The two exited the craft and were instantly greeted by the stench of burning oils and waste. Shades of grays and yellows stained every wall of every building; the terrain was stewing in its own filth. Darious' initial breath led to him cough several times. "I'd advise against breathing here," Zoe bantered.

Above the tarnished structures, Zoe noticed several high-rise highway tubes in the distance transporting heavy machinery. Nearer, podways connected every building and many converged to the largest—an off-white tower, beginning as a smooth sloping structure, pleasing to the eye and topped by an obdurate cube with uniformly placed windows. *That must be the central hub,* thought Zoe. For their purpose, it would be a good access point.

Their landing pad was one of many. Each was slightly elevated, circular, and connected to a railed podway. Zoe and Darious stepped into an awaiting pod. It noiselessly closed its doors behind them and swooshed onwards to the towering main station. Zoe motioned for Darious to look back at the port they were rapidly receding from.

"Did you notice the entire port resembles a 2D grape bushel? And guess what—that is on purpose. Many ports throughout the galaxy have such a design. Random as the distribution of grapes may seem, they are not." With her index fingers, she outlined a group of circles as she spoke. "Nature has found a particular fractal-based algorithm where each singular berry of an entire branch has the opportunity to have a complimenting amount of light—space for outgoing and incoming flights—and a proportional lifeline to the ground—distance to the main station." She paused for dramatic effect, but saw no awe in his eyes and so continued, "The algorithm, a very delicious one," she smirked, "has aided in both fruitful endeavors of nature, and of society. Stations such as this, are allowed to remain compact and efficient. This same algorithm is also utilized for shipping, manufacturing, raw material production, and even to guide some educational programs of students." Darious seemed now a bit impressed, but not to the point of physical excitement.

He asked, "And what about raspberries?" Before Zoe could answer, the pod reached the inner station and the door opened with a chime.

"Ah, here we are." She scooted Darious out first. The pair was welcomed by a grand sight from the central interior of the tower. Pseudo-timber arches extended out from white polished floors, stained in places with yellow like the rest of the planet. They arced twenty stories high, curving sharply and coming back down again. They reminded Zoe of pictures she had seen of cathedrals, but somehow, they were missing that ethereal quality. To Zoe, this place reeked of the self-imposed sanctity to which the business-world assigns to its purposes, in addition to its many unidentifiable foul odors.

Darious was turning in circles, his mouth open and eyes dazzling. Zoe looked around herself and saw byways leading to many other pods and out and away from the building. She spotted a control console at the leading edge of a nearby beam. She motioned to Darious as she repositioned the backpack upon her shoulder.

When Zoe accessed the screen, a motion graphic of the 'Millipede Manufacturing Company' zoomed into view and then flew off. "Welcome" a woman's robotic voice announced and lowly echoed throughout the empty hall. Zoe again motioned to Darious who was still mesmerized by the dizzying height of the open architecture above him.

"Come check this out." He walked over and stood next to her. A video tour began, showing the different operations around the planet—metallurgy and circuit printing to the south, civil construction northward, manufacturing and assembly to the west, packaging and shipping to the east, and metrology and pressure testing at the planet's core. The rendering of the planet became translucent, presenting a view of its structured interior. In addition to overhead tubes circumscribing the planet, there were tubes within for fast travel from one sector to another. The globe then flattened out and red dots lit up, signifying all the hubs around the planet. "We are here." Zoe pointed to just below the equator. The screen magnified on that dot, showing a 3-dimensional local map, including bathrooms and eateries. "Oh, that's useful." She scrolled around the map, zooming in and out. "Somewhere like this may do us some good." She had centered on a grouping of presentation suites within their hub.

"Sounds good," said Darious. Just then, they heard a chime behind them as another pod entered the station.

"Come on, let's go."

They made their way past the arch entrance to the building's large commercial center, comprised of a central overbearing hallway with rows of double doors on either side, each giving way to large company conference rooms and presentation auditoriums. Zoe peeked through the open ones and saw all were empty. They hadn't even passed by a single person thus far.

"I guess this place isn't really a popular vacation spot, is it?" she rhetorically asked. They winded through several smaller corridors, ending up at a sector having secondary presentation suites. Zoe poked her head in one and saw it had a central projection screen and several rows of elevated seats. "This will do.

Please close the door behind you." Zoe flipped on the lights, fully illuminating the mauve carpeting and fabric chairs. She stepped to the podium and began busying herself with its digital interface. "Take a seat Darious. Get comfortable." She brought out her lightcard and set it on top of the podium, periodically checking it whilst navigating through the factory's digital infrastructure. She quickly found, to her relief, that this station was indeed connected to Pantheon Industries' servers, but the firewalls were stratospheric. Zoe brought out an electronic module from her sack and connected it to her lightcard. "Darious, this may take a bit of time. Can you do me a favor and keep an eye around the door? It would be quite inauspicious for someone to come snooping."

Right then, the same mechanical woman's voice sounded from the podium. "I'm sorry, I can't let you do that."

"Shhh!" Zoe uttered to the screen as the ringing voice echoed momentarily.

Despite a few more similar interruptions, Zoe was slicing and dicing her way through the online system, but she had to admit it was very well done. She soon came upon a set of files which sparked her curiosity. "Ah, I think I've got a bit of something."

"Zoe," whispered Darious, though he had done it so loudly it came off as husky, "I think someone is coming." He eased the door shut from the crack he had been peering out from and slowly backed away from it. Zoe searched with even more rapidity.

She whispered back to him, "Darious, Erik was not the only one; there are dozens of deleted spatial-time points just in the last couple years. If I could just—"

"I'm sorry, I can't let you do that," came the woman's voice again, shattering their chalice of solitude.

Heavy steps sounded just outside the door. Zoe wiped the screens and typed in a quick command into her lightcard, shutting down the podium's computer. With one quick motion, she scooped up her things into the open backpack and jumped off the stage next to Darious, just as the door opened and a heavy-set man with a tucked in white-striped shirt and navy-blue slacks entered in.

"Hey! You two! What are you doing in here?"

A security guard, Zoe quickly surmised. "Sir," she said in her most innocent voice, "my aide and I are a bit lost. These displays don't work like the ones at the station. Oh, can you help us find our way back?"

"Ma'am, step out of the room." She did so, Darious following behind her with his head bent low. The security guard gave him a stiff push forward as he passed by.

"Sir," Zoe tried to resume, "what a wonderful establishment you have." She noticed the man was gripping his pistol holster at his belt.

His stern demeanor was unyielding. "Ma'am, please." He held out his arm, gesturing for Zoe and Darious to start walking. "I will take you back to the station."

They were escorted in near silence for some time. Zoe pretended to be lost at every turn and the security guard only used the single words 'left' or 'right' to direct them. Zoe peeked over her shoulder several times and offered him a cheerful smile, but he remained at the ready, as if all he needed were the excuse that one of them had tried to make a run for it to shoot them dead. To her relief they were shortly upon the central station.

"Oh, thank you, thank you sir!" said Zoe. The security guard held up his hand to silence her and brought out a tablet. "Your name, designation, ID, and of course," he eyed her sardonically, "your reason for being here." She supplied him with a false name and a set of generic identification nodes from her lightcard—which she had previously created for a rainy day—and set to tell him a tale with such girlish prattle and such length that he soon lost interest and waved them off. As soon as he did, Zoe gestured to Darious with her eyes and they quickly made their way back to the pod.

As its door closed with a chime, Darious spoke, "Zoe what did—"

"Hush." She leaned in very close and whispered in his ear. "I have no doubt we are now being watched."

She straightened up and Darious slowly nodded. As soon as the pod had deposited them at their landing pad, Zoe unlocked the gangway with her lightcard and bounded up the ramp with Darious following right behind her. Once they entered in, she swung around in the captain's seat and ignited the thrusters, roaring upwards.

CHAPTER 10

TWO EYES, ONE NOSE, AND A FORKED TONGUE

The phone rang. A serpentine finger teased the handle for a moment before quickly grasping it and pulling it into the shadows.

"Yes?" The question was posed with extreme authority and provocation. Murmurs could be heard on the other end. "Yes." again was the response, with enough animosity to condemn an entire race. There were more submissive murmurs at the figure's ear. The voice died away and soon there was a silence on both ends, though from the shadows, the silence had a crushing force comparable to the vacuity of space. The sound of some seething snake escaped from the figure.

He leaned forward, exposing a square jaw to the ambient light from an etched window with silk brocade curtains. As the top of his necktie touched the light, it reflected with blue hues only capable from the finest pigmented platinum polymers forged by mankind. Its brilliant richness of color could have dazzled ancient people of Earth-1 to the point of worship.

"I will take care of the issue."

He placed the auriferous phone back in its engraved cradle. The snake slithered once more. With a sudden outburst, he banged a balled fist onto the 20th century cherry wood desk and then slowly slid back into the shadows. After a moment, he reached for the phone and spoke into it.

"Kappa Iota Lima."

"Yes sir," a cheerful attendant's voice responded. There was a clicking sound on the line for several moments, then the other end picked up.

"Kappa here."

"I have a job," said the shadow man.

"Yes sir."

"The particulars will be sent to you. I want you to observe them, at first. If those two, and yes, I am counting the clone." He wheezed in abhorrence as if the word despoiled his tongue. "If those two are bleating, then shear their heads from their bodies." There was a mechanical yet primal tone to his voice. He did not wait for a response and hung up the phone. Venom dripped from the snake's mouth.

CHAPTER 11

A FUNNY THING HAPPENED ON THE WAY TO TROY'S BANNER

As Zoe's ship reentered the vacuum of space beyond the factory's sphere of influence, Zoe and Darious both couldn't help but take several much-needed deep breaths in. Zoe sniffed her arm and then Darious' hair.

"Ugh. We reek of that wretched planet."

Darious nodded. "And that security man—"

"Also wretched. I know." Zoe sat in the captain's chair but quickly stood up again. "I'm going to rinse off." She looked him over. "Afterwards I suggest you do the same. I will see if I can find ya some clothes." Darious smiled; such niceties were not commonly bestowed upon him. "See if you can put the ship's filters into overdrive to help clear up this stench while I'm away."

"But..."

"No worries. Fiddle with the controls. It's the best way to learn the system." She smirked. "It's how I learned. Anyhow, what's the worst that could happen? The airlocks disengage, depressurizing the ship? The side thrusters activate, spinning us beyond the stabilizers' capacity and into a fine goop? Or perhaps the ship spontaneously self-implodes by an accidental over-clocking of the arc reactor?" Darious stared at her wide-eyed. "No worries." With that, she turned and left the cockpit.

Darious slowly sat in the hot seat and paused with his hands above the virtual keyboard as if his unworthy being was about to pick up the holiest of grails. He closed his bar-coded eyes, opening them again and accessing the first layer of the ship's computer systems.

"Let me see."

He soon navigated to a routine titled 'Aeration Sequence 1-99.' He opened it and suddenly heard a gurgling sound from elsewhere in the ship. He gasped and popped out of his seat, running to the central chamber. Darious paused all motion and listened. Zoe was in a side room behind a closed door. The gurgling stopped and started several more times, originating from this washroom. He exhaled with relief, now recognizing the sound for what it was—running water through the filtration system. He walked back to the cockpit and wiped sweat from his brow. Sitting once more, he read through the command lines for the routine package he had opened. The text read: 'Brew Aeration Sequencing System. Version: 1. Edits: 99. Purpose: digital analysis aid for determining the correct amount of froth to be applied to a cappuccino.' He did not recognize the last word.

Ah Zoe, he thought. Darious' mind lifted to new heights around her and his memories of lowly hitchhiking, and before that, of laboring in the mines, faded into dust. He recalled his initial hesitation when first witnessing her 'methods' but her heart seemed to be in the right place. Something new had sprung up in him. He was beginning to trust her, to believe in her.

Darious backed out of the program and navigated to other routines. He soon found one labeled 'Ship Thermostat.' As the program opened, a graphical user interface appeared, transposed across all screens around him with many options, command line cues, and charts. Off to his left, a virtual screen overlapping part of the cockpit window, read 'Onboard Filtration Settings.' In the command line, he typed 'enter.' The central screen instantly came back with text in red stating: 'are you sure?' He typed in 'y.' The left screen expanded and whipped across all other displays, presenting a plethora of options. Dazed, though optimistic from the progress made, he began reading through the list of options, using his finger to guide his sight through the many lines of text.

He stopped at one which read 'Internal Filtration C.O.D. Central.' Darious entered it and suddenly a shrill yelp erupted from the washroom. "No!" he gasped and frantically searched the screens for an 'end' option before quickly abandoning it and ran to save Zoe from whatever he'd done. "Zoe!" he yelled through the door.

"Damn that waters' hot. Surprised myself. I turned the heat too high. Everything okay out there?"

He opened his airways and panted. His face was pale, and his hands were shaking. "Yes," he said, his voice strained. "All okay. No problems here." Darious sighed and marched back to the cockpit, physically shaking off the certain doom he had faced. Sitting once more, he read over the subroutine and his heartbeat soon returned to normal. He carried on and navigated through more appealing options, spending time to read each thoroughly. He was slowly working his way down the list, being sure not to touch the keyboard until he was certain the right option had been found.

Presently, he entered into an enticing subfolder which brought up 5 items, each one containing a command line prompt. There were no descriptions, just titles and a line to type in dialog. He twiddled his fingers for a moment, rationalizing the possible catastrophic consequences. Feeling confident, he typed 'enter' into the option labeled 'Configure Central Air Purification.'

Suddenly, an alarm rang to life. The cleaving oscillatory siren made Darious leap into the air.

This was it, the end for Zoe and himself. How could he have done this? How could he have been so careless? Sweat from every pour of his body beaded up and rained down his body, cleansing his smog-stained skin and replacing it with a newer unpleasant odor. The many screens emptied themselves of menus and command prompts and were replaced by a single red statement outlined by a bold rectangle: 'Incoming Call.' His mental convulsions ceased, and he sucked in precious breath.

"Oh."

Darious was about to go to the washroom door to ask Zoe if he should answer, but as he turned she was already entering into the cockpit. Her hair was still wet from the shower, shining and adding to the radiance of her cleansed face. She was wearing a new set of clothes, similar to what she had on before, but the shirt contained a different graphic. Zoe looked at the screen and then at him, no doubt noticing his pallid, shaky composure.

"Did, uh..." Her grin was nearly splitting her face in two. "... did you see a ghost?"

Darious tried his best to compile himself. "You have a call," he sheepishly responded and pointed a shaking finger to the screen.

"I can see that." She continued to smile, now kindly moving past him with shimmering elegance. Zoe typed in a command, turning off the alert and engaged the call. The two circular blue lights on the left and right of the console lit up as the stereoscopic microphones rose. "Hello. This is Zoe." There was a low static on the other end. Zoe waited a moment. "Hello," she repeated.

A tinny and slightly distorted male voice came through. It spoke slowly, "Zoe... Zoe and the clone." The voice ceased and only static was heard. Darious suddenly began to feel very uneasy.

"Yes?" asked Zoe as she took her seat. Darious leaned in close behind her.

"Sto...stop what you're doing. They..." the voice paused. "They have marked you. You...you need to stop. And hide."

The voice was quivering worse than Darious had felt during his recent foray into the ship's computer systems. From the few lines the individual had spoken, Darious picked up on his truly tremulous manner, as if he were shaking from heart to fingertip. However, Darious thought the statements had sounded constructed, though clumsily delivered. Had the individual practiced these words?

"Interesting," Zoe stated, "Care to elaborate?" She silently began to touch-type. The voice on the other line did not speak, but the channel remained open. Zoe cleared her throat. "Okay then, whom am I talking to?"

Static crackled. "No one." The voice fidgeted. "Pl... please Miss Zoe and co... company, please end your activities into this mat...matter."

Zoe continued typing and suddenly paused. "What the hell?"

Darious looked down at her and whispered, "What is it?"

She muted the line. "The call is coming in through an FTL Fubier interstellar wave algorithm."

Darious scanned out to the horizons of his mind. "I am not familiar with the term. What does it mean?"

"It means he's calling from a very long ways away."

Zoe resumed the call. "Sir. Who is this? I can see your Fubier algorithm intertwined within the communication signal."

The call abruptly ended, and the blue encircled microphones slid back into the console. Zoe was already typing away. "He was using a proxy line shrouded to look like a normal communication signal. We can assume in order to mask his location, but the depth of the attenuation means it was sent from a very far location." Her fingers typed as an orchestra, harmonizing each keystroke into the next with a precision of steps that Darious thought could rival the great musicians of Earth-1. He knew they too had played instruments of keys and he had read their rhapsodies could produce such melodies that would stir the heart and even end wars. Zoe had that gift, though the melodies produced by her tapping of keys were not for the ear, but for something even more fundamental.

Zoe ended the concerto with an arm raised high and brought down her pointer finger to the control panel, engaging the program. "Well, that was an interesting call. I'm running a trace on it now. We shall soon see where our new friend hails from. Go ahead and shift our coordinates. I don't wanna be caught off guard."

Darious swallowed, producing an unintentional burp. His meandering cognizance suddenly snapped to attention. The events of the last hour all at once seized his mind, as if a Trojan horse had just opened and he was the lone fool staring up at a thousand men. He could feel his skin go cold and once more he became a washed-out version of his former self. Zoe looked over at him expectantly but her face eased.

"Darious, how about a nice hot shower?"

He nodded and made a strained smile. Zoe took his hand and led him to the washroom. She pointed to the left temperature control. "Careful with that one, it's a bit touchy."

CHAPTER 12

SOME PEOPLE JUST HAVE TOO MUCH TIME ON THEIR HANDS

Darious soon joined Zoe in the cockpit where she was pouring over the results of the call analysis. She was huffing continuously, having to read and reread entire strings of results. Without looking up she asked, "Did you find the clothes I put beside the door?"

"Yes Zoe. Thank you very much."

She turned in her chair and looked him up and down. The brown pants seemed a near perfect fit. Darious had tucked them neatly into the black boots she had also scrounged up. Of the three shirts she had laid out, he had chosen the ashen one and wore over it a leather vest that had slightly-worn trimmings, giving him the appearance of a veteran semi pilot. Darious' exposed, tanned arms revealed the coded tattoos on each ligament. His muscles were now apparent and larger than Zoe had first assumed. Seeing him cleaned up and in fresh clothes, she began to wonder about the 'clone.' The word was fluttering; he was a human being. Darious stood tall and proud, beaming at her. The statement continued to free-float like an autumn leaf in her mind. Human. Though she had never agreed with the way clones were treated, she had never had the chance to converse with one, and now to hear his story and his dreams, to share commonalities and to have his companionship was simply... Zoe searched for the word... nice.

"You look... nice," she said with an emphasis on the word and instantly realized how it must have sounded. She finished by saying, "they look nice on you. The clothes, they fit you well." She turned back to the console, palming her face in her mind. "Okay, so I've completed my first round of analysis. I say first round because it turns out this call has done some fancy flying on its journey to us and it's going to take more time to find this fella."

"What can I do, capt'n?" Darious asked. She turned and was met with a smirk.

"I take it you feel better after your shower?"

"Yes! And the clothes! Thank you, Zoe."

She bowed to him in her seat. "Come, check this out." Zoe scrunched over and Darious took up the spot next to her. "So, this guy was probably pulling our transmitted responses from a precision antenna pointed toward us." She then pointed to a segment of overlapping mesh of symbols and text. "However, his transmitted Fubier signal was curved around three—yes three—neutron stars! The resulting vector was through four bismuth rich planets en-route to us, in addition to many other objects, which I assume was all done purposely to further distort the source. I'm having a hell of a time untwisting and detangling his signal."

Darious bent forward, reading the results she was describing, but it was evident he was not absorbing everything. She herself was a bit lost. Zoe acquired her position on the screen again. "So, the main problem now is I can't see the source of the signal before that last neutron star. On my current simulation, if we follow that curve, the signal leaves the galaxy. Though, if I bend it by any minor amount, it intersects any number of objects. Like a needle in a haystack."

Darious chortled at the phrase. "Maybe..." he started. Zoe typed a request for the computer to simulate. It came back momentarily.

"Nope." She threw up her hands. "I have no idea."

"Well, what if the signal did originate from outside the galaxy?" Darious asked.

Rockets ignited within Zoe. "Genius!" She began fanatically typing. "Darious! Simply genius! That accounts for the stretched-out attenuation of the signal. Simulating now." After a minute, the main screen dropped down new meshes of coding. "Ah-ha! Darious, you're right. The fade amplitudes match perfectly! The signal was sent from beyond the galaxy. In fact, it was sent from our galaxy out to the Andromeda Galaxy and looped around its central black hole back to us!"

"Yes indeed!" His expression lit up but began shifting downward as some perplexing contemplation edged in. "The signal was not even in the haystack. Though..."

She continued his statement, engrossed in her own thoughts, "Though, this person would need quite a powerful antenna or an array of highly localized antennas. The specificities and harmonics are mind boggling. This man is a genius. Luckily for us, now that we know the signal's general direction and distance, the algorithm he used becomes apparent. Each node you see here is just to compensate an anomaly in space—like a comet or planet." She typed in several cues and continued working out loud, "With the major known ones gone, we can now see the general power curve," she pointed to a flowing green graph at her right, "and where the point reaches '1' is the signal's source. Now to go from a general direction to the pinpointed location." She typed for several more minutes and waited for the computer to simulate the response. "Phew! Over 3 million subjacent nodes edited out. Good thing we aren't using a slide ruler, eh Euclid?" Zoe playfully jabbed Darious in the side with her elbow. "Okay, just a couple more tweaks and we should have it. Gotta get rid of all this noise." She paused for a moment. "But can you consider all the work that would have gone into such a phone call?"

Zoe began to think as the computer finished up cleaning the complex signal. For her to unravel this communication algorithm, it was basically straightforward; for the person who initially calculated it, it must have been a feat worthy of a Z-Prize. Zoe's mind was juggling about a dozen compounding variables—just off the top of her head—necessary to attempt this sort of communication. *And not just that,* she thought, *the resonating algorithm would be required to hit just the right nodes at just the right points along its entire winding journey of*—her mind went into after-burner mode—*of a million floating-parsecs.* Just to attempt such a communication; Zoe now saw an ocean of variables. Her mind did another summersault. *Oh, and the dimension of time!* To take into account all that scalar skewing... it's not like one could simply dial a destination *across the cosmos* to the precision of a human hair and press 'Call.' Calculating the path through the many many-body problems would take a long time to compute. *And plus!* Plus the fact that they were moving and everything else in the universe was moving, and influences from obstacles would constantly be coming and going in-between the signal's starting point to its destination. Zoe's thoughts were now free floating in space. *Astounding.*

"Zoe?" asked Darious, bringing her back to the ground. "This genius, though irregular, did warn us to stop. One must assume he was referring to our current investigation. But why? Also, how did he know?"

"Well" she inflected his tone, "how about we go find out?" With fleet fingertip movements, Zoe unbound the last of the transmission distortions and the computer homed in on signal's originating location. She enlarged it. "The moon Iros, of the world Ios." She brought up a fact sheet on it.

Darious began reading segments out loud. "Uninhabited. Near zero atmosphere. Calcate rock..." he stopped reading. "It seems like an out of the way place for a genius to be living."

"To each his own I suppose."

"Shall we?" Darious asked with a glint in his eyes and the hint of a shy grin upon his lips.

"Yes sir!" responded Zoe. She input the coordinates and the ship bound into high speed. "13 days to rendezvous."

CHAPTER 13

THE 13TH DAY

Zoe switched off the bass-filled electronic music as they reached the periphery of the planetary system containing Ios and Iros. She engaged the ship's midrange tracking hardware. Darious was in the central chamber studying. Zoe had given him reading material covering a range of topics including engineering, physics, history, and sociology.

"Darious," she called over her shoulder. He put the books away and joined her in the cockpit. "It would seem we have arrived. No unusual readings from the scanners yet. I'm willing to bet we won't get any until we're right on top of him."

"This man is showing typical behaviors of a recluse. Perhaps a posttraumatic stress disorder." He waved his finger in the air. "No, perhaps a social anxiety disorder, or an avoidant personality disorder. Though I doubt the last, as he did reach out and send us a warning. In any case, I suggest extra caution as he may be..." Darious searched for the word with his finger, "...unstable."

Zoe smirked. It seemed someone had been reading a bit of psychology. Darious was soaking up all she could give him at a rapid pace; soon he'd be teaching her.

"Agreed Darious. I will put us into orbit around the moon and continue scanning. I'm assuming we will also be looking out the window for signs of life." Darious nodded in the affirmative. Zoe had further integrated his computing station into her ship's infrastructure now that he had a bit of training of the ship's systems. "Set up a 40% electro-static covering on the outer hull. 'Caution' is the word of the day." Darious nodded once more and entered the command into his computer terminal and then rejoined her, leaning on the arm of her chair.

The display to Zoe's right remained blank. Even as they entered in the orbit of Iros, there was still not a single ping to evidence any human activity, not any out of place signal on any channel nor any ectopic radiation emissions of any kind. According to the ship's sensors, this entire solar system was completely uninhabited. But Zoe was sure of her calculations. She salivated at the questions she would ask this man once they had found him. The ship started a controlled descent to a low anti-synchronous orbit.

"We will loop around all quadrants of the planet. Keep your eyes peeled."

"Eyes peeled?" ask Darious

"Indeed," she replied.

About a half-hour later, a sheen on the horizon caught both of their attentions simultaneously. Zoe was quick on the control console and adjusted course to intercept. The bright spec grew into a structure as the ship neared it. Darious continued staring at the foreign object while Zoe attempted in vain to get a reading off of it.

"Oh my," Darious said.

Zoe paused her digital probing and looked out. Three stout towers were now decipherable on the dusty, cratered moonscape. As the ship neared, Zoe could see their semicircle tops arching down to cylindrical bases and each connected to the next through tube-like corridors. Adjacently, a landing hangar was joined to the structure. The colors of the entire ziggurat matched the ancient soil around it, save for a slight metallic patina that lined its edges.

"Well that's obviously natural, let's move on," said Zoe, rolling her eyes.

Darious pointed. "Look beyond it."

As the ship came closer, revealed behind the structure was a vast array of small circular dishes, all flush with the ground, probably 200 or 300 in number, and arranged as a geometric pentagon.

"Oh my!" said Zoe. "A genius indeed."

She commanded her ship to slow and stop, hovering high above the complex. At their height, the horizon of Iros carved out a perfectly pale semi-circle into speckled space. Everything looked so washed out, so desolate, and yet so pure, as if the sands of this moon were hallowed ground; an aggrandizement of thurible ashes shot into space and coalesced at this final destination.

Zoe flipped on the close-range scanners and adjusted their parameters accordingly. Silence came back. The ship could not recognize the building from the natural lunar surface. Perplexed, Zoe rescanned twice more but, to the ship, it was just a normal patch of soil on the satellite. Nevertheless, there the structure obviously stood.

She turned on the microphones and initiated an open broadcast on all shortwave channels. "This is Zoe of the ISS Caution." She shrugged at Darious, recognizing the tacky choice of name. "Anyone there? We require assistance... our oxidizing manifold... system... is leaking." She waited a moment. "Okay, I can see your base. We're right above it. You called us 13 days ago."

The other end suddenly picked up. "Don't...don't...," the voice stammered, now much clearer than before, though sounding just as afraid. "Don't co... come any closer. Le... leave!" There was such fear in his voice; to Zoe it rung of a tone not just terrified of them, but of every particle in the universe.

Darious quietly muttered, "PTSD." Zoe waved him off with her hand.

"Or what?" she asked into the microphones.

The voice on the other end attempted to articulate something but failed miserably. It began again, "Or... or..." The line hung up.

Zoe knew that was not good. A phrase she had once heard suddenly popped into her mind: *Don't poke the bear.* Though she had never seen a bear in real life, she knew plenty about them. This man was no bear on the outside, but on the inside—his precocity—there was the bear and she had just disturbed him in his deep, dark lair. Zoe raised defenses to maximum and strapped herself in.

"Darious, ignite the main thrusters!" A momentary pulsing static resounded from the ship's speakers and the main console flickered and died. "Crap" she muttered. All the lights went out and the ship plummeted.

CHAPTER 14

A BEAR ON THE MOON

Straining against the enlarging downward G-force, Zoe swung her fist with all her might toward the left wall of the cockpit, aiming for a mechanical pushbutton. She had just barely managed to tap it, shutting off all systems for a complete reboot. Darious had not been so quick as to belt himself in and had been flung upward into the air, smacking against the ceiling. The downward acceleration of the ship continued. Zoe's whole body felt as though it should belong on the ceiling where Darious lay sprawled. She yelled, gathering her vitality to hit the red button again. With another punishing stroke, Zoe hit it on the nose. The ship suddenly roared to life. Its automated systems all turned on at once: gravity power, engines, on-board lighting, controls, and defensive and offensive systems. Darious fell from the ceiling and landed hard on the floor. Zoe instantly began engaging multiple commands on the newly lit console. The ship shook wildly as all thrusters fired, working to counter the free-fall.

The ship finally came to a stop. Zoe was panting and could hear Darious groaning behind her. Layers of error messages were popping up all over the console. Zoe paid them no mind and rushed to Darious.

"I am okay," he said as he slowly sat up and put a hand to his head. "I think my face absorbed most of the fall." He made a small smile.

Zoe helped him to his feet and went back to her chair. She whooped as she looked out of the cockpit window. The ship had settled just several meters above the ground. Dust, kicked up from their decent, was settling all around them. Looking out, just about 20 meters to the front was the structure, now standing tall and mighty before them. Zoe grit her teeth.

Onscreen showed an alert of an incoming call. She could feel Darious grip her seat. Zoe opened the call with a snarl. The voice on the other end seemed more tremulous than before.

"Th... that craft you... you have. It's... it's... fantastic."

"Thank you," said Zoe flatly, still slightly panting from exertion.

"You... You're the first ship I've ever seen sur... survive a neutrino C pulse."

"You're the first to have disabled my ship so," replied Zoe. She then lost her cool. "And what the hell! What did we do to you!? And what the hell was that? A 'neutrino pulse?' How can neutrinos do that!? Damnit!"

"Ye... yes. I am Doctor E... Earl... Doctor Earl... Docto..."

"Damnit!" she cut him off, "You stuttering idiot! You almost killed us!" Zoe was fuming. Darious placed a gentle hand on her shoulder which cooled her red-hot spirits. His hand was warm and comforting. Zoe sighed. The voice on the other end had gone quiet. "Look Doctor, we are not here to hurt you or anything, just to ask a couple questions." The stuttering man did not speak. "That array you have and the trick of utilizing a Fubier harmonic. It was—"

"A bub bub bub bub" interrupted the other line. "Sh... shhh!" Th... they are always listening. Always... always."

"This is a short-wave transmission Doctor. Who is—?" Zoe began to ask.

"A bub bub bub," he interrupted again and abruptly ended the call.

Zoe threw her hands up. "What the hell is this guy's problem?"

Darious gave a similarly perplexed look. "Do you think he will call back?"

"He would be so lucky if we answered."

Zoe initiated a ship-wide diagnostic to see what had been damaged from the fall while elevating the ship to get a better physical view of the complex.

'Call incoming' displayed across the main screen. Zoe picked up the line.

"Hello," she said robotically.

The doctor began to speak, "Th—"

"I'm sorry; you have reached the answering machine of Zoe and Darious. Please leave a message after the beep." She paused and yelled "BEEP!" into the closest microphone and ended the communication. She continued tinkering with the ship's systems. After a minute the screen notified: 'Tele-call incoming.' "Ah," Zoe perked up. "That's more like it."

She opened the call. Her main screen projected a gaunt man standing and facing them with a laboratory in disarray behind him. "Why can't scientists ever keep a clean workspace?" Zoe muttered. As she eyed him, she noted he was indeed very skinny, to the point of malnourishment. He had an unkempt beard and drooping facial muscles. His plain clothes looked as if they had not been washed in years. It was as if his entire being was the product of a lifetime of tribulations. In her intense scrutiny, she suddenly realized he looked to be no more than 40, or perhaps 45 years old. He lifted a shaking hand toward the screen and slowly waved.

"He... hello."

"Hello there." Zoe made a small obligatory smile. "I am Zoe, and this is Darious." He looked them over. Zoe could tell he was eyeing Darious in particular.

"You... you're an interesting looking fell... fellow."

Darious' eyes wavered and fell to the floor.

"Doctor," Zoe said, regaining his attention, "we have traveled quite a ways to talk with you."

"Who... who are you?" he suddenly asked.

"Err, excuse me?" She then articulated, "I am Zoe. And this is Darious."

"Yes... bu... but are you... you? Who... who sent you?" He began to jitter, and his composure turned sour. "I... I warn you I... I... have killed before!"

"Wow. Wow. Doctor, no one has sent us. We come of our own free will." Zoe and Darious exchanged quick worried glances.

Dr. Earl made a quick incoherent sound and shut down the call. Zoe wasted no time and put the ship in full reverse, establishing a good distance between them and the doctor.

"Okay, maybe a little PTSD," said Zoe.

The pair peered out of the cockpit window toward the structure, expecting the worst. Then, they observed the top bay door of the hangar open. It retracted into the building, exposing a dimly-lit interior of grey walls. Zoe and Darious braced themselves.

A blue glow appeared and sparked several times, multiplied by reflections on the interior walls and then, with a speed so fast it was hard for her eyes to follow, a ship no larger than her own, burst out and off, straight up and away from them.

"Damnit!" Zoe shouted and pulled open all thruster menus, setting all to maximum. Darious smartly strapped himself into his seat. Her craft rocketed upward, following the rogue ship. Zoe winced as the stabilizers fought hard to even out the force of their ascent. She spiraled the ship upwards through the thin atmosphere, weaning off drag. "Darious, track that ship!"

"Aye captain!" he yelled back through the chaotic reverberations and thundering engines.

CHAPTER 15

CHEERS, MY FRIEND!

As soon as Zoe's ship broke free from the bounds of Ios, she set the engines to overdrive. "Hold on to your butts," she said and pressed 'Enter.'

Zoe and Darious were both instantly halfway devoured by their seats while their muscles, both physical and mental, endeavored to perdure working. The Doctor's ship continued its unrelenting acceleration ahead of them. Now long behind, the moon of Ios became an afterthought as both ships rocketed into the night of space.

"200 kilometers distance!" yelled Darious. Zoe snarled; the chase was on. The great thrusters of her ship were working harder than they had in a long time and she could feel it. Everything in the cockpit was rattling, even her digital display. "Heading: 501C by 14.02. He is headed clear of the system. Current linear destination: let me see..." Darious' fingers fumbled as his hands shook over his console. "Port Silenus in 3.1 floating-parsecs."

Darious had been sending a continuous stream of tracking dialog to Zoe's main screen, which she input into the steering system. Dr. Earl's ship seemed to have that same non-existence thing as his lunar lodging and Darious was only able to track it thermally from the thruster's exhaust, but even those readings were sporadic.

Finally, her ship's stabilizers overcame the initial leap forward and the pursuers eased in their seats as all was calm again. Zoe's scrunched face did not allay. Try as she might, she could not close the gap between the two ships. In fact, she could see the Doctor's ship becoming smaller.

"Distance increasing," Darious stated as if reading her mind. "250 kilometers and growing."

"Noted," Zoe responded through grit teeth.

She was manually tweaking the engines to pinch their acceleration curve without overheating any drive components. Her ship's bow gravity fields were working hard, having to shoulder every cosmic pebble, each with the potential impact energy of a world-ending asteroid. They soon crossed through the heliosphere of the solar system and entered into ethereal space. The two ships were reaching inimical speeds; a lesser ship would have been excoriated at the seams. *Like a banana*, thought Zoe. She was starting to have trouble compensating the many strains on her ship.

"It might get a little bumpy!" she shouted over her shoulder.

The Doctor's ship was now just a bright blue dot, its main features obscured by distance. Zoe could feel him slipping away, despite the prodigious speed of her own ship. She quickly set up a zoomed-in view in the lower corner of her screen to visually track his ship and pushed hers further into overdrive. A low gurgling started from the bowels of the craft. Vibrations from its center resonated outward and rattled the entire ship. Zoe did not yield.

Suddenly, Dr. Earl's ship made a sharp turn, veering to its left. Zoe altered her own trajectory with a stiff drift, outdoing her ship's stabilizers from the immense force, flattening herself and Darious to the sides of their seats. She whipped the sternside out, directly lining them up with the Doctor's new course and sending piqued shrills and alerts throughout her main console. Their speed was insane; the two ships were passing entire star systems in mere seconds.

"New course heading plotted!" yelled Darious. "Heading 739 by... oh!" Zoe's eyes darted out. Far out in front of them, though quickly enlarging, she could see an oncoming globular region.

"I see it!" Zoe yelled back.

She recognized it as a nebula by the bright hues of its gasses, but was not sure of the dark specs all over it—thousands of menacing dark specs. Darious shot over a summary to her display. Indeed, as she had surmised, stretching for nearly a parsec, this region of space was a primordial soup of newborn stars, densely packed with planetoids and marked as an absolute 'No Fly Zone.'

The nebula soon filled her ship's view with its immensity, stretching from edge to edge, as far as the sensors could reach. Looking into it, Zoe could not see through to the other side. Those oncoming dots were rock debris, most sized between Earth-1 and Jupiter, scattered like a galactic minefield. Zoe saw the Doctor's ship pass into the nebula and its bright peripheral rockets flickering as it began smartly maneuvering through the colossal obstacle course. Zoe's mind was racing. They were traveling too fast; those planetoids were too big and too plentiful, but there was no time to go around or they would definitely lose him. No, she had to keep him within her sights. Zoe tightened her harness and called for Darious to do the same. Determination trickled through her fingertips as they jittered upon the console, initializing many predefined routines as her ship entered into the naissance grounds.

"Darious, prep bow thrusters! Fire 75 percent at my mark, every mark!"

From their first oncoming obstacle, Zoe maneuvered the ship upwards, bringing them low in their seats and curving alongside a planetoid until they had regained the Doctor's trail. Warnings glared in bright red all over Zoe's many screens. They jetted by the next rocky mass. The ship's monitoring system was nearly overloaded with incoming object warnings. While maneuvering the ship with one hand, she flipped several switches with the other, disengaging all safety protocols and resumed two-handed control just in time to avoid two more calamitous asteroids. She dipped the ship low and arced around the next giant rock. *There!* Zoe spotted the Doctor's ship, likewise weaving through the masses before disappearing once more behind herds of free-floating mountains. *How was he*—Zoe thought, as she wound up an oblong rock half the size of Earth-1 and gasped as an equally sized planetoid revealed itself just beyond it.

"Mark!" she yelled.

The ship rattled severely as it fired from both back and front. Zoe used this quick confused moment of inertial forces to make a dire course change and swung left of the oncoming mass. The perilous maneuver effectuated just a momentary lapse in speed and saved Zoe from sacrificing the finely tuned settings of the thrusters. She boosted again as the ship swerved back on course, sighting the Doctor once more.

Another dozen space rocks cannonballed by as Zoe's ship pitched and rolled with all the agility its nimble-fingered aviatrix could command. Zoe and Darious were impelled in all directions and had to use their legs and elbows to stay in place whilst operated their consoles.

"Mark!" yelled Zoe and executed another harrowing maneuver, narrowly avoiding vaporization by way of ship—near-warp speed—versus planet. "Mark!" she yelled again, using the gained microsecond to roll the ship on its side and threading the fine gap between two enormous proto-planets. Darious gasped a string of vowels. Zoe rolled the ship back around, nearly grazing its belly upon the flat back of another rocky mass. Meanwhile ahead, Dr. Earl's ship was cleanly avoiding all obstacles and continuing to distance itself from them.

The two ships were now completely engulfed in the gulf of yellows and oranges. Classic space had all but disappeared, replaced by a dreamlike evening glow of a nightmarish cemetery; a birthing boneyard where each planetoid was an available grave with a complimentary tombstone to carve their fate upon.

"Craaap!" Zoe yelled as she reared up the ship to its physical limits, marginally clearing a dense string of asteroids.

She sent the ship into a mad spin, spiraling around the space rocks and then evening out into a transitory clearing, free of hazard. Zoe took the opportunity to draw in a much-needed breath. The entire universe seemed to slow in that moment and all of time exhaled with her. She looked out for the Doctor's ship and spotted it just below her horizon, continuing to make mincemeat of the nebula. Zoe cracked her knuckles.

In the next moment, chaos resumed. Zoe piloted her tiny craft dynamically, only just being able to avoid rock after rock. "Mark!" The ship bounded downward and twisted through a maze of smaller asteroids, each whizzing by just shy of them. "I really do not like this guy!" she yelled and then gulped as they narrowly missed a mass shaped like one of her food packets.

"Nebula boundary in less than .01 floating-parsecs!" shouted Darious.

"We can make it!"

Zoe lifted the ship over a considerable planetoid and then weaved through the next group. The haze in front of them was clearing. She saw the Doctor's ship burst though the nebula and rocket onward, free of the proto-planetary hindrances. In a moment, Zoe and Darious too surged through in a blaze of glory, spewing forth from the globular structure like a comet with a trail of shimmering dust.

Dr. Earl was now ranged at a quarter parsec and even on Zoe's zoomed screen he was little more than a bright speck.

"Heading!" demanded Zoe.

"Heading 501C by 14.02!" yelled back Darious.

They both snapped, "Port Silenus!"

Zoe could no longer keep up compensating the overheating engines. Transferring excess energy from one section into another was becoming overly complicated for her to do in real time. They now were barreling at a speed of .32 floating-parsecs per hour. The Doctor's ship was evidently even faster.

"Darious! I gotta slow the ship down."

"Aye captain!"

She knew Darious could see on his screen the readout of the over-clocked engines and was probably eyeing it nervously like her. Zoe began slowly diminishing their speed, being very careful to dump energy in a progressive manner. At this velocity, even slowing down was a dangerous maneuver. Soon the deafening rattles of the ship began to subside. The Doctor's ship completely disappeared from view.

"My thought is he will be at the port! Hopefully we will catch him there!" Zoe yelled. Her voice came out much louder than necessary, now that the cockpit had grown quiet again. "Ahem. Sorry." She could still hear her ears ringing.

"Try as I might, I just cannot track him," said Darious.

"Ya," replied Zoe. "Whatever cloaking mechanism he has is amazing. I saw you were tracking him based on his heat trail; smart, I must say. I was trying to visually track him."

Darious came over and leaned on her chair. "Have you ever seen anything like that?" She looked up and could see the apprehension in his eyes. Zoe felt it in herself too.

"No."

Within a half hour they caught sight of the port. Darious read out an info sheet on it. The port was stationed in deep space; the only things near it were small mining colonies. It edged on a minor transportation byway and thus, as Zoe stated, it was more of a poor man's 'hey-hey let's get crocked' spot. As they approached the space station, no more statements from Zoe were necessary to describe the sort of place to Darious. Old mining and delivery ships floated about; the ones inbound flying were with vigor while those departing lumbered on in a slower, undulating motion. The port was grimy and dilapidated with exposed and corroded cables floating around it, as if it was some moribund space squid. Dirty, patched ships were docked at nearly every receptacle. As a drunk itself, the port gulped down ethanol in overabundant and inefficient quantities, expelling the combustion byproduct from its bottom in continual bursts of inky flatulence.

"Ah, a fine place to be," remarked Zoe with mock cheer. Darious had an expression of quite the opposite. "Let's fly around a bit and see if we spot his ship." Zoe could sense the uneasiness emanating from Darious. "Trust me, I'm hoping as much as you we do not have to go in there. Langer miners. Pe-ew!" She waved a hand in front of her nose.

Zoe crept her ship around the port as the pair searched through the cockpit window. Their eyes fluttered about, briefly landing on each ship before darting to the next in search of that elusive floret.

Zoe was first to espy Dr. Earl's ship. "Ah, bingo!" It was docked at the lower end, tucked away in the even dirtier underside of what was undoubtedly an already underside space station. She brought them close in until the view of the craft nearly filled her cockpit window. "It looks like a modified M-4 intra-galactic ship. But those gull wings..." she paused in fascination "...and those thrusters are unlike anything I've ever seen." Zoe tiptoed her ship closer.

Suddenly the Doctor's ship roared to life. Stunned and momentarily blinded from the flare of his thrusters, Zoe recoiled backwards and Darious half fell over the console. With a frantic alacrity, Zoe put her ship in full reverse and prepped a high thrust combination. The Doctor's ship broke away from the dock, ripping away metal and cabling and sending shrapnel flying into space. His modified craft pivoted and faced Zoe's, pausing for a moment as if sizing her up, and then rocketed off, nearly crushing the top of her ship as it flew by. The hurricane whipped up by the Doctor's Herculean engines reverberated throughout the cockpit.

"Damn maniac!" Zoe cried out as she whirled her ship about to follow the madman as Darious took up his post. They blasted off in pursuit.

To absolutely no one's surprise, the after-hours pub took no heed of the bizarre and sudden happening. Rusty vessels continued lazily sauntering by, those inside continued quaffing their hard-earned concoctions, and those few who had noticed were too inebriated to care, simply waving off to the two ships as if to a friend, and then clinked their glasses and drank heartily.

CHAPTER 16

THE RIOTOUS DR. EARL SAKNUSSEMM

"What is this guy's problem!?" exclaimed Zoe, once more throttling the engines to speeds greater than that of supernovae flares. Beholden by interstellar space, the hunt continued. Both ships burned bright, both burned in defiance of the other. "Man," Zoe said to herself, "he's gonna attract the attention of the Copper Force if he doesn't stop."

Darious spoke up just then. "Doctor Earl Saknussemm," He sounded like he was reading from his screen. "Otherwise known as Nero. Otherwise known as Nero the Purist."

"What?"

Darious synced his display to Zoe's side monitor and shot over a document with a picture attached, exactly matching the emaciated man they had met on the moon.

"He is a galactic criminal," said Darious. He scrolled through reports littered by encounters with the law. "There are pages of unlawful acts. Inciting riots. Public dissonance. Sedation. Murder. It states here he killed an ambassador of Trenzalore ... in addition to many others." Darious' voice suddenly became quite shallow, prompting Zoe to read through the dossier.

Doctor Earl Saknussemm, a believer in Purist Exceptionalsim, received his undergraduate degree in astrobiology from the University of Renaul, in the Luat Sector. Afterwards, he was taken on as a pupil by Neomarxist Dr. Shie Shralow and earned his masters in natural science law and genetic recombination, while being published in major journals for his work on genetics. Mr. Saknussemm continued to study under Dr. Shralow when he was transferred to the University of Duke, in the Aurka Sector, where he earned a PhD in natural science law. After the untimely death of his mentor, Dr. Shralow, Dr. Saknussemm recused himself from the university, ceasing his post doctorate studies and fulltime academic role, and began publishing anti-clone literature under the pseudonym 'Nero.'

Zoe sighed.

Upon Dr. Earl Saknussemm's direct link to the bombings of several clone plants, he was indicted by a grand jury, though due to the uproar by the following he had accumulated through his writings and public speeches, he was sentenced to a minimal work facility in the Distol Sector for 9 years. During Year 2 of his incarceration, Dr. Saknussemm escaped and has the current status of a Category 9 fugitive. Since his escape, Dr. Saknussemm has taken responsibility for multiple attacks on clone facilities, including the property damage of 9,000 clone deaths in the GenSol manufacturing plant of the Klein Solar System.

Zoe sighed again and shook her head.

Recent literature from Dr. Saknussemm suggests a large underground effort to claim a section of the galaxy, assumed to be near the rim of Quadrant 4 on the outer regions, for his following of 'Purists.' The plan proposes the mass expurgation of the nearly 400 million clone bodies in the area and the installation of colonies fully run by humans. Dr. Saknussemm's movement has gained much traction within the past decade while rumors are abound of dissident groups weaponizing to lay claim to these lands.

Zoe cleared the text from her screen in disgust. There was a sudden, albeit subtle jolt to the ship and it shook momentarily. She took one look at sensor readings and resumed her thoughts of Dr. Earl Saknussemm. Meanwhile, Darious, still synced to Zoe's screen, was hurriedly checking the ship's systems for what had caused the brief turbulence.

"No need to worry, it happens sometimes. Stars are constantly shedding their layers. Sometimes they end up far flung. How's the Doctor doing?"

Darious cleared his throat. "He is leading us at about 70,000 kilometers. No course changes thus far."

"I suppose you noticed; I'm weary of running my ship so fast after him, especially in light of all that has happened today."

"An agreeable pursuance," Darious responded. "His trajectory does not seem to be toward anything in particular, for thousands of parsecs. Where do you suppose he is headed?"

"No clue." Zoe shook her head.

The gap between the two spacecrafts continued to increase, though the Doctor's dot of a ship remained within her ship's visual tracking range thanks to the linearity of its course among the unwavering stars beyond. Where was he leading them now? Zoe speculated while typing into her console.

"Darious, I'm going to send you a routine. Insert it into your trajectory program." He did so, and both their screens lit up with a flurry of colored text. "Now, go ahead and remove our emissions from the sensor parameters. See if we can discern any sort of trailing information from the Doctor's vessel. Meanwhile, I'm going to try something..." her voice lingered, "...something probably not so good for the integrity of the ship." She just knew Darious had winced at that comment. "But no worries."

The pair went to work, busy at their stations and each perking up for brief moments in thought before once again energetically typing. Zoe's ship continued a modest acceleration in the direction of Dr. Saknussemm. Their linear flight path reduced a lot of strain on the stabilizers and it was as if they were floating on pacific seas. Every so often, Darious paused his work and called out the increasing distance of the Doctor's ship. 80,000 kilometers. 90,000 kilometers. 100,000 kilometers. Her ship's optical tracking system was starting to error and the approximations from the readings were growing exponentially.

"Okay. All set. Let's try this," said Zoe, and without waiting for a response, engaged the newly scripted routine. Her ship coughed for a moment, jerking the pair brutally forward and then back again. After that, her ship resumed its silent flight.

"What was that?" asked Darious, coming over to Zoe with a hand rubbing his neck.

"We shall see in about 5... oh there it is." Her display notified them of a sudden and dramatic deceleration of the Doctor's ship, beyond the optical tracking system's error approximations, and thus his ship had certainly been stopped dead in its tracks.

"What did you do!?" Darious uttered in bewilderment.

"Sent out a super high-pulse demodulated resonance beam of energy in the waveform of a communication channel, which his ship apparently allowed so it subsequently fried all of his electrical wiring until it found a suitable ground. It's an old-school hack. I'm somewhat surprised it worked." She looked up at Darious. "In essence, it's a giant middle finger." Darious stared wide-eyed at her console.

"Zoe! I do believe you have received his attention!" He pointed to the inbound dot on her display. Dr. Saknussemm had changed course, heading directly for them.

"Ah crap!" she shouted and initiated an emergency deceleration of her ship. Darious leapt to his seat and strapped himself in. With their massive momentum, Zoe began arcing upwards, hoping to gain time before the Doctor was upon them. Her efforts were in vein; his devilishly deft ship was matching her trajectory at speeds thrice her own. "Darious, all defensive systems, online! Now!" Zoe saw page after page of subsystems engaging. "Anything that could be of use!"

Impact warnings covered Zoe's main display and as the Doppler sirens became nearly imperceptibly close together. She squeezed her eyes shut in anticipation of the impact. Just as the tone condensed into one long beep, it eased and began to elongate with a lower pitch. Zoe opened an eye. The Doctor's ship had passed them by, just several meters from her craft, and was now rapidly receding from them. Zoe grabbed the controls, ignoring the alerts onscreen. She continued to arc her ship upwards while modifying their trajectory to match the Doctor's and rocketed after him. Her ship surged forward; its engines were resolute and left in their wake an ion trail, nearly a solar system long, of radiant whites and blues.

"Course heading!" yelled Darious, "712A by 02. 59! Port Auborne in .04 floating-parsecs!"

Zoe looked onscreen; they would be upon it in minutes, though at their present speed, it would be a momentary dash of light. From what she had witnessed of Dr. Saknussemm's ship, it was no doubt nimble enough to stop in time; hers, however, would require an immediate deceleration to be able to catch the port. She quickly introspected their options and action probabilities.

"Darious! Can we assume that's his target?"

"I would conclude so!" he responded.

"Okay! I've got to slow the ship now, so we don't overshoot it." She began ramping down the engines. "About half an hour and we'll be dockside."

"Aye captain."

CHAPTER 17

MANIFEST DISCREPANCY

"Any luck tracking some sort of signature?" asked Zoe peering over Darious' shoulder at his work.

"Sorry, no." Darious didn't move his eyes from his screen or his fingers from the console.

"Who is this guy?" she asked. Her mind was in conflict. Two formulations had permeated deep into her thoughts, though only one could be correct: an oppressed, genius scientist or an insane, outspoken zealot. Each had its own discrepancies, but on the whole, respectively, both could not possibly be simultaneously true. "Doctor Earl Saknussemm," she slowly muttered. The gears of thought turned, the many teeth of facts linking with others. She bit her lip, chewing on her ruminations. *Granted, the galaxy is big, but not that big.*

Zoe and Darious soon were upon the port, a typical interstellar stopover used by transportation agencies and people of all types.

"Hopefully the Doctor has decided to take a bit of repose from all this running," Zoe said. Darious, still busy tinkering with the tracking program, did not answer. "Don't bother with that anymore. It won't work." He turned towards her and grimaced.

"Hey, practice makes perfect." She patted him on the shoulder and motioned for him to join her. "Let's play a game, I-spy."

Zoe sat in her chair, with Darious on the armrest leaning in, and the two began looking out the cockpit window for the ship belonging to the Doctor. After just a couple minutes of surveying the port, Zoe squeaked with excitement. Darious had evidently spotted it too and pointed to the docked vessel at the same time as Zoe. They chuckled at their mirrored motions and Zoe brushed his arm away from hers.

"I saw it first!"

She then, very heedfully and very slowly, brought her ship next to the Doctor's with a finger on 'Full Reverse,' anticipating the worst. Darious was likewise firmly gripping her seat. They waited a few minutes in silence, though there was no sign of life from the ship.

"Hmmm," Zoe puffed. "What to do. What to do." She rapped her fingers on the console.

"Perhaps he did indeed dock," Darious said. "Seeing how you agitated his ship, perhaps there was certain 'frying' that required repairs, or perhaps he is planning on evading us by some other means."

Zoe considered their options. "Perhaps. Perhaps his ship doesn't have a bathroom." She typed in a command and set her ship to auto-dock at the empty parking space next to the Doctor. They rocked slightly as grapnels fastened to both sides of the ship and a walkway tube connected to its hatchway. There was a distant sucking sound as the pressure equalized.

Zoe noticed Darious looking solemnly at the floor.

"I know!" she said and snapped her fingers. She went to the main cabin and pulled open a myriad of drawers, shuffling through mounds of gear. "I have a hooded sweater somewhere in here you can wear." Zoe heaved an armful of garments and dropped them to the floor. She reached her arm deep within a compartment. "Bingo!" She tossed him the sweater—an over-sized pale-russet pullover with a stretched-out hood. Darious put it on over his clothes and flipped down the hood. It fell just below his nose. "Ha! I like it."

Darious pulled up the hood, revealing his tattooed eyes. "Thank you."

"Now, let's go catch us a madman."

The pair exited the craft and made their way through crowded byways, heading deeper and deeper into the depths of the spaceport. Darious kept his hood low and his hands in his pockets, though with quick upward glances he looked around. Zoe owled about on constant lookout for Dr. Saknussemm, but an hour later neither had caught sight of him.

As they were completing their second circuit, Zoe spotted a thin figure, dressed much like Darious, with a casual cloak covering all extremities and a too-casual demeanor, evidencing the want to stay unnoticed in the open. *Funny how purposely blending in makes one stand out.* She steered Darious toward the figure, who was within a shop peering out its window at the flowing masses. The man pulled out a rectangular object and surveyed it. Zoe's suspicions were confirmed, and not from the device but from those distressed, fidgety fingers.

"Do you see him Darious?"

Darious shot a quick glance outward. "Yes. Do you suspect it is him?"

"Perhaps," she said, winking at him.

Whether or not the figure had noticed them, Zoe could not tell; he had not moved from his post even as they neared. Zoe tried her best to act casual as they crossed the threshold into the convenience store. She walked shoulder to shoulder with Darious and they both feigned interest at a shelf of snacks.

"Oh, the purple one looks good!" She picked it up and examined it. "Pickled eel skin." She shoved it back in its spot. "Not what I was expecting from the packaging." Zoe peeked over at the figure and then down at his hand clasping the device.

Crap, she thought. It was similar to her lightcard, though a bit wider. She would have to be mindful of it, knowing the capabilities of her own card. *Screw it, here goes nothing.* Ignoring further pretenses, she straightened up and walked over to the man.

"Ahem. Doctor Saknussemm."

The hand jittered, almost dropping the card. He turned to face Zoe and lifted his hood, revealing himself to indeed be the Doctor. His eyes and lips trembled, and his brow narrowed, evidently not too thrilled to have been found.

"I'm... I'm—"

"Doctor," Zoe cut in and held up her hands to show that she meant him no harm. "Please, can we simply talk?"

He brought out his card and Darious quickly stepped in-between him and Zoe.

"It's okay. It's okay," said Zoe. "Be cool. Everybody be cool, this isn't a robbery or anything."

Dr. Saknussemm drew his arm back and, in a quick motion, grabbed the tall shelf behind him and pulled it forward, bringing it down on Zoe and Darious. It flattened them both out on the floor and a hard can of jellied beans smacked Zoe on the face. She cursed. Of course he would run; she should have been more on her guard. Zoe's arm immediately began to throb. The shelf was pinching it against the opposite counter. Darious lifted and they both wiggled out from under the mess.

"Ugh," said Zoe, brushing herself off and then Darious. He had quickly replaced the hood over his head, but a crowd was already stirring.

"Damn it." Zoe was looking out beyond the scowls. "Now where did he go?"

"I see him!" Darious grasped her hand and pulled her with gusto out of the store, and down the busy corridors. There was momentary shouting, but it was quickly drowned out by the sounds of the never-ending claptrap of travelers.

Darious half-sprinted through the hallways with Zoe close behind, closing in on the clumsy cloaked man, who was knocking into people and pushing others out of the way. There were some peeved voices and many condescending sneers, but no one physically intervened. Darious and Zoe nimbly navigated and were converging on the Doctor.

"Doctor Earl!" Zoe called, but her voice was overthrown by the crowd.

"Doctor Earl!!" shouted Darious with a great might in his voice. The Doctor turned back with wide eyes. He dodged into an ancillary hallway. Darious and Zoe made the same turn just fifteen seconds later and found themselves fighting through a white-water current. Zoe noted the sign above them displaying 'Outbound Flights,' and they soon came upon the station's main shuttling service area with multitudinous entryways at every angle, each with a numeric indicator above it including flight details. Both of their heads swiveled about through the crowds. Zoe could not sight him.

Darious suddenly grabbed her hand and they were they were off again.

"Did you see him?!" Zoe shouted from behind.

"I believe so! This way!" Darious ran down a passage and made a left turn down a narrower hallway. He paused, quickly shifting his gaze from person to person.

Zoe leaned on his back, taking a quick breather. Darious led them a few paces deeper into the corridor, stopped-up with throngs of waiting people. Zoe could see it dead-ended into an outbound flight carrier. There was an attendant next to the doorway, resting her elbows on a podium and lazily processing the people passing through. Though slightly out of breath, Zoe's mind continued racing. Was this a dead end for them? For the

Doctor? If Darious was right, surely now they had him. Why was Dr. Saknussemm putting up so much of a fight? That baleful moniker which had troubled her since she had read about him kept repeating in her head: 'Nero the Purist.'

Green arrows lit up on the ceiling, pointing towards the outbound flight entrance. An intercom crackled. "Flight 603c, Port Auborne to Polestar 7, now boarding." The message ended with a tone, sending the crowd into an uproar around Zoe and Darious. They spun around but were centered within a single-minded mob and about to be washed away.

"No. No. Sorry sir. Excuse me. Excuse me." Zoe and Darious attempted fruitlessly to ease away from the crowd but to no avail. They were pushed and prodded forward, like two black sheep in a transhumance herd. Before Zoe knew it, they had passed through the gate, the attendant had scanned their faces, and they were onboard the great space carrier.

Zoe and Darious finally washed up on fabric seats deep within the craft. Zoe stamped her foot and sat with a scowl, arms crossed. Darious shook his head under his hood, still being shouldered by bustling travelers.

"Have you ever...," he began.

"Damn it. Damn it Damn it," Zoe repeated. She looked up at him. "I am sorry Darious."

His eyes eased, and he looked at her with compassion. "It is alright Zoe." He held out his sweatered arms. "Look, I still have all my limbs."

She earnestly tried for a smile, but her insides were still steaming too hot. Zoe stood up and looked back from whence they had come. Though people were quickly dispersing to any and all available seating, the fast-flowing madness still could not be weathered.

A voice broke in from the ship's speakers, stating in a calm, though slightly mechanical voice, "Boarding complete for flight

603c: Port Auborne to Polestar 7. You may feel a slight bump as the ship exits the bay. Your pilot today is Captain Malley O'Hare. For your convenience, in Sections A through E of Floors 2 through 6 you will find amenities, including snacks, drinks, and everything you may need to make your flight comfortable. We hope you enjoy your flight onboard Epsilon Spacelines. Star light. Star bright. May Epsilon be the star that guides you tonight."

Zoe, Darious, and the entirety of the passengers slightly swayed back and then forth as the ship lifted up from the enormous bay of the port and started its long journey though the emptiness of space. Zoe sat with a slump and exhaled.

"Well, nothing to do now but enjoy the ride." Her blood was still settling from being outmaneuvered by such a senseless man. Darious took a seat next to her.

Zoe began mulling over recent events. After some time huffing and puffing, she turned to Darious and whispered, "You know what is so odd about all this?" She did not wait for him to respond. "Nowhere did that report mention the Doctor's apparent prodigious knowledge of intergalactic communications, or being a master mechanic with insane ship modifications, or that unexplainable, so-called 'Neutrino pulse' technology."

Darious thought for a moment. "I suppose his followers could have aided him."

"Sure. But he is such a scared, distraught man. I don't know Darious. I smell a rat."

"A rat?" Darious sniffed the air and then paused, turning to Zoe, and nodding in understanding of the metaphor. "Ah. I do agree. I have never heard of this man, or of attacks on GenSol facilities."

"Me neither. The galaxy is a big place," replied Zoe. "But not that big." She bit her lip. "Something is not right here. There is no way the man we met today is that man. This has implications, you know."

"Indeed so," responded Darious.

Zoe sighed and stared out the window into space. Her eyes became self-guiding, lazily searching the outside blackness and shifting from speck to speck while her mind's eye zoomed in and drew fuzzy scenes about each one. She could feel her back muscles relaxing. The seat was comfortable, and the contours of its plush cushions reticulated until they exactly matched her body.

"Now if only I had a Carnegie Cosmo."

Darious smiled at her. "Here you are, my lady." She looked down at his empty cupped hand and smiled.

As the boat sailed through the eternal night, the two enjoyed a few more laughs and inside jokes while deep in their minds a new scene was drawn, starting from a speck, and expanding into a full sun with the warmth to endear all the planets of the galaxy. They then sat together in tranquil silence for a long while as the soft sway of the ship cradled them, alleviating the many aches of their journey. Together their eyes fluttered and soon sleep became them.

Some time later, Zoe awoke and shifted in her seat, waking Darious. She yawned. "I'm sorry, nature calls." She got up and scooted past him as he tucked in his legs.

"Let's see," she mused to herself, tapping a finger to her chin. "Was it two floors down, three rows to the right? Or three floors up and 2 rows to the left?"

Zoe made her way to a broad staircase leading to the deck below. "And down we go." She walked with a skip to the lower level, pausing at a directory which starred her location and pointed to various amenities and restrooms. "Ladies Room. Bingo." Zoe moseyed on while teasing a lock of hair, strolling as if on a cruise.

Feeling much relieved from being relieved, she began to wander the ship. Most seats were occupied, though some people were also stretching their legs. As she made her way from floor to floor, she overheard gossip, snores, and the munching of chips. Without realizing it, she walked through a curtain and into a service cabin for flight attendants. A casually dressed man in a short-sleeve shirt with overbearing muscles paused his conversation with a female attendant in Epsilon's azure collared skirt. She eyed Zoe with disapprobation.

"Ma'am," the attendant spoke up, "this section is for personnel only. If you have an issue, please press the call button above your seat."

Zoe nodded and backed out, already mentally retracing her steps to rejoin Darious. Then she overheard the man speak the words 'Dr. Nero' and she sharply spun around, putting her ear close to the curtain as it whooshed closed.

"No worries, ma'am," said the man in a low voice. "The situation is under control. I've been instructed to keep an eye on him, but not to alert him. He's not armed."

"But you just said he's a fugitive. An extremist," the attendant whispered back. "A murderer," she hissed.

"No need to worry. There is a team on standby that will take him into custody as soon as the ship lands. Professionals."

"That's all well and good, but they are not here."

"Ma'am, the situation is under control," the man grunted.

She muttered flatly, "Thank you for informing me, Marshal."

"You're welcome, ma'am. Now please, be calm. I will be keeping you and your crew up to date."

Zoe flopped down in the closest seat to her and buried her head in a magazine as the curtain spread open. The brawny man strut out and past her. Her heart sped up at the thought that Dr. Saknussemm was onboard. She turned and watched the Space Marshal work his way to the end of the isle toward a flight of stairs. Zoe got up and followed him, being careful to mind her distance. They went up two more levels and then through a long section of the ship with many rows of seats, most of which contained sleeping passengers. The Space Marshal seated himself about a dozen seats shy from the very first row. *The Doctor must be somewhere close by*, thought Zoe. She regained her bearings and quickly made her way back to Darious.

Zoe paused as she reached him and smirked. Darious had fallen back asleep and was half slumped over her seat, his hood covering his head with his hands cradling it underneath. She felt bad for having to wake him, but this was an urgent matter. She sat next to him and softly nudged his shoulder.

"Darious." There was no movement. "Darious," she whispered again with a slightly harder push. He momentarily spasmed and slowly sat up, yawning.

"Ahhh. Yes Zoe?"

"Doctor Saknussemm," she whispered in excitement. "He's onboard." Darious jolted upright, his eyes staring deep into hers.

"What? How do you know!?"

"Shh. Shh. I overheard a space marshal talking about him. Seems he has been found out. They have police waiting for him when we land. They..." she looked with dismay. "They also called him a murderer."

Zoe could see puzzlement on his face. "But how—" Darious began and then lowered his voice, "how did he get onboard if he is wanted?"

"He does seem quite capable when it comes to getting around. Plus, consider his knack for sciency things. I suspect he simply bested the security systems." Zoe came closer to Darious. "Look, we gotta ask the Doctor some questions. He seems to know all about whatever is going on."

"Should we even approach him? Especially now that he is being monitored?"

"I do agree we don't want to be seen with him. Being detained by the CF is not the sort of thing that would make my day."

"What should we do?" asked Darious. "Once he is taken, it will most likely be even more difficult to talk with him."

Zoe's eyes glinted and a smirk crossed her face. "I have an idea."

A short while after, Zoe heard an overly-dramatic fainting gasp. *Right on Cue.* She would have to remember to give Darious a Galactic Emmy later. The Space Marshal had also taken notice. He sternly got up and jogged his way to the downed individual. Meanwhile, Zoe quickly eased in between rows of seats, working her way closer and closer to the Marshal's seat whilst being careful not to wake any of the sleeping passengers.

She coolly sat in his seat, as if it had been hers all along, and craned up to be at the Marshal's sitting eye level. In the direction straight ahead was a clear view of Dr. Saknussemm. He was just 5 rows ahead, lounging back and ostensibly asleep. Though his hood was covering his head, Zoe was sure it was him. She could hear Darious groaning behind her and turned to see the Marshal had caringly turned him over, caringly enough until he pulled back the hood and saw the clone. The Space Marshal suddenly let his hands go and Darious' head smacked hard on the floor.

"Ow," Darious muttered and opened his eyes. "Oh, thank you. Thank you, sir."

He quickly stood up, grasping the Marshal's hand in both of his and shaking it vehemently. Zoe turned back to her target and quickly worked her way low around sleeping travelers to the Doctor. She very, very delicately slid herself into the seat next to him; he made no movements. Maybe he was actually sleeping. *How do I wake him and talk to him without having him run again?* She knew there was no time to muck about.

Zoe grabbed the Doctor's hood, and forced it downwards into her lap while pinning his arms back. He flailed in surprise and kicked out his legs.

"It's Zoe. Hey. It's Zoe. Remember me?" she whispered. "Listen, you've been found out by a space marshal onboard. Not by me. I'm here to help." Dr. Saknussemm twisted, attempting to regain his arms, but Zoe pushed them back harder. His frail body wriggled in pain. "Listen. Listen. We only have a minute. I'm going to let go. Pretend you're still asleep." She tested him by easing her grip slightly. He did not wiggle any more. She fully released her hold and he slowly sat back in his seat, facing her, though keeping his hood low. Zoe sagged low in her seat, hoping it would appear to remain empty from the perspective of the space marshal, and put her hand under her head to cushion it.

"I... I do apologize," Dr. Earl Saknussemm whispered. Zoe could see such terrible fright in the Doctor's eyes. "I... I...." He tried to pull back his hood, but his hand was shaking too much.

Zoe shook her head. "No. There is a space marshal about five rows back. He's got you." The Doctor fidgeted in his seat. "Stay put. He's not going to make a move until we land. Just act like you're sleeping."

"Who... who are you?" The Doctor stuttered.

"Look, I feel...," Zoe slowly started in a low tone with eyes now closed, as the Space Marshal had surely returned to his seat by now. "I feel as though I'm on the cusp of something. Something that I don't yet understand. Something hidden, though somehow right in plain view. I just can't put my finger on it." She realized the obliqueness of her words. Even in her acute mind, she did not know exactly what she and Darious were on the trail of. Zoe was unsettled. "Something strange is going on," she said. "And Darious and I are going to find out what it is."

To this the Doctor jittered a moment before settling once more. "Dar... Darious. He... is that young man as de... determined as you?"

Zoe had not expected this clone-murdering man to ask about the feelings of one he had purportedly killed so often.

"He is," Zoe whispered back.

"Th... then per... perhaps... perhaps," he trailed off and started again. "Perhaps you are right." Zoe was not sure how to interpret this. "Per... perhaps the galaxy is not... is not as it seems. Per... perhaps you two are cor... correct. Th... then what?"

"Then we keep digging until we are satisfied."

"If... if it's dangerous Mi... Miss Zoe?"

"Danger is my middle name," she coolly replied.

"Zoe. I... I am, and I am not wh... what I am." Zoe turned the paradox around in her mind. "I... I... am Doctor Earl Saknussemm. I... I... am a phys... a harmonics phys... physicist of the fi... fi..."

"Ah," said Zoe, "then you and I have more in common then you may think." The Doctor shifted his head and seemed to be easing a bit. "And can I assume what is on file about you is not true? You don't murder clones and preach of purity?"

He did not stir, but only made a stifled sighing noise. "You are... are cor... correct."

"Doctor, you are in good company."

Dr. Saknussemm did not speak for some time, perhaps analyzing what she had said.

"I... I was forced to... to work for Pan... Pantheon Industries," he whispered with both abhorrence and fear. "I tried ex... exposing them. But they... they threatened me. And... and they followed through on those threats. I.... I am not a co... cold killer." His voice sounded tinny. "Though I had to survive." The Doctor's bearings suddenly seemed to fade away and he did not say anything for several seconds. He began again, "Th... they want me dead. Though I... I had to survive. Years I... I have evaded them... all of them."

"It is quite the home you've built for yourself too," Zoe said.

"I... I... am alone."

Zoe did not move, but her heart drifted toward the Doctor. She believed him. "What can you tell me?"

Suddenly the ship's intercom broke in. "Good day. We will be landing in approximately five minutes. Please prepare your belongings and take your seats. You may feel a slight bump as the ship docks. We hope you have enjoyed your flight onboard Epsilon Spacelines. Star light. Star bright. May Epsilon be the star that guides you tonight."

"I... I cannot," said Dr. Saknussemm.

Zoe knew time was running out.

"Earl. Please."

He quivered in his seat and stared at her. "Help... help me," he said, as defeated as she had ever heard anyone.

Zoe's mind immediately began plotting and was already raising alarms of the tough, if not nearly impossible, challenge of sneaking the Doctor past the Space Marshal, the waiting police, all prying eyes, and past such a frightened state that he may actually be able to articulate answers to her questions. She nodded her head, mentally preparing for the task ahead.

"Okay," Zoe said.

CHAPTER 18

DOORS

The lunar station, Polestar 7, was comprised of many connected structures over the surface of its moon. It had become,
over hundreds of years, a central hub for many people as they
continue on to their final destinations. It was a sorting labyrinth
and its occupants navigated it expertly. Outbound and inbound
flights filled and empted; hallways ebbed and flowed. It was like
a colony of bees—a haze of flying ships around a hive while or-
ganized chaos filled its interior—and so Polestar 7 had commonly become known as the Hive. At the center of the Hive—the
source of its continued efficiency—was an integrated computer
bank, both powerful and intuitive, keeping the colony in order,
and had been thus appropriately nicknamed, the Queen.

━━╼╀ ╀╾━━

That is the spot, thought Zoe, as she reviewed the specs of the station on her lightcard to arrange their escape. Though it may very
well be under security and most likely overseen by the Queen
herself, it was the only place she could, ever so slightly, tweak the
station's protocols, diverting attention away from her party and

procure a path to safety. That ratiocinative machine would be watching, analyzing, and worst of all, anticipating. It would be quite the task not to be stung on the way there.

The flight carrier elegantly heaved its massive body toward the docking bay. Zoe had left her seat with the Doctor and had reconvened with Darious to explain the escape plan. He wore an understandably long face. She responded with her own enthusiastic look, though underneath was a similarly long face.

Zoe was just finishing up a coding sequence on her lightcard when the ship swayed a moment and then stopped moving.

"We're here," she said and quickly stood up. Darious took her by her hand.

"Wait," he said. She turned and looked in his eyes, those magnetic eyes. "Be safe Zoe." She nodded and quickly left.

Upon reaching the Doctor's floor, she saw he was no longer there, as planned. The Space Marshal was no longer in his seat either, also as planned. Then suddenly Dr. Saknussemm stepped out of the stairway corner, right next to Zoe. This was not planned. She stared at him wide eyed.

"What are you doing!?" she whispered in a strained voice.

"I.... I've lost the Marshal."

He kept his hood low but spoke with a slight confidence she had not heard before from him. Perhaps there was indeed a bit of anarchism within the Doctor. Zoe scratched her chin. This was not at all part of her machination, but there was no arguing at this point. She turned and accessed the directory on the left wall. Other passengers were stretching and preparing their bags.

"Well, since you're here, be a lookout. This may take a minute or so."

Zoe and the Doctor stood back to back, him staring out while she opened up a small panel below the directory. Zoe could hear increasing murmurs and huddled her body closer to her work so people wouldn't see what she was doing. She navigated to the root menu of the directory and placed her lightcard near the exposed service panel. She wirelessly sent her newly written code into it and waited for the prompt to show up.

'Initiate Theta Protocol?' the computer screen flashed.

"Why yes indeed," said Zoe as she typed in a 'y' and pressed enter.

The hack was easier than she anticipated and suddenly the ship slightly rocked. Passengers all paused and looked around. The Doctor, though aware of Zoe's plan, fidgeted at her back.

"That'll do it," she said as she replaced the panel.

Dr. Saknussemm crouched over her, surveying her handiwork. She tapped on the directory screen, returning it to its normal function and turned to the Doctor. He raised an eyebrow at the lightcard and then at her.

"Well Mi... Miss Zoe, i... it seems you've done this before."

She let loose a small giddy smile.

The carrier vessel picked itself back up and gently wobbled as it lifted its great burden back into the air. Confused passengers were quick to retake their seats as it begun lumbering forward. A voice came in through the intercom, the same female voice from earlier.

"Sorry folks. It seems we have been redirected to a new bay. We will be docked shortly." There a slight groan from the crowd. "Thank you for your patience."

Zoe and the Doctor hurriedly made their way toward the exit on the first level where a waiting Darious sighed with relief. The craft swayed once more as it again landed, and Zoe could hear the final diminution of the engines. Unlocking clamps thudded on the outside of the ship and its exit doors opened. The three departed and hastily made their way from the outbound corridor to the main passageway among the crowds of the Hive. *So far, so good*, thought Zoe.

Though they had been so fortunate as to avoid any extra attention thus far, that run of good luck was now over. The Queen had evidently been a busy bee. Black uniformed bodies synchronously appeared at opposite ends of the bumbling hallway. Their large statures and jet-black regalia clearly set them apart from the crowds. Darious gasped at the sight of them to the front and Dr. Saknussemm likewise at the sight of them at the rear.

"There!" Zoe spotted a maintenance door. They quickly worked their way through the crowds to the door. She fumbled with the electronic lock at its handle. "Come on. Come on."

Darious and the Doctor teetered over her shoulder, their close nervous breaths disrupting her concentration. She kept the lightcard low in one hand while the other manipulated the lock. The mechanical bolt made a scraping sound and the door opened. Zoe thrust the frail Doctor in first, followed by Darious. Once she was through, she quickly closed the door and deleted its electronic communication protocols. Darious propped up a metal beam to the door's handle. The three took a team breath in and it was now when Zoe realized they were in a dingy, neglected service hallway. It was empty, save for a few discarded items here and there, no doubt from workers too lazy to actually put them away. Zoe looked up. No cameras either. Good. The hallway went on for a short distance, about 50 meters or so, before leading to another corridor.

Zoe urged the group forward and they hustled through to its end, exiting at a large maintenance tunnel. She peered left and right as they entered in; they were still alone.

"Man," she stated, "security sure is a big deal here."

"Did you see the rifles those men carried?" asked Darious.

Zoe had not. "They were armed?"

"Yes."

She shook her head. *Then they were not typical port security.*

Darious jogged over to a digital sign on the wall. "According to this map, the central computer is that way." He pointed to the far end of the large passageway. "Then we take Corridor 405 to its end and left through Door 22."

"Okay," responded Zoe.

Once more, the three were off. Darious led while Zoe held up the rear. It was evident the Doctor was straining to keep up; he seemed to have a limp about him. His whole body seemed so much older than it was. He looked afflicted and maltreated. *Perhaps from Pantheon making good on its threats,* she thought. In her mind's eye she repulsively imagined the Doctor turning away from some evil research and being beaten in response. Imprisoned perhaps. A slave perhaps. Though at some point he must have procured an escape. She played out Dr. Saknussemm's subsequent life as they continued to hurry through the corridor. Zoe imagined the Doctor hiding in his solitary outpost, eroding away year after year and shuddering from the memories of what had been done to him. Conceivably, that trauma mixed with his precocity and a dash of paranoia had been what nourished his ingenious inventions. The long duration of terrified tinkering in his lab had no doubt led to the worsening of his condition, both mental and physical—an atrophy of sane mind and staunch muscle—with the final result being the broken man now hobbling in front of her. Zoe elutriated her mind. It was all conjecture; she had very little facts to work with. One thing was certain though, *something extraordinary* had happened to this man.

Upon reaching Door 22, with thankfully zero resistance, they paused while Zoe started deciphering the lock. The Doctor was taking wheezing breaths in. The ceramic sapphire door had a small, oblong porthole at eye level crisscrossed with security wiring. Zoe noted the thickness of the window. *Nothing of importance beyond here...* In any case, she would make short work of the electronic lock.

"It's... it's...," Dr. Saknussemm began.

Zoe heard the distinct sound of heavy boots. They were echoing from far down the corridor and were certainly getting louder. Urgency impelled her to work with unparalleled legerity. Just ten seconds later, she had hacked the door open and the three clambered inside. Darious tore a safety poster from the wall and applied it over the porthole. Zoe nodded with approval.

"Seems you too have an undiscovered knack for anarchy." Zoe winked at him.

The room they had entered was narrow; the floor was composed of old steel grates and the ceiling revealed ventilation tubes. At the opposite end was another door with a larger porthole and a security card reader near its handle. Zoe walked up to it and eyed the room beyond. Several rows of computer hardware created neat shelves with blinking lights. She spotted a control console.

"Bingo."

Darious and the Doctor stared at the door they had come through as if at any moment it would explode and soldiers would fusillade into the room like shrapnel. Zoe worked the voltaic latch, but to her dismay it countervailed all her efforts. *Crap,* she thought. Darious must have noticed the worried expression on her face, for he came forward and pressed a boot to the card reader. Putting his weight behind it, he thrusted forward and the force from his leg cleft the mechanism from its wall mount.

"Ah," said Zoe. She had not thought of that.

She took up the newly exposed wiring and made quick work of it. The door slid open. Inside, Zoe quickly took a seat at the computer console. Her agile fingers navigated through the vast framework of the Queen.

All she could hear was the soft hum of cooling fans within the core room and the typing from her own fingers. Her thoughts were concentrated on the single task at hand. Darious entered in and began walking around, surveying the equipment. The

Doctor appeared a minute later, his vision keen on the door beyond with the poster. From the corner of her eye, Zoe could see his hands were shaking.

"Just a moment more," she said calmly. "I'm setting up a sequence I can initiate from my lightcard." The Doctor coughed several times and leaned up against the wall. "It'll falsify our whereabouts, tricking the computer to think we're at the East end," Zoe cracked her neck, "while we will be rendezvousing with a ship being autonomously prepped on the West end." Zoe was suddenly submerged in a torrent of coding. "The Queen has so many verification subsystems. It's like a giant balancing act with her. There we go. All set. Would you like a ship with cup holders or with massaging seats?" Darious came up to the control console and looked at the ocean of data Zoe had been swimming through.

"Oh, a massage will do." He waived his hand in a nonchalant manner. Zoe giggled in amusement. The Doctor did not partake in their good humor; he continued his death stare at the door. After a minute more, Zoe finished coding and stood up.

"Okay gang. Time to go." Zoe and Darious huddled at the sapphire door and listened intently. No sounds came from the other side. Zoe brought out her lightcard, which had on its screen a large neon-green square with the words 'Press Me.' She did so. A moment after, a clear yell broke the silence from the other side of the door and footsteps were heard coming and then going from one end of the hall to the other.

Then all was silent. They carefully opened the door and the three made their way down the opposite hall. They came upon a doorway leading back into the masses. With a deep breath in, Zoe opened it and once more they were among the clamorous crowds.

The group crossed the busy hallway and headed for the departing flight back to Port Auborne. The crowds were thinning in this direction.

"We're flight 0-20," Zoe said to her companions.

Darious pointed to a sign above one of the hallways and Zoe and the Doctor followed. The final corridor to the awaiting ship was empty, as the only occupants who knew of the flight where the three currently rushing toward it. When they reached the pale white door, Zoe manned the podium and opened it. A cold gust blew out. Placed before them was a small spaceliner parked at the center of a huge enclosed bay.

The three wasted no time and hastened toward the craft. Just then, a loud submerged bang resounded somewhere from Zoe's left. Looking towards the sound, she saw a sealed hatchway a ways away from them along the perpendicular wall. There was another hollow bang and the door burst open. A single man stepped out, posing heroically for a second and then turning his gaze towards them. Stepping into a run, he raised a long pistol from his side. A shot rang out.

The three froze. Zoe stared at the man wide eyed. He had the stature of a military roughneck and wore a dark cloak with a darker vest and an eccentric brown headgear. It took Zoe a moment to call to mind the elongated brim and its front folded center. *A cowboy hat.* The face under it seemed machine-like with deadened eyes and a square jaw overlain by shadowy stubble.

"Run!" shouted Darious, snapping Zoe out of her stupor just as another shot fractured the air.

Zoe could feel the heat from the plasma bolt pass near her cheek. At this she bound back in surprise and then leapt forward into a full sprint. She pulled out her lightcard and activated the ship's boarding sequence, via falsified command from the confused Queen. Lights from underside of the craft out to its wingtips blinked on and its primer thrusters ignited. An entryway on the private vessel's side began to slide open and a ramp extended down to the ground.

Two more shots boomed, prompting the group to run faster. The Doctor was falling behind. Zoe slackened her pace and heaved him by the arm. They were nearing the ship, though the man in the cowboy hat was quickly gaining on them. A loud shot came again, this time hitting flesh.

"Agghh!" yelled out Dr. Earl Saknussemm, twisting and falling to the floor. He rolled over once and onto his back, his arms and legs sprawled out. The shot had burned through his upper torso.

"Shit!" cried Zoe.

She grabbed his arm with both of hers, attempting to hoist him back up. Another gun blast hit the Doctor's midsection, instantly scorching cloth and flesh to black. He screamed, and his eyes darted about as panic took hold.

Darious was far up ahead, already making his way up the ramp. "Zoe!" he called.

She slumped to the Doctor's side and propped up his worn face in her palms.

"Doctor." Her eyes were beginning to puff up. Doct..."

He coughed and blackened saliva drizzled down his lips. "Zoe." His face spasmed in pain. "Here... here.... poc... poc..." He tried at his breast pocket with a hand, but it fell to his side. "It's... it's..." Another shot rang out, this time evidently aimed at Darious as it ricocheted off the ship. "...the... the... truth." Dr. Saknussemm's head slumped back and he lost consciousness.

Zoe, through watery eyes and a thumping heart, reached in the Doctor's front pocket and withdrew a small rectangular object. It had been grazed by one of the gun shots. She gripped it tightly in her hand, blackened by the Doctor's wounds. Zoe looked up and saw the man nearly upon her. She gasped and lunged forward into a sprint. In moments she was up the ramp and yelling for Darious to take off.

The spacecraft quivered as it lifted up from the ground with quick, uneven thruster pulses. The ceiling of the great dome split in the middle and the two halves began retracting. At this, red alarms and sirens blared all around the docking bay. A great wind blew out from the closing hatch of the ship to the bay and then out to the vacuum of space. Zoe clung on to the nearest seat until the ship's door was completely sealed and the air settled. Outside, the bay was quickly depressurizing and the gap above widening, fully exposing the bay to the cosmos. Zoe sat in the chair and panted, looking out of the passenger window. The figure with the gun had turned around and was sprinting back toward the door from which he had come. His clothes flapped wildly about him while a hand firmly held the hat to his head. Dr. Saknussemm was on the floor, unmoving; ash rising from his body and out to eternal space.

The ship lifted higher and higher, up through the great door, tilting portside as it aligned itself with its course and shot out from the station. Zoe became conscious of her daze and ran to the cockpit where Darious was strapped in to the captain's seat, manning the spacecraft. She sat in the copilot's chair and stared out at space for a minute before wrapping her arms around him and burying her face in his chest.

CHAPTER 19

DON'T EXPECT COMPLIMENTS FROM A SERPENT

Rock-like fingers typed on a projected number pad. The signal connected. A brawny hand interlocked with its counterpart and muscular arms pushed the entanglement out, causing a deluge of cracking. A gentle woman's voice came from the other end of the line.

"This is Mr. Achan's office. Mr. Achan is not in—"

"This is Kappa."

There was a pause. "One moment please."

Kappa stretched out his shoulders and eased his back in the seat. Firmly gasping his head, he twisted it sharply to one side then to the other, creating more crepitate sounds. The cabin of his spacecraft echoed with tinny chirps. Kappa smirked as he considered the sounds not as echoes but as the actual ship itself flexing its couplings. He looked around the single quarters of the small superluminal space fighter, lacking any sort of creature comforts. He sighed. *Where had it gone?* At least he had his own musings.

The other line crackled, and Kappa quickly set himself upright. Then it went silent again. He relaxed and lazily extended a leg onto his console and set the other atop it. Kappa stretched his arms over his head and waited. After a few minutes, the call clicked and a harsh, merciless voice spoke through his speakers.

"Yes?"

From the one word, Kappa could sense such disdain in it, such power and such ire, an ineffable scorn, as if each microsecond was too much to waste on the plebeians. Kappa quickly leaned forward to the microphone.

"This is Kappa."

The voice on the other end callously hissed, "I know." There was a pause and it smoothed out. "What of the two?"

"Oh, much better than the two." Kappa waited, primed for that teaser to perk up Mr. Achan. He realized though it was probably in vein. "I've located and retired a 'Doctor Saknussemm,'" he said confidently.

There was a momentary static. "Do you have the body?"

"Yes sir. Though, it sustained a bit of... suction."

Mr. Achan's voice remained unmoved. "Bring his corpse to the lab."

"Yes sir. The other two continue to be mobile. Orders?"

"Dispose of them. By any means you deem necessary."

To this, Kappa smiled. It had been a long while since he was granted such autonomy. Moreover, it had been a long while since he had the opportunity to use Bessie. Kappa bent low and retrieved her from under his seat, placing her in his lap. *An open kill order.* He walked his fingers along her massive polysteel barrel with wandering thoughts.

"Well...," Mr. Achan broke in, his voice now returning to its original sin, "...keep hunting!" The slamming of the speakerphone made the speakers of Kappa's ship send out a loud shrill note. He winced and then shrugged his shoulders.

Kappa eyed the private craft he'd been tracking on long range scanners. It looked to be headed toward a spaceport not too far from the one it had set out from. He ignited the thrusters and stared out the cockpit window as the stars around him bounced and then began to drift faster and faster around his ship, like droplets on the windshield of a speeder bike. He approximated they would be there in six hours. He would be there in three. Perhaps there was time for a drink. He tipped his brimmed hat to the space beyond. He'd have this job wrapped up before sundown.

CHAPTER 20

THE WITCHING HOUR

Zoe did her best to rinse off in the parsimonious lavatory. Upon returning to the cockpit, she sat with a slump next to Darious, who was focusing all his energies on the controls.

"The ship does have an autopilot," she said and then turned her attention to the view of outer-space. After some time, Zoe spoke again, continuing to stare outward, "When we were young, darkness was quite an unnerving thing. And you know what? It wasn't the dark per say, it was the unknown it represented. The unknown is always so unjustifiably scary." She turned to Darious. "It's black out there. As black as it gets." She then added light-heartedly, "but, the ship can maneuver just fine on autopilot."

"Yes captain," he said without shifting his eyes from the console.

"No. No. Today, you are the captain. Captain Darious."

Darious succeeded in putting the ship in autopilot and looked over at her, his expression easing. He smiled, and they exchanged a quick hug.

"So, Captain Darious," said Zoe, "how long 'till our arrival?"

He turned and fumbled with the controls for a moment. "Five hours, 14 minutes."

"Good. Darious, I'm going to take a nap. It's been one hell of a day." Zoe's stomach started growling. "Actually..." she licked her lips. "...let's see if we can find something to eat first."

With the ship speeding steadily on course, the two made their way to the dining area of the private spaceliner. Zoe spotted plates and handed one to Darious while proceeding to rummage through the cabinets.

"Ooh! Mashed potatoes!"

Zoe grabbed three vacuum-sealed bags and plopped them on her plate. She tossed another on Darious'. He was busy reading the labeling on a package of mixed beans. She stuck out her tongue.

"Ugh. Nope."

Zoe pulled the package from his hand and tossed it back in the cupboard. She then pulled out a large silver package in the shape of a 'T.'

"This is what you want," she said, nodding emphatically.

Darious held up the package and turned it over. It was without markings.

"What is it?" he asked.

"Steak." Zoe smiled broadly. "Oh ya. Nuke that baby for 2 minutes in that oven over there and you're good to go." She pointed to a small appliance on the counter. He looked over at it and then paused, looking down. He seemed to be hesitating for some reason. "What's wrong?" Zoe asked.

"Well," Darious stiffened up. "I've never had a steak."

"What!? Oh Darious. Oh, Captain Darious, you're going to enjoy this!" She took the package from him, popped it in the oven and set the timer. She snapped her fingers. "Needs sauce." She shuffled through the open cupboard. "Oh yes."

Zoe picked out a small glass bottle with a screw top and handed it to him. Darious inquisitively examined it. There was a cartoon animal with hooves on the label, posed with its rear legs kicking high in the air and a shocked look on its face. Flames were shooting out from its buttocks. Zoe couldn't help but smirk at Darious' utter confusion.

"Guess what it is?"

"I... I have no idea," said Darious. "I did not know a creature existed that could propel flames from its underside. Why have a picture of such a grotesque beast on food rations?"

Zoe couldn't help but chuckle. "Rations, no. This here is hot sauce, a topping for your steak. And that there," she pointed to the animal, "is a donkey. Farting fire."

He looked down at the bottle and over at her several times. Zoe was adoring his expressions. He would curl one eyebrow up in deep thought, then look at the bottle, stare at it for a few seconds, and then come back to her with that same perplexed look. Zoe burst out laughing.

"Okay. Okay," she said, "Put a dab on your finger and taste it."

Darious did so and his eyes began to widen further and further. His face turned a light shade of pink. Then, a smile started forming. It broadened. His white teeth slowly began revealing themselves, sparkling with glee.

"Oh yes," Darious said with an equal glint in his eyes. "That is good."

The oven beeped once. Darious carefully removed the package and opened it via the pull string, liberating the steak from its broiling chamber. Mouthwatering aromas of freshly roasted meat filled the ship. Next, Zoe heated the mashed potatoes and the two sat down for a proper meal in the front cabin.

Darious doused his meat in the hot sauce and carved it into large portions. With each new forkload, sounds of elation escaped from him. Zoe also hungrily ate, using a ladle to spoon mushy masses into her mouth. They ate together in silence, though for Zoe, this mute moment said more than any words could have.

She looked at her plate, at Darious, at the Jackass Hot Sauce, and out at space. She was happy.

Five hours later, the pair reached Port Auborne. Darious was at the helm with Zoe coaching him through the docking procedure. As copilot, she had plotted their landing vector, checked over the spaceliner's docking systems for any potential issues, scanned for space debris, and sent out a broadband beacon with their landing credentials. Zoe had found a parking spot near her ship's docked location.

"Careful. Careful," she said slowly as Darious manually shuffled the ship into its final anchor position. He eased the craft forward and backed it off again, over and over. It rocked back and forth, as if it were a boat on water, until he had it aligned just right. "Perfect." Zoe leaned over him and flipped a number of switches. A loud clamping noise echoed and then the craft was completely still. "And we're here." As they got up, Zoe noticed Darious take up the half-empty hot sauce and pocket it. She smirked. Zoe held out her hand as he lowered his hood, and the two entered the passageway together.

To her, and most certainly Darious', relief, they came upon only little resistance in the hallways from other travelers and were soon entering into her ship. Zoe closed the hatch and exhaled a deep sigh of relief. Darious took off his sweater and did likewise.

"Home sweet home," she said, leaning on the hatchway. Darious nodded in agreement. Zoe left the central chamber and took up her captain's seat. She wriggled in the familiar crevices and relaxed low in the chair.

From here, Zoe wasted no time. She flicked her wrists out and began initiating the flight procedure. Darious took his post as the mechanical docking couplers released the tiny craft. While system checks were autonomously ticking off, Zoe slowly turned the ship around, outwardly facing away from the port. Alarms suddenly blared bloody murder and her console lit up with red warnings. Zoe quickly looked at her screen and saw her ship had been locked on.

"Port bow, 300 meters off!" Darious yelled.

Zoe looked out the cockpit window and saw in the lower corner, a small ship. It was hard to make out. The craft was dark—very dark against the backdrop of space—blending in with its celestial surroundings. *Blending too well.* Zoe immediately initiated prompts for circumrotating maneuvers. As the unidentified ship came forward, she could make out its tinted, grinning cockpit window.

"Port bow, 250 meters!"

Zoe continued squinting at the vessel. It had no markings. The belly seemed to be the whole of it. Connected atop was a pair of wings bending low around it, with the wingtips splitting into multitudinous razors. To Zoe, it looked like some sort of space bat, if there was such a thing. It had such a menacing look about it. Zoe had her fingers on the console, ready to engage thrusters. Why was it engaging them? Where had it come from?

Darious declared, "100 meters. It is now stationary!"

The two crafts stood in the dead of space, staring at each other; one backed against the space station, the other with infinite freedom behind it.

Zoe opened a channel and hailed the ship. No response. Her skin began to feel prickly as she continued to leer at the ship. Darious came over next to her and peered out at the craft. He was about to say something when another siren went off and he spun back around, reading from his console.

"Thirty-six additional lock-ons!"

Zoe saw now, under the wings and close to the belly of the craft, the outlines of many rockets and an assortment of ordinance hardware. Blue lights began encircling each as they came online.

Zoe suddenly remembered where she had seen that craft, or one like it anyway. It was a Drak-9 interstellar fighter—a retired military vehicle for special operations, capable of flight speeds much faster than her ship and much, much faster than the light she was observing it with. There would be no outrunning it.

"Darious," she called back through a storm of typing. "I'm engaging the Middle Finger Protocol." She could hear Darious take a deep breath in. Zoe pressed enter and the power levels of her ship momentarily dipped as the high energy pulse charged and was shot toward the Drak-9. Staring out, Zoe was hoping with all her consciousness it would work. Just a second later, the resulting effect was apparent.

The Drak-9 violently jerked from its stationary position and completed a series of rapid twirls in place, somersaulting over and over. Zoe was sure glad she was in her ship and not in that one. A sudden bright spark flashed from within its window and the spinning craft came to an abrupt halt, completely dead. A puff of smoke expanded out from the ship and dissipated in space, causing it to drift slowly out from the port and away from them.

"Old tricks are the best ones," said Zoe. As the paralyzed vessel floated away, she got a good look at the engines on its stern side. "Wow," she said lowly.

When Zoe had first decided to construct her own craft years ago, she had researched many vessels. She knew the engines of the original Drak-9s well. This was something far beyond those. Zoe flipped several toggle switches above her. Seeing the danger was over, as the ship was completely disabled, she swung her ship about and brought the two cockpits eye to eye.

Zoe and Darious leaned in close to try and make out its interior. It was dark on the inside due to lack of power, though she could see a faint blinking red light in the corner, signifying emergency systems were still online. Suddenly, a man dashed forward at the cockpit window, striking it with his head and fists. Zoe and Darious jumped in near terror. The man's eyes narrowed as he fixed his gaze on them. He grabbed the rimmed hat on his head, flinging it away and continued banging closed fists to the glass. His mouth opened wide and shut many times; Zoe almost thought she could hear his furious shouts through the vacuum gap of the two ships.

Zoe blinked. Damnit. He must have been tracking them since their last encounter. With a few keystrokes, she probed the exterior of his ship and found a small array of antenna at the junction between the two overbearing wings. She smirked; if the man in the cowboy hat did not like that last trick, he would definitely not like what she was about to do. Zoe engaged thrusters and propelling her craft forward, ignoring the proximity alerts. She ignited secondary boosters and pitched her craft upward just before impact, grinding the hard, metallic underside of her ship against the antennas, pulverizing them to dust. As the grating sounds resounded in her ship, she fired all thrusters to full, sending the Drak-9 into a mad horizontal spin, and she blasted off into deep space.

The rush of escape had sparked the joints around Zoe's body, but soon her lips began to slide downwards, and her heart bottomed out. She looked at Darious who had an equally sour expression on his face. Zoe knew the same thought had undoubtedly connected them: They were in deep.

CHAPTER 21

GOOD THING NO LITTLE ONES ARE PRESENT

"Damn fucking hackers! Fucking damnit!" Kappa smashed his forehead into the window toward the deviant ship. A meteor of a punch flew forward and flattened against the cockpit windshield. "Fucking mange of the... the garrh!"

Kappa's enraged words crumpled into unintelligible sounds and guttural rumblings as he pounded more fists into the window. The two of them stood there, just staring at him, like deer caught in terawatt excimer headlights. He grabbed the hat off his head. "Fucking damnit!" Kappa crushed it in his hand and threw it away. "You fucking hackers!" He continued mashing his fists, each blow sounding with dull tinks.

The woman, Zoe, was now typing. Kappa paused, staring at her. She would kill him now that he'd been rendered powerless. It was over.

"My hat?!" he cried and looked to where he had thrown it in his fit of rage. He picked it up, dusted it off and replaced it on his head. Now he could die.

Just as he finished adjusting the pointed rim forward, there was a shock to his ship, rocking it backward and causing him to lose his footing. Kappa quickly spun around on his hands and knees, looking out the window, and was blinded by the sudden burst from an exceedingly bright rocket blast.

"Ahh!" he yelled as his vision was seared white through closed eyelids.

In confusion, he scrambled to his feet, covering his eyes. Then, as if thrown by an invisible opponent, Kappa was suddenly hurled sideways. The ship had been spurred into a wild spin. Kappa's fluttering, flustered flight through the cabin abruptly ended with his gut wrapping around a structural beam. All the air from his lungs was immediately expelled. He wheezed and attempted to release himself, but the centrifugal force was too much. Pushing with his arms, Kappa was only able to slightly ease himself off, allowing breath to partially return, but was unable to fully relief himself of the horseshoe posture that had him pinned. He let out a half-breathless yell. The bright light was gone now but the blurriness and stinging sensation lingered in his eyes. His stomach was compacted and now disorientation filled his senses as the breakneck spin continued.

Oh, he did not feel good. With minimal gravitational stabilizers, with minimal everything for that matter, there was nothing to slow the spin.

"Ugh."

His stomach writhed; his mind whirled. With another aggressive push, Kappa released himself from the beam and collapsed next to it, falling flat on his back against the wall of the ship. His stomach heaved once more but he forced the bile back down.

"Fucking. Hackers," he choked.

Kappa strained to look down at himself. He couldn't even make out his own booted feet through his burning eyes. What a rodeo this turned out to be. He let his head go limp and it slammed against the metallic wall. He allowed the spinning to overtake him.

"You. Win. For now." Kappa shut his eyes and let the blackness come.

It was some time later when Kappa awoke to the feeling of being lifted up from his backside. As he opened his eyes, he hit the floor. He let out a surprised yelp and strived to get to his feet, stumbling as the rotational forces continued to draw him outward. The ship's revolutions had slowed; perhaps it had grazed something. He sure felt sick. Holding his midsection, he slowly made his way to the rear of the ship, toward the computer bank. He had to assess the damage those two mooncalves had caused and then assess his options.

Damn they were determined. Smart too. How long had it been since anyone had put up any resistance? And stealing corporate documents... who did that sort of thing anyway? This was the first time he had come across someone who'd done it. All he ever dealt with nowadays were drunks who pissed off some suit at Pantheon. Wasn't the galaxy big enough for everyone to just leave everyone else the fuck alone and go about their merry little way?

Kappa slumped next to the computer terminal and took in several long-needed breaths. The spinning could last for days if he didn't get the ship properly started, or worse he could crash into the port, and who knows where it was. Surely that would happen before anyone bothered to stop and help him.

He bent low and felt around for the latch on the wall. With a push of his thumb and a mechanical click, the drawer opened, and Kappa began sliding out the ship's central processing core. It was an open-top black module containing many vertically aligned boards. He immediately smelled the distinct odor of newly soldered connections and grimaced. No longer did he feel the pains of his stomach; it was now the box that received his full

attention. That smell was not good. Once the core was fully extracted, he delicately brought it down to the floor, continuing to
hold it with one hand. Peering in, Kappa could see scarring along
the inner walls, no doubt from an overloading of the ship's electronics. He muttered several short curses. Reaching in, Kappa
removed one of the rectangular boards. He held it up to the dim
glow of space, complimented by an intermittent red light, and
his face creased inward. The intricate circuitry, originally green,
was now brown with black streaks strewn throughout it like petrified lightning. He turned it over; the same etchings were present
on the other side. The computer board suddenly gave way in his
hand, crumbling into countless tiny bits and pouring through
his fingers like grains of sand. Wisps of ash went up into the air
as the ruins settled on the ground.

"Damnit."

Kappa crushed the last fragments of the circuitry in his hand.
It was as frail as a 100-year-old derby horse. He looked down at
the box of remaining processor boards and though he already
knew their fate. He inspected each in turn and then replaced
the box into its compartment. He was not going anywhere for a
while.

CHAPTER 22

REQUIEM FOR A DOCTOR

Zoe twiddled the sable bequest with her fingers. The silent dirge from it inspissated the air around the captain's seat. Though cool to the touch and colder still by memory, the small cenotaph warmed Zoe with the speculations of what it might contain. One side bared the epitaph of the deep scar from the encounter with the man in the cowboy hat. She thumbed at it and could feel the fracture extending across the surface. A melancholy sigh left her lips, meant only to be audible to those in the cockpit; Darious was studying in the main room and her pensiveness was hers alone.

After ensuring the ship was on course for the Doctor's homemoon, Zoe set the data stick onto the instrument panel and guided the computer to extract its contents. To her surprise, it contained only a single file of coding, though considerable in length. Zoe read through the first few lines of overlapping numerals, symbols, and text.

"Hmmph."

At first glance, she had no idea what she was looking at. A ploynumeric method for interstellar communications? Didn't seem to be. A comparative morphologic study of sea cucumbers and fractals? Nope. She scratched her chin and internal cogs began to slowly turn. *Wait a minute...* The idling flywheels rotated faster and faster, interlocking with further gear heads, and expanding into a critical thinking machine. Zoe flipped on her revered, low-toned music and shifted her mind into overdrive.

Zoe became a dizzying sight, a human-powered pure computational engine; her fingers indefatigably typed away on the console while her eyes scanned layer upon layer of coding. Her body constantly left to the central chamber, returning with books and materials of everything from cryptocalculus to The Epic of Homer. Her mind never strayed from the enigmatic program of Dr. Saknussemm. All parts of her were in concert, working as one toward a single goal.

Many hours passed. The console was strewn with books and her screens were filled with multitudinous pages of coding. Zoe was tinkering with a particularly puzzling string of content when she heard Darious come up behind her yawning. She did not look up from her work. He bent over her and peered at the virtual monitors. He placed a hand on her shoulder.

"How is it going, Captain?"

Zoe sighed and finally paused her work. With arms stretching high, she cracked her back and adjusted her sore neck. The central display suddenly flashed 'Error' in big letters. Zoe sighed once more.

"That's how it's going." She removed the data stick from the console. "It's been damaged." Darious took up the small rectangle and examined it. "Glanced by gun blast it seems," she said.

Zoe held out her hand and Darious gingerly placed it in her palm, as though it was the last remnant of an extinct world.

"I've worked my way through much of it. It seems to be some sort of synchronized resonance for some sort of globular protuberance. What it does, or how it does it, I have no idea. This particular section here," she flipped through several virtual pages of coding and pointed to the middle of an intricate, multilayer sequence, "is completely corrupted. So, in addition to figuring out what the program is, I have to fix what seems to be the crux of it. So... yay me."

Darious smiled and squared his stance. "Oh Captain, my Captain. I fear our trip is far from done." He reached out a hand high to outer-space, presenting his sentiments to a congregation far from his center stage. "Your ship has weathered every crazed man; the prize we seek is near won. Oh Captain! My Captain!"

"Haha!" laughed Zoe. "Ah. Walt Whitman. I think I like your version better. So, seems someone has been doing a bit of classic reading."

"Yes! Zoe our forefathers saw the world with an amazing, poetic mindset. They created. They attempted and endeavored. They..." He fumbled for the word, "...they dreamed."

Zoe smiled warmly. "Indeed." With the cessation of her work, she now realized how fatigued she had become. Her mouth opened wide and a noisy yawn leapt out. "I think we could both do with a much-needed break." Darious nodded.

Turning off the harmonized warblings and minimizing her work from all the displays, Zoe laid back in her seat and stared out at fully revealed space. Though the text was gone, her mind kept recapitulating her work, overlaying the eternal night of space with strings of coding. Darious let out a complimentary yawn and settled with her in the seat. It was a snug fit, perfect for the two. The grandeur of the cosmos, just an arm's length beyond, soothed their weary bodies and minds, and they slept.

CHAPTER 23

THE FURY AND THE ANTHROPOS

"Wakey, wakey Mister." Zoe playfully tapped on Darious' forehead. "Wakey."

He stifled a yawn. "Ahhh. Are we there?"

"Just about." Zoe was manning the console with her one free hand, as the other was locked behind Darious.

"Oh. Excuse me." He bent forward, freeing her arm.

"Thank you." Zoe lifted the limb, but it remained limp. "Asleep." She wiggled it and giggled. "Ah! That always gets me." With her one functioning arm, she picked her way through the navigation systems. "Let's see, we are about 1.6 million kilometers from the system of Ios..." She fumbled with the controls as her other hand slowly regained responsiveness. "The weather seems fine; it's not raining toads just yet. Wait a minute!" She sat straight up and typed with both hands, ignoring the fatigue of the one. Darious quickly scooted out of the way and booted up his station. She flung the new information through cyberspace to his monitor.

"Oh my," he said upon reading it.

Zoe engaged a full stop of her ship. Forward thrusters ceased, and reverse thrusters ignited, sending the craft into a hasty deceleration. Ios' moon was infested with ships encircling it. In fact, the entire system was interwoven with ships of various sizes and makes, all bearing the single identifying signature of Pantheon Industries. Here laid a company armada of galactic-enabled ships.

Darious spoke up, "I think it would be best if we did not venture further as we are not sure where the corporation stands in all this."

"And considering the kind words the Doctor had of them," added Zoe. "Man, they are everywhere, as if they are scanning the entire system." She reflected on this for a moment. "Hopefully they are scanning inwards and not out at us." A blue light on the projection screen signified her ship had come to a full stop and was holding its position in space. Zoe pivoted the ship around and launched them away at high thrust from Ios and Iros.

The two sat in a long silence. Zoe's skin was tingling, no longer from awakening circulation, but from nervous anticipation. After several minutes, it was apparent no ships interior to the star system had taken notice of them. "Well, there goes that." Zoe was looking at her original scans of Dr. Saknussemm's moon abode. "We need more information of his work. Dang! I bet his home was a goldmine. What can we do now?"

"Well, I suppose we could just ask them for it," said Darious, lightheartedly.

Zoe snapped her fingers. "That's exactly what we will do!" Though she was turned away from Darious, she could just picture his face dropping. "Well, except for the asking part," she added.

"I already regret what I have said."

"Too late!" Zoe rebutted, smirking. "Okay, here's the idea: All the information they find from the Doctor will be stored, right?

In some database, somewhere. So, we go to the filing center," she put up air quotes with her fingers, "and 'borrow' what we need, and get out of there. All before tea time." She could now sense Darious glaring at her. She turned towards him and her supposition was indeed true. "Aww come on. It could be fun..."

"It is a very dangerous idea, Zoe. We will be directly in harm's way. Some man has tried to kill us. Twice now."

"I know. I know. Darious, I need to do this. I need to know the reason for Dr. Saknussemm's death."

Darious took a moment and then solemnly nodded his head. "I understand. You are right. I too feel a certain allowance must be made in this direction. You are not alone, Zoe. I am in."

"Yay!" She stood up and wrapped her arms around him. "Okay. Let's see where Pantheon keeps their data. This time, we are going to the source." Zoe compiled a quick search. "Ah. Turns out it's at their headquarters. Planet Kratos in the Pantheon System. Of course they named an entire solar system after themselves. It's in the Veritas Sector. Ugh. 3 hundred and—ugh—twenty-nine floating-parsecs away."

"That will take several weeks at high thrust; time for us to prepare," said Darious.

"Indeed sir. Let's start from the top. Find who the head of the corporation is and if they have their office there. If they don't, go down the list to the next highest-up person. Map out everything you get. The safest way to gather information is to access public databases through a coupled proxy line, like I showed you."

"Aye Zoe. I suppose I will also have time to finish this." He held up a book, 'The White Whale,' and smiled.

Zoe swiveled back around and surveyed the mess of papers on the console. "I suppose it gives me more time to ponder this code. Then it's settled," she said authoritatively. "Set course for Pantheon Industries."

"Aye."

⊷⊶

The ship swept upward in a great arc. Transfusing in its ionizing wake, a passing cloud of nearly microscopic dust ignited and burst into a flurry of sapphire and amethyst, creating a spectacular trailing glow. The effervescence shimmered for some time before dissipating and becoming once more obscured by sempiternity.

Zoe meanwhile was transformed into an Erinyes of furious proportions, wholly transfixed in her work. Days passed. Soon weeks sailed by. The Fury and the Anthropos always remained assiduously dynamic; always learning, practicing, formulating, and most importantly of any two-bodied system—creating new inside jokes.

⊷⊶

With the arrival at Pantheon Industries' headquarters just a day away, Zoe had finally narrowed her scope of research and was applying it to the missing sectors of coding. She had brought the craft to a complete stop and scanned the entire surrounding area. Darious was with her in the cockpit, looking over her shoulder and offering his thoughts on the test she was prepping, most of which were related to their safety and the safety of the ship. Still fresh in Zoe's mind was the Doctor's amazing technology of his home and ship. As such she heeded Darious' warnings and placed all principal systems on a redundant standby in case of the worst.

As Zoe wrapped up the last bits of work, she reflected on how the culmination of weeks of nonstop effort was to be this single experiment that would probably last no more than a minute. Among her thoughts, she noted how adept Darious had become at working on her ship with her, on both soft and hard-ware; he was a great help.

"Okay Darious, let's boot up this bad boy." He held the back of her seat. Zoe noticed his fingers flexing and understood; in fact, she was probably more apprehensive than he. "So, supposedly, assuming I understand what the Doctor's algorithm is supposed to do, we are about to generate a resonant node through two pulsers I've modified, the node being of what I understand to be of infinite size—which, I'm not sure how—vibrating at near infinitesimalness—again, which I barely understand how—in a supposed contained volume—to which I've set to be a meter diameter sphere in front of the ship—that does… something. So… ready?"

"Yes. Wait!" exclaimed Darious. "What about the secondary inter-airlock seal?! Is it—"

"Checked and double checked. I've put it with the rest of the systems in a separate parallel program. I think we're ready." With that, Zoe initiated the stitched-up program from the late Doctor.

A low hum started from under their feet and the floor lowly vibrated, as if Zoe's bass had been turned on and was slowly being dialed up. "That's normal. Just the exigency bay opening and the signalizing Z-Pulsers warming up."

"Z-pulsers? What is this?"

"Well, there are two of them. They're both below us, aiming forward into space. I worked up the Z-Pulsers from what I could gather about the Doctor's program. There were some coded blueprints; most of which were intact. Also, knowing—mostly—the parameters of his inputs made it a fairly easy task. Basically, take your standard zepto-second pulse generator, couple it to an antenna, pump up the power, and restrict certain waveforms. Add a bit of other magic and then run the program. Viola. I dub them, Z-Pulsers. The Z stands for…" She gave Darious a wanting look, but it was evident he was not in a jesting mood. She playfully waved him off and continued anyway, "No not zepto, for *zero* things to worry about." She smiled.

Lights onboard the ship suddenly dimmed and Darious nervously shifted. "Still normal. Capacitor banks charging." Zoe could feel his grip on her seat increase, matching the increasing quivers of the ship. "Program fully online. Initiating sensors." A readout display began pouring data packs to a screen on their lower left. "Stable. Stable. Check. Check. All normal." The humming continued to increase. "Norm... errm." The scrolling information flooded by at rapid speeds. The vibrations were now no longer at their feet, but all around them, reverberating the walls as if they were on an old steam train. The ship's recessed lighting began to flicker and go out completely for entire seconds at a time. Zoe and Darious peered out at the empty space in front of the ship. Nothing was happening.

"Wait!" Zoe gasped. They simultaneously bent forward and stared. It was as if a faint haze was coming into focus just ahead of the ship. "What is that?" asked Zoe. The diffused light barely shown, as if it were obscured by clouds. In fact, it looked as if the light itself was the globular shape. Zoe squinted harder, trying to understand what it could be. "How is it doing that?" she trailed off. In her mind she could not connect how the pulses being sent out were creating this sight. Sure she was dumping energy out into space, but the program was specifically alternated pulses so that each Z-Pulser did not interfere with the other. There were no energy collisions happening. What were they reacting with to make the light? The test medium was a vacuum, verified by her ship's sensors to be a pure section of space and now, something was being created from it. Out of nothing, something.

Sensor readouts were now spewing forth feedback too fast to read. The low-level humming was still increasing, now becoming a prominent noise rather than a background annoyance. The amplitudes of vibrations within the ship now made their feet bounce on the ground, creating tapping sounds. Books and tools throughout the ship vibrated from their pedestals and rattled on the floor. An entire disconcerted concert was taking place within Zoe's craft. The cloud of light ahead remained unchanged.

Zoe's vision remained fixed on that golden hue. "It's so—" multiple electrical pops resounded from somewhere. The ship jerked, and the humming ruptured into mashing clashes, as if an entire world of machines had all lost a sprocket at the same time, and everything completely ceased. The ship stabilized, and all systems returned to normal. However, Zoe and Darious were left wheezing between white teeth and even whiter faces. Zoe looked out; the glow was gone.

She lifted a shaking hand to the keyboard. "It... it looks like we blew a couple ancillary fuses. The ship auto-decoupled the Doctor's program as soon as that happened." She leaned back and sighed. A similar sound escaped from Darious. The sensor readout had stopped its text-based voluminous vomit. Zoe scanned through the resulting summary.

"Wow!" She snapped up from her seat and intently read with both hands on the console. "Darious look! On a micro-scale we were changing the space in front of us, actually modifying it!" A deluge of abstractions suddenly filled the canvases of Zoe's mind, having just witnessed the impossible made possible.

Darious read and his eyes widened with astonishment. "At the atomic scale...." He shifted his gaze back out to space. "But to what?"

"That, I have no idea." Zoe sat back down, making sure to save the information and then checked on the status of her ship. "Well, everything else seems intact. The fuses are back there."

She thumbed behind her towards the main compartment. "It'll take a minute to fix and then... more science!" Just as Darious was lifting a finger in admonishment, Zoe sprung from her seat, and was off to grab several spare palm-sized fuses.

CHAPTER 24

LET'S TRY THAT AGAIN

U pon the prompt completion of repairs, Zoe took up the captain's seat and set about preparing the computer to once more initialize the Doctor's program, ensuring that all primary and, now, secondary systems were safely tucked away. Once ready, she stretched her arms out, interlocking her fingers, and pulled the cartilage zipper apart. Zoe shook off the weariness from weeks of labyrinthine work and wiggled her fingers in front of the console with anticipation.

"Darious."

"Yes Captain?" He came and stood by her side.

"Starting now."

The buzzing below them began once more. This time, Zoe had spaced the power dumps at half intervals to better compensate energy repercussions of the pulsating antenna outputs. She had also tweaked several lines of the algorithm. Her craft once more started the low rhythm, deep from within its mechanical core. Zoe now knew much more what to expect and she kept focused with cool logic. As readouts began to flow back, she continuously shifted settings of the Z-Pulsers while altering coding bits. She was quickly learning how to adapt the fluctuations arising from both the experiment and her unestablished fixes of the broken program. On the whole, this run was going much more smoothly.

"There it is!" she said.

The first traces of the shadowy glow appeared, as if there was some unknown ether in front of the ship. It remained reticent as before, contained to a small quadrant directly at their center bow. Its luminosity barely registered, but from Zoe's keen eyes and the keener sensors of the ship, the ball of light was absolutely observed. If it wasn't for the blackness of space, human perception alone might not have been able to perceive anything.

The experiment soon matched the energy levels of their last attempt and was now reaching new, untested depths of the Doctor's program. The humming of the ship increased, as well as the intensity of the object. Zoe was mystified by it—an anomaly created by an electronic algorithm and the essence of space.

The object shone like a beacon in the night sea. Zoe and Darious were pegged to their spots, mesmerized. *What is it?* Zoe once more thought. The light seemed as if it was thickening. Zoe looked over her ship's sensors readings. They were now of little use, constantly communicating that both infinity and nothingness were present in front of them, so she diminished the readouts to get a better view. It looked as though singular rays of gold were being extruded from the spheroid. Still confined to the programmed volume in front of the ship, the beams continuously grew and diminished. Soon they appeared to be solidifying, like forged rods of light. These rods condensed and stretched out at intervals, warping into conical shapes. Zoe typed into her console and commenced an approximating routine, sampling the spaces in-between the experiment. As she adjusted its parameters, she could now read that, indeed, on a micro-scale, events were occurring incongruent with normal, physical reality.

"What is it?" asked Darious, the wonder in his voice matching Zoe's thoughts.

"I don't know." She was reading through the summaries while trying to direct the data to make more sense. The ship's sensors were receiving terabytes of information every second. "Energy levels are rising too high. I'm going to have to shut it off here in a second." Zoe stared out at the glowing orb, filled with transfiguring ingots, and then flipped a switch, powering down the entire experiment. The rods and cones immediately vanished, though the diffuse glow lingered for several moments before disappearing altogether. The hums from the ship lowered and faded away. All returned to normal, though the air about Zoe and Darious remained electric.

After a few seconds of silent bewilderment, Zoe exclaimed, "What was that!?" Her voice was pitched with excitement.

"Zoe! That was amazing! Ha! I have no idea!" Darious laughed and Zoe joined him.

"Ha ha! How crazy was that?!"

Darious nodded, his smile still growing. Zoe herself was feeling astronomical. Though she had no idea what they had done, she knew deep inside, from some imperceptible part of her, that they had just accomplished something incredible. Zoe was hoping with all her being that their imminent visit to the homeworld of Pantheon Industries would yield the answers to this enigma. *Pantheon Industries*, thought Zoe. She was ready.

CHAPTER 25

KRATOS SNUBBED

Assumed to have once been a planet of natural origin, orbiting around its central star, though now the region's true center of force, the longstanding headquarters of Pantheon Industries completely obscured the globe of Kratos. Not a single spot of indigenous terrain could be observed; the entirety of the planet was inhabited, built up, and populated with overreaching towers, terminating at the upper limits of the atmosphere.

When strangers neared the confounding object from space, it bore semblance to a needle spire as seen through a kaleidoscope. Upon closer approach, the oncoming spires seemed to take on the appearance of an armory of lances, daggers, and scythes, externalizing the weapons of pens, contracts, and economics incorporated within. Down, down the gapers plunged; the arsenal ascending higher and higher. As the ground below came into view, reverent warmth and the purity of pellucid sunlight became obscured behind the broadsword. Here, artificial light was necessary to illuminate the way. The many buildings, walkways, and landing pads all shared complimentary leaden grey tinctures. Having finally landed and looking out, the sky was seen in xanthic tones, though not a single cloud existed. The ascendancy over nature was complete; the ascendancy over man was well underway. One may gulp and nervously ease his collar; indeed, this was no place for such a man.

A woman, slim, short-sleeved and short-panted, strolled through the auto-reticulating doors and was greeted by an automated voice from above. "Welcome to Pantheon Industries." Directly ahead of her, at the far end of the ostentatious entrance, was a considerable receptionist desk, marbled and accented in shining gold, matching the large backlit Pantheon logo on the wall behind it. The woman casually walked up to it and greeted the secretary.

⟨+ +⟩

"Hello there."

The receptionist made eye contact and upon seeing Zoe an eye twitched, though the smile remained plastic and intact. "Welcome to Pantheon Industries. What may I do for you?"

Zoe feigned a smile back. "I'm here for a meeting with Mr. Alfred Achan, though I suspect I'm a bit early."

The secretary's eye seized again, and she took to typing on her computer console. Her agreeable countenance faded. "Ahem. I'm sorry for the inconvenience. It seems Mr. Achan is out for the week. Are you sure you have the time and coordinates of the meeting correct?"

It was Zoe's turn to act snippy, though she quite knew that Mr. Achan, and his associates were thousands of floating-parsecs away at a diplomatic function. "Oh yes, I'm quite sure." At this, the receptionist seemed to growl under her skin, prompting Zoe to try another approach. "Oh dear. Oh dear," she said, looking truly, truly upset.

The effect was null, but nevertheless, the secretary began checking through the digital agenda of the company with rapid fingers and squinted eyes. It was obvious this 'diligent' check was as authentic as her demeanor, but Zoe stood patiently.

"I'm sorr—"

Zoe cut her off. "Ma'am, Alfred was to give me documentation of a contract I am currently helping to legislate. I'm sure he left it in his office. I talked with him not two days ago when he told me the papers were prepared and I could pick them up from here."

The receptionist paused in thought. "I'm sorry, I cannot enter his office while his personal assistant or he is away."

"Oh. I understand." Zoe gave an affable smile and placed an arm on the counter. "Would you mind if I took a quick peek to see if perhaps the documents are there?"

"I am sorry. I cannot allow that."

"His office is just down this hallway, right?" asked Zoe retracting her arm and dissolving all niceties. She made her way to the left of the secretary's desk, towards the administrative wing.

"Miss! I cannot allo—"

Zoe immediately interrupted her. "It's quite alright, we are very close, you see—Alfy and I—he won't mind one single bitsy iota."

The secretary stood up in protest and moved to block Zoe's path, but Zoe brushed past her, flinging her arms back to ward off her off.

"Miss!"

Zoe paid her no mind and began running down the hallway. The receptionist did not pursue her, instead loudly phoning security from her desk.

Zoe quickly read the labels above the doors and byways as she sprinted through the highfalutin hall. "Nope. Nope. Nope. Nope. Ah, bingo!" She came to an abrupt halt and reached for the handle only to find it was locked. "Damn." She pushed against it. To her surprise, it felt like genuine wood. It would easily give way with a decent amount of force. She looked up and down the corridor; she was alone for now. Zoe stepped back and leaned in with a heavy kick, aimed just next to the door's handle. The wood gave way and the door swung open with splinters scattering inwards. The locking mechanism dangled from the remaining fibers. She would have to thank Darious later for showing her that little maneuver.

Zoe entered into a small empty receptionist's office with yet another door across it. She ran to it and tried the handle. *Yes! Not locked.* Inside, she zipped her gaze around the prodigious office. The ceiling first caught Zoe's attention. Three floors high, it rounded off into a painted scene of a blue sky with Cumulonimbus clouds and rays of sunshine beaming around their perimeters. Gold laced curtains came down from this great height, like a waterfall from the firmament and curled on the floor as volutes. The carpet was patterned with intersecting fleur-de-lis of crimson and blue. She looked over at the single imposing, intricately carved desk at the far end. Upon it rested a black phone, audaciously gilded like the rest of the executive office, and a computer console.

"Bingo."

Zoe set herself down in the padded seat and two armrests greeted her just as she was powering on the computer. She stretched in the chair. It seemed to be fluffing around all of her sore areas just perfectly. She'd have to get one of these. So far, the plan wasn't going half bad. Zoe checked her lightcard; she could see Darious had finished readying the ship in case of a quick exit. He was getting good. *Well, time to get to business.* Zoe smiled; no better place to access the information than from the head of the titan itself.

She set the lightcard on the table and opened its wireless ports. It began autonomously resolving the security protocols of the computer. Thirty seconds later, Zoe was in. She found it wasn't too difficult to find the sectors of information relating to Dr. Earl Saknussemm, as the closer she got, the bolder the red warnings barring entry became. Breaking into the boldest, reddest division, she found a set of subfolders directly relating to the late Doctor.

As the lightcard began assimilating information from Pantheon Industries, Zoe picked out a couple files which caught her eye and expanded them one by one. The first was marked 'Project R.E.A.P.E.R.' Flipping through several of its pages, it became evident it was for some sort of automated work droid. *Interesting, but far off.* she thought. She closed it and moved to the next, titled 'Origin Gravesite.' It was marked all over with 'Unlawful to Open' and 'Classified' which only served to increase Zoe's interest. To her dismay, it only contained a set of spatial coordinates. Nevertheless, she noted them and moved to the next document in the same subfolder, 'Kapteyn Material Provider.' Zoe recognized the word 'Kapteyn.' Kapteyn was the base hull material for galactic ships which allowed for their superlumious space flight due to its unique properties in the hostile faster-than-light environment of space. It was the statement 'Provider' that had caught her attention. She had never thought about where that magical substance had originated. The file contained a recent board review of the market.

"Hmmm," Zoe reflected. She expanded the document. "Oh wow. Seems you guys are the sole supplier." Certainly there were many companies selling it, but it was now evident they were actually subsidiaries of Pantheon. Even the freighters around the galaxy distributing Kapteyn, and not just the large ones such as IQS, were all under control of the corporation. Expanding the document further revealed comprehensive lists for every Kapteyn-manufactured vessel. *You completely own the market.*

It was then she noticed a bracelet at the far end of the desk. Picking it up and examining it against the backdrop of the curtained window, she could see it was forged of Kapteyn. The chain glinted in the light, showing an interwoven pattern of ghostly chromatic hues, as if reflecting the colors of the office through penumbral gems. Though Zoe had been familiar with this substance for years, she now peered at it with renewed interest. She slipped the thaumaturgy on her wrist. It was cool against her skin, as she expected due to its exceptional qualities.

A tone from her lightcard signaled the transfer was complete and it was time to go. There would be no more snooping for now. She shut down the computer and looked once more around the grand room before exiting. Upon reentry into the corridor, Zoe noticed something, or, as she corrected herself, the lack of something. All was very still. She could not hear any noises from the secretary's end of the hallway and the other end was completely silent. Zoe's skin crawled. This placidness was a farce and she knew it.

Zoe began running towards the reception area and came to a screeching halt, her sneakers skidding on the floor. With trailing cloak and one hand on his hat, the cosmic cowboy stepped out from the hallway's end, blocking her path. Zoe spasmed as her heart skipped and her mind replayed, in graphic detail, the death of Dr. Saknussemm. In that same spasmodic motion, she flung her arms around her, attempting to gain traction from the air, and whipped around seeking another exit. There came a yell from the man, but it only served to further shock Zoe's system, sending her into a mad rush down the hall.

It seemed within mere moments she reached the hallway's end and turned with it left, fleeing far down further grand corridors until she found herself in an open area of cubicles, filled with arched automatons typing into their consoles. They sat, without the semblance of ever having legs, while their mechanical digits clicked on keypads of further digits. Zoe had heard of such places, where market aggrandizements were evaluated to decimal places beyond human comprehension and far into the mundane. It was somebody's gained quadrillionth of a slice from somewhere.

At first Zoe froze for fear they would pounce on her, but none took heed of her. None even slowed their labor. She resumed her run, past the rows and rows of workers encapsulated within white cubicles. The compilation of their clicking emulated Zoe's fervor. She did not pause to take further observations of this place, instead remained focused on putting distance between the cowboy and herself.

Darious and she had prepared a plan B and Darious was no doubt tracking her movements within the building via the ship synced to her lightcard. They had parked as normal inhabitants of this world, with falsified credentials. Darious would be moving the ship to intercept her on the roof. Her lifeblood was a yarn being stretched by the galaxy's loom and he was the weaver. Just as Zoe reached the final doors exiting the enormous room, there was another yell behind her. Looking over her shoulder, she saw the mercenary standing at the opposite end, gripping a large cannon of sorts with one muscular hand. Zoe's mind did a complete summersault. He shouldered it, with an eye upon its scope, and raised his free arm vertically, unfolding his balled fist into a 'V' with his index and pointer finger.

Zoe burst through the double-doors and into a pivoting stairwell. As she made the first step onto the upward-bound flight, a mortar shot resounded from behind her. She vaulted herself upwards, knowing that impact was imminent. The rocket exploded at the stairwell's entryway and Zoe was flung into the wall. Smoke and debris filled the air. She had luckily made it high enough to avoid the direct blast. She got up coughing, her senses on fire. Looking over the warped railing, she saw the huge hole generated by the blast, as well as the obliteration of the first part of the staircase. With a face full of soot and trifling cuts around her body, Zoe continued her sprint up the stairs.

"That was. Way too. Close," she muttered between quick drawn breaths.

Grasping the handrail and using it to further propel herself forward like a triped, Zoe soon passed upwards of ten floors. Smoldering ash from below had diminished at this distance, and Zoe didn't hear any more shouts or explosions. Each new inhalation drew in another gust of vitality as she went up and up. From what she could remember, the building was some eighty stories tall. She had entered in at the thirtieth floor. *Not far now,* Zoe thought, though even her thoughts did not waste energy on sarcastic mirth.

After what seemed an endless tirade of flat and perpendicular cliff faces, Zoe paused and peered through the security window of a door. Into it she saw a similarly large cubicle area. Her eyes darted around, looking for some signifying mark so she could surmise her vertical whereabouts. She did not spot any floor level markings, though her eyes paused at the Eastern windowed wall. On a structural beam, in-between the view of neighboring buildings, there was a wooden clock with both hour and minute hands. Both dials pointed directly up. Zoe nodded and after a quick glance down the stairwell and seeing she continued to be its only occupant, she once more took lunging steps upward.

Zoe huffed between greased gradations, "Oh Darious. It's. Time to go." No sooner than eons had passed, she made it to the final floor.

With a similar explosive force to the canon that had nearly ended her, Zoe burst through the rooftop door and stumbled onto its surface. She was alone; her ship was not waiting for her with an outstretched gangway as she had hoped. However, between hard earned breathes, she could hear the familiar whir of her ship. It was crawling up the skyscraper to her and would take her away; her knight in shining armor come to save the day. She dared a glance behind her; all was quiet on the southern front. *Where did he go?* Although Zoe's mind speculated, her body was well done with this place and ran near the building's ledge, eagerly awaiting her ship.

Its silvery top first appeared, and next the cockpit window. Darious waved from within and Zoe looked once more behind her. All safe, for now. The ship swayed a bit as it swung overhead and clumsily eased onto the roof. Zoe motioned for Darious to open the hatch. She then heard the welcome clacks of internal locks being released and sprung toward the entryway as it opened. The ship had not yet evenly landed, and it needed not, as Zoe had already leapt onboard and was yelling to Darious.

"Go! Go! Go!"

He swiveled the ship about faster than it had come; the centrifugal forces nearly tossed Zoe back through the aperture. She scrambled into the cockpit.

"Zoe! What hap—"

"No time! Seat!"

Darious quickly moved and Zoe took up the reins. The ship evened out under her skilled grip. It purred from her touch and roared as she brought it up from the rooftop, continuing Darious' swing with fluid vigor and arcing down around the side of the building.

"That man," her lips murmured.

"The man with the brim hat?"

Zoe nodded, her mind too focused on pulling her appendages about the virtual console to form a snarky remark. She initiated various systems and compiled others in the short few seconds before the ship reached the ground level of the executive enterprise. A screen to Zoe's left lit up and a red rectangle outlined a nearby parked craft.

"Bingo," Zoe declared, and a grin followed. She typed into her console. "Weapons locked."

Zoe centered her craft to face the black falcon perched on the landing pad before them. To her left, Zoe flicked open a black cover, revealing a toxic green switch. She flipped it forward. Two booms from both sides of Zoe and her companion resounded in the ship. Two rockets, both painted the same toxic green, shot out from her ship and spiraled toward the Drak-9. Darious stared wide-eyed. Zoe was already plotting a course for far, far away. Two explosions, both hitting the port wing, ignited the whole craft into a vortex of flames. Zoe's ship veered away, and the cockpit window no longer gave a view of the explosion, though readouts continued the explanation to which eye was now blind to. They boosted away from the scene, leaving a dissipating plume of smoke in the wake of the engaged target. One target destroyed.

"Ye-ah!" cried Darious, the second half of his triumphant, arm-raised hurrah, dwindled and turned to a whimper. Zoe too paused her inbound self-approval. Her hand reached out, like death's own, and pointed toward the display readout.

Damage: minimal–moderate
Summary:

Aft Spoiler:	*44%–48%*	
Starboard Wing:	*Intact.*	
Port Wing:	*45TW conduit nulled; auxiliary ionizer nulled.*	
Ballast Thrusters:	*68%–73%*	
Force Thrusters:	*Primary Array:*	*Limited operations; inconclusive.*
	Secondary Array:	*Limited operations.*
	Ancillary Array:	*Inconclusive.*
Life Systems:	*Inconclusive.*	
Gravitational Systems: Inconclusive.		

Conclusion:	Operations limited; space flight capable; reduced .6 f-p/hour estimated maximum speed.

Zoe, as pale as Sirius, gulped. "We had better go."

She turned the ship fully skyward and shot through the sepulchral undergrowth of Kratos, out from its metallic tendrils and soon beyond its gravitational grasp, though she knew they were now unescapably being pulled in by its real sphere of influence.

CHAPTER 26

THE STORM OF THE CENTURY

A gold tooth grated against its biological neighbor below. Swift, hot breaths rushed out through the gaps of the entire city. Above, the glare of the clouds signaled a storm was coming. In fact, the storm of the century was inbound.

⟞⊹ ⊹⟝

Kappa grit his teeth harder, looking at his craft. The stench of burning oil from ruined fuel lines did not concern him as much as the inevitable conversation with Mr. Achan. He tipped his hat back and looked up at the dull sky. High above him, the smoke from his battered craft was mixing with noxious vapors of the corporate wasteland. *What a fucked-up place.*

With a huff, he slackened his muscles and dropped down to the cement, landing on his rear. He sat for a moment, relaxing his vision, and gazed through the hull of his ship to its crippled heart and slowly tipped his brim, sympathizing with the vessel. He picked up Bessie and detached a signal generator from the gun. He unclipped its two pieces. The first was an earpiece, which he put in his ear and the second, a type pad, which he used to initialize the call to Mr. Achan.

The sound of crumpled paper came through the earpiece as the call connected. The voice of the familiar circumspect secretary answered.

"This is Mr. Achan's office. Mr. Achan is not in right—"

"This is Kappa."

"Ah, Mr. Kappa. Mr. Achan has spoken to me. He has been monitoring the... situation."

She paused for several long moments, Kappa assumed for dramatic effect, which did indeed have an effect upon him. She then continued, "Mr. Achan has instructed you to extirpate the two. He insists..." She cleared her throat. "... you do so 'fucking soon.'"

"I understand. Please give Mr. Achan my apologies. I'm on it."

"Mr. Achan has also instructed me to tell you, if you ever feel the urge to use such weaponry inside his office again, he will place said weaponry inside your rectum posthaste."

"Understood."

The call abruptly ended. Kappa took in a deep breath and exhaled. A cold wind blew around him, making his overcoat flap around his arms. After up-righting himself, he stared at his ship. Kappa placed an open hand upon his chest and closed his eyes. *Where had it gone?* He sighed and straightened his hat.

Kappa's eyes narrowed and his mind refocused, trained thoughts replacing his wandering visions. He slung the gun around his back and proceeded to the craft. He forced open the damaged hatchway and looked around the cabin. He knew it would fly; uncomfortably, but it would do. There were still burning embers within her and within himself too. He slammed the door shut. The ship screeched to life as its massive engines drew in monstrous breaths and exhaled fire. Kappa set the ship to autonomously seal the biggest of errors and it lumbered up from the ground.

CHAPTER 27

PROFUNDITY AT ITS SIMPLEST

"Aha!" sounded a rejoicing Zoe. "Yes! YES!!"

Darious, hearing the commotion from the cockpit, paused his studies to see what the hubbub was about. Upon entering, he was greeted by piles of books spread everywhere and all projection screens opened with layers of coding. Even Zoe's lightcard was on the console, plotting out segments of the algorithm. He was glad to see Zoe's determination, though if she had been a stranger, he might have described it as an almost unreserved enthusiasm.

After their pillage of Pantheon Industries, Zoe had scoured the captured files, not surceasing her investigative venture for days. Unfortunately, the 'borrowed' data had yielded little. Dr. Saknussemm's prior work with the corporation was near completely redacted. As for his personal research, most of what was available Zoe had already solved herself. The last bits were jumbled and useless. As she had told him, the Doctor seemed to have gone through great measures to protect his work.

"Zoe, you have not left the cockpit for several days now. Are you okay?"

She swiveled around. "Me Zoe. Me make fire."

Darious smiled awkwardly. "Zoe, not to be the bearer of bad news, but I do believe fire was discovered many thousands of years ago."

"Oh, but Darious dear, you see, I have discovered that the multifarious tessellation of sectors A through E Gamma are in fact correct. It was the corresponding infinitesimal phased array subsystem that was corrupted." Zoe pointed to a section of text on her main screen. "By replacing the stringed Eigenvalues with their complex counterparts, I was able to extract the missing pieces and create a routine recomposing their basic values. Now," she said triumphantly, "the computer is running a quadrilateral simulation to see if any other flaws exist, but initial results show perfect harmony of the algorithm."

"Fantastic!"

"Yup, yup."

"Sooo... what is next?" he asked.

"Well, it looks like we will be at the coordinates of the 'Origin Gravesite' within the hour. Sooo... tea?" They both smiled.

"Aye, aye Captain," replied Darious as he set about preparing tea for two.

"I'll clean up in here," Zoe called over her shoulder as he left the cockpit.

Darious returned within a few minutes and saw that all the books had been thrown toward a corner of the cockpit. With his foot, he scooted a short pile away from his console and handed a steaming cup to Zoe. Darious took up a seat on the arm of her chair, sniffing at his herbal blend. He looked out to space.

"It looks to be quite barren out here. What else did the 'Gravesite' file say?"

"Nothing. And there's indeed nothing on all scanners, just vast space. There's no traffic, not even shipping lanes for thousands of floating-parsecs."

"A desert in the sea."

"Indeed," said Zoe sipping her tea.

The two sat in silence for some time before Darious broke from the hypnotic view. "I have been meaning to ask: I recently finished reading 'The States of Bose-Einstein Condensates' and a particular chapter near the end briefly went into hyper-fluidity at regions where gravitational forcing nears infinity, and—"

"And you're asking what is going on?" Zoe finished for him.

"Yes. I mean, how does it occur?"

"Well, simply, the strings in atoms become non-interacting with their surroundings due to the super resonance nodes reached at such small amplitudes. The strings slide around freely, and quantum motions become apparent at a scale we can measure. Add gravitational force to the mix, lots of it, and you get a phenomenon of physically moving large amounts of matter from impossibly small spots of space. See, that's the mousetrap; this state only occurs for massive, massive things confined in tiny lots."

"Interesting. So, could it be considered as teleportation?"

"Yeah, I'd say so. But remember, it's also all theory. Actually, do it and you'll definitely earn a cupcake from me."

"I believe I understand," Darious said. "The book inadequately described the topic. My next question is, hypothetically speaking, what happens if you brought a large amount of these quantum nodes together, by some means of a mega-forcing device, and harmonized them?"

"I'm not sure. First off, you're right, a lot of force would be necessary; like the sort that black holes are associated with. Then, of course, the nodes themselves would have a tendency to become very unstable. Phew, the real-time calculations to control the whole thing would be staggering. But I do suppose," Zoe tapped her chin, "if you could tune that crazy hypothetical mass of yours to the natural frequencies of certain space-time locales, then you could 'teleport' it. Oh, and how about this: yourself too, if you could make a shell with it. Now that would be cool. But that all seems just a bit beyond our time"

Zoe set down her tea on the console and took up the bracelet from her wrist. She stared at it for a moment. "You see this, Darious?" There was a sudden seriousness to her voice. "This is Kapteyn. I found it in Achan's office."

"I have noticed you wearing it since we left," said Darious.

"This material allows for humans to pierce through the barriers of space-time for speeds faster than light, as I'm sure you've read about. It's in every ship everywhere, mixed right in with my ship too. I had never thought about it before, but this too has to be beyond our time. I've been doing research since we left Kratos. This alloy, if that's even the right term for it, has missing links pertaining to its scientific development. They may not be evident, but they're certainly there. It's like one day, nearly two thousand years ago, it was just realized, created and mass produced. But the formation of the material was really, really advanced for those days and even still today."

Zoe held it out to him and he peered at it closely. It relayed the colors from her digital console into complimentary, yet submerged, hues. It didn't look metallic, nor of any material he had ever seen; its appearance alone had led him to theorize it was a very unique substance. Zoe hung it from a U-bar on the ceiling and continued exuding uneasy words.

"Even in laboratory conditions—extreme conditions—this material would have been a galactic feat to initially conceive. Granted mankind is awesome, but looking into it, I now feel that this is really above and beyond. The gaps in development leading to this are too wide. The published theories for Kapteyn's creation came after its construction. I mean, have I missed something here? Usually the theories for something new come before its actual creation, not after. After pouring over lots of research, I could see that publicly available information has been so scattered that there is no way its lifecycle could be reconstructed by anyone. I've come to the conclusion that this has been accomplished on purpose."

Zoe paused and took a deep breath in. "We may be further down the rabbit hole than we think," she said. "The pertinent information I have found regarding Kapteyn came from the Pantheon data catch; it's not public information. It's hard to say, as much of the information has been blotted out, but there is a definite link to Dr. Saknussemm. We know the material was made way before his time, so he didn't invent it. But it looks like he was definitely involved."

"Perhaps working on its next-generation iteration?"

"No," replied Zoe. "At least not from what I can gather. It looks like they had him researching its natural occurrence. Whatever their purpose, it seemed to have been something bad. From what I've been able to put together, it seems they were studying how to destroy the source of Kapteyn. But Kapteyn is manufactured. By them. I mean," Zoe rapped her fingers on the control console, evidently disconcerted. "I don't know what it means. Pantheon Industries appears to be the only entity capable of making the stuff and it's very apparent that they want to keep this all secret. To remain ahead in the market makes sense, but there is something more going on. Too much secrecy. And the deletion of certain semi travel routes. Which, by the way, from the records I've read through, seems to have been a recent undertaking by them and they have quite the thorough deletion protocol—from all information servers everywhere. What is up with that? Oh, and how about trying to kill people who are just a tiny bit curious. They are certainly hiding something, something much more than a line of products. I... I..." Zoe trailed off, aggravated.

Darious, trusting in her, felt a bit anxious of what was so unknown, even to her. "What are you thinking, Zoe?"

"I don't know. I just—"

A soft ding came from the center console.

Darious reached across Zoe and brought up the itinerary message with his free hand. "We have arrived."

"We can discuss it later," said Zoe. "Let me make sure this sector of space is still clear"

The ship came to a stop and Darious took up the drinks to clean in the main chamber.

"All is well," she called to Darious.

He shortly came back, wiping his wet hands on his shirt and looked out the window to the blackness. "An interesting expanse of space, Captain!"

"Yeah, yeah. I wasn't expecting much either. Though I was hoping a little, considering our recent run-ins with Pantheon and its goons."

Darious nodded and another ding sounded.

"Ah, the compiler is done!" Zoe said. She brought up a menu, with Darious looking over her shoulder, and centered on the resulting summary. "Complete with less than a millionth of a percent corruption. Now I'd say that's a success. Everything comes with just a bit of a fudge factor. So, what do you say we fire up the Doctor's program one more time for old times' sake? This is as good a spot as any." Darious put both hands on the back of her seat. "We should make some handholds for you there." Zoe smirked. "So, do we attempt it again?"

"Certainly. I presume all safety precautions are primed?" asked Darious, to which Zoe flipped a few switches. "What do you think it will do?"

"Other than a cool, paradoxical light show, I have no idea. Let's find out!" Zoe began typing away madly. "I've created a complete routine to run the program. Just gotta double check the Z-Pulsers..." her voice trailed off as her typing became more rapid. "...and complete," she said, with one last encore from her fingers on the projection console. A scrolling checklist appeared to their side and autonomously ticked off its line items. "All safety procedures double checked. Okay. Here we go."

The floor began to vibrate softly. "Door open. Capacitors loading," said Zoe. Darious clamped on the seat and firmed his stance. "Initiating."

A similar readout as before popped up and began running through sensor feedback.

"I've set it for the same meter cubed in front of us."

Darious read the summarizing display to ensure that the moment something odd was perceived they could react. Though, thus far, Zoe's revamped program was handling things magnificently. "All operations normal," he said. Then the shaking under his feet began to intensify.

"Look," said Zoe, in a breath of awe.

Out in front of them, a light, an eerie twilight of white and gold, began to appear in the programmed volume of space. Its nature, so unnatural, did not come forth evenly but as a shifting haze. Coinciding with larger vibrations and humming within the ship, the globular light began to take form. It condensed and wheezed. It seemed to Darious to be spinning, though in what direction he could not tell.

"All normal," said Zoe through the resounding vibrations of the craft. "Oh man, it's sucking a lot of energy."

The bound haze convulsed and surged outward with a sudden bright burst, so bright that Darious could no longer read from the console and was forced to cover his eyes. "Captain!"

"Damn, that's bright!" shouted Zoe. A moment later, the cockpit dimmed by degrees as if being dialed down. "I've turned on the star shades; should auto-reduce the light coming through the cockpit window."

Darious let down his hands and marveled at the scene outside. Through the artificial tinting, he was staring at corporeal light. It was about a meter in length, glowing brightly and nearly holding its shape as a triangle with a cupped point at one obtuse corner. "Wha—"

Without warning, the radiant object exploded again in a frenzy of light, startling Darious, though the star shades were quick to adapt. The vibrations and noises were now so prevalent that Darious could barely hear Zoe yelling, even though she had turned toward him and was nearly in his ear.

"It's producing more light than a Category 4 Pulsar!!" She turned back to the control console just as another brighter blast shot out. "Ten-fold luminosity!"

Darious leaned in to her ear. "Danger?!"

"No!" she yelled back. "It's not generating any heat!"

Darious was confused by this. *How can an object be so bright, yet not generate heat?* Then a final bright wave bounded from the object and the Doctor's program went dead. The ship jerked forward, giving both Darious and Zoe immediate whiplash. The vibrations ceased and only a minute humming from deep within the craft remained though was quickly dissipating. Darious looked out and there was once more normal space with its stars and all of infinity, though this was not what his eyes, nor his mind, were keen on. Centered in his perception was a triangular object, once a glowing haze and now, definitely a physical object floating peacefully in space, heedless of the hellfire from which it was born. Zoe made a long-intrigued sound. She typed into the console and brought up a scanning display.

"It's..." she trailed off as words seemed to fail her.

It was now Darious that picked up her thoughts, "...it is... it is..." He was reading through the summary. "...it is metal?!" Looking out at the floating triangle, it now just looked like a piece of space garbage.

Zoe cleared her throat as Darious wiped away sweat from his brow. Engaging a program, she turned on a spotlight to the object. "What do you suppose that is?" she whispered. "We are out in the middle of space. Space, Darious."

The object had retained a similar shape as its bright cocoon, though it was now about half the size. Staring at it, Darious noted it did indeed have a metallic tarnish; it was worn away and its edges were very dull. As the triangle floated in space, it slowly turned and gave the viewers a full look at its inscrutableness. As the edge came to parallel view with the cockpit, Darious saw it was nearly flat. From this view, he could see a smaller triangular architecture within the edge and even smaller concave dimples fitting within each gap.

"It's a structure!" said Zoe. "Look at that, it has a support system underneath. It's been exposed." She paused. "Darious this is a piece of something. Look at the edge, it's been ripped off of something." Darious only nodded. "Good thing is, it doesn't appear to be a piece of my ship." Zoe smiled.

She typed on her console. The spotlight swiftly shifted through many filters, collecting data by each, which was then output to a side projection screen. "Good. Darious, let's bring it in and get a better look."

Slight apprehension momentarily took hold of Darious. "Zoe, we do not know what it is. It could be contaminated, radioactive."

"Eh. Wouldn't be the first time." She looked over at him and winked. "Anyhow, look at the scan results. It's a polytitanium ceramic. Nothing biological detected. Nothing life-threatening detected. But you're right, there's only so much we can decipher through the looking glass." She smirked at him. "For the most part, it just looks like a hunk of space junk."

Darious nodded. "I had thought so too. However, it was not here a minute ago." They both stared at the object as it slowly turned in space. He began to feel an itch deep within his mind. Zoe's curiosity was so very contagious. "Yes, let us bring it in."

"Alright, that's my Darious! But, before I do," said Zoe, "I want to show you something." She scrolled through several screens and expanded one, highlighting a section of collected data in soft blue. "This was taken during that last bright episode, just before this little guy showed up. Look, the radiograms went, for a moment, beyond measurable scales both in negative and positive directions. The same is true for the directed spatial accelerometer, active flux-barometer, diodic equalizers, and particulate drivers. That last one doesn't even make sense! How can we have an overload of negative particulate flow in space!? That thing out there is definitely in no way normal." She stared at Darious with eyes like full moons.

"It would seem then," said Darious with a grin of almost unreserved enthusiasm, "all the more reason to bring it in and take a look."

CHAPTER 28

LET HISTORY MAKE ITS OWN JUDGMENTS

The itch, concentrated at the pharynx, though having originated from peregrinate aspirations of youth, was ever-present, at least as far back as anamnesis could affirm. The withered throat stifled a cough and a long wheeze was let out from parched lips. Crevices of age led from this dry well, surfacing the cheeks toward the eyes, hazy in the dusk of life. Captain Daggar once more cleared his throat. With a rheumatic hand, he gently stroked his neck and winced. The shaky hand laid back down on the armrest and he became an entirely motionless mass, motionless except for the ebb and flow of slow, strained breaths upon his chest. His eyes lowered, and consciousness with them, as the tide of torpidity rose.

The potential, now realized under a diadem of buttons and switches, was centered in an ellipsoidal throne room of shadowed indigo. Commandeering atop the tired-out throne, a single denizen remained at the helm—no internal lighting to see with and no skylights to be seen from, albeit from the bow where a single window carved a forward view into deep space. Shown through this aperture were the furthest sights any man had ever envisaged. Though Captain Daggar, at his waking moments knew this, the joyous celebratory times had elapsed and his heart no longer palpitated at this grand achievement. *Oh, how long had it been?* His crew, his coequals, had long passed. He, the original captain of this exploratory vessel, was the last and would be with it to the end.

The human race; oh, how proud they had left their brethren; how glorious the ceremony and the crowds were at their departure; how noble a position such as his—to lead the first deep space mission past Alpha Centauri and countless interstellar objects and to witness firsthand which only mirrors and silver had observed before. The spacecraft he was to command was the paramount achievement from the disciplines of both physics and engineering. The ship could almost fly alongside the colors of the rainbow, reaching with its wingtips for that universal speed. *How long had it been?* Captain Daggar had not turned on the computer console in some time; the panorama of pure space was all he desired; time need not apply. The crew had all known, as they hugged loved their ones and shook hands with those come to wish them farewell; icy space would be their final tomb. But they had not shed tears, for they had dedicated their lives to their purpose—to the advancement of mankind beyond that single watery globe.

Years and years of service on behalf of humanity passed. Old age became them, and elderly corpses were jettisoned with heartfelt salutes. The Captain alas was the last. *Oh, how long had it been?* A terrible cough ignited from the withered man and he erupted into a coughing fit, bending low in his seat. It passed soon enough and once upright, Captain Daggar leaned his head to the side and stared, as he did at nearly every waking hour, out to the black yonder. The mission was over. It had been for many years. Success. Now, to simply enjoy retirement. He had no apprehension about this as it would surely be a peaceful death, an honorable one, and a courageous one. Multitudes of years had passed since he had last contacted Earth, or they him. All the goodbyes, farewells, and salutes had been expressed. *How long had it been?* Captain Daggar's eyes once more shuttered and dreamless sleep became him.

Unbeknownst to the great Captain, a glow had begun to infuse the cockpit with diffused lambency, slowly increasing over the last several days, though hidden from him by the gloom of glaucoma. The light had been thickening as an inbound waterborne fog, and like such fog, it remained unbound by a linear trajectory, seeming to fill every crack and void by its own volition. Densest at the cockpit window and even greater beyond, it wafted in like vapors of cardice from a bottle, heedless of the glass barrier.

A low snore instigated a cough and once more the old man was bent low wheezing. From this agony, shrills of pain were sent forth from each guttural outburst. His hands trembled about his face as he sought to capture expulsions from each cough. Though his skin and throat were deserts upon the living terrain, the pain squeezed from this draught land a single tear.

Even in such a long-expired state, he was not woeful; his life had not been forsaken. Of all the places he could be, this was undoubtedly the one he would choose—amongst the stars. The coughing slowly subsided and he was soon able to lean back in his seat, sucking in much needed air. With renewed cognizance, he now secerned the glow enshrouding the cockpit. It had suddenly surged in strength, as if it were the coming dawn. Captain Daggar's mind indeed deceived him for a moment, as he saw himself striding through the wheat fields of his childhood; the morning sun stretching toward and then past him as the golden rays reached for the horizon. The Captain quickly regained his temperance. His heart thudded as the light continued to increase with exponential luminosity. Had the navigational systems erred? Was the ship plummeting into the heliosphere of some star? Had all the crew gone? He thought to call out to them. Where had they gone? The great white light, now blinding all senses, completely enveloped the ship. Captain Daggar's heart beat faster. Where was Marissa? Where had she gone? Like a tsunami towering above a schooner, the prodigious light swelled with immeasurable power and nullified the ship from existence. *Oh, how long had it been?*

CHAPTER 29

A SPARKLER IN TIME

"2,179 years!"

Zoe held the metallic piece in her hand. "2,179 years! Darious! Look at the carbon readings!" She turned it over, revealing the lined metallic body. "Look at this construction! And pulled from the vacuum of space!" They peered in as closely as their eyes could focus.

"What is it?" Darious finally asked.

"It has to be a relic. From the dating, it could only possibly be from ancient Earth-1." She handed it to Darious, who took it cautiously and rotated it, so the light reflected at different angles. "We must experiment!" she stated and was off to the central chamber, collecting components from the ship's multitudinous drawers. Though Darious' body had followed her, his eyes and mind remained fixed on the object. Zoe emptied drawer after drawer, tossing gizmos and cables over her shoulders.

Darious had the sudden worried thought that the bright light which had borne this object had possibly been emitted far through space. "Zoe, do you think perhaps we should move from our current location?" His eyes never left the relic in his soft grasp.

"Good idea," responded Zoe, still turned away from him. She tossed an old computer console backwards, which landed with a foul crash and fragmented into several pieces. "Oops," she said apathetically. She looked down at the broken electronics and then over at Darious as he frowned. "Darious, what only matters now is properly identifying that space debris; exactly when and exactly where it came from." Darious understood. He knew he was holding something very special in his hands, he could feel it. Zoe continued digging deeper through her things. "Take us starboard about .05 floating-parsecs out, so we can continue to monitor the site but are far enough away to be a speck to anyone else."

"Aye Captain. ahh... what shall I do with this?" She turned and smiled upon seeing Darious coddling the object.

"Oh, you two continue to bond. Just, don't drop it." Turning back, she was once more absorbed in her search. Darious went and seated himself at the captain's chair with the metallic cherub in his lap and navigated the craft as instructed.

Zoe soon came into the cockpit, hauling a large gauge cable. "Darious, mind opening that portside panel for me?" Setting the relic on the console, he bent low and gripped the top of the panel with his fingertips. He pried off the clamps, exposing various connection ports. Zoe dropped the heavy cable and sat on the floor next to him. "Let's see..." She fumbled around inside, pushing around wires and peering into the depths of the craft.

"Here Captain." He thrust his arm deep into the organs of the ship and pulled out the proper coupling line.

"Ah bingo! Sharp eyes, Sir." She happily took it from him and connected it to her own. A buzzing began from the central chamber.

"What are you preparing back there?"

"Come look." She paused. "How far out are we?"

Darious helped up Zoe and looked over at the console. ".048 floating-parsecs out. I've set the ship to auto-stop when we are there."

"Good. Good. Okay, come on. Oh, and bring the... baby." She winked at him.

Perched upon a telescoping table in the center of the room with equipment all around it, as if offerings to an altar, was a black machine. A myriad of cords rounded out from this box, circumnavigated it, and reentered at other sides. There were many dials on all faces and a large projection display along its long end.

"Mind the cables," said Zoe, pointing downward. She fiddled with the machine's controls and a depressurizing sound escaped from its backside. Then, the device's top opened, revealing a hollow interior with dotted white walls and a silver grill on its bottom. "Set it in there."

Darious eased the relic into the cradle. "I'm going to perform a Sparkler Test to determine this object's origin, hopefully without vaporizing it since it wiggles the molecules of the test item." She typed into the controller and the box sealed shut. "Basically, I'm going to fire resonance nodes of high voltage waves throughout it and collect the data three-dimensionally. The real magic comes through the programming of this little guy. "It may take several minu—" A ding sounded from the machine.

"Oh. It's done." The machine's lid opened, releasing steamed air smelling of soldered wires. Darious reached in to grab the relic. "Wait!" exclaimed Zoe. He quickly pulled back his hand. "It's going to be very hot. Excited molecules equal heat."

"Indeed so," he replied, cupping the hands that were almost no more.

"Give it a few minutes; it'll cool quickly. Onwards! Let's see where our little friend hails from." Zoe headed to the cockpit with Darious trailing her. She took to her seat and brought up the results from the test. Many screens appeared around the console with virtual data covering from the top of the cockpit's window to the floor. Darious bent forward, reading the box of information closest to him.

"It says here," said Darious, "that this piece was made from a metal level treatment technique used thousands of years ago. Date of material cohesion was 2064."

"That concurs with our initial test. So far, so good." Zoe read from another information box. "Database analysis suggests it was manufactured by a Space-Z Incorporated plant in the northern hemisphere of Earth-1. Ah-ha! Told ya it was from Earth!"

Darious skipped over to the next projected box. "It is from a ship called the 'Origin-X.'"

Zoe diminished all screens and searched the term. Shown large and centered in front of them was the data sheet for the spaceship Origin-X along with its mission log. "Oh my," Zoe said, leaning in as she read. "I've heard of this ship." She turned to Darious, her eyes beaming into him until the heat of her gaze nearly made him melt. "Darious, this is a piece of Origin-X. It was the first deep space mission from Earth! Oh my!"

"Wow!" Darious was wide eyed. "How... but how!?"

Zoe continued reading. "'...sent out to observe several exo-planets and study the impact of deep space on organic life. After completing its mission, with the legendary Captain Daggar at the helm—' I've seen him before in history books..." Zoe seemed to lose her vector of thought as if reliving an echoed memory and then shook it off. "I remember it was a one-way mission. They had traveled the furthest any human had ever gone, and they held the record for some time after that. I believe it was something like twenty-five floating-parsecs; a real achievement in those days. It says here the ship was never recovered." She held her hand out to the text. "I guess I assumed it was in a museum somewhere." She looked back up at Darious and in a mesmerized tone asked, "What the hell is going on?"

He shook his head. "I have no idea."

"'Soon after Origin-X's mission retirement, contact was only deemed necessary if specially requested and after a 6-month sleeper period, contact was lost. The flight path had been thought to have been precisely extrapolated. Optical and radio telescopes were utilized by the global community in hopes of spotting the vessel, though there were no confirmed sightings. Once the region of its course was inhabited, in the year 2459, an effort to locate the craft was undertaken. Specially tuned echo-location probes searched the region but no remains or any evidence of Origin-X were ever found.'" Zoe brought up the flight path for the ship and whipped through many screens. Darious tried to follow her swift work but became lost as she compiled batches of information faster than he could interpret. "Jeeze," she said. "Do you realize its trajectory was in the opposite direction from us, on the other side of the galaxy? According to its route, it should have never even been in our current quadrant of space. It should be half the galaxy away from us!" She typed a quick search into the console. The result came back momentarily. "No combination of heavy star swing-bys can naturally account for it."

Zoe got up and returned with the triangular piece of Origin-X in her hands. "How did you get here?" she nearly whispered at the object.

Darious brought back up the result screens from the Sparkler Test alongside the digital schematics of the craft. "This looks to be the starboard wingtip of it." He then brought up a file photo—a promotional shot of the ancient craft docked at a rudimentary space station. The ship was long and narrow, outfit with many large archaic rockets utilizing liquid fuel. It had several wings at different angles along its fuselage. Toward its aft side were the two largest wings, extending far beyond the others. A single black strip lined the perimeter of each edge. Atop the wings were numeric identifiers, as well as several symbols from the time period. The vessel shimmered in the sun, just beyond the photo's line of sight, and seemed to be glowing by the sanctity of its maiden voyage.

"Wow," said Darious. Zoe handed him the fragment, which he took up with great care and great zeal. "Zoe, this is an amazing find."

"So," she said, "any idea how we pulled it out of thin air, or in our case, complete lack of air?"

"No. None at all." He sniffed the piece and then gently brushed it with his fingers. "I have never held anything from Earth-1."

Zoe looked at him. "By all means, keep it Darious. I hereby declare you 'Keeper of the Relic.'" She bowed to him. Darious smiled from the inside and a happy chirp escaped his lips, making him blush.

Zoe laughed. "Alright then. I'm glad we both agree." She turned back to the computer's analysis. "Hey look at this." She expanded the internal molecular analysis. "It's very, very slight, but these numbers don't match up with what the materials should be."

Darious, now holding the piece of the ship as if it were certainly his baby, read through the analysis. "You are right. But… how?"

"It's like it has been ever-so-slightly altered at the micro level…," Zoe said, rubbing her chin. "…or something." She expanded the results further, which in turn equally expanded the confused look on her face. "The ionic bonding is off. No wait…" She expanded the fundamentals of the results further. "The molecules themselves are off-angle. What the hell!?" She stood up and grabbed the piece from Darious. "What are you and where did you come from!?"

She tried shaking a response from it, but the relic maintained its stubborn pose.

Zoe sighed and looked over at Darious. "It's cool. Everything is cool." She handed it back and he took it up with open arms as she slumped in her seat. "That's as far as the analysis can go. We need help on this Darious. This is beyond me."

He stuck out his tongue as a sudden obscure thought seized his reasoning that the sense of taste must not be left out in the analysis of the mysterious Earth object, but he sucked it back in, thinking better of the taste-test at the last moment. He then absorbed Zoe's last statement. "I suppose you have someone in mind?"

"I have seen artifacts from Earth-1 before, at my ol' university. I know a professor there that may be of help. Anyhow, if he can't, then no one can. Care to check out my old stomping grounds?" Darious merely nodded in the affirmative. The thought of a new crowd in a foreign place made him uneasy. However, he knew it must be necessary. "Professor Timonay Kring was my main mentor during my graduate studies. A great man. You'll like him. No worries, he has an open mind with people like us." She wiggled her finger at herself and Darious, smiling and, in doing so, eased the wrinkles on his brow. "And," she stated positively, "it's a college university. Everyone there is an oddball!! Trust me. Some people are... well you'll see."

Darious chuckled. "I would be glad to join you, Zoe."

"Wonderful!" said Zoe. "So, who's gonna clean up? Nose goes!" With a finger on her nose, and the other hand pointing to Darious, Zoe laughed as he stared at her perplexed.

CHAPTER 30

SYZYGY

They arrived at Newton-Maize Sector University several days later. As the ship came down toward one of the institution's landing pads, Zoe quickly noticed much had changed since she had last been there. For one thing, they had added a lot more blue sculptures. *Those soi-disant artists*, she thought sardonically. Her craft descended comfortably and smoothly under her control. There was just the slightest jostle as it touched ground.

"Welcome," said Zoe, patting Darious on the shoulder as she left her seat to prepare a bag. She shortly returned from the central chamber and saw Darious peering out of the window. "Don't worry," she said. "The air is most certainly breathable out there."

He turned and looked flatly at her. "That is not what I am apprehensive about."

Darious took the sweater from on top of his chair and pulled it over his shirt. Zoe carefully packed the triangular piece from Origin-X and put a couple knickknacks in the bag's pockets. Throwing the strap over her shoulder, she looked over at Darious.

"You ready, Mister?"

He nodded. Zoe opened the port and lowered the gangway to the ground.

The pair was greeted by the brilliant irradiance of a noon sun with wistful clouds high above. Zoe shielded her eyes until they adjusted. A mid-summer's breeze of warm air tickled her skin and she took in a deep breath, smelling the keen scent of fresh cut grass along with other familiar smells. She stood and looked out, watching for a moment as two black birds passed overhead, fluttering together, and chirping all the while.

Zoe and Darious made their way past the small planetary parking lot and onto the main stone walkway, which served to guide students from their transitory households to their classrooms.

"They call this the 'Interstellar Mall,'" she said.

Darious lowered his hood as a group of students passed by. Zoe stopped and took him gently by the arms. "Darious. It's okay." She lifted up his hood and placed it at his shoulders. She stared deep into his eyes. "Trust me." Zoe could see the trepidation that had been driven into him for years and couldn't help but take his hand and give it a squeeze. They began to walk together. "Plus," added Zoe, "it's way too nice of a day to be all covered up."

They made their way past many numbered buildings, most of which were speciously constructed with the personality of adobe, giving the university a nice earthen compliment to the deep blues of the sky and lush greens of the flora. Grassy areas filled the gaps around and between buildings. Pristinely trimmed bushes and flowerbeds were present on both sides of the Mall. Their little blossoms guided the explorers' steps. Zoe had many fond memories here. No singular one encompassed her thoughts; it was their compilation which made her feel lighter than air: evenings of laughter with co-students, one-on-ones with professors discussing fractal mathematics, and all those little adventures and misadventures sprouting from adolescent behavior.

"Darious," Zoe said demurely. She thought for a moment he hadn't heard her.

"Yes, Zoe?"

"Thank you for coming with me."

She gave his hand another squeeze. As they continued their stroll with a soft current aiding their movement, a student rounded out from the entrance of an oncoming building, using his back to prop open the door while his hands and eyes worked a tablet. His turning motion became a brisk walk up the Mall. As he was about to pass by, he happened to glance up and made eye contact with Darious. Zoe felt Darious' intertwined hand jump.

"Hello there!" said the student and shot a hand forward to Darious.

Zoe and the clone stopped, the latter in more of a frozen state then an actual amiable pause. She nudged Darious with her shoulder.

"Oh!" said Darious in a most urgent manner and shook the student's hand. "Hello to you sir." The student nodded once, as if to a longstanding friend, and continued up the pathway, once more enthralled in his tablet. As Zoe and Darious resumed their walk, Darious turned to her and gave an impressed look.

"Ha! Oh, Darius, you're too much. You know, the campus sure is pretty empty today. It must be the weekend. Or perhaps summer break. I always liked how college campuses aim to retain the traditions of classic inspiration."

Zoe let go of his hand and began marching ahead half-singing, half-chanting, "School's. Out for. Summer! School's. Out for-ever!" She circled back around, looping Darious' arm with hers and gamboled with him at her side. She bumped him with her hips, continuing her happy melodies.

The pair soon came upon a group of students in their mid-twenties. Each of their eyes widened momentarily upon seeing Darious, but smiles quickly followed. They each shook his hand in turn and he graciously wished each a 'good day.' Zoe whistled her song and soon, Darious was swinging his arm in time with hers and the two walked with a skip in their steps to the sound-less beat.

"Make a left here," said Zoe, pointing with Darious' hand in her own. They rounded a concrete side-path, with several equal-ly-spaced buildings and a planetarium. "This is where I spent most of my graduate studies." Darious looked all around him. "Just up ahead is where I first studied thermodynamic tensor flow. They have a superconducting maser spectroscope in there." Darious gave her a blank look. "Trust me, it's awesome. Oh, and right over there," Zoe pointed to their right, "is where they do zero-point metrology. Also, very cool."

The pair walked on, past lecture halls and buildings of never more than a couple floors tall, with the smell of redolent flow-ers under a hot sun filling their noses. Every so often they would pass by people, each always very courteous to Darious. His stride elongated, and his shoulders seemed to broaden. If Zoe didn't know any better, she'd say he was strutting. *The things he could ac-complish.* she thought.

"Up ahead and to the left," Zoe said. "That's where Professor Kring has his office—or had. I hope he's still here. You know, in the years I attended Newton-Maize I never saw him stray from that building. It's like he lived there. I've never seen a man love his work more."

As they were entering into the grey building, with many satel-lite dishes peeking over its roof, a man came out from the double glass doors wearing all black leather and having a purple mo-hawk nearing half a meter long.

"Good day," said Zoe as he held the door open for them. "Love the hair."

He ginned, revealing silver teeth. "Hello." Upon seeing Darious his smile broadened, followed by a more enthusiastic 'hello.'

"Hello sir," said Darious taking the door from him. "Thank you."

Inside, they were greeted by refreshing air conditioning.

"It's a hot one today," said Zoe.

They stood, centered in the great corridor with staircases on either side, curving around the hall to the second floor and then double-backing to a third floor beyond view. Darious did several complete turns, taking it all in.

"Yup. This is the astrophysics building."

All at once, three sets of doors to their left opened and students began flooding out into the corridor.

"Excuse me. Oh, excuse me," said Darious as students hastened by. Zoe could hear numerous 'hello's and saw hand after hand extended out to him. "Oh, man," she giggled to herself, "he's never gonna wanna leave." The crowd soon passed, and the hallway was once more barren, save for a few stragglers.

"Well," said Zoe, "I guess summer courses are in session. Let's go up to the second floor. Professor Kring always lectured in one of the rooms there near his lab."

Zoe guided Darious up the broad steps and through the long corridor. There were portraits of faculty along both walls, though overall, the hallway seemed a bit worn, as if it could use a nice face-lift; just how Zoe remembered it.

"Let's see, Room 204... 205... ah, 206."

She opened the door just a crack and they both poked their heads in. Zoe and Darious beheld a great auditorium, with rows and rows of seats leading downward to a central stage with whiteboards covering its three oblique walls, each filled with blue-ink pictograms and formulas. Zoe could tell, just from the writing, this was an introductory class on spaceflight. She noted the rudimentary propulsion formulas and drawings of gravity slingshot assists. The amphitheater was about a quarter full of students evenly distributed and all writing furiously, attempting to keep up with the professor at its focal point.

"As topsails collapsed to rockets," he lectured through a microphone, "humanity sought new tools to aid in their renewed exploration. But with such distance between worlds, new science had to be adopted. Misunderstood superluminal motions from quasar jets had instigated scientific debate in the 1970's, which was renewed with sincere interest after the first microton telescope was constructed in the 2080's. By 'superluminal,' I mean, of course, faster-than-light travel.

"The fundamental superluminal theory, later to become the first of the Grand Unified Laws, was first mathematically proven by Dr. Elborus Fischer, who in 2142 was the first to work out the long-held conjecture that space is indeed non-linear for all dimensions and for the first time, all aspects of reality had a base formula for its causality. An experiment was quickly created to test his theory."

The professor opened a digital picture on the board directly behind him which showed an array of low structures on Earth-1 soil, each a multiplex of antennae and mirrors. He pressed a button on his podium, changing the image to a birds-eye view of all the buildings, now clearly arranged in a great circle with woodlands and a small-town crossing through the experiment.

The professor continued, "In accordance with the prerequisite conditions from Fischer's ecumenical theory, superluminal and subluminal light wave transmittance and absorption were observed. By this experiment, and many more following it, superluminality came to be widely accepted by the scientists of the time. They found that indeed natural light waves have a non-linear velocity, especially noticeable at very low and very high energy frames of reference. This became even more apparent with communication breakthroughs—enabling near-instantaneous communications along any vector— the advancement of fusion energy and new space construction media some forty years later. Physical crafts were, for the first time, able to travel many times the speed of light. Thus, a modification was necessary for the common light-year, the previous standard form of distance measure. As such, floating-parsecs were to become the standard, as is now." He took a side step from the podium and surveyed his class. "Whilst traveling abroad on a ship of today, onboard virtual controllers, by method of probability algorithms, set up 'floating' points," the professor enunciated the term, Zoe figured to help his students absorb this root meaning, as most had probably never thought twice about the term, "on opposite sides of the ship and quantify length by method of parallax within a universally singular frame of reference. Understand, though the method for distance quantification via parallax had been utilized by centuries past, it was erroneously based on the flawed light-year. Ergo, it was quickly and irrevocably replaced by the floating-parallax-arcsecond. After the light-year, the floating-parsec became the..."

"Hey Darious," Zoe whispered, "Why don't you sit in on this?" She urged him forward to the closest seat. "I will check back after I'm done." He accepted and sat, leaning forward and instantly engrossed by the lecture. Zoe noiselessly closed the door and continued on her way.

Down the hall and through a passage to the left, she was soon upon the lab spaces of Professor Kring. Looking through the glass walls connecting the lab area to the corridor, Zoe quickly spotted him with his back turned to her, in a bronzed overcoat and hunched over whatever experiment must have caught his fancy this day. She swung a door open without saying anything, quietly winding her way around lab tables while being mindful of the backpack slung over her shoulder. She was now just behind the Professor and leaned over to get a glimpse of what it was he was peeking at through the monocular microscope. Zoe could see a small metallic crystalline object, probably some allotrope of bismuth.

"Mind handing me a pipette of oxy-propylene?" asked the Professor in deferential tone. His gaze still had not strayed from the eyepiece, so Zoe, not wishing to disturb his work, looked around for the syringe. She spotted a stand containing several of them and took up the one called for. She then handed it to him and he pressed the clear liquid onto the sample. After a few moments, Professor Kring let out a disappointed huff and set the pipette down.

"What's up, Doc?" said Zoe.

He suddenly straightened up and looked at her, a broad smile lifting his face.

"Zoe, my dear! How are you?" He gave her a tight hug and then looked at his hands. "Pardon me. Let me wash this oxidizer off and I will be with you."

He quickly departed into the adjoining washroom. Zoe took up a circular seat and spun around, looking at the laboratory. Equipment of all sorts filled every table and half-opened metal cabinets along every wall showed even more experimental apparatuses. It was like the lab of a mad scientist; however, the white color scheme and décor gave the room a pure quality. Good science happened here. Perhaps sometimes redundant, but nonetheless, the Professor was a decent, dedicated man. Zoe had always respected him. From early on, they had clicked. He had been the one to sponsor her graduate studies and when she confided to him that she had learnt all she wanted and would be departing for the next stage of her life, he had wholeheartedly supported her.

Professor Kring came back momentarily, drying off his hands on his lab coat. "How have you been?"

"Great Professor. How are you?"

"Doing well. I've recently picked up a grant to further my research on negative-fermi particles. I'm also now teaching electrochemical courses. Well, I start next semester."

"Oh?" said Zoe surprised. "No more quantum harmonics?"

He smiled. "Not as much these days. They don't make these students like they used too. Now, if I had a room full of pupils like yourself, I could really do something." He gave Zoe a genial look. "I remember when you first came here; even then your perspicacity of harmonics was amazing. Of all my students, you were one of the brightest, one of the youngest too."

Zoe blushed. "Oh ya! That reminds me, remember your position on Tuned Spatial Rings and the debates with Dr. Ginsberg?"

"Oh yes," responded Professor Kring. "Did you know he retired last year? Anyhow, despite my best efforts, Spatial Rings are still unproven; hypothesized for nearly a century now and never experimentally verified. I was never able to do it. They have the potential to make shipping and traveling across the galaxy nearly free and at speeds unheard of. Imagine: many of these tuned plasma rings lined up like highways and connecting planets across the galaxy, from which a ship or container could be jettisoned through and in hours, not days or weeks, reach its destination. Some people still don't think it's possible. Neophytes. We had a proof-of-concept once built here, as I'm sure you remember, but it never worked. Perhaps I should resume my efforts after I finish this work, although I feel Spatial Rings' elusive nature will forever keep them contained to paper. What of them?"

"I made one," said Zoe.

"Zoe, that's a bold claim." He leaned in and a small giddy smile broke across his lips. "Tell me more."

"Oh, you'll love this: I used a dirty ethanol base for the vibrational catalyst. Then I synced the two counter-nodes. I hope you don't mind but I used your working algorithms, along with some additions based off the work of Dr. Brahms. And it worked."

Professor Kring took a seat next to her and sat in deep thought for nearly a minute. His eyes then rose and shined. "Of course! That would moderate the entropic fluctuations. Oh, you are a true genius Zoe. What happened when the signal loop completed?"

"I don't know," responded Zoe. "The experiment failed at 82 percent from attenuation. The computer was unable to construct the final outcome. However, I ran an extrapolation with inputs from your prior work. It was leaning toward a self-folding, resonant circle, tuned just as the theory requires. Could you imagine!? With the right tooling, it may be possible to get it to the 100 percent mark and keep it stable. Then once shrunk down, it would usher in the next generation of travel across the galaxy! Though at some point, you'll have to explain to me how one slows down once in such a slipstream..."

"Eh, shrunk down?" the Professor inquired.

"Sooo, it was much bigger than I thought. I'm not sure if the theory needs a bit of updating or if my alcohol-base might have had something to do with it, but I'm guestimating the loop would have come full circle at around sixty million kilometers. I was working in space from my ship to keep it cool, but I had limited—"

"You have a ship! My dear girl! Captain, eh?"

"Yes sir." She smiled back at him. "Made it myself."

"Ah, Zoe. It's been too long."

Zoe pulled out her lightcard. "If you have an NFC interface, I can give you the info from my experiment. I've taken it as far as I can. Care to take a look?"

"Yes. Thank you, Zoe." She could tell he was brimming with excitement, though his professional deportment kept it contained. Dr. Kring pointed to a computer console. Zoe went over to it, synced the data from her card, and returned to the seat next to him. "Zoe, I will be sure to mention your name on any paper that comes from this. This is exhilarating. Young woman, you have made my day."

"Thank you, Prof, but that's not actually why I'm here."

"Oh?"

Zoe set the backpack on the table and opened the zipper. "I need help with this." She extracted the triangular fragment of Origin-X. Dr. Kring carefully took it up in his hands, bringing it level with his vision. He murmured several things Zoe couldn't make out. The Professor finally pulled his eyes from it and looked at Zoe.

"Well, I can tell it's old. The stress marks along here," he pointed to the exposed trilateral subsystem, "show me that it's made from die-cast components. He rapped a knuckle on the relic's flat top. "It does not contain Kapteyn. Let's see, I would place this piece somewhere around 2100. Besides looking like space garbage, this might just have some value. What is it you are curious about?"

"Are you familiar with Origin-X, Professor?"

"Yes." He held the piece up high, his eyes remarking its reflectance. "Do you mean to tell me you think this is a fragment of that vessel?" He observed her with that factorial dean's stare.

"Dr. Kring, it is."

He set it on the table and now gave her his full attention. "You do know that vessel has never been located? May I enquire as to where you came across this item?"

"In this quadrant, just a few days ago. I... found it just floating in space."

He lowered his gaze. "I do know you Zoe. So, I'm assuming you've performed spectral and sparkler analyses on the object in question?"

"Yes sir."

217

"How close were the sparkler approximations?"

"99.999... well it goes on. It's a match, Prof."

Dr. Kring's expression eased and he became animated. "Well, well dear! I did not know you had become a treasure hunter. Congratulations. I see why you've come! We will have to confirm everything. Zoe, this may be quite a find we have here. You have come to the right place for such verification."

"Professor Kring, that's not really why I'm here either. I'm no treasure hunter, well not until recently, but unintentionally. This fragment... it's... well, please take a look." Zoe walked over to the computer console and synced the data from the Sparkler Test. Dr. Kring came over, pulled out a pair of horned-rim spectacles from his shirt pocket and began reviewing the data. Zoe could see his demeanor grow disengaged as he delved through the layers of data. He took up the seat at the computer and slowly scrolled through the plethora of recorded information and calculations.

Twenty minutes passed before the Professor finally sat back and nodded to himself. Without saying anything, he stood up and walked over to the door, locked it, and then flipped a switch, turning all the windows opaque. Dr. Kring resumed his seat and closed his eyes with a hand over his mouth. He seemed calm on the outside, but Zoe knew within him a great storm was churning. She would give him all the time he needed. He sighed, relaxed his shoulders, and placed both palms downward on the desk.

"Zoe. I now understand. Please, take a seat. I have several questions for you."

Zoe did so. Suddenly, she felt somewhat uneasy and a low nausea crept up. *What if...* She near panicked for a moment. Could she trust Dr. Kring? What if he was in league with Pantheon Industries? *No,* Zoe reaffirmed herself. She could trust him.

"I will answer the best I can Prof, but I am at a loss as to what it all means. I take it from your expression, that I didn't miss something; it is indeed... abnormal."

"Yes Zoe. First, who knows about this?"

"Myself and my copilot." Zoe then quickly added, "I also have a secure remote backup capable of self-distribution." She was not sure why said that last part.

"And your copilot, do you trust him?"

Zoe thought of Darious and it comforted her. "Yes. With my life."

"Okay. Secondly, and take your time on this one: how did you obtain this fragment?"

Zoe knew she must be careful here. Too much information of Dr. Earl Saknussemm could endanger the Professor as well as make him a cognizant accomplice. There was no doubt the less he knew, the safer he would be. "I have been working on a resonant fractal routine. The purpose was to... test a sort of teleportation concept I've been tinkering with. I was experimenting with quantum strings at the exajoule range and trying to elongate their nodes toward infinity. I was not sure what the result would be, but somehow from it, I now seem to be the owner of a genuine piece of Origin-X." Zoe shifted her gaze to the fragment. "Prior to obtaining it, there was nothing around me. This wasn't a quantum tunneling effect, as there were no special movements recorded at all. I don't understand. Like, did I pull it from some parallel universe?"

Professor Kring lowered his glasses and narrowed his vision, apparently chagrined by her last comment. "I strongly feel further analysis must be completed before attempting to hypothesize on the extraordinary nature of this object and whence it came from. Zoe, please remember, we are practitioners of science. Jumping to conclusions too prematurely will lead us to the same pseudoscience phenomenon that plagued the twentieth and twenty-first centuries. Thermodynamic laws always hold. Fundamental laws of physics do not break. All of these are filaments of indestructible, golden threads. Surely, we will come to an understanding of the phenomena at work here. Zoe, this wreckage is too important to be subject to preconceived notions, as they could cloud one's impartiality. Clear your mind. Let cold hard logic guide you."

Zoe felt slightly embarrassed. The Professor contracted his frown and added, in a mollified tone, "A piece of an ancient craft, lost for millennia, is right here on this table and you are right, the vibrational state of its constituents does not correctly correspond to that of their classical counterparts. Considering the analyses I have reviewed, I can say that indeed something very special has happened to this material."

"Agreed," said Zoe.

"Good. We cannot yet determine where it has been or what forces it has been specifically subject to, though we do know this item is indeed significant. Now, let us proceed along the vector of fact. Your Sparkler Test has confirmed it to be from Origin-X. The elementary particles it's composed of are all showing evidence of vibrating at a previously unknown stable energy state. There is something here like carbon, but it is not classic carbon. There is something here like titanium, but it is also not. I believe this is to the point at which we stand now." He nodded to himself. "This is all quite intriguing. You were right to bring it here." Professor Kring thought for a moment. "I'd like to run a few tests, if you don't mind."

"By all means Prof."

"Thank you. I will, of course, seal this lab up. This is an exceedingly cultural and scientific find. Ah, you may have been right all those years ago; space still contains hidden marvels. What was that mantra you always recited?"

Zoe grinned. "'Verve, nerve, and adventure.' It's from an old Earth-1 comic."

"Indeed? Words to live by." Professor Kring stared at the ceiling for a moment with a finger in the air. "You know, the last time

I was confronted by a conundrum that evinced such curiosity was the Zeta-Prime Incident. Ever hear of it?" Zoe was about to shrug her head, but the Professor was already continuing on. "I didn't expect so. Come, I will show you." He got up and opened a door to a side room, within which was his personal office. It was in complete disarray with piles of papers stacked on piles of papers. It looked as if his whole desk was composed of countless wafer-thin layers. He shifted around piles and thumbed through folders. Zoe risibly thought for a moment, *this is what my ship must look like to Darious.*

"Ah, here we go." Professor Kring pulled out a yellowed folder and flipped it open on the desk. "Let's see, it was about 20 years ago. Time flies, as they say. The CF was testing a new experimental craft. Always better and faster." He scanned through a small leaflet of handwritten notes and put it aside, revealing pages of bound content. "The craft was partially composed of zeta-prime plutonium, so it was exothermally hot, and they had been playing with the resonance of the ship, as a whole, at very large nodes. Sound familiar to your experiment? Anyhow, an incident happened. During a test flight, the ship became completely and utterly unresponsive. Even independent and shielded redundant operations went offline. The pilot died due to life support systems failing.

"A special team was assembled to assess what had happened. I was part of that little group. We knew immediately they were not informing us of everything, by the obvious fact they had called upon harmonics experts, instead of electrical and mechanical engineers. No matter. We were set to receive the ship at a CF dockyard but unfortunately the craft had been destroyed by clerical error." He smirked at Zoe. "It was instead sent to a salvage yard and vaporized. Nevertheless, our instructions were to go ahead. We modeled countless spatial scenarios, attempting to recreate an event which could account for such a cataclysmic error, but we were never able to generate anything substantial. I believe the program was canceled after that." The professor flipped over a page, dropping a photo to the floor. Zoe was quick to pick it up and froze upon seeing it. "Yes," Dr. Kring said, "That was a file picture from just after the incident. The craft was entirely un-marred, save for two small circular ingresses near the port wing. Unfortunate. We presumed that was the flashpoint at which all major electronic systems were severed. It's the only photo I have; perhaps the only one that still exists."

Zoe stood up. "I have to go."

"Oh? You seem startled my dear."

"I have to go now." She went back to lab room and slung the open backpack over her shoulder.

"My dear," said the Professor, following her. "What is it?"

"I will leave the remnant here." she eyed the piece of Origin-X for a moment and then looked at the Professor. "I have seen those markings before. Recently."

A look of concern spread over his face. "Are you sure?"

"Yes. I need to get Darious and then I need to go."

"Okay. Okay. Please, be safe my dear. I will update you the moment I get results in. May I assume your contact information has remained the same?"

Zoe pulled out her lightcard and typed in a couple quick commands. "I just sent my new info to your computer." She gave the Professor a hug.

"Technology these days. Okay, thank you, Zoe." Dr. Kring ad-justed his overcoat and gave her a short smile as she turned to go. "Be safe" he said as she exited the lab.

"Farewell," she said in a hushed voice. Zoe quickly made her way through the auxiliary hallway and into the main corridor. Her mind was racing. The holes in Captain Henry's ship; they were exactly the same. What was going on? She thought of the fragment from Origin-X. Somehow, it was hiding within it some clue, some truth that was at the center of this cosmic quandary. She then thought of Darious, that epitome of humanity. She had to collect him and find Henry.

Opening the door to the auditorium, Zoe peered in, scanning for Darious. There were only a few students within and the tactful voice of a lecturer filling the great room.

"...a syzygy is the spatial alignment of two celestial objects around a central one. For all these..." he spoke on.

Zoe looked around, realizing it was the wrong room. She carefully closed the door and saw she was one lecture hall early. At the next one, Zoe quickly opened its door and saw the class had been dismissed and the lighting had been turned back up. *Ha!* she thought, spotting Darious at the base of the auditorium, speaking with the professor. The professor was sketching things on the board. Zoe made her way down the steps toward them. *Indeed, a true epitome of humanity; curiosity and all.* The instructor was explaining the finer points of theoretical wormholes and Darious was producing question after question.

"Good afternoon," said Zoe.

Darious paused his query, smiling at her with sparkles in his eyes.

"Ah Zoe! Dr. Thane here," he motioned to the professor who shook Zoe's hand, "was just enlightening me on Einstein-Rosen Bridges. Can you believe the concept has not been touched in fifteen hundred years!? There is so much we could look into with the tools of today!"

"Interesting," said Zoe quickly. "I am sorry to cut the party short, but we need to go."

"Okay, may I—"

"Darious, please. Now."

He evidently sensed her urgency and nodded.

"It was a pleasure, Dr. Thane," he said, shaking the professor's hand.

"Likewise. It is refreshing to see such an enthusiastic student. Come by my office anytime. Do you know where it is?"

"I am actually not a student here," said Darious, a bit abashed.

"Oh? Well, I must insist that you do join us."

"Thank you. Thank you," said Darious, very graciously.

He shook the professor's hand again and was still bowing as Zoe took his arm, pulling his livened soul up the steps. They exited out onto the Interstellar Mall, the dry heat now fully saturating the campus and instantly making Zoe perspire. She did not notice, no longer saw the verdant blossoms, or the passing, cordial students; her mind was laser focused on the task at hand. Zoe's thoughts were already within her ship, establishing action items to force contact with Captain Henry.

Onboard her craft, Zoe straightaway took her seat, sealed the aperture, and began prepping for takeoff. She shifted in her chair, realizing she still wore the empty backpack and put it on the floor. Darious took his seat.

"Captain, what is it?"

"We need to locate and contact a 'Captain Henry.' In lieu of contact, as I'm supposing he does not leave his communication lines open, considering his hauls, we will need to locate him and rendezvous as soon as possible. Darious, finish the preflight setup." Zoe tossed her screens over to his dashboard and pulled up her saved files of Henry's damaged semi. She centered in on the image of the two holes on his craft and zoomed in. *Exactly the same.* Zoe diminished the screen and pulled up internal files from the semi. While synced with the ship during repairs, she had downloaded most of its digital innards. She scanned for any documents or calendars pertaining to the Captain's future engagements. *Bingo.* To her luck, he had an upcoming meeting scheduled not far from them. They could be there within a day, hopefully in time to catch up to him.

"Zoe?" spoke Darious from behind her.

"Yes?" she said, reconstituting the most likely route Captain Henry would be following.

"I… I am very grateful for your companionship, for the places we have seen and the experiences we have shared. I would never exchange any of it, ever."

She paused her work and turned toward Darious. He was already looking at her and wore the most beholden expression she had ever seen. It was heart melting.

"Darious," Zoe said with manifest tenderness, "Anytime." Turning back, she added, "Sounds like you already got a recommendation for enrollment next semester." She could just picture the smile on his face.

As they left the planet's ionosphere, Zoe pinged the communication satellites enroute to the planetary region where Captain Henry should be. A few moments after, she got a hit.

"Found him—the Opici System—looks like he's orbiting around a Class-H planet with a single moon. Humph. Well there are no spaceports nearby. It should have been a pass-through system for him." *But*, she thought, *with a bootlegger, secret midnight meetings might not be that out of the ordinary.* In any case, caution was necessary. "Once we get close, I can track the signature from his ion trail to get a precise location."

Zoe sighed and got up from her seat. "Darious, the man we are traveling to meet has had an anomaly onboard his semi. The same anomaly I was just informed that Professor Kring had witnessed some twenty years ago. I have left the Origin-X artifact for him to do further analysis on. It is undoubtedly associated with all of this. I can't put all the pieces together just yet, but I am formulating a hypothesis." Zoe was speaking through that cold hard logic. "The Professor will contact us soon with his results. From there, and from our meeting with Captain Henry, I will begin to finalize my suppositions." She paused a moment, captured by Darious' pacific gaze as it pacified her own recent tensions.

"Darious, it is our duty to see this through to its end. We must be heedful of where we are headed. Pantheon can't be far. I doubt they have stopped looking for us. But I'm not too worried; our trail is kept minimal, thanks to the construction and form of this ship." A grin of self-triumph formed on her lips, though her smugness was soon outshined by stronger emotions as she continued staring at Darious. It was like she was being pulled in. *Those eyes; those mystical eyes.* "Darious I.... thank you. It is I who is grateful for your companionship."

He stared back at her without saying anything for several seconds. "I suppose then we are unequivocally lucky to have found each other."

"In all the gin joints of all the worlds," said Zoe with a smile.

CHAPTER 31

AFTER ALL, WE'RE ONLY ORDINARY HUMANS

"The ion trail ends at the far side of the moon," said Darious as their ship neared the barren planet-satellite system.

"Moonshine by moonlight," replied Zoe. "I do hope we are not too intrusive."

She gracefully arced her quicksilver ship around the satellite and delighted at how the oncoming sunrise reflected a phosphorescent glow from the lunar sands below to her bow. As hills and basins were being revealed by leaping jetes of sunlight, sirens suddenly bound to life within the ship, sending forth loud wales.

"Oh crap! It's the Coppers!" Zoe squirreled the brakes and stalled the ship in dead view of three large CF cruisers. "Crap. Crap." Zoe began furiously typing away.

"Captain? What are you doing?"

"Gotta tuck away all those ill-tempered codings I keep around." Her fingers were a haze over the keyboard. "Aaand good." She looked out with Darious as he leaned over her shoulder. "What's going on out there?"

Three Interplanetary-Class Copper Force ships, gigantic 'U' shaped vessels of stolid greys, were situated around a comet field. Zoe spotted a smaller fleet of micro-crafts interacting with the cloudy mass.

"Ah, do you see those little oblong guys moving throughout the comet?" ask Zoe.

"Yes."

"Those are 3D geometric compilers. Basically, little robots. One is a neutrino generator and rotates all around an object. The other follows opposite its motions, acting as the receiver. Together they can create a three-dimensional map where EM rays cannot penetrate. I always liked the genius of these 'bots. Seriously, they can virtually reconstitute a whole object way down to near microscopic precision, even working out a blast's source. You see, usually they are used for investigations of zero gravity explosions, not comet resear—" Zoe stopped, and her heart dropped like an exoplanet doomed to an infinity of falling into a black hole.

An intercom began ringing. As if pulled by some arcane force, Zoe got up and brushed past Darious. She picked up the wired communicator as he took a seat at the helm.

"Yes," Zoe said and then listened. The man's voice on the other end was strict and inquisitive. He rapidly fired questions in quick succession. Were they aware of their location? Was the pilot onboard licensed? Did they know this sector was currently off-limits due to an investigation? On and on the fusillade of questions shot through the handset. "Yes. Yes. No, but... I know but..." The man cut her off, continuing the verbal onslaught until his questions began to blend together into an indistinct globular cluster.

Upon the culmination of dominating vociferation, he firmly requested that they proceed to the central CF ship. Zoe's mind began to anneal. She stared at Darious, her life force being restored. Zoe was once more dynamic and functioning. "Oh..." she said, her own indomitable will sharpening the steel of her tone and a fiery smile edging upon her face. "Oh, yes sir."

The man sternly responded, "CF Investigation Unit A dash 9. The docking bay will be marked. Disengage all offensive and defensive systems."

"Yes sir." She hung up the phone. "Darious, prepare to dock with the A dash 9 Cruiser ahead."

"Captain?"

With renewed vigor in her voice she said, "We are going to find out what happened here. And hell hath no fury like a woman."

"Aye-aye Captain," said Darious and he typed in the command.

Ten minutes later they were landing in the bay of the police ship. Zoe was pacing back and fourth behind Darious as he monitored the final steps of the arrival process. Her hands massaged one another as thoughts thickened and congealed in her mind.

"Darious, grab your hoodie and prepare to board with me. Say nothing and do nothing onboard the cruiser."

"Will we be okay?"

"I imagine so, but we must tread carefully when in the forest of the wolf."

She gave him a mild smile and held out her hand. The two moved off the ship together and slowly made their way down the ramp. The bay was a pale white with exposed structural beams and sonic rivets. Two armed guards were standing at attention, waiting for the pair at the base of the gangway. Zoe stopped short, giving Darious' hand a firm press. She produced a reassuring look and stepped off the ramp onto the hunting grounds.

The door directly ahead susurrated open, prompting the two officers to switch rifle hands in unison with a concerted clatter. From the aperture and with a pace signifying interminable punctuality, an officer in blue police regalia with gold passants and a triple-barred gold emblem on his left shoulder advanced toward them. His boots pummeled the floor and in a moment, he was upon Zoe and Darious, stopping with such intensity that his body momentarily vibrated like a flagpole in the wind. The officer looked them both up and down.

Through a brown beard and gruff voice, he said, "I'm Sergeant Duvel. Follow me." He turned on his heel, to which the two guards once more shifted weapon arms.

Past silent corridors, the marching Sergeant led the party. Zoe was doing her best to remain calm, but by each turn, deeper and deeper into the ship, pangs of nervousness intensified. She forced the feelings back down; she would hold out for Captain Henry's sake. The CF ship was a dizzying maze of corridors to Zoe, with a minotaur awaiting them at its center.

"Here," said the Sergeant, suddenly stopping before a door.

He eyed Zoe and Darious once more and then operated a control panel, to which the door slid sideways, revealing a large room in direct view of the debris field with the little robots zooming throughout it. The room was dimly illuminated by blue lighting behind every shadow. The empty walls did not reflect with pristine whites like the rest of the CF vessel but instead shone with dull hues, further emphasizing the great view of space from the enormous panoramic window. Above the glass were several screens displaying the ongoing physical analyses outside. Holding Darious' hand, Zoe entered in.

"Sir, the two, Ms. Zoe and the clone, as requested."

Zoe nearly jumped when she saw a male figure stir near the viewing window. He had blended in so well that she had not noticed him against the midnight backdrop. His back was turned to them and he said nothing, merely shifting his stance while continuing to stare out. Sergeant Duvel turned and departed, the door closing behind him.

Zoe and Darious stood motionless. A few minutes passed before the man shifted his weight again and then cleared his throat.

"Please, come here," he said with military hardness, though Zoe could definitely note a slight tinge of compassion.

At this, she eased a bit; perhaps the wolf had already consumed his meal for the day. Her prior meetings with the CF had never really been... positive. Zoe led Darious to the viewing aperture, stopping abreast with the man, and all three stared out at the cloud of detritus. If that was indeed Captain Henry's vessel, it was nothing more than ash now, millions upon millions of scattered pieces drifted amidst a dense nucleus. Bits of metal shrapnel glinted in the sun while the many pairs of robotic compilers scanned their every millimeter.

"I am Sheriff Edward LaBarre Vere, the commanding officer of this investigation unit. I have been leading vessel incident investigations for over 20 years now." Sheriff Vere secured his stance. "Miss Zoe Halloconst," he said slowly. "I need you to be very honest with me. Please understand, we at the CF hold all incidents with the highest of seriousness. We have an abundance of intelligence from which to draw on during our investigations. I have a hunch why you are here, but I need to hear it from you."

Zoe solemnly nodded, still taking in the great debris field in front of her.

"Cid 'Zephyr' Henry," the Sheriff said. Zoe twitched at this, now knowing without a doubt the inevitable truth that was looming. "He was not a colleague of yours, correct?"

"Correct sir," said Zoe.

"He was a friend?"

"Yes," said Zoe, her heart nearly giving out.

"I see. I am sorry to say that Mr. Henry is dead. Before us are the remnants of his vessel." The truth of it all sank to its fullest effect within Zoe. The officer turned his head toward her. She could feel his eyes attempting to compel some declaration from her, but she didn't move her gaze from the scene beyond. Sheriff Vere cleared his throat. "We have already confirmed he was a bootlegger, trading and selling illicit goods. Did you know of this? Zoe, it is imperative you answer honestly."

"Yes. But I—"

"That is fine. We at the CF already know. You are not in any trouble."

He then turned to fully face her. Zoe finally looked over at him and saw a man with such a chiseled profile that he seemed to actually be carved from bedrock. The Sheriff looked to be in his mid-50s and in amazing shape. The uniform he wore was silvered at the seams, though remained the same blue as the other officers. An insignia of a starred rank was stitched upon his left shoulder. Zoe could see within his eyes a man of pure principle, of unbreakable duty.

"I am sorry for your loss," he said. "All untimely loss of life is sour to the heart and acidifies our society."

"What happened?" asked Zoe.

He exhaled. "Ma'am, I am sorry. Our investigations are underway. I will say however, we have confirmed a single occupant was onboard and it was Mr. Henry."

"I understand," said Zoe quietly.

"Please also understand, we will do everything we can to discover the fault of this unfortunate incident. You may trust in my abilities and in my crew's abilities."

"Thank you, Sheriff."

He turned and looked out, putting a definite hold on the conversation. Zoe did not care to look at Captain Henry's gravesite anymore and instead turned her attention to the monitors above them. Scrolling text from the 3D compilers showed the various elements being digitized from the debris field. *Oh, Henry*, she thought. *What happened?*

A minute or so passed before the Sheriff spoke once more. "Space," he said, in singly the most epic tone Zoe had ever heard. She looked at the stoic officer, but he continued staring out beyond them. "The CF is here to uphold peace and neutrality throughout it. People like Mr. Henry undermine these efforts." He paused, seemingly lost in the stars. "However, he is one of the citizens we have vowed—I have vowed—to protect. As such, it is my personal responsibility to alkalize the conditions of his death, which I uphold with the sincerest authority."

He turned to Zoe. "You are free to go, Miss Zoe." He stared at her as if analyzing her.

She nodded once. "Thank you, Sheriff Vere."

"I must go attend to my duties. You may stay as long as you need and then you may depart. Your ship is in Hangar 3."

From one last look out at the cosmos, he turned to leave but then paused, eyeing Darious. "Before I depart, may I ask one more question?" Zoe nodded. "I am intrigued as to why one would travel with a working clone. I assume a servant for your more cumbersome tasks? It's an interesting idea, I must say."

"No Sheriff, I—"

"Say no more." He evidenced a twinge of disapproval, said nothing more himself, and left.

Zoe turned her attention back to the wreckage and the pair stared in reverent silence for several minutes.

Darious soon became somewhat fidgety. "Shall we go?" he asked.

"Yes," said Zoe.

He turned and began walking to the door, but Zoe remained. With somber steps, she walked up to the window and pressed a hand to it.

"Goodbye, Captain Henry," she whispered and gave a soft kiss to the window, the profile of her lips imprinting the glass and sending out an everlasting kiss into the cold of space toward the final resting place of the late moonshiner.

CHAPTER 32

AN ABSOLUTE RESOLUTION

Once relieved of the investigative task force and onboard their ship, the pair set sail in hallowed space. For the next hour, Zoe and Darious worked in silence at their consoles; Zoe, in particular, was avoiding the poignant spirits brewing from within. As she typed on her digital keyboard, her rational mind was attempting to console her rueful soul. Captain Henry, as effectual as any captain before him, had been set upon a pyre and sent out into the medium of his cruising. There was a sort of nobility and sanctity in this. But in the means of his death, there was treachery—murder. The fact that the destruction of his ship was so complete as to reduce it to such small bits had to have been done on purpose. This was obvious. What's more, the job was done by a very thorough explosive device. Zoe's heart wrenched. How could this have happened? Pantheon Industries? The CF? Were they in it together? Or was the CF innocent in all this, putting the pieces together itself? One particular thought, stemming from her meeting with Professor Kring, bore deeper and deeper into her: what if, by back-tracking her movements, Pantheon had found Captain Henry and his ship containing, unknowingly to him, that direct evidence of their secret? Was this all her fault?

As if Darious could sense the invisible, albeit thick, cloud of self-destructive rumination about the captain's seat, he came to Zoe and offered her a warm smile and gentle hand upon her shoulder. He then moved behind her, placing his other arm on her opposite shoulder and began working away the tension from her muscles. Zoe looked down at the tattooed fingers and followed them until they disappeared behind her. Darious worked along the curves of her shoulder blades, pressing compassionate hands into knots and then wiping them away into nothingness. As he massaged his way back up and was again at her shoulders, Zoe placed her hands over his.

"Thank you," she said softly. Darious grasped her hands tenderly and then resumed kneading through her melancholy disposition.

Zoe soon drifted far away from reality, off in abstractions of a mid-summer's dream. Darious' hands warmed her skin like sunlight's embrace. The feeling was as pure as dawn's first rays. It was as if she could feel the dampness of an early morning being pulled up from the ground while plants began to extrude their aromatic oils. Everywhere, life was being lifted skyward by some remarkable force—something more fundamental than the thermodynamic laws of heat. Something like… a sudden beeping began from the center console. Zoe lifted the sun-kissed veil from her eyes and looked onscreen. It was a call from Professor Kring. She sat straight up and opened the call.

"Hello Prof—"

"Zoe!" he said excitedly. "Zoe this is no doubt a piece from the craft Origin-X. A truly wonderful find!"

"That's great news professor. What of the—"

"The nature of the artifact?" he finished for her. "Amazing indeed! I must tell you, at first, I had thought one of the graduate students had been fiddling with the calibrated settings of my equipment. But no! Alas, all was functioning properly. Well, I did have to modify the signal guide for the tetra-reflectron. Then the ionization matrix on the—" Now the eager professor interrupted himself. "—I'll send you my full report." A faint typing echoed in the background. "Sent. The conclusion of my analysis is this," his exhilarated breathing came through with unabashed clarity like the diamond planet of Janssen, "Zoe, this object has spent time beyond the physical confines of our reality. I'd liken it to an affine space, similar to the postulations put forth by Dr. Baez in his published works. My analysis points to an undiscovered stable energy state for matter and forces, one where objects would seem impossibly lighter than air to us and very much impossible to perceive or interact with. Oh Zoe, what a find!"

Zoe had brought up the files and was scanning through them. "Professor, you validated these experiments four times."

"Thorough, yes. I had to be certain."

"Thank you for lending your expertise. This is no small amount of work."

"It was my pleasure dear! When the task is this stimulating, the term 'work' simply does not apply." Zoe could hear a muffled fumbling, as if the professor was bringing the microphone close to his lips. He then whispered, "I have cancelled all my classes since you left. I told my students I was ill." He quickly laughed and went back to speaking in a normal tone. "They can look up all of the requisite information anyhow. Shall I get started on the competency curves the university has set standard for these students? Bah. They all pass." He paused. "I digress. Zoe, I have encased the relic in a fluorocarbon layer and sealed it in a faraday vacuum chamber."

A sudden thought occurred to Zoe and she nearly fretted for a moment. "Prof?"

"Hmm?"

"The piece doesn't pose any physical threat, does it?"

"Oh, no my dear. The artifact is completely inert. I've secured it as such for safekeeping. Go ahead, read through the study. In fact, it's quite possibly the closest thing to being negatively inert!" He made another quick laugh. "What is most fascinating is, wherever it has been, it does not seem to have completely returned from. In a small way, on a scale beyond that of micro, this artifact has reached a pseudo-physical qualitative state. Go ahead, read through the report."

"Oh, I will Professor. I'm scanning it now."

"No, give it a good read. I know you're like a bullet from a gun, but this is one, Zoe, needs to be sifted and washed so that its pearl may be best observed. Anyhow," he continued in a tone Zoe was quite familiar with from the distinguished professor, "I trust you will read it."

Zoe nodded at the Professor's words and felt the old influences of her teachers. Though she had graduated with top honors and Professor Kring had said she knew enough to teach his classes for him, she couldn't help but feel a bit nostalgic about her past learnings. That period of her life at the university, with the Professor included, had kept a piece of her, in much the same way this new version of space still held on to the ancient fragment.

The professor continued on, "Have you been able to locate the gentleman you so rushed to find? I am most curious to see the boreholes of his vessel."

This was the bubbling-over point for Zoe. She let out a soft whimper before stating in choked words, "Captain Henry... he's dead."

There was a pause. "Oh, my dear. I am so sorry. What a true tragedy. He was a friend, I trust?"

"Yes," said Zoe, stifling a sniffle. Darious was at her side; his own face was somber though he had never met the late captain.

"And tell me," asked the professor, "is that chap you mentioned so fondly with you at the moment?"

"He is." Zoe grasped Darious' hand.

"Sir, I apologize, I forget your name. Was it Darren? Das—"

"Darious sir," he spoke into the nearest microphone.

"Ah, my boy." The professor cleared his throat. "You be sure to take care of that girl. Now, normally under such circumstances, I would say to her she is in good hands with such an individual as yourself—a trusty companion at her side—but I know Zoe and it is you whom is in good hands. She is strong. Stronger than you or I. Stronger than the bonds of lead." Zoe could feel herself start to smile.

"Sir, I do know it," said Darious. He gave Zoe's hand a squeeze to which she reciprocated, and her smile widened.

"So, you two wanderers of our great galaxy, though I cannot leave my post as I have been absent from by duties for too long, I request that you visit the Copper Ephemeris Station."

"Professor?" asked Zoe.

"I have some follow-up research to be done, which cannot be accomplished here. This facility has such capabilities and I have a colleague there which can assist you. Do you accept?"

"Certainly sir!" Darious blurted and then quickly looked at Zoe for an approving signal.

Zoe smiled at him. "Yes sir!" she rejoined.

"Excellent. I'm sending you the coordinates now. I will let Dr. Wright know to expect you and I will send him the work to be done. Now, let me calculate..." his voice drifted to quick ramblings. "You're at Sector Beta Prime 932A by... with dual fusion thrusters... 45.38 998—"

"I also have four high-speed proton thrusters," Zoe said.

He paused. "My dear! It is a wonder you haven't pierced through the fabric of space-time yourself."

"Haha! Oh, Professor Kring. It was good seeing you."

"And you as well, Miss Zoe. Next time, be sure to have Mr. Darious with you. I'd much like to meet the lad who dares to share the stars with such a trailblazer."

"You as well sir," Darious responded.

"So, Prof, based on the coordinates you just gave, we should be arriving there in about 4 days, 3 hours."

"Thank you, Zoe. Please keep me up to date. See you two around. Zoe: verve, nerve, and adventure to you."

Both Zoe and Darious gave a cheery 'goodbye' and hung up the call.

Zoe sat in thought from nearly a minute while teasing a toggle switch. Darious meanwhile had begun reading through the report on her screen.

"Darious," said Zoe. He turned to her and she stared deep into his eyes. "I pledge to get to the bottom of this and I accept whatever risks may come along. I accept the uncertainties and a possibly hazy future due by my actions. I pledge this to you and to Captain Henry and to Dr. Saknussemm—whatever hand he might have had in all this."

"I too pledge. To you Zoe."

"I wouldn't want anyone else by my side." She smiled and then added solemnly, "It is no doubt going to continue to be dangerous Darious."

He nodded and resumed his seat. "I can navigate us to the monitoring station. I would also like to review the work from Professor Kring, if you don't mind."

Zoe sent over the coordinates and the research. She then silently stared out at space, her recent tears lubricating the ever-present gears of her mind, building steam towards her absolute resolution.

CHAPTER 33

WHO WATCHES THE WATCHER?

Four days later, Zoe's ship was on its final approach toward the massive space monitoring station. Telescoping antennas of every size and shape protruded from all sections of its skeleton-like body. More than just a nerve center with many vertebrae, to Zoe, it looked like a beast with a billion backs, a complex set of instrumentation for snooping in every nook and cranny of the galaxy.

Zoe turned off her music. "Darious, everything is scrutinized here. Everything." She took her feet off of the console as he came over to look out at the station. "It's a CF facility. We should heed what we say here." Zoe tapped her fingers on the armrest. "I sure hope Professor Kring is right in moving us in this direction."

"The Copper Ephemeris Station is quite a human achievement," said Darious. "I read that it collects petabytes a second of galactic information."

"Ya, more or less," said Zoe with a hokey scoff. "I already received the docking info. We are set to land at Bay 11. Care to guide us in?"

"Aye Captain," said Darious as they switched positions.

Darious made his smoothest landing yet and in no time, they were ready to disembark. The gangway was lowered, and the pair made their way down.

"Jeeze," said Zoe. "Do they ever decorate these places? The same white everywhere. It's enough to bore a rock."

They were soon past the landing bay and entering into the main lobby. Zoe put on a cheerful smile and strolled to the front desk.

"Greetings, fellow carbon-based biped!" she exclaimed. A plump woman in a white coat with the CF science insignia smiled at her.

"Hello. May I help you? Ah, wait, Miss Zoe I presume?"

"Yes, ma'am."

"You are scheduled for a meeting with Dr. Wright at 3:30."

"Yeah. How did you know it was me?"

"We don't get many visitors," responded the receptionist. "I will let Dr. Wright know you are here. Would you like a water or tea?"

"No, thank you."

"None for me either," said Darious, earning a scolding glance from the secretary. He pulled his hood down low over his face.

"Come on," whispered Zoe. "Let's take a seat."

She took up a chair at the meager waiting area and stretched out her legs. Darious perfunctorily sat beside her. Looking around, Zoe noticed the somewhat decrepit state of the place. The waiting room was of a wholesome white, but from each corner a slight discoloration was creeping outwards. By this, Zoe came to the conclusion that though this station was a hub for the CF's monitoring activities, its funding might not be what it once was. The secretary's desk evidenced the same dilapidation. From Zoe's experience, she had known how it was common for departments of the CF to replace their furniture every few years; they gotta make sure to spend the whole budget, lest they chance getting a smaller amount the next time around. Zoe was tempted to ask the secretary about the state of things, but decided against it. The receptionist hung up the phone.

"Dr. Wright will see you now," the woman said, standing up. "Please follow me."

Zoe promptly rose and followed the lady as she waddled through a series of corridors. Zoe's hypothesis gained traction by each step as she noted the many empty offices. After a few minutes of silent walking, they stopped before an open office door.

"Miss Zoe is here to see you Dr. Wright."

"Thank you," said a voice from just around the corner of the door. The secretary smiled at Zoe and then left. They entered the office and were greeted by a balding man with a long, gray beard. He shook Zoe's hand.

"Welcome."

"Hello Doctor Wright. I am Zoe, and this is Darious." Darious held out his hand, which the Doctor languidly shook and then went back to ignoring his existence.

"Please have a seat, Zoe."

She motioned for Darious to sit next to her. Dr. Wright took a seat behind his desk.

"I'm sure Professor Kring apprised you of his current studies," said Zoe.

She had spent the better part of the last four days reviewing the Prof's work alongside Darious. The Professor had ingeniously found a single resonant harmonic which stood out from the piece of Origin-X, due perhaps from part of its matter being slightly attenuated and missing in that higher energy state. The harmonic was subtle, but definitely perceivable. Dr. Kring proposed that the same phenomenon could exist elsewhere, thus any chance of finding corroborating evidence should be at once investigated. It was a good idea; a single identifying signal could crack this whole thing wide open.

Zoe looked at the library of books behind Dr. Wright, layered from floor to ceiling. It was an impressive collection of everything from EM synaptics to tactile bioengineering. She tilted her head, reading through the imprinted spines.

"Yes, he has," said the Doctor, bringing Zoe's attention back to him. He spoke with an air of superiority. "I have prepared the prerequisite annotations for us in the Stellar Lab. I must say though, before we begin, when Dr. Kring described the intricacy of the problem and an associate coming to perform the work with me, I envisioned someone a bit… older."

Zoe couldn't help but grin. "Should we get started then?"

No reciprocating smile came from the Doctor. It seemed her age really did bother him.

"Yes, Miss Zoe. Please, follow me."

He led Zoe and Darious through the office section of the space station, past its many vacant labs, to the stellar research area. They entered into a large hollo-plotter, similar to the one Zoe and Darious had used at the Majora Station, though Zoe estimated this one to have somewhere around 1,000 percent better precision in addition to having the ability to scan the entirety of the galaxy with a multitude of waveforms.

"Here we are," said Dr. Wright. He turned toward Zoe. "Have you ever visited our Stellar Lab before?"

"No," replied Zoe. "I. Am. Impressed."

She turned to Darious with an approving nod. This was indeed a state-of-the-art facility. If there was any place to find an odd signal, it was definitely here. Professor Kring was smart to think of utilizing this station's capabilities. They just might get a better clue as to what had happened to Origin-X.

"Before us and around us is the Stellarizer-2206, version 3.0. Utilizing compound emission bands and special compilers, we are able to visualize the entire galaxy at all wavelengths in a true 3D fashion."

"Damn," said Zoe.

They centered themselves in the room around the podium. Dr. Wright turned down the lights and closed the door. As he continued to operate the console, the room vanished and soon they were surrounded by unobstructed space. Darious stiffened his stance as the floor became seemingly null underneath them. Zoe was looking all around, positioning herself in the clouds of stars. She quickly recognized their location; they were standing where the Copper Ephemeris Station would have been.

"Dr. Kring sent me the protocols by which to search. I'm loading them now. He did not specify to which emission bands we should constrain the search."

"Stick to x-class bands."

"Setting the parameters now," said the Doctor.

Suddenly, they were transported out from the star system and rapidly away from innumerable celestial bodies with speeds impossible by any spacecraft. As they zoomed outwards, space seemed to recoil inwards. Just a few seconds later, the cosmic ride slowed and stopped. Displayed at their feet and extending all around them was the whole of the Milky Way Galaxy. Its many great arms of golds and blues dazzled Zoe. She had never seen such an immersive view of her home.

"Oh my…," she said.

"Yes. Please be mindful of your balance. It can be disorienting for first-timers."

"No, it's not that. It's so… beautiful."

"Oh," said Dr. Wright with zero enthusiasm. "We can see from here it is simply billions of stars and matter in orbit around a gravitational sinkhole."

"Sir," said Darious in a very serious manner. "'It' is 'simply' prodigious. Though," he added, "I may need to sit down."

The Doctor ignored him, so Zoe gave an empathetic nod. "Feel free to, Darious. The ground is still there like normal. Okay Doctor, let's clear up the clutter and get a better look."

Dr. Wright coughed and typed into the podium. "Shifting bands," he said. A wall of text appeared to their left, hovering in space, closest to Zoe. She read through the scrolling data.

"Can we decrease the theta background noise?" she asked.

"The computer is already collecting samples of cosmic background noise to remove," responded the Doctor, with slight condescension. "I'm editing the filamentary protuberances. Please apprise me of any anomalies you may note."

In the slow-moving data Zoe had read through, so far all was normal. "Nothing to report yet."

A blue square appeared, containing several lines of text. "The background noise has been fully isolated and scrubbed," said Dr. Wright. "The resolution is now at the micron level for all x-class emission bands. The time-scale is from the present to the last fifty years in steps of microseconds, as dictated by Dr. Kring. Querying now with the provided harmonic waveform."

Zoe couldn't help but hold her breath. This was it. What else was hiding in their galaxy? What were they about to find? Minutes went by with Zoe reading every letter from every line of data. Nothing.

"Scan complete. Preservation with less than a total of 100 microns of error. What do we have here?" The Doctor perked up from the console and went over to where Zoe was staring at the resulting information.

"Nothing," she said.

"Ah. As I suspected."

Zoe turned to him and couldn't help but give a slight scowl.

"I did a preliminary scan before your arrival. I am not entirely sure of what Dr. Kring is hoping to accomplish. I gather he is looking for some sort of unusual, previously unnoticed signal. I would hate to think the university is dabbling in metaphysics." Zoe was fighting off the urge to glare at Dr. Wright until he turned to stone. "No abnormalities. No odd signals. Miss Zoe, please relay to Dr. Kring, if I were to ever discover any unidentifiable abnormality, to which I highly, highly doubt, you can be sure I will forward the information to the university for further study. Dr. Kring is an old colleague after all. Anyhow, this was an odd request to begin with. I cannot provide further services. As it stands, I shall be billing the university for my time. What is it Dr. Kring is researching exactly?"

Zoe ignored the question; the one within her own mind was too loud. "Doctor, allow me one more request; then we will get out of your hair." *Or what's left of it...* "Can you complete the same scan, at your highest resolution, for a particular location I have here?" She brought out her lightcard and with a few commands, synced it to the hollo-plotter. "There are the coordinates and the time-stamp." Surely here, the Stellar Lab would recognize what Zoe had held in her own hands.

"Scanning now," said Dr. Wright, with an opprobrious exhalation.

Their view of the galaxy zoomed in at a fantastic speed to the spatial location which Zoe and Darious had pulled that recondite relic from the vacuum of space. In a moment, the scan was complete, and a floating data square showed the same null results.

"No," said Zoe calmly, almost prepared to laugh at the absurdity of it all.

"Pardon me?" said Dr. Wright.

"No," repeated Zoe. "It's wrong."

She should have expected this. The data was undoubtedly manipulated, the same as the Majora Station. Pantheon Industries had undoubtedly even edited the entirety of CF's galactic systems. There was nowhere to go. She looked out to the billions of bright specs and suddenly space felt so closed, so compact, as if it were squeezing her.

"Ma'am," said Dr. Wright. "This is the galaxy's finest spatial monitoring station. If we cannot detect it, it simply doesn't exist. I am sorry for whatever hypothesis Dr. Kring has you naively spending time on."

Zoe went over to the console and turned the lights on. Darious was on the floor and looked up at them. She helped him up and turned to the Doctor.

"I am sorry," he repeated apathetically. "Any further questions?"

"Yes," said Zoe, with a sudden gust of unrestrained inquisitiveness. A theory was building up in her mind, past what Professor Kring would be comfortable with. "Has this station ever found any anomalies that couldn't be accounted for?"

"Anomalies? No. Every signal accounted for; everything in its place. Can you be more specific with your question?"

Zoe firmed up her voice, "Have you ever intercepted any transmission which couldn't be defined as... from mankind? I mean, a transmission not natural and not man-made?"

"What are you alluding to, aliens?" The word resonated a chord within Zoe. "Miss, there is no such thing. Humans have been all throughout the galaxy. We've inhabited over a million star systems and have thoroughly scanned the rest. There have never been any signs of other intelligent life or any evidence to suggest there might have been in the past. There are simply no aliens... except, of course, if you count the primordial bacteria that are found throughout the galaxy, which can barely even be categorized 'life.' No. We are unique."

"I know," rebuked Zoe. For her, it was difficult to argue. It was such an abstract idea, so full with nothing. She was struggling to rationalize the concept and yet, at the same time, a piece of her was becoming dedicated to it.

"I do not like to have my time frittered as such. Tell Professor Kring that he or any future 'associates' will have to follow proper

CF proposal protocols for future use of the Stellar Lab. We are quite busy. I'm beginning to think he was being generous and you are simply a student. He may be falling far from the tree these days. Shame."

Zoe wanted to growl and pounce on this man. "Dr. Wright," she said. "I do think we are done here. Thank you for your time."

Her sudden and formal valediction caused the group to straighten up.

"You are welcome Miss Zoe. Please, see yourselves out." He motioned to the door. "I must recalibrate the settings of the Stellar Lab for the next user." The Doctor then held out his hand. Zoe was lifting her own to reluctantly shake it when Darious sprang and grabbed the outstretched hand, giving it a stiff shake, and causing Dr. Wright to wince. Zoe could have given Darious a high-five.

"Good day, Dr. Wright," he said.

Zoe nodded. "Good day," she muttered as they left the Doctor to his toys.

They began to make their way back down the corridors to the front lobby.

"Zoe," Darious said, "your statement about ali—"

"Darious. Not here. Let's depart before we talk further. I already feel I have said more than I should have."

Her own statements from the hollo-lab sunk in deeper as they wound through the outbound halls of the monitoring station. Even the secretary's 'goodbye' was met with a distant echo from Zoe. It was not until they had boarded her craft and were exiting the bay that Zoe became cognizant of her surroundings.

"Darious."

"Captain?"

She set her hands on the armrests and turned to him. Her mind was resolute, but her words were broken and unsure. "Even the CF has been infiltrated, completely. Pantheon seems, to me, to be the culprit. This secret of theirs... it's above and beyond everyone, everything. This secret of theirs..." Zoe bit her lip and stared into Darious' eyes. They had become her one earthly comfort in all the cosmos. "Darious. I don't think this secret of theirs... is entirely theirs."

⊨ ⊨

Deep within the unfathomable depths of space, the bantam ship, with its two occupants, traversed the stars. At some unbeknown point of inflection, their journey had been noticed and had begun to be undone, such as infinity becomes undone when its inverse is granted, enlarging values. Thermodynamic recklessness is no longer possible. Instead, cosmic mountains arise, and the travelers slide in the only direction possible with infinity rushing past them.

Of all its theorized forms, none is truer than space's paradoxical nature. It is a fabric stretched as reality, whose single fibers have no endpoint, no middle, and only a supposition of a beginning. Its intricacies are only fathomable by conceptualizing the lack of it. Nonetheless, one single truth of space's enigmatic nature remains steadfast, to which its occupants must always succumb to: the true force of nothing—a force harnessed to create the extreme, and extreme by its own right. This harness, created by metal and polymers and ridden by corporeal creatures erroneously thinking they hold the whip in one hand and the reigns in the other, is not a harness at all but a cage. When considering the abysmal complexities of infinity, unbridled space does not follow their path, they follow its. Inhabitants of the galaxy, take heed, as its strands had been woven long before your day. What is the noble lie?

CHAPTER 34

KAPPA IGNITES

About an hour after departing from the Copper Ephemeris Station, as Zoe was fiddling with a piece of coding to clear her mind, an inbound call from Professor Kring appeared across her screen. She answered the call.

"Zoe!" declared the Professor, evidently in an excitable mood. "I could not wait to get an update from you. My duties here have distracted me long enough. We old men, as you know, are quite impatient when it comes to our research."

Zoe couldn't help but smirk. "Professor, perhaps next we should invent a time machine."

"Indeed, my dear. Have you arrived at the Ephemeris Station? I'm positive Dr. Wright is preparing for your visit."

"We just left."

There was a pause. "Ah. Zoe, I can tell by your tone it did not go well."

"I am sorry Professor. Results were zero for the entire galaxy."

"Hmm. I was sincerely hoping for some further clue. That is fine." He sighed. Zoe knew he was not displeased with her, but rather, disappointed that the search had not yielded anything new. "Well, Dr. Hubert Wright was the one to do such an examination, a true wizard at these things. I trust he was helpful?"

"He was," said Zoe. She did not want to talk about the last bit of their meeting. She then giggled at remembering how oddly he had first looked her up and down. "Though I think he was expecting a man, a much older man."

"Ha! Gave him a bit of a shock, did you? Well that 'ought to have woken the old boy up. Genius comes in many forms; a university will sure teach you that."

Zoe looked behind her and saw Darious very much absorbed in a textbook in the main chamber. He had quickly taken up researching her 'alien' hypothesis to which she spoke no more of. Zoe turned back to the microphone.

"So, Prof, how has Origin-X held up?"

"Safe and locked away. We must now think of alternative solutions. I would like to ask your permission to bring in more minds on this project, but first, I must tell you of a gentleman that came by looking for you a couple of days ago."

Zoe immediately bent toward the microphone as if electrically prodded.

"Who?"

"He did not leave a name, but he did ask for you by name. Do not worry. I know that any friend of Zoe would already have her contact information, thus I proceeded to tell the chap that I did not know where you were or when you would be visiting the university again. I understand your need for secrecy. I suppo—"

"Professor, what did he look like?" Zoe interrupted.

"Well, let's see, he had a large brim hat. Like one of those cowboys from the western era of Earth-1. Is that coming back in style with the boys?"

Zoe felt herself go pale. She closed her eyes and let reality whirl all around her. Opening them once again, she let out a long breath. At least he didn't harm the Professor.

"Zoe, do you know him?"

"Professor..."

Zoe suddenly felt as though her lungs weren't able to provide enough Oxygen. She tried to shrug off the feeling. Dr. Kring immediately seemed to pick up on her strangulated state.

"Please, please dear, be safe."

"Professor, I will try."

"Dear?"

Zoe could not tell him about all that had happened, she just couldn't.

"I'm sorry Professor; I've just been a bit on edge."

"I understand. I can't help but worry. Anyhow, back to my question, may I bring in more brainpower on this project?"

"No!" Zoe then blushed. "No, not yet. Give me a bit more time."

"As you wish. If I think of anything new I will be sure to call."

"Thank you, Professor."

"I need to go now. It was a pleasure talking with you Zoe."

"You as well."

As Zoe hung up the call, she couldn't help but feel a bit contrite from her tone with the Professor. She knew he had seen through her poor guise, but she couldn't let down her walls; after all, it was for his own safety.

Then it hit Zoe like a fusion bomb. Dr. Kring had not told the man in the cowboy hat where she was, but he had just called her through an unsecured channel. If that man was this close to her trail, then he would no doubt be monitoring the Professor. Dr. Kring had just inadvertently given away her exact coordinates.

"Darious!"

Zoe began prepping all thrusters for a rapid kick. Darious came running into the cockpit.

"Captain?" he asked, while taking a seat and readying his projection console.

"I just spoke with the Professor. The man in the cowboy hat, he's—"

"He has found us," said Darious in a manner that made Zoe's skin burn cold.

Long range sensors just then came to life, having picked up a craft heading straight toward them. Zoe immediately scanned the ship. It matched the one she had torpedoed on Kratos. With her two hands and ten digits, Zoe quickly calibrated the thrusters and fired a pre-burst to warm them up. The craft leapt forward, and Zoe fired all engines at maximum, in the opposite direction of the oncoming vessel.

"Darious! I need you to go into the cooling routines and relay power from everything we aren't using."

"Aye, Captain!"

Zoe could see his quick work on her side screen while she fervently set the ship's thrusters to pulse like clockwork in order to maximize power without burning up any of the engines. She looked down at the long-range scanners and nearly jumped from her chair. The mad cowboy had already halved the distance to them. He would be upon them within minutes.

"We won't make it," said Zoe breathlessly. She looked out to the stars surrounding her, surrounding the harbinger of death, and surrounding all things. "No," she said. "Not today."

Surely by now the assassin had modified the communication protocols of his ship so her last trick would not work again, and he would undoubtedly be prepared for any frontal assault, not that she had any torpedoes left anyhow. There had to be another way. Then it came to Zoe. Oh, this time he would get his. She had something for him, something with much more... flare.

Zoe eased off the throttle. The low of rumblings of her craft subsided and the cabin felt calm, that same faux calm that comes right before a storm, when the conscious mind only comprehends stillness, but the body knows something is amiss and skin tingles as hairs stand on end.

"Captain, why are you slowing the ship!?"

"It's okay Darious. You can let up on the cooling systems. I'm bringing us to a stop."

"Zoe!?"

"We will burn up trying to outrun that Drak-9. Instead," Zoe began loading Dr. Saknussemm's program, "we are going to give him a taste of what the good Doctor left behind. You might want to strap in."

There was no response from Darious, but she could see her ship's cooling systems return to their automated configurations. Zoe had made a couple tweaks to the Doctor's program since they had last tried it. She was a flurry over the projection console as she prepared all the routines. This should be their best light-show yet.

Her ship came to a full stop. Zoe turned it about, directly facing the oncoming bird of prey. She stretched the focal point of the Z-Pulsers as far out as it could go in order to intercept the oncoming craft's trajectory, though it was still going to have to come quite close. Zoe loaded the last of the sequences. The Drak-9 was momentarily upon them, having also stopped about half a kilometer away, and was now slowly creeping forward. The cowboy was evidently being more cautious this time. Zoe reveled at the thought that perhaps their last meeting had riled him. She opened the Z-Pulsers' small bay door and began charging the capacitors for one big burst.

"Darious, track his weapon locks. We don't want any surprises."

"Aye, Captain."

Zoe brought up her visual array to take a closer look at the enemy craft. The zoomed-in view on her screen showed the demonic vessel in all its unyielding viciousness. Some metal patchwork had been completed since their last meeting, giving the vessel a more barbaric look. In addition, all along its low-bending wings, the Drak-9 was armed with missiles, guns, and plasma cannons. Perhaps the CF would like to have a word with this gentleman regarding his armory, that is, if they were not the ones doing the arming.

"Quarter kilometer and continuing approach," called Darious. "14 weapon locks on us."

"Any powering up?"

"No," he quickly replied.

Zoe stared at the ship. "Come on. Come on."

The two vessels continued their standoff while space around them seemed not to take heed of the scene unfolding. The stars shined just as they always had. Here, Zoe and Darious were alone. No judges, no jury; just the cosmos to bear witness.

"Weapons loading!" yelled Darious. "20 percent powered!"

Zoe grit her teeth. "Just a little closer..."

"65 percent! 85 percent! 95 percent!"

"Now!" shouted Zoe, engaging the program and sending a nova of a shock through her ship.

The repercussion nearly threw Zoe from her seat. She could hear Darious scrambling behind her. A massive bolt of white light seared through space, ripping across the void, and striking the Drak-9. Zoe saw it happen. Through the near-blinding light, she saw arcs traverse the exterior of the vessel and spark around its aft spoilers. There was an explosion. In the next moment, thick smoke consumed the Drak-9.

Suddenly, loud popping sounds resounded within Zoe's craft and the interior lighting went out. A plethora of alerts appeared across her screens. As she brought up the error menu, her ship veered to its starboard side. She strained to hold on while typing on the console. A dozen fuses had been blown. The Z-Pulsers had gone offline and the feedback energy had ruptured part of

the central power conduit. She quickly shut off the damaged segments and circumvented their circuits. The ship soon stabilized,
and the lights returned to normal. Zoe breathed a sigh of relieve.
That was almost really bad.

"Are you okay Darious?"

She turned back and saw him regaining his seat.

"Yes, Zoe."

"Okay that time, you can't say I didn't warn ya." She smirked.

"You are correct, and we are still alive. What is the status of
the other ship?"

Zoe had already turned back and was rotating her ship to
face the Drak-9.

As it came into view, Zoe was simply stunned. The fiery glow had
subsided, and smoke was mostly dissipated. The Drak-9 seemed to
have lost power and was now slumped over. It reminded Zoe of when
she had first seen Captain Henry's vessel floating in space. The ship
looked abandoned. It had sure taken a beating since meeting her.
As the Drak-9 slowly turned, Zoe got a good look at its thrusters.

"Darious! Take a look at that!"

He immediately came over and gawked at the view.

"On my!"

An entire chunk of the vessel was missing. It was like a spherical bite had been taken from its main thruster and the two connecting boosters.

"Haha!" exclaimed Zoe. "Take that!" She compiled a quick
scan and read through the results. In addition to the engine
damage, that large explosion had been from one of his missiles erupting during the event, further damaging the aft wing
of the vessel. "Luckily, our damage was minimal. A couple fuses and I may have overloaded the Z-Pulsers. Let's get out of
here."

"Aye captain," said Darious, patting her on the shoulder. "A
good idea."

Just as Zoe was plotting a course for far, far away, the Drak-9 sprung to life. The whole ship rattled, and black exhaust blew out from its thrusters.

"Oh shi—," Zoe started.

"Zoe! It is rebooting!"

With the Drak-9 powering up, Zoe scanned its propulsion system. The results came back in a few seconds.

Summary:

Ballast Thrusters:	*Online.*	
Force Thrusters:	*Primary Array:*	*Significant damage. 53% operational; inconclusive.*
	Secondary Array:	*Operational; inconclusive.*
	Ancillary Array:	*Inconclusive.*

Conclusion: Estimated .51 f-p/hour maximum speed.

The chase was not over, not by a longshot.

"Darious, find a way to close the Z-Pulser door. The main circuitry to it is fried. Find a work around. I'm ramping up thrusters."

Zoe brought up an interactive display of vacuum-to-fuel ratios for all her thrusters side by side. With her fingertips on the projection console, she slowly raised the bars upward. Her ship began a smooth, yet rapid acceleration. Zoe kept a keen eye on the cooling systems and on the Drak-9. It was evidently still rebooting but had turned to face them as they passed it in the night of space. Soon the ship was a speck in the distance.

"Darious, status?"

"Door sealing now, Captain."

"Thank you. That was one thing I did not want to lose. Speeds approaching .2 floating-parsecs an hour; continuing acceleration."

A red light on Zoe's console signaled the Drak-9 had begun its own acceleration in their direction. The cowboy had not given up. Zoe continued ramping up power with moderate enhancements to the thrusters, ensuring they could fly as long as possible at high speeds.

"Captain."

"Yes Darious?"

"Good work back there."

Zoe smiled and for a moment the chase seemed to glaze over, as if Darious and she were merely out for a Sunday cruise to see the rings of Saturn.

"Aw, it was nothing, Hot Sauce."

"We are approaching a planetary system 30 degrees from the port bow. It appears to be heavily populated. Perhaps a good place to lose the man in the cowboy hat?"

Darious sent the information to Zoe's display. They were near the Agora Bazaar System. Indeed, it was densely packed with many inhabited planets, planetoids, and space stations.

"Good call," said Zoe. "Changing course to intercept." She continued to monitor the Drak-9. It was slightly gaining on them, though its distance was currently too great for it to be a threat.

Within twenty minutes they were upon the Agora Bazaar. As they passed into the boundary of the solar system, Zoe had to reduce their speed dramatically. The solar system was absolutely crammed with other spaceships. Zoe slowed her ship to a stellar crawl, just as a proximity alert went off and a massive trader vessel flew just overhead. She looked out at the busy surroundings; it was truly a human wonder to behold. From the alert, Darious had come over.

Zoe's computer was quick to scan the system and overlaid her screen with dozens of ruby and orange-swirled planets. Lanes of interplanetary vessels flowed from one world to another and even more led out from the system. Zoe swiped away the digital view and stared outward. Massive fleets of cargo ships swooped and arced all around them. The entire star system was a living hive of trading. Zoe had never seen such a sight. Hundreds of thousands, if not millions, of ships were present in the Agora System. Who knows what treasures passed through its hands every day? Zoe wound gracefully around a 100-kilometer-long cargo vessel. Painted red on its side were markings from the Terenginar System. She knew that system was in another quadrant from where they were. *There must be people here from all over the galaxy.* Zoe bisected a double lane of vessels, noting the various insignia on each. She chanced to look over at Darious who was still absorbed by the sight.

"I know," said Zoe. "I have never seen such a place either."

"It is humbling," he said.

An alert shot across her screen. Darious was first to read it aloud.

"Locked on. Ship: Drak-9. 10,000 kilometers. Engaging."

"Darious, take your seat!"

Zoe braided through several lines of vessels, keeping tabs on the Drak-9 with her sensors, but it remained locked on them.

"Damnit!" said Zoe. The pursuing ship was advancing quickly, too quickly.

"6 locks! Powering up!" shouted Darious.

They were approaching a large vessel with antennas splayed around its central fuselage. She brought her ship toward it and matched its speed. Proximity alerts rang, but she turned them all off. Zoe piloted down toward the craft to be as close as she could to its hull, hoping to blend in with the confusing metal structure. Though just a meter from the vessel, the lock-on alarms continued to sound; her ploy would not work. Zoe smacked her forehead.

"Of course!" She quickly typed in her console and retrieved one of the programs she had tucked away in a cryptographic folder during their recent meeting with the CF.

"Weapons powered at 75 percent!"

Zoe flew upward from the trader ship. The Drak-9 was nearly upon them and warnings signaled all across Zoe's screens. She loaded the program and turned off power to the wings, diminishing her ship's electromagnetic signature, but also drastically reducing its agility capabilities.

"Weapons powered!" yelled Darious. "Weapons fired!"

A large alert on Zoe's screen overlaid all others.

Incoming Projectiles

Zoe began winding her ship through space. Trader vessels strayed from their lanes to avoid impact from her erratic flight path.

Zoe could see on her screen that six rockets were fixed along her route, twisting as she was. In mere seconds, their needled points would be upon her, but Zoe knew this was not the end. Her sensors had shown the missiles were of an older and outdated—probably black market—model, no longer in use by any fleet.

Just as the rockets were about to contact her ship, she flipped on the program, turned off the main thrusters and banked hard to her left. The projectiles missed, continuing their twirling tirade in the wrong direction, now chasing nothingness.

"Huzzah!" chirped Zoe.

"What was that!?"

"One of those 'ill tempered' programs," she replied. "The CF would be pissed if they knew I had that one. It throws out bogus resonant nodes of my craft's energy signature—like a ghost ship. In empty space it doesn't work all that well, but here our chances are much improved. Not a bad one, eh?"

"Indeed Captain!"

Zoe arced around another lane of travelers and wove through a grouping of several hundred ships. She purposely flew her ship into the thickest of craft thickets. *There's no way he can lock onto us here,* she thought.

"Weapons locked!" yelled Darious.

"Damnit!"

"One rocket fired!"

Zoe did her best to pivot her ship upward as its wings were still powered down. They passed just above a fatty semi with a triple wide cargo bay. She could see the single rocket incoming. It too was a fatty one.

"Oh Darious, this is gonna be bumpy."

The rocket dexterously dodged around many trader ships, heading right for Zoe and Darious. She curled her ship beneath another vessel and again engaged the ghost ship program. For a confused moment, the rocket shot upward, but it quickly recovered and swept back toward them.

"Damnit. Too smart for that trick..."

Zoe banked again, as hard as she could, around a massive freighter. The rocket was rapidly approaching them. Zoe reengaged her ship's wings and shot around the vessel's mighty starboard side. The missile was not so nimble and tipped the cargo ship's wingtip, exploding on impact. The gigantic exothermic blast sent metal debris into the back of Zoe's craft. Loud crashes echoed, and half of her screens went blank as numerous systems went offline. Half the thrusters spasmodically fired, sending the craft into a mad spin. Zoe had lost control of her ship.

Through the chaos, she remained at her post, flipping switches and rebooting systems as fast as she could. Fires within the engines were autonomously put out by the ship's safety hardware. The recently circumvented circuits that were now corrupted were once more circumvented. Zoe regained what was left to command of her craft, but it was now beyond flight. She strained to correct multiplicities of malfunctions, but new ones were continuously cropping up.

"Darious! We gotta land!"

"Aye, Captain!"

Zoe could see on one of her side monitors that Darious was also fervently working away to compensate the errors of the ship.

"A planet is just off our port bow!" he yelled back.

Zoe used the last bit of her navigational thrusters to aim for the oncoming planet while engaging landing protocols. The planet drew into view as a wide semicircle of oxidized deserts and shining cities. They plummeted toward it. The Drak-9 slowed its pursuit and was no longer locked on. It would seem the cowboy would rather watch them go down in flames.

CHAPTER 35

VERVE, NERVE, AND ADVENTURE

Zoe was typing as fast as she could, her face hardened with concentration through the tense tremors of her craft. The great red planet filled the view of the cockpit window. Its atmospheric ring gleamed as a bright halo in the sunrise. Zoe managed to reboot the fore heat dissipaters just as they entered through the thick atmosphere. Red alerts continued across all screens. Zoe's face hurt from the vibrations. Her fingers had trouble keying in commands. Twice she mistyped, almost losing the fine balance that kept the ship from tumbling end over end.

It was a very steep descent. The hull remained intact, but within, components were flaking away. System after system encountered faults. With much finagling, they finally broke through the clouds to the lower atmosphere. The rubicund desert of the planet shone in long stretches reaching to the horizon. Arid cities spackled the lands. Zoe was signaled by the nearest establishment toward a large airstrip and she quickly accepted the request. At least they would have vehicles there to put them out if they did end up a fiery mess.

"We're coming in hot!" yelled Zoe, gripping the console.

As the ground came very near, Zoe forced the nose of the ship as high as it would go. She engaged all the landing and reverse thrusters that were still operational. The ship jerked violently, and Zoe was nearly thrown onto the console.

They skidded on the ground, leaving a trail several kilometers long on the landing track, usually reserved for mammoth vessels but had been designated for her failing craft. The ship came to a final stop. As it shifted backwards to its ultimate resting position, one landing strut seized and the whole ship leaned down on its port wing.

Zoe looked out through the window. They had made it. Around them was a trader's city, a bustling metropolis matching the desert panorama surrounding it. Ships continued to fly above them; business as usual. Zoe could see several emergency robots rolling toward them to take care of any fires that might exist.

"Darious!" she leapt out of her seat.

He was still in his chair with his fingers unmoving at his console. He slowly turned and looked at her.

"We made it," he finally said.

"Ha ha! We did! We have to get out of here. I'm sure the cowboy will be making sure we're nothing but ash. Come on!"

Zoe wasted no time packing up things. She ran to the main chamber and worked the panel next to the gangway. The door slowly opened, letting in a hot gust of wind. Once halfway detracted, the door squealed and jammed, but it didn't matter. The pair jumped from down the opening and onto steady land.

Zoe looked at her craft. It had certainly seen better days. Suddenly overhead, loud engines boomed and bellowed in their direction. The Drak-9 was coming down right at them.

"Come on!" yelled Zoe, taking Darious by the hand and the two entered the merchant city.

They were soon among other people in a poorer part of the municipality where shop tents lined the pathways and voices loudly haggled. Zoe and Darious ran through the busy streets, constantly taking lefts and rights, hoping to obfuscate their trail.

Zoe began losing breath. Darious was gaining ground ahead and she called to him.

"I need," she said gulping in air, "I need to stop. For just a moment."

They attempted to get out of the way as people pressed around them. Zoe and Darious took to a narrow alleyway that was shadowed from the sun and Zoe leaned against a crumbling brick wall. With hands on her knees, she sucked in several large breaths.

"Perhaps. We can procure. A shuttle?" asked Darious through heavy breathing. "Or a place. To hide?"

"I don't know," said Zoe. "He won't stop. He just won't. Come on. We gotta keep moving."

They continued down the alleyway at a rapid pace. It emptied out into a larger back area with garbage bins and scrawled writing on grimy walls.

"Stop!" a voice shouted from behind them.

Zoe spun toward the voice and froze. It was the cowboy.

He was standing in his overcoat and hat. Now face to face, Zoe noticed the unusual nuances about his face, in particular around his brow line and long, muscular chin. He was from the Laconial System. Zoe was familiar with that system. It was very military-like and many from it served in the CF, that oxymoronic peacekeeping force. *So,* she thought, *they must have branched out to contract killing.* The cowboy was smiling, an unusually large smile for a Laconian. Someone from his recent family history must have been from somewhere like the Rimaldi System. Only these two places could have added up to the unique and relentless character standing before them.

"You two!" he roared, his long grin fading. "You two have been hell for me!"

He took a step toward them and flipped back the flap of his overcoat, revealing a large pistol. Zoe quickly looked around. He had them cornered and defenseless. There had to be something of use around them or some way of escape.

"What the hell did you do to my ship back there!?" he furiously shouted at them.

Zoe looked at him defiantly. "I sent it to a better place."

"What the hell did you...," he repeated, growling.

"Who do you work for?" asked Zoe, snarling. "The CF?"

He cocked his pistol. "Naw. Not these days."

"So, you had? And now what, you're a killer for hire!?"

Zoe was in a state of fury and panic that she had never felt before; after all they had been through, just to die in an alley like this. Her mind was screaming. The cowboy took another step forward and then stood stolidly.

"Tell me!" she shouted.

His eyes narrowed, and that elongated smile crept upward from his lips. "I was in the CF for some years. Now I am a private contractor."

"Wow, so you went from helping people to murdering them!? Just like that!?"

"He-ey," the cowboy responded, in a tone not the least bit offended. "The job has always been the same. Receive orders, get the job done. Explanations were rare even before I went solo. The difference is now the pay is much better." His grin broadened.

"Well, do you know why you've been hired to kill us?!"

"Yes," he said coolly. "You've been stealing corporate secrets, which is illegal in the first place, but from Pantheon Industries— from its headquarters—phew! What did ya'll expect would happen?" He brought up his sidearm.

"Corporate secrets!?" Zoe shouted, astounded. "Pantheon has been murdering innocent people. We are trying to find out why!" Darious held steadfast next to Zoe.

"Innocent. Not innocent. It depends on who's giving the orders really. The people on the wrong side of the CF always said the same thing. And yet on their own side, no one ever has any quips about the lives they take. Tell you what, it's been a while since someone has given me such a hard time, even though there are now just two of you..." Zoe bit her lip at his gibe while the memory of Dr. Saknussemm being murdered flared in her mind. "...and although I can't let you live, I'd say you have earned a little reprieve." He twirled the gun around his finger. "Tell me why you and your clone deserve a quick death instead of a slow one and I will comply."

Zoe and Darious were equally wide-eyed. Doom filled Zoe's heart. A deep survival instinct was coming to the forefront of her consciousness, that age-old fight or flight response. But they, cornered and without any weapons while he was holding the only gun and had it aimed directly at them. There was no way to maneuver, nowhere to run.

The lack of response agitated the cowboy. "Either way," he said cruelly, "your bodies will be pieced and disposed of. No one will ever be able to identify you. I'm sure you understand." Zoe took a slow step forward. He aimed the gun at her chest. "Yes?"

Water began to fill her eyes. She stood, hands at her side, trembling. "Three words."

He considered a moment and lowered the pistol a bit. Zoe breathed and then said, "Verve, nerve, and adventure."

"Well I suppose technically that's four, but I'm an easy fellow." He then paused, evidently taking in her words. "Wait. Verve you say? Nerve? Adventure?" His expression began to change. No longer was it a smile or a frown, but altogether something very obscure. His muscular jaw tightened and his eyes strained, as if his mind was being gassed. "Zoe and the clone. Verve. Nerve. And adventure."

The cowboy moved several steps back. While still holding the gun toward them, he used one hand to drop his overcoat and then diagonally removed his shirt. His exposed skin revealed a muscular torso of various scars, but moreover, of many tattoos. In the center of his chest, curved over one brawny pectoral to the other, were letters formed into three groupings. The characters were odd, and Zoe could not understand them.

"Ancient Latin," he said and point to each in turn. "Verve. Nerve. Adventure." Zoe was beyond taken aback. The cowboy raised the gun to her head. "Who are you?" His grip around the pistol tightened. "Who are you!" He took a step foreword, bringing the firearm less than a meter from her face. Darious took Zoe's hand. She made eye contact with him and then looked back at the contract killer.

With her throat choked up she said, "I am Zoe, and he is Darious."

The three stood for a long while, not moving, not saying anything. Several tears were making their way down Zoe's cheek. The mercenary's nostrils flared, and his lips curled as if he was beginning to smell something foul...

⊷⊶

...something undeniably foul. Within Kappa, his top-notch military training was being sidestepped by a sensation he had not felt in a long time. Something was not right; this was all too rotten, like kipple. He could feel his eyes began to squint, producing an outward glare and an inward one too. Verve. Nerve. Adventure. These were the three words which had resonated within him all the way back to his youth. At night his grandfather would recite stories of fantastic voyages from Earth-1. In almost all, some lone explorer or captain had uttered these words. It was the motto of the greatest men who had ever lived.

These were the three reasons why he'd left his homeworld years ago. They had stoked his own voyages from one end of the galaxy to the other, after which he had joined the Copper Force, with still enough steam to be installed in their elite division. Those three words had faded; the spark had faded.

That particular word 'adventure,' it was such an underused word these days, practically forgotten. He himself had not heard it in years. A tiny ember ignited in his soul, the likes of which had been not felt since those daring days. He teased the trigger of his cobalt six-shooter, but did not apply any pressure to it. The renewed flames of that deep yearning began to warm his entire being.

⚒ ⚒

"Bah!" he said suddenly, ending the stalemate. The cowboy spun the gun around his finger and holstered it. "Zoe and Darious, you say?" His facial muscles relaxed; his rigid stance loosened. The cowboy held out a hand to shake. With a big smile he said, "I'm Kappa."

Zoe and Darious burst out sobbing. Zoe nearly crumpled to the floor but Darious had wrapped his arms around her and was holding her tight. It took several minutes before their tears subsided. Kappa stood unobtrusive the entire time, though he wore an even wider smile than before. To Zoe it looked a bit awkward on him, a man of his stature and composition, grinning like a boy with a new speeder bike. She let the last of her sniffles cease and slowly shook his hand. Darious did likewise, albeit a bit more cautiously.

"Ha-ha!" shouted Kappa and grasped both of their bodies, pulling them in and giving them a giant hug. He squeezed them and nearly lifted them from the floor. Releasing his grip, he bent down slightly to be at eye level with Zoe. "So, Miss Zoe, adventure you say?"

Zoe looked at him, still somewhat tense, but her mind had soon rationalized enough of the new, unexpected state of things and she began to ease.

"Yes, Mr. Kappa, care to join us?"

Kappa simply beamed. Soon a smile born of relief began from Zoe and she could see the slightest evidence of one from Darious. She knew he was thinking the same thing as her. Their brush with the contract killer of the stars, the mercenary of death, was over.

CHAPTER 36

A SOMEWHAT GOOD
MAN GOES TO WAR

There was a momentary crackling of the phone communicator before the other end picked up.

"This is Mr. Achan's office. Mr. Achan is not in right now."

"This is Kappa."

All traces of enthusiasm dissolved from the secretary. "One moment please."

Kappa patiently held the phone and breathed with slow rhythmic breaths. The call crackled once more.

"Kappa," said a gruff, seething voice. "Status?"

"I'm in the MICA-10 Sector."

"Status?" asked Mr. Achan, in a more indignant tone.

Kappa held the silence as long as he could until he sensed the transceiver's speaker was about to detonate.

"Sir," said Kappa, "the two have proven to be quite the hunt." He let in another long pause and then added, "Sir, I have never failed a mission... yet."

Static rained from the phone. "If you fail," said Mr. Achan with a primal growl, "I will send a hundred ships from the CF to cleanse those two. I will have them condemned as terrorists and drowned in whatever rat hole they are hiding in. And then, I will do the same to you."

"Ah. Mr. Achan, I am glad you will not have to go to such great lengths. I am pleased to report that both subjects have been terminated with active prejudice."

"Good. Fucking good," said Mr. Achan with grizzly pleasure. "Payment will be sent as usual. You keep your head low."

The call abruptly ended. Kappa turned off the transceiver and put it back in his pocket.

⊱❦❦⊰

Zoe was staring wide eyed.

"Now we know what he's willing to do," said Kappa. Zoe continued to stare bewildered. "Miss Zoe? What is it?"

"That's Achan! Alfred Achan!? That's the man that wants us dead!? I was in his office!"

"You sure were," replied Kappa coolly.

"Oh man! If I had known that, I would have at least broken a lamp or something."

"Ha ha!" bellowed Kappa. "I like your spirit. Trust me, just you being there rankled him enough. Now, where do we stand?"

"You killed Dr. Saknussemm," said Zoe bluntly.

"Yes. There is no undoing that. I am very sorry for my prior actions."

"And Captain Henry?" asked Zoe, cringing.

"Uh, no, ma'am. I have never killed any Captain Henry." Kappa leaned against the alley wall and sighed. "If I had a cigarette, I'd sure offer ya'll one and have one myself too."

"Dr. Saknussemm was innocent in all this. Pantheon Industries twisted his identity like they are ready to do to you and I," said Zoe.

"I understand. I understand to the fullest extent. I am sorry for Doctor Saknussemm and I am prepared to do what it takes to recompense for my wrongdoings."

It was Zoe's turn to sigh. She took Darious' hand and the pair stared in silence at Kappa.

"It will take some time," she said.

Kappa nodded. "Whatever it takes." He tipped his brimmed hat forward. "I am grateful for your amity. I, Kappa, offer myself to your cause. Whatever that cause may be. May I ask, what is the cause?"

This time, Zoe put out her hand for him to shake, which he fervently accepted. Kappa then offered his hand to Darious.

"Sir," said Darious, bowing slightly and accepting the shake.

"So," said Zoe, beginning to walk around in a circular pattern while staring at the stone floor, "Pantheon—they manufacture and sell, though countless subsidiaries, Kapteyn. Kapteyn, as you probably know, enables superluminal flight. It's in all of our ships. Pantheon Industries has the complete market hold over it."

"Yup," said Kappa leaning back against the wall and adjusting his hat.

"Here's the kicker, we have evidence there is something else going on regarding the stuff. Something hidden."

Kappa eyed her with interest.

"When I 'disappeared' a piece of your craft, it may have disappeared to us, but it's actually still there, existing in a higher reality than ours, that is, in a higher vibrational stable-state. There is no doubt that Pantheon knows of this, and has for some time. They had hired Dr. Saknussemm some time ago to crack this egg. There is something in there. Something that they are willing to murder people to keep a secret, yet they seem to want it destroyed and it's all tied together by Kapteyn. We are simply trying to get to the bottom of all of this."

"I see," said Kappa. He spit on the floor and stood up from the wall. "Well Miss Zoe and Mister Darious, I will help however I can. I will atone for silencing your friend and all I have done to you."

His sincerity, though untested, did bring some closure for Zoe. This was one outcome she had not foreseen when he first had them cornered. They now had an ally. Together, maybe they could find out what Pantheon was really up to.

Kappa leaned back against the wall and continued, "To make sure the right foot goes in the boot, I may have certain skills to help. As I've told you, I worked for the Copper Force. I was part of their Hyper-Security Division. Sometimes we saw things, never anything to do with Kapteyn or disappearing things mind you, but nonetheless things that were intriguing to a simple guy like me. Anyhow, I had joined for the adventure, but everything always became political."

"You should have been a scientist," Zoe interposed.

"Naw. Too mind-numbing. After my second-round contract with the CF was up, I retired and went private. I've been working for Pantheon almost exclusively for some years now, mostly rustling up people or uncooperative businesses, but as you know, sometimes the assignment is... more than that. I suppose today, I retired again. No more bridle for me."

"Well Kappa, we are glad to have you on board," said Zoe.

"Indeed," said Darious with a nod. "What are we to do now?"

"I don't know if you noticed Darious dear," replied Zoe, "but my ship is in no way flight-capable. The main spoiler has been nearly bent in half, struts are dead, half a dozen systems require complete overhauling, the—"

Kappa sprung from the wall. "Hey, ya'll are in luck! We are, after all, in trader nation. All you'll need to fix up your ship is right here, and then some. Plus, I have a credit pass here, courtesy of your buddy Achan, now loaded with mula. What do ya say? This one's on me."

"Kappa! Thank you!" exclaimed Zoe galvanized. She smoothed out her electric comportment. "It will also give us time to plan out our next step."

"Sounds good," said Kappa. "I also need make some repairs to my craft after the hell you've put it through. I tell ya what, I have never met a girl with more spunk than you, Zoe."

CHAPTER 37
OUT OF THE FRYING DEATH RAY INTO THE SUN

The Magister sat in Mr. Achan's guest chair with his emerald robe draped around its curves like the ethane falls of Titan. The robe, an ornate green garment with gold cuffs, was nearly the same hue as the Magister's skin and nearly as imperial as his voice. He held himself while flicking out the foot of his crossed leg every so often. His gaze slowly turned to the silk curtains and he eyed them with pompous displeasure.

"I am of the opinion," he began patronizingly, "that those curtains are ill-fitting with the decor of this office. They come down in long straight lines, affronting the canvas above and the curves of this desk. The lines are all wrong." Mr. Achan, already sitting very straight at the head of the desk, sat straighter still. "Don't you think?"

"Why yes, now that you say it," replied Mr. Achan, setting aside the speakerphone he had just been using.

"Ah!" said the Magister. "See. All the same—spineless." He stood up, rewrapping the robe around his plump body and tucking it in around his arms. It seemed to pour down from him.

One sleeve was momentarily caught upon a gold brooch on his chest, but he easily shrugged it off. "The man you were just talking to, how loyal is he to you?"

"Very."

"No," the Magister sternly corrected Mr. Achan. "Your bounty hunter is no longer in your service. We both listened to the same phone call, but we heard two very different exchanges." He stared again at the silk curtains. "All the same. In fact," he walked over to the closed door of the office, "your service to the Magistrate is no longer needed."

"Sir?" asked a meek Achan, like a snake upon crossing paths with a mongoose.

The Magister's voice intensified. "Your service to Pantheon Industries is no longer needed." His face flushed with power and pink showed through his jade skin. The Magister's breathing soon evened out. His expression settled, and he locked eyes with Achan. "The entire situation is no longer in your hands. I will now deal with it personally. You have done enough; your risked exposing too much. You..."

The Magister seemed to lose enthusiasm for the subject and moved closer to the office door. He knocked on it just once and it promptly opened. A man of healthy proportions in a spectacularly polished suit came in. The Magister placed a fatty hand on his shoulder.

"This is your replacement."

Achan stood up abruptly. The man pulled out a small sidearm and shot Achan in the chest. Crimson blossomed from Achan's own perfect suit and he fell backwards.

"All the same," remarked the Grandeur as he adjusted his robe and left the room.

It was several days into repairs and Zoe thought they were making fantastic progress. Kappa was true to his word and didn't spare a single credit on repairing their crafts. More than that, he'd hired a local crew to help and had bought additional upgrades for Zoe's ship. Every day he was offering something new. Darious was coming around too. Several times she saw the two laughing. It was such a relief to stop running and to have a chance to gather up her thoughts.

Darious was taking a break under the wing of her ship, avoiding the hot noon sun. He no longer wore his hoodie, instead, opting for a fit white shirt. Zoe wasn't complaining. She took a seat on the dirt next to him.

"So, Mister, how goes it?"

He swallowed a big bite of his hot sauce-smothered sandwich. "It goes very well. We just finished up on the sinuous boosters. We will be test firing them this afternoon."

"Great. I just installed that new theta amplifier Kappa brought over from the market."

She watched the workers laboring around them. Lifts were attached to the thrusters and cables ran from her ship to diagnostic machines. Components and tools of all sorts were scattered about. She stared outward and shielded her eyes as a desert wind rose and swept across them. They had been towed to the outskirts of town, the best place for open work on the two custom vessels. Beyond were desert dunes, baked by the sun and echoed as far as the eye could see. Zoe shifted her gaze back to Darious' sandwich.

"Mind if I take a bite?"

"By all means." He handed it to her and she took a large mouthful.

"Iffs weally good," she said chewing.

Zoe swallowed it all down and coughed once. Leaning back on the soil, she looked over at Kappa's craft parked alongside hers. The Drak-9's engines were being completely stripped down and rebuilt. Kappa was on top of his ship, carrying a large pipe when he chanced to spot Zoe watching him. She waved to him. He tossed the part into a junk bin and jumped down from the craft.

"Sure is a hot one," Kappa said taking off his hat and brushing the dust from it. He dropped to a sitting position, opposite Zoe and Darious. Pointing to her ship with his hat he asked, "What do ya call your vessel?"

"Um," said Zoe. "I usually call it 'ship.' Or sometimes 'spaceship' or ..."

Kappa looked stunned. "You call it 'ship?' Surely you could have named it something more imaginative. Like..." He paused, and his eyes widened as if some cosmic revelation was about to be spoken. "Starchild." He brought up his hands with spread fingers. Kappa's expression quickly turned flat as he stared at the faces of his dull audience.

Zoe smirked. "What hippy planet did you fly off from?"

Kappa puffed for a moment like a newly blown out candle and cooled. "Think of a good name. It's important ya know." He stood up and began to walk away when Zoe suddenly jumped to her feet.

"That's it!"

He spun back around with a surprised look.

"That's it!" Zoe repeated, full of excitement. "I know how we can find out what Pantheon is hiding! Come on! Come on!"

She heaved Darious up and quickly made her way up the new gangway with he and Kappa following.

Upon entering the main chamber, Zoe tugged open a drawer and an old monitor unfolded from it. She fumbled behind the screen, pulling out a physical keyboard. She blew the dust from it and held it up.

"That?" asked Kappa. "That is what you are going to use to outsmart the multi-quintillion credit, galactic conglomerate of Pantheon Industries?

"Ones and Os baby," said Zoe, pulling up a chair and setting the keyboard on her lap. She flipped a switch behind the monitor. The screen turned blue. Lines of coding quickly scrolled upwards and then the screen went black. A white command prompt appeared in the upper left corner. It contained a single question.

Password?

"Turn your heads guys," said Zoe. She looked back and saw them staring. "I'm serious."

They did so, and she quickly typed out *'notsofastoryoullmissaletter'* and pressed enter on the mechanical keyboard. The monitor rolled through more pages of coding. At its end was a list of folders in alphabetical order.

"Okay gentlemen, you may look."

They turned and peered at the screen. Darious leaned in very close, reading through the listing.

"I do not understand Zoe. What is it?" he asked.

"This is the backbone to a program I scripted a couple years ago." Zoe looked at Kappa. "Let's call it Wiggles. Wiggles was too dangerous to keep on my ship's mainframe, so I decided best to keep it on an old computing machine. Nowadays no one even knows how to operate one of these bad boys. Pretty smart eh?"

Darious nodded.

"So, what is it Miss Zoe?" asked Kappa, standing straight and crossing his arms.

"It's basically a communication worm. It exists within a transmission—like a phone call or a download—pieced up within each data packet and acting as a whole where the communication's harmonic nodes exist. While pieced up, the worm has the appearance of the normally accepted corruption margins in interstellar communications and is thus ignored by the receiving ship. Now, I originally built Wiggles to duplicate information of a receiving ship's computer, but I can program it to do other things. You see, it's meant to copy and send back all those captured data bits in the same pieced up manner to one predetermined point—aka my ship. Once the data from the poor sap has been assimilated, the worm replicates on from that location, via the next transmitted signal. If it can't go anywhere, it simply shrivels up into nothing. At the end of the day, the worm is gone—no evidence—just sweet, sweet data gems. Though, I've only tried it with relatively close communications in a closed test, as I have to know the identifying protocol of each ship for the worm to move on."

"Alrighty," said Kappa. His expression led Zoe to believe it hadn't all sunk in. "I still don't see why ya keep it on this antique?"

"Well," she said, reminding herself of the tone Professor Kring often used with his pupils. "Imagine if this worm was sent out from a transmitter station capable of sending both high and low communications—say a CF broad communicator—and having a large catalog of buddy CF ships." Zoe put out her hands, mimicking a ship with each. "Buddy ships allow communications to and from other buddies, like a highway right to the heart of each ship. This happens in the background of all our communications networks; once your ship is allowed to talk to another, it's basically there. As far as anyone is concerned, it's an unbreakable technology; makes sense too because any extra burden—say eavesdropping—on a communication line is easily distinguishable and would be nulled by the ship. Not Wiggles. Wiggles is special. Wiggles can ride those waves and not be seen.

"Back to buddy ships; Wiggles gets transmitted out to buddies. It duplicates and is sent onward from those ships to more buddy ships and more ships. Any identified friend becomes another target for Wiggles. Now do you get it? I don't want to be responsible for accidentally hacking the entire galaxy. That's just a bit illegal. It's simply safer being tucked away."

"Son of a gun," said Kappa.

"Zoe," said Darious, "this program is very clever. However..." He paused but she motioned for him to continue. "However, isn't the program limited to a vector of transmission? In your example, the worm, I mean Wiggles, is sent by a CF ship to other CF ships and so on. This could potentially be crippling for the CF, which is more than reason enough to have this program separate from any computer capable of communicating, as you have done, but I believe it would stop there. Once Wiggles has exhausted a friend registry, it is done. My thought is Wiggles could possibly penetrate a portion of the galaxy, but thankfully hacking the 'entirety' of the galaxy would require a good deal more ships, id est, many that are non-CF associated and independent."

Zoe smiled throughout his irrefutable ratiocination. "Young Padawan, I have trained you well. So, you're saying I would have to have a friend list of nearly every ship, CF or not, in the galaxy to pull off such a feat? Well, as it turns out, I do." Darious and Kappa both stared at her. Zoe had to work hard to keep her eagerness contained. "When Kappa mentioned names, I remembered that I have such a list. While I was in Achan's office, I saw on his computer the many, many companies operating under Pantheon with regard to Kapteyn, including records of all the ships manufactured with the stuff—records of each's internal identifier." Zoe looked at Darious and Kappa. "I downloaded the database when I was there. Practically every ship everywhere is manufactured with Kapteyn and we have each's identifier. We can target all of these ships! I'm talking about millions of ships!"

"And where will that get us? Besides on the Copper Force's shit list?" asked Kappa.

"Instead of using Wiggles to capture computer data, I will load it with a sensor feedback routine to find matches of that harmonic Dr. Kring was able to identify—with some tweaking. I am confident I can have it just focus on objects in the higher energy stable-state space. Each ship will simultaneously scan its local region for such readings. All that data will then come back to us and we will basically have a galactic map of that higher resonant version of space, more importantly—of what's in it."

"I believe I understand," said Darious.

Kappa still had a blank expression, so Zoe continued, "We currently have a tool to search for matter that has spent time in that odd form of space, thanks to Dr. Kring, who I do believe you have met." Kappa gave a slightly sheepish look. "We were recently at the Copper Ephemeris Station searching for such signatures, but their data had all been edited.

"I am proposing, instead of searching for things that have been pulled out of the higher resonant space, I'd like to make a map of everything in it, get a good picture of what's going on in there. I am confident I can modify Dr. Kring's work to accomplish this. Having Wiggles securely send back the information to my ship won't be a problem either. Kappa, this is the only way to get real-time, real data."

"Okay," began Kappa, walking around the cabin, "but you would have to be able to send the transmission out on all communication frequencies. And plenty of those are secured CF."

"Yup," replied Zoe. "All we need to do is access a top-level CF craft with the transmission clearances coving all possible vessels. The transmission can simply be a CF system test alert, or something like that, with Wiggles wrapped up inside of it. Once the worm is sent out, I suspect it will take a day or so for it to gather the data and send it all back. My ship will then auto-compile all those little mapping bits."

"Wow," said Darious. "An entire model of an invisible galaxy within our galaxy."

"Yes! Then we shall see what Pantheon is up to and what is going on, once and for all."

Just then, Kappa paused from his pacing. "And just what are you expecting to find in this 'invisible galaxy?'" he asked.

Zoe looked at him but did not answer.

Darious blurted out, "Possibly aliens."

"Aliens?" repeated Kappa flatly.

Zoe stood up, facing Kappa. "Yes," she said, in a tone with space-cold seriousness.

"Ah. Okay then," said Kappa, and he continued pacing.

Darious put an arm on Zoe's shoulder. "How are we going to access a top-level CF ship?"

"That part I'm not sure—," she began, but Kappa cut in.

"And what if these aliens are malicious; a threat to humanity?"

Zoe turned to him. He stood motionless, staring at her. It was difficult for her to read him. "Well," she began, "I suppose, if there are indeed aliens, they aren't too bad, considering they prefer to stick to a higher, invisible state and would have done so for the entire existence of humanity. But if Pantheon, and possibly the CF, have been exploiting them, or worse, as Pantheon's archives allude to, have plans to destroy them, then we have a duty intervene. Anyhow, that's one theory."

"I see. I've never seen or heard anything 'bout aliens. But hey, there is a first time for everything. If you think Wiggles will get the job done, then I'm in." Kappa tipped his hat upward. "For the communications link you're talking about, you'll need access to a Copper Force Galaxy-Class Regency Station. It's not too easy getting on one of those. The way I see it, you will need two things to get onboard." Kappa staunched his stance and lifted a finger. "First, you'll need a disguise, something like a CF technician. I'm sure ya'll can whip something up."

Zoe nodded her head. She liked where his mind was at.

"And the second?" asked Darious.

"The second," he said, lifting another finger and making a 'V,' "A distraction." Kappa smiled that great big smile of his.

"A distraction?" asked Zoe.

"Oh yes. The more eyes turned away from you, the better your chances will be. ...Oh, and the Slough Force Shield of the Regency Station will have to be disabled. Once that's done, their breeches will be so knotted up they'll be barking for maintenance. That's when you slip onboard."

"How do you suppose we accomplish such a distraction while terminating the shielding?" asked Darious.

"Leave that to me." Kappa's smile never faded. "I've given a lot of blood and sweat for the CF. I've done some things for them that I'm not too proud of. It's about time I made a little hell for 'em."

CHAPTER 38

I'M A FAN OF THE DOPPLER EFFECT

Kappa twirled the sonic riveter in his hand and looked his craft up and down, admiring the work that had been completed. In just one week, his ship had been fully restored. It looked brand-spanking new. He put the riveter in the chest with the other tools and motioned for a worker to pack it with the rest of the outbound carts.

The head of the crew came up and spoke a couple words in that trader slang, nearly too garbled to understand. Kappa nodded and held out a hand to shake with a large bonus in it. The supervisor hungrily went for it and when his hand contacted Kappa's, Kappa stiffened his grip on the little man and pulled him in close.

"You've done a good job," Kappa said lowly. "And I've overpaid." He clamped down harder. "You never saw any of us."

The supervisor nodded in agreement with a smile and a strained eye. Kappa instantly let go and grinned. "Well then, off you go."

The supervisor whistled, and he and his entire team piled into their transport craft with a dozen tow rigs of equipment behind them and were off toward the city. Kappa smirked and shook his head as they drove off. He turned and spotted Zoe admiring her own craft.

"Zoe," he called.

She came over, wiping oil from her hands with a rag. Kappa surveyed her ship.

"The ships look damn good."

"Oh ya," Zoe replied.

Darious, having just showered off, joined them and the three stood watching the setting sun gleam across the vessels.

"So, what's with this?" asked Zoe, pointing to the large black bars spread horizontally across the hood of Kappa's ship. Two considerable spikes pointed outward from either side of the assembly.

"Rammin' plate," replied Kappa.

"Oh?" asked Darious. "For what purpose?"

"For ramming. Made from the hardest stuff available. Should get the job done."

"Darious, better not to ask," said Zoe.

Kappa placed himself between the two and put a brawny arm around each's shoulder. "It looks like we're all set here, folks. Everythin' else in order?"

"Ya," said Zoe. "The CF maintenance vessel you found is waiting for us at the local spaceport. Darious and I had a chance to check it out. It'll do the job. We have some jumpsuits ready to go too, CF logo and all. As for you, Kappa—"

"As for me, I'll be at the Regency Station that Darious located, stir up some trouble and skedaddle before ya'll arrive."

"Yes sir," said Zoe. "Be safe out there."

She motioned for Darious.

"Goodbye Mr. Kappa," said Darious, offering a genial hand.

Kappa shook Darious' hand and then Zoe gave him a hug. Kappa thought to himself, *she's a great gal. It's an honor to work with someone of her caliber.*

They saddled up into their respected vessels, Kappa with a course plotted directly for the Regency Station while Zoe would be traveling to the nearby hangar. As Kappa's ship sealed tight with a hollow thud, he took to the pilot's seat and pre-fired the thrusters. He looked over at Zoe's cockpit. She was busy at the controls and soon he heard the second ship's thrusters ignite.

As the two vessels slowly lifted from the ground, the thrill of the hunt began rising through Kappa's body. *Oohrah!* He tried prying open the port window. The magnetic lock held firm but then he remembered the switch underneath it. Kappa flipped it and the window swiveled outwards. He stuck out his torso and roared with clenched fists in the air. Zoe likewise made a muscle from within her craft. He pulled himself back in as gusts of wind became overwhelming. With the sensation of that fire burning deep in his soul, Kappa gnarred and centered his sights on the invisible pole star.

"Let's do this."

He pushed his ship's accelerator forward. Thrusters erupted, sending a booming shockwave through the atmosphere. His ship quickly lifted up and beyond the confines of the trading world. Soon the vessel crossed through the black dawn and was rocketing among the stars. Kappa's grip was steadfast on the controls; his mind was level and focused.

Kappa looked down at the readout for his destination; ETA was less than two hours. Already, his long-range scanners were picking up throngs of crafts around the central brute. He figured he'd first disable a few of the outer CF ships, grabbing the fleet's attention, before setting his sights on the bigger fellows. This was going to be one hell of a ride.

An hour and a half later, Kappa slowed his vessel as he came into view of the CF fleet with the Regency Station at its nucleus. Swarms of ships circled around it while smaller clusters monitored the perimeter in highly coordinated patterns. Immediately his ship was hailed. He ignored it, instead pulling his brimmed hat low and setting his gaze on an outer group of pint-sized CF crafts.

Multiple warnings and hails flashed across his screen. He entered further into the military space. A warning shot flashed across his port bow. The green plasma bolt shined brilliantly for a moment and then evaporated.

"Well that didn't take long."

Kappa's ship began counting up the multitudes of weapons locks on it. Kappa flipped several switches at his side and engaged the power-plus mode of his craft. Two joysticks popped up from the console. Kappa fired the main booster once for a burst of speed and spun forward, cutting just behind a small CF craft. He squeezed the left trigger, sending a blue wave of light out to the craft. Its little engine sparked and went out. The ship rolled over onto its belly, rendered harmless.

"Ha! They don't make 'em like they used to!"

He gyred his ship around the next one and performed the same maneuver. The continual hails to his vessel became a nuisance so he shut down the communication system. His circular tirade continued as he picked off ship after ship. He saw that several large CF cruisers had detached from their flight patterns and were heading toward him. He took out another group of small ships along his course and prepared to be intercepted by them.

A shot came from one of the cruisers. This time, it was not a warning. The searing red beam burned right through his starboard wing, but the damage was minor. Kappa quickly stabilized his ship and began spinning towards the large craft.

He definitely had their attention now. The full firing capabilities of the cruiser rained upon Kappa and he spiraled his ship through the plasma shots and missiles, continuing on toward his target.

A squad of small ships attempted to block his way.

"Not today guys," he said, pushing the accelerator down further and splitting the gap between them.

A small explosive projectile hit his right wing again, this time sending shocks throughout his ship, forcing Kappa to pull left with the joysticks to maintain his course. Plasma fire of all colors tore through space, all centered on Kappa.

"Yaw baby, yaw!"

He leaned forward in his chair, spurring his craft onward as fast as it would go. He was nearly upon his final target, a giant space-carrier vessel and also a key-commanding vessel to the locks of the Regency Station. A dire warning spread across his digital display.

Impact Imminent

Just mere seconds away from collision with the enormous ship, Kappa flipped a switch above him. He crossed his arms and took in one last deep breath. His ship plowed into the CF carrier, horns first. It cleft through the exterior hull and burrowed deep into the craft before coming to a halt. In the process of the collision, the interior of Kappa's craft had erupted into a flurry of ballooning coils, protecting the cargo within.

Kappa coughed and strained to focus his sight. Momentarily, reality came back in its fullest abstraction. He tore away at the deflating bags and looked out of the windshield. Through the scoring on it he could see his ship had stopped halfway through a large corridor and a couple of fires were burning. There were pulsing red lights along the hallway; probably alarms were ringing too but all he could hear were those in his ears. Kappa performed a quick diagnostic of his ship's systems. All in all, the damage was quite minimal; he'd be able to reverse and fly out once his work was done.

Kappa drew out a bandana from under his shirt and pulled it up over his nose. He opened the exit door and looked around the corridor. It was full of debris but clear insofar of opposing forces. A mighty wind rose in him and the kindling in his eyes ignited. He clenched his fists and held up both arms, hardening his muscles to the point of cementation. Kappa started marching forward and took a huge breath in.

"For...," his words and his steps stumbled. "My hat?!" he cried. He frantically looked about and spotted it on the ground. He propped it on his head. "For Leeroy Jenkins!"

Kappa ran with a mighty yell onto the CF carrier. He recalled from memory the general layout of such ships and quickly began making his way through its corridors. His cloak flapped behind his fleet-footed steps. Along the upper edges of each wall, lights continued flashing. Speakers crackled overhead, and the occasional numeric order was sent out through them.

Kappa rounded a corner and instantly dove back upon seeing a line of soldiers kneeled with rifles pointing down the corridor, right at him.

"Surrender!" a voice shouted.

Kappa leaned against the wall and pulled out a sidearm from his cloak. He peeked around the corner, spotting the corporal behind the blockade of troops. He pressed a button next to the trigger, charging up the gun. A single ding sounded from it. Kappa flung out from around the corner, gun blazing. A dozen or so shots came from Kappa before just two had been discharged from the opposing force. He had aimed low, hitting the crouching soldiers in the legs. Their shots had entirely missed him.

As the troops toppled, unraveling the cover of the corporal, Kappa raised the gun to the man's face and calmly said, "Surrender?" with a pitied look.

The squad corporal, a man of slender build with a long nose, stood agape. Kappa walked the few steps to him and smacked him on the forehead with the butt-end of his pistol. The corporal fell with a slump alongside his moaning, injured soldiers. Kappa snickered and resumed his sprint past them.

He followed the metal conduits on the ceiling toward the ship's main bridge, soon coming upon a guarded door with two soldiers on either side. They raised their guns as soon as they saw him, but he dispatched the two with posthaste. He used the badge from one to open the magnetic door. It slid to the side, revealing a room of a dozen waiting troops. With instincts built from training, he dove in right amongst the thick of them and popped up, brutally under-cutting the nearest soldier with a closed fist. Chaos erupted in the room as soldiers broke from their positions and strived to stop the intruder without shooting or hitting one another. Kappa was a flur-ry of fists, head butts, and kicks. Soldier after soldier was dropped by his might while he dodged and rolled away from oncoming attacks. One trooper pulled out a large serrated knife. Kappa grabbed him by the arm and flung him at another man who was slowly getting to his feet after a severe blow to the head. The two soldiers fell flat and attempted to get up. Kappa initiated a single kick, hitting one's head into the other, which bounced off the wall and rebounded back into the first soldier like a Newton's cradle, knocking both men out.

Kappa stood at the center of the pile of unconscious soldiers. He surveyed his work and ran to the opposite door. Past it, he judged he was getting very close to the ship's bridge as the walls had a slightly shinier glean and the floor was well polished. While making his way down the curving corridors, he took out two more guards, knocking each out even before they could raise a firearm or a finger at him.

Kappa slowed and silently crept to the large entryway for the bridge. He stopped just before it and peered around the corner. A single guard was standing at attention in front of the doorway.

He marked Kappa and in a single quick motion had raised his rifle. Kappa ducked back just as a shot split the air. There was shouting, but Kappa paid it no mind. He peeked back around the corner and two more shots rang out. One grazed his shoulder. He backed against the wall, wincing in pain. Upon a quick inspection, he saw it was just a minor flesh wound.

Anger started building within Kappa. Instead of the wound weakening his resolve, it enhanced him, enraged him. He ran out from the corner bellowing obscenities. The soldier flinched, missing a key opportunity to stop the intruder. That half-second was all that Kappa needed. He was momentarily upon the soldier, roughly tackling him to the floor and rendering him unconscious.

"Ha," Kappa breathed from under the bandana.

Kappa took the man's badge from his uniform and stood up. He withdrew his two large firearms from their holsters at his sides and pressed the badge to the door.

Hell was waiting for him within. Kappa's eyes widened as he saw the senior officers already poised and readied with weapons raised at the open door—at him. Kappa dodged to the side of the doorway, avoiding the barrage of gunfire. Smoke filled the entrance as plasma bolts melted the walls around it. About thirty seconds after, the gunfire ceased. Kappa waited motionless with his pistols at the ready. Several men called out. He did not answer.

Kappa took a quick peek through the entryway and the gun blasts surged again. One caught the tail of his cloak, instantly burning it black.

"Oh, hell naw," declared Kappa, looking down at it as gunfire continued to bear down on his position.

Kappa's eyes narrowed to small slits. The entire area was charred black and still plasma blasts continued to impact deeper into the burnt structure. As soon as the shots once more subsided, Kappa raised his guns and in one motion dove in front of the aperture, aiming his pistols mid-leap, and fired a single round from each.

The two plasma shots hit their mark, igniting the central console into fiery brimstone. A new alarm wailed on the bridge as vacuum systems autonomously worked to expunge the fire. Kappa utilized this moment of discord, while officers shuffled around to avoid being either burnt or windswept, to leap into the room. A few shots flew in Kappa's direction, but the majority of the officers were unprepared. Kappa was quickly upon the closest, giving him a firm punch to the gut and knocking the air from him. As the man was in the process of bending downward, Kappa used his own momentum to turn with the man, creating a human shield. The gunfire immediately stopped, except for one last delayed shot, which hit the asphyxiated man in the midsection. Kappa, holding the officer with one arm, brought up a pistol over his shoulder and began firing. He turned from target to target around the room, hitting each in various limbs, and sending all to the ground. His aim was true enough; in just a few seconds he had dispatched the entire room.

Kappa then quickly went around the bridge, knocking all those out who still presented any possible threat. He proceeded to drag all of the officers out of the room. Kappa saved the commander for last. He was outfitted in a silver uniform with many pins about the breast and shoulders. Kappa pulled the badge from his collar and flung him out of the room with the others, sealing the door behind him.

Kappa looked around the now empty bridge. Though the red flashing lights continued, a calm had entered the control room. On the floor, a dozen trails of blood led to the closed door. The walls were charred black from gunfire. He looked out of the excessive viewing window, presenting an imposing forward view of space. Kappa was completely surrounded by CF crafts. They had set up a giant blockade around him with countless ships.

Kappa sat in the commander's seat, a lavish chair centered in the bridge with a control module on either armrest. Kappa put the commander's badge on his collar. He was now in charge of this steed and free to pilot it as he wished. With two hands on the control consoles, he quickly set about powering up all of the carrier's weapons. He scrolled through the list, checking off entire categories of armaments.

"Thirty aft 30-centimeter phaser cannons. Forty-five 45-centimeter quad cannons. One hundred 10-meter plasma mortars. Scalar torpedoes. Boltzman multipliers..."

In minutes, he had over 1,000 weapons of the CF carrier under his command. They were located all along the exterior of the gigantic craft, capable of targeting enemies at any angle. He set each to fire in a circular pattern at random intervals. Kappa grinned and pressed '*Enter*.'

The result was amazing. A lightshow of gunfire shot out from the vessel. Plasma beams and artillery shells fired randomly in all directions. CF ships broke from their formations, attempting to dodge the chaotic gunfire. Kappa saw several even collide with each other.

"Amateurs," he muttered.

With the confusion outside fully in motion, Kappa went to work using his new rank to disengage the Slough Force Shield around the Regency Station and remove as much of its secondary encoding allowable in hopes of unbalancing the system and frying some relays to give Zoe and Darious more time. When the computer asked him to confirm his order, Kappa affirmed with a bang of his great fist on the '*Enter*' button. The shield dissolved and went completely offline. He smirked as he thought how such an armada as this, when just a bit perturbed, could become such a muddled mess.

Next, Kappa prepared the carrier's weapons for a focused burst directly forward. The spinning turrets swiveled dead ahead and fired in unison. CF ships scrambled to get out of the way and in doing so created a clear path for Kappa. He punched the thrusters to maximum, blasting forward and away from the Regency Station, with the entire CF fleet following right behind his spurs.

CHAPTER 39

COLD WAR

Zoe had synced her lightcard to the CF maintenance ship's meager speakers and her bass music—upbeat battle tunes for the occasion, echoed through the craft. Darious was in the copilot's seat, reading a textbook he had brought along. He paused his reading and looked over at Zoe who was playing a game on the console.

"Zoe?"

"Yes, Darious?" she did not look up from the rows of ships she was blowing away with pixilated fury.

"The program we are set to install on the CF Regency Station..."

Zoe diminished the game and looked over at him. She could see he was in an introspective mood and recognized his concerned expression.

"The program," he tried again. "It is no doubt ingenious. It is a perfect marriage of your resonance physics skills and your love of coding. However, I feel sometimes, we as humans can dig wells too deep for our thirst of knowledge and risk exposing the hellfire beneath."

"Well said," Zoe responded.

He tapped gently on the console. "I understand the worm's necessity for our current use. But beyond that, I am worried if it happened into the wrong hands, it could be utilized too easily for malevolent purposes."

"I agree with you. If programmed with other directives, it could send us into a galactic dark age. I should have dumped it a long time ago." She looked deep into his tattooed eyes. "Darious, after we are done here, I promise I will scrub it from the computer systems. It will be no more." She could see his expression ease. "Aw, it ain't no thing. And you're right. Thank you." She gave him a big smile. "So, Mister, how far out are we?"

He manipulated the console. "We should be arriving in a couple minutes."

"Good, just enough time to finish this level."

Soon enough they were upon the Galaxy-Class Regency Station. As it came into view Darious uttered his amazement. Zoe whistled.

"That is one large boat," she said.

The enormous CF station, shaped by a spherical hull, floated stationary in space. It glinted with a pearlescent silver sheen and dim green lights glowed from its many levels of windows. The station was completely by itself. Zoe reflected that there should be an entire fleet of vessels around it. The Regency Station was, after all, a galactic base of operations for the CF. Then a piece of spaceship debris passed by their bow.

"I dunno' what Kappa did here, but he seems to have gotten' the job done," said Zoe.

"Indeed," said Darious, reading from the console. "The shield is offline and according to the long-range scanners, this is the only vessel in the region."

Just then, they were hailed by the Regency Station. Zoe quickly accepted the call.

"Good day," she said. "This is CF 232-C repair ship. We have been instructed to fix an error associated with the security systems of the station."

"Good day, CF 232. Prepare to dock at gate 1 dash 23." The speakers crackled, and the voice added. "It's been a bit of a wild day for us here."

Zoe could only assume to what the traffic controller was referring to. She sailed the clunky maintenance craft to the Regency Station and let it auto-dock when they were within range. Zoe double-checked Wiggles the Worm on her lightcard and tucked it away in her shirt. Darious left the cockpit and returned with the two blue jumpsuits. He handed one to Zoe and zipped his up over his clothes. Zoe did likewise. She smirked upon noticing the large oil stain across the stomach.

The ship lightly rocked as it landed in the bay. Zoe flipped off the engines and grabbed a clipboard-style tablet from the captain's seat pocket.

"Shall we?" she asked Darious, who nodded in the affirmative.

They walked off the ship and were greeted by a single officer.

"Hello sir," said Zoe, saluting him. Darious copied her motions and the man saluted back.

"Good day." He undoubtedly noticed the markings on Darious and grimaced. Looking past them to the CF ship, his face turned even more sour. "Ma'am," he stated. "Your craft..." he walked over to it and peeled off a piece of flaking paint. "Your craft should be better maintained."

"Certainly sir," Zoe chirped. "We had been scheduled for a re-fit and were en-route when we received priority orders for security repairs on this station."

"I see. Please, follow me."

He turned on his heel and they followed him into the passages of the Regency Station. Despite the military air of the ship, the corridors were very broad and well-lit with glossy flooring that looked like metalized marble. It hardly seemed like a space-faring vessel at all. The Regency Station's numeric indications made little sense to Zoe. How had they gone from Section 101 to 193 by only passing through a dozen junctions? The officer could be leading them in circles for all she knew. She shrugged off the discombobulation sensation and sped up to be alongside the officer.

"Sir," she said, "when landing, we were informed there was some sort of hubbub recently."

The officer turned toward her and nodded. "There was an attack earlier."

"An attack!?" asked Zoe astonished. "On this station!?"

"The attacker was unable to penetrate into the station. Instead, he fled with the fleet in pursuit. I'm sure by now they have captured the anarchist."

"I've never heard of such a thing—an attack on a galactic station. A single attacker you say?"

"Yes, ma'am."

The officer pivoted and stopped abruptly in front of a metallic door. He saluted them, turned, and left. Zoe and Darious stared at the door.

"Well," said Zoe turning to Darious, "I suppose we're supposed to go through."

She pressed a button and the door slid open. The pair entered midway into a service corridor with many conduits along the walls. Zoo looked down one way then the other. It seemed to go on forever.

"Ugh. We don't have time to figure out where we need to be going."

A voice called out from behind them and Zoe turned to see a man jogging toward them. He wore a similar blue jumpsuit as them, though his was much more well-kept. As he approached, Zoe noticed the rank upon his chest—he was the head mechanic.

"Hello," he said with a quick salute. The head mechanic was a burly man with a full beard and mustache covering much of his face. "I was just informed you'd arrived. I'm surprised you came so quickly. The call went out for maintenance support only a hair ago." He looked at both of them. "Just you and a utility aid?"

"Yes sir," said Zoe.

"Well then, let's get started."

Zoe walked abreast with the mechanic through the maintenance corridor while Darious followed closely behind.

"What a day," the mechanic stated. "Would you believe it? Now the crazies are targeting CF bases. I've seen some things in my day, but nothing like this. Phew."

"Indeed? What happened?" asked Darious.

The mechanic turned back and gave him a dirty look and then responded to Zoe as if she had been the one to ask the question.

"I was told a single man in a single ship came through, flying right into a Stellar B8 Carrier. He then went about shooting up the place and took control of it. At the same time, our force shield went down. It was anticipated he was going to use the B8 to fire on the station, but instead he got wise and ran."

"Wow," said Zoe. "Those crazies."

"I just filed the report to get the shield up and running again. I guess you two must have been in the area. It looks like a dozen systems have been corrupted. Even the back-ups are down. No physical damage thankfully. Even still, I had asked for a full specialized shield team to support with repairs."

"Have no worries, we can fix it," said Zoe happily.

He eyed her skeptically, prompting her to pull up the tablet and type some notes onto it. They turned into a new corridor with brightly marked fuel lines.

"You looked a bit lost when I caught up with you."

"A bit," said Zoe.

"Ever been onboard a Regency station?" he asked.

"No," said Zoe.

"But, you have experience with CF Slough Force Shielding Systems?"

Zoe winced at her verbal error. "You see sir, ahem, we have been recently training at the Sector Ceta Command School. My coworker—aid—and I scored top marks with regards to shield programming. We're the ones for the job"

The mechanic did not respond, and they continued on for some time in silence. Eventually they came to an octagonal door with a control panel. The mechanic typed into it and the door opened, revealing a large room full of cabling under the grid floor. It was somewhat dark in the room. The majority of light came from the wall of computers and workstations.

The head mechanic sat before the largest computer console and logged onto it. He navigated to the shield sectors as Zoe and Darious looked on. Zoe handed the tablet to Darious and took a seat next to him. Using the console next to his, she began piggybacking from his work and soon surpassed him. About a half hour later, the mechanic leaned back in his chair and exhaled.

"My lady. You are certainly apt."

"It's all in the wrists," she said.

"'All in the wrists;' that's a good one. Every single new subroutine I look into, you've already repaired. You're far too quick for me." He swiveled in his chair toward her. "I suppose I was wrong about needing a team, you are a one-mechanic army. I can see I am of little use here. And it's not often I get to say that, so I guess you're one up on me."

Zoe jumped at the opportunity. "Would you mind getting me something to drink? I'm so parched I can barely think." She smiled as big as she could. "A cold water would be nice!"

"I too would like one," added Darious.

The mechanic nodded once in a stilted manner and left. Immediately, Zoe pulled out her lightcard and synced it to the workstation. With a few keystrokes, Wiggles began downloading in tiny bits, masked within the station's own data streams. The download took just one minute to complete.

"Annnd done," said Zoe, snapping up the lightcard from the console and tucking it back under her clothes.

The worm was now being transmitted over all channels, everywhere. It would take a day or so for the data of their invisible surroundings to be acquired and be transmitted all back to her ship. That was the thought anyhow. Zoe heard the mechanic's steps on the metal grating just as she was navigating backwards to the shield's programming section that she was supposed to be working on. He came in, holding a bottle of water in each hand. He sat next to Zoe and handed one to her and then drank from the other one.

"Thank you much," Zoe said. She gave the chilled bottle to Darious. "We are just about finished here. Just a couple more..." She faded off, typing into the console. "Ah. Finished." Zoe turned her chair around, facing Darius. "How's the water, Sir?"

He was about to respond but was interrupted by the mechanic.

"Done?!" the head mechanic looked at the console. "Shit! Miss, you are something else." He reviewed the diagnostic logs. "It all looks good. My regards to your instructors; I will have to put in a good word for you." He stood up and offered a hand to help Zoe up. "We could use someone of your talents onboard. Your designation?"

"I'm sorry?" asked Zoe.

"So that I may put in a good word for you."

"Oh." She laughed him off. "Not necessary, just doing my duty."

"Designation please." The niceties of the head mechanic's request fell away. Just then, the phone at his belt went off. He promptly answered it. "Yes sir."

Zoe could only make out incoherent murmurs from the other end.

"Yes sir," he repeated. The mechanic replaced the phone at his side. "The guys upstairs say everything looks good; all systems are back online."

Zoe simply bowed and ushered Darious to the door.

"Hey," she said, hoping to put another mental block in the mechanic's mind, "got any good tricks for getting a stain out of this thing?" She pushed out her paunch and pointed to the brown blob.

"Ha. Sure do," responded the mechanic. "Throw it away and grab a new one. Why waste time cleaning it?"

"Ah, good call," said Zoe.

The three began walking down the corridor. The mechanic was typing on his phone's screen and Zoe didn't attempt to stir up further conversation. As they rounded a corner, his phone rang again.

"Sir?" the mechanic spoke into it. He immediately straightened his stride. Zoe pretended not to notice, but put a nonchalant ear toward the call. An uneasy feeling began creeping up in her. "Sir. Yes Sir. Thank you, Sir." He put the phone back into its holster. "The Commander would like a word before you depart."

Zoe's blood ran cold. The Commander? The Commander of this colossal station with an entire fleet under his control? What could he want to say to her, a mechanic? 'Oh, thanks for fixing our ship?' Should they make a run for it now? Zoe swallowed her fear.

"The Commander," she said. "Our pleasure."

"I will take you there, as this is your first time here."

He guided Zoe and Darious through more never-ending corridors, finally ending at a lift. The trio entered in and it propelled them some three hundred floors up, to the highest point of the craft, where the Commander of the station and of the local fleet was waiting for them. The door slid open.

"Good day Miss," said the mechanic as he saluted them off.

Zoe and Darious slowly entered into the semicircle room with the lift doors closing behind them. It took Zoe a moment to take in the inspiring sight. The spacious bridge had two tiered rows of three seats and a larger seat elevated like a throne behind them, no doubt for the Commander. All the chairs were vacant, and a single man was standing at the control room's front, staring out of the single window that wrapped around half of the bridge. It was as if they were in a helmet and were given a visor's view of outer-space.

The Commander, wearing a grey uniform with hands placed at his back, turned when the elevator door clicked closed, revealing his neatly shaven face and authoritative eyes. His expression was hardy, though Zoe noticed his nose was quite pink. He began walking toward them, but stopped halfway, taking a handkerchief from his pocket and sneezing into it.

He sniffled loudly. "Excuse me."

"Sir," said Zoe.

She and Darious saluted him in unison. Without further acknowledgment, he passed by them and took a seat at the helm. Zoe gave Darious a quick awkward look. She turned to face the Commander.

"Sir?" she asked.

He sniffled and blew his nose again. "Excuse me. Please do come up."

They did their best to march like soldiers and then stood at his left side. For some time, the Commander did not speak, instead choosing to gaze motionlessly at space. He reminded Zoe of starry Vere. Perhaps all captains of the CF were a bit star struck.

"I was told you did a stand-up job repairing the Slough Field. It is much appreciated. After the fiasco we've had today, it is a bit of a relief."

"The head mechanic informed us of an attack earlier."

"Yes. An unusual one too. Nevertheless..." His voice seemed to doze off.

"Sir," started Zoe, letting curiosity get the better of her, "Where is the rest of your commanding company?"

He surveyed the bridge with a slow eye. "They all are aiding in the chase of that maniac. I just kept a skeleton crew here to manage Regency."

"I see," said Zoe. *Wow. Kappa must have stirred up quite the storm here.*

"I thank you for your concern."

"All for the CF, Sir."

"Yes," said the Commander as he gave her a short smile. Zoe felt comfortable enough with his tone to push the conversation into a new direction.

"Sir, may I pose a second question?"

"Yes Miss. You have secured my vessel faster than calculated. I am at your disposal."

"It has nothing to do with Slough fields, but rather with intangible integrity. In your opinion, Sir, would you say that the CF's integrity could ever be influenced or corrupted? I mean—"

One swift look from the Commander told her that he fully understood. He turned back to space and thought. Then, he stood up, regarding the stars beyond in more of an open manner, as if he was among his oldest friends. He spoke absolutely.

"The CF remains very compartmentalized at lower levels of service, for the integrity of its own personnel. Departments, though separately coordinated, have certain powers over one another to ensure a total system of checks and balances. Do you understand?" He looked at Zoe.

"Yes Sir."

"With that said, at higher levels, pieces tend to interlock, forming larger controlled assemblages with smaller controlling parties. It allows for a forward stream of orders than can be enacted swiftly. The higher you go, the broader the influence of the reduced party. Perfectly sensible. This is the correct system to have cohesive efforts with minimal possible wasteful outflows.

"However—," he sneezed into his handkerchief, "—excuse me. We may stop revolutions with cannons, but internally, no shots need to be fired. Politics and so forth. We do what we can, and we must trust the system. After all, there is balance throughout the galaxy." He again eyed her. "What prompted such an inquiry?"

"Oh, CF politics has always been a small fascination of mine. And it's not every day I get to speak with a Commander, Sir."

"Ah. I thought I had gone far beyond your question and your clone was giving you a hard time, so you were looking for some sound way to have him extinguished." He laughed, and Zoe smiled, but it was a completely hollow smile. The Commander sneezed and quickly pulled out his handkerchief.

"Excuse me." He sneezed once more. "This damn cold."

"Sir," Darious said, "the common cold, most likely a strain of the ubiquitous rhinovirus, requires rest. Hot chicken soup is recommended. I would additionally suggest a—"

"Ah-hem," Zoe cleared her throat, prompting Darious to abandon his medical rejoinder. "Commander, this is a magnificent vessel." She surveyed the amazing view of space in the same way he had. "And we thank you for your generosity in allowing us to be onboard the bridge with you. Thank you so much. With your dismissal, may we return to our vessel? We must attend to other duties, Sir."

The Commander returned the handkerchief to his pocket. "Certainly"

He saluted them, to which they reciprocated. As they entered the lift, he sneezed out loud once more.

"Damn cold!"

CHAPTER 40

SCUTTLE!

As they entered into the lift, Zoe couldn't help but feel a bit ill at ease. That vinous gut-feeling ate away at her stomach and dizzied her mind. She wasn't exactly sure why; the plan had worked and now the worm was being sent across the galaxy. They glided downwards, leveling off at the hangar floor where the maintenance vessel was parked. The lift door opened, and they entered into a long corridor.

"Straight ahead," said Zoe.

As they walked, Zoe was glad for the lack of personnel, though the vast emptiness was a bit creepy in such a large craft; perhaps that was why she had that disquieting feeling. At the entryway to the bay, Zoe paused. This was it; they had made it. The door slid to the side with the press of a button, revealing two waiting guards with rifles. Panic momentarily struck Zoe and she looked over her shoulder for a possible escape route.

"Ma'am," said one of the officers in a tone that confirmed this was not a coincidental encounter. She slowly turned back. Darious stood motionless. "Ma'am and clone, you are to be held, by the order of the Commander, under suspicion of illicit activities."

Zoe cringed. She then saw, over the two men's broad shoulders, several more soldiers exiting from the maintenance craft. Evidently, they had searched it. The officer who had spoken stepped through the doorway and glared down at Zoe.

"Nice and easy now, turn around."

He pulled out a pair of handcuffs. Zoe and Darious complied and their hands were bound behind their backs. Darious gave Zoe a defeated glance but she kept her own insecurities within.

"Follow me," said the soldier.

The other man took to the rear, blocking off any chance of escape. Zoe and Darious were led once more deep within the craft, down into its furthest pale caverns. Eventually, they stopped at a door which required the officer's authentication. Within was a large room with a control console at its center and four heavy metal doors on opposite walls. *Holding cells*, thought Zoe. She was prodded forward with a rifle as the officer opened one of the cells. When Zoe and Darious entered in, their bindings were removed.

"Sit there. Do not move."

The man pointed to a metal bench along the far wall. Zoe nodded, without saying anything. He closed the metal door, leaving Zoe and Darious sitting in the while-walled cell with no windows or any indication of what the future was holding for them.

"Zoe?" asked Darious in a strained voice.

"Shh. They may be listening." She then raised her voice. "We did our job repairing the Slough shield. I'm not sure why we are being held. Perhaps the military is not a fan of efficiency."

Just then the door opened, and the Commander entered in. The relaxed expression he had worn earlier was now gone and all Zoe could see was a man of anger. His eyes were narrowed, and only little black beads of lead shone through. The Commander closed the door behind him and held out a scanning device. He waved it up and down in front of Zoe and then did the same to Darious. It beeped once.

"I am confirming your identities," he said.

A second beep sounded from the device. He continued to fiddle with it and sneezed into his arm. Zoe looked at Darious and then back at the Commander. What could she do?

"Comman—," she began.

"Do not speak!" he bellowed. A third beep came from the device and his face turned from bitter to rotten. "You damn kids."

He turned on his heel and left, the door slamming shut behind him. Zoe could hear him yelling at the officers outside. He sounded livid. There were several 'Yes Sirs!' and then the noises died down. Soon it was all quiet. Several minutes passed by in complete silence.

"Darious, I'm so sorry." Zoe put a hand over his. "I am so, so sorry."

He looked at her with a somber face. His eyes pierced through her soul. Then everything went black.

A second later, the lights turned back on, though now with the addition of cyclic red flashes.

"What the?" asked Zoe, standing up.

"Zoe, what is this?"

"I have no idea."

Could it be Kappa? Was the station going into some sort of lockdown? Then a low siren began, shattering all of Zoe's thoughts, all except one.

"I know what that siren is. I know it."

She could feel her face go white.

"Zoe, Zoe what is it!?"

"The self-destruct mode of the ship has been activated. We need to get out of here."

"What!?" Darious exclaimed in pure astonishment.

Zoe ran to the door and quickly scrutinized its hinges and weld seams. There didn't seem to be any weak points or any electronic service panel to hack. She leaned on the door, putting an ear to it. To her amazement, it began to creep open. In his rage, the Commander must have forgotten to lock it! With both hands on the cold metal, she gently pressed it forward and peered out. Zoe then pushed the cell door fully open and bound into the room. It was empty. She looked back at Darious, stunned. He had the same expression upon his face. Zoe ran to the computer podium and quickly started into Regency's systems. It was as she already knew: the station was in an auto-destruct sequence. There was no way to stop it. She navigated through the station's files.

"Craaaap! The escape pods are all leaving. Everyone is abandoning ship." She delved deeper into the station's directives. "The auto-destruct, it didn't come from the Commander." She hurriedly typed. "It was remotely activated. The command came from up high... a dignitary... Magistrate high!"

"A dignitary? A dignitary did this?" asked Darious.

"No, not just any dignitary, someone from the Magistrate, the highest presiding dignitaries in the galaxy." Zoe thought for a moment, *it couldn't possibly be because of us; could it?*

"How much time do we have?"

Zoe continued typing into the console. "Nine and a half minutes. I'm locating an escape pod for us. ...there! Okay, mapping the quickest route now."

A map filled the screen with an orange line leading from their current position across a good portion of the Regency Station. It was mostly a straight shot. Zoe typed one last command, pre-igniting the escape pod, and grabbed Darious' hand. The two took off from the room and sprinted down the corridor.

The entire station was empty. Under the red flashing lights and sirens, Zoe and Darious ran, retracing much of their way, though soon diverging toward the escape pod. As they ran, Zoe pulled out her lightcard. *Two minutes left.*

"Faster!" she yelled, forcing her legs to alternate even quicker and ignoring the burning sensation in her chest.

Darious kept up, taking long strides alongside her. They rounded a corner and dashed down the next corridor, arriving at a lift. Zoe quickly accessed its controls and they were taken six stories up, emerging on the correct exit floor. Zoe looked at the time on her lightcard. Thirty seconds. They still had to cover nearly a kilometer to the awaiting pod.

"We're not going to make it," she breathed.

They started sprinting, but Zoe wavered. She began to feel heavy and at the same time as though she was coming undone. Without her ship, without any means to defend or evade, and without time; not even against Kappa had she felt such futility, like the surface of her being was crumbling away into an abysmal sinkhole. There was always something... something... nothing. Her hands felt numb. She tried balling them into fists, but that did not help. *This is it.* Zoe stopped running.

Darious, a few paces ahead, slowed to a jog and looked back.

"Zoe!" he called and ran back to her.

To Zoe, everything seemed so far away. She could hear his voice, but it seemed more like a specter's wail. She no longer felt the floor under her feet or the air around her. Nothing.

"Zoe!"

She slowly looked down at her lightcard. "Ten seconds," she whispered.

Darious grabbed her by the hand. "Zoe, we are getting out of here!" He cupped her face with both hands and brought his mouth close to hers. "Zoe!" She made no acknowledgement. "Zoe!" His tone was still exasperated but his eyes softened. "Zoe, I cannot live without you."

Darious then grabbed her hand and yanked her forward. His sudden heave freed Zoe from her stupor and propelled her forward. Together, they were again at a full sprint. When they had made it just halfway down the corridor, the low-pitched siren ceased.

From within the depths of the Regency Station, there was the sound like a metallic bar of epic proportions being bent. The ground shifted under their feet. Echoes of twisting metal resounded all around them, inducing the pair to run even faster.

An explosion boomed from the bowels of the station, warping the floor underneath them, and hurled them into the corridor's walls. Zoe scrambled to get up, but could only lurch forward as the air had been knocked from her lungs. Darious was quickly up and lifted Zoe to her feet. Another thunderous explosion ripped through the floor, tearing the entire corridor into a giant fissure. Zoe was thrown backward and swallowed whole by the avaricious mouth of fire.

CHAPTER 41

TO THE END

Darious awoke and shook the dust off himself. He slowly
got to his hands and knees, shell-shocked, bloody and battered. He gradually became aware of the great fiery cavern next
to him and how close he was to its precipice. The hallway had
been completely split in half. He was on the side that still existed. The missing half opened up into the raw structure of the
Regency Station, exposing a fracture some-twenty stories deep.
From across the gap he could see many levels of burning rooms
and corridors. The sensation of hearing returned, and continual
explosions echoed from unseen locations all around him.

"Zoe?"

He coughed and stood up. Bullets of pain shot through his
body. He did not see her anywhere.

"Zoe!"

Darious heard a faint cry and rushed to the edge of the chasm.
Looking down, he spotted her, and his heart jumped. Zoe was
dangling above the fiery abyss, holding onto a protruding metal
wedge. She yelled something, but a loud explosion from behind
him cut the words from the air. The intense heat scalded his
back and nearly sent him over the ledge.

Clenching his jaw, Darious withstood the pain and looked on the ground for something rigid to hold on to. There was a rectangular panel jutting slightly over the edge with a bar through it. He pushed at it with his foot and it felt secure. Laying flat on his stomach, he eased forward, holding the makeshift handle with one arm while thrusting the other downward toward Zoe. She was looking up at him, her body swaying from the blasts below. Darious called to her to grab his hand but he could already see the distance was too great. He pushed himself further down, feeling for her hands.

"Darious!"

Zoe released one hand and gripped his outstretched hand. Another explosion rocked the station, sending debris over the escarpment. Zoe lost her grip on the wedge and momentarily hung with just one hand connected to Darious. Her full weight on his arm made it hurt incredibly. She swung her other hand upward and firmly gripped his wrist. He pulled as hard as he could, but the weight proved to be just too much. Suddenly, there was a hissing sound from below, like a giant tank was rapidly depressurizing. The sputtering abruptly ended with a deafening boom, sending great orange flames up from the abyss.

"Zoe!"

Every muscle in his body strained in the supreme effort to pull her up.

"Darious, go!"

He grit his teeth and pulled harder.

"There's no time, go!"

The edge of the panel was cutting into his arm and he could feel his grip failing.

"Darious, you need to get out of here!" she shouted up at him.

"No!" Darious yelled back, exerting all his strength just to maintain his hold on her.

"Go!"

"NO!"

A massive explosion shook the rupturing station, sending Darious further over the edge and further stressing his hold on Zoe. Tears were streaming down her face.

"Darious..."

"Argh!!" he yelled and pulled with the might of all the spliced millenniums of humanity within him.

Having one hand firmly fixed on the metal bar, Darious heaved Zoe toward him. His eyes became red giants as blood vessels burst. He hauled Zoe up little by little. As soon as she touched the pointed ledge, she let one hand go and was scampering for something to hold on to. With one final great heave, Darious pitched both Zoe and himself onto the hallway's surface. Darious laid panting with Zoe next to him still in tears. They turned their heads towards each other. Zoe gave him a small, soft smile.

Another explosion rocked the failing station and the two quickly got up, knowing that time was short. Darious took the lead, running towards the escape pod with Zoe close behind. He forced his way through a broken door and they entered into the pod bay.

"There!" shouted Zoe, sprinting to the small pod.

As they entered through its circular door, Zoe quickly started the separation sequence and they both strapped in.

Just then, explosions flared all around the pod. From the small aperture, Darious saw flames engulf them. In the next moment, the escape pod shot out into space and away from the exploding wreckage that was once the Galaxy-Class Regency Station. Darious got a good view of the entire station, now cleft in half, with its two sides drifting away from each other. Then, the entire mass exploded into a single expanding inferno. A huge wave of debris accelerated outwards, outmatching the escape pod's speed.

The little craft shook and rolled. Darious knew that if it wasn't for the force-bearing dampeners, Zoe and he would be an oscillating mush from floor to ceiling. Zoe reached out her hand and Darious took it; together they endured the silent hurricane in space. Pieces of the station ricocheted off the pod, relentlessly knocking it back and forth. Then, a large metal fragment glanced the craft, knocking it into a spin. This was too much for the dampeners. The forces exuded on Darious and Zoe were extreme. Outside of the tiny escape pod, the universe was deaf to their cries.

Darious' eyelids kept floating over his pupils as the spinning challenged his lucidity. He continued to hold on to Zoe's hand through the chaos. He looked at her face, her lips, and the tears on her face. A sudden hard shock knocked her unconscious. Darious never took his eyes off her. As the pod thrashed them about, he remained unmoved from her. He would be with her to the end. A massive pipe came into view from the small porthole, directly lined up to strike the pod like a battering ram.

"Zoe..."

CHAPTER 42

THE PHOTON, THE GLITCH, AND THE COSMOS

*B*eep. A long silence passed. *Beep.* On the console, a dim red light pulsed in sync with the droning sound. *Beep.*

"What? No, no more tea. It's been a long winter..."

A loud snore drowned out the next beep. The sound changed to a boisterous double tone. The Captain gargled and immediately sat up in his seat coughing. He caught sight of the flashing red light on his console.

"Eh?"

The double beep rang again. He turned off the alert and pulled up the radar log.

"What's this?" The readout showed a small piece of debris in the shape of a cracked egg. "Rotten space garbage..." He shook his fist at the display. "...wakin' me up." The Captain made a mental note to recalibrate the sensors later. "It's too small to be worth my time ya damn ship. It's just a..." He trailed off as he read further into the report.

The Captain's eyes widened. He was instantly fully awake as he realized the object before him was not just irrelevant space trash. He quickly typed on the worn-out keyboard. Then, he forcefully stretched a flex-mic to his face.

"Attention. Attention all personnel. We have a Code S3. Prepare portside Cargo Hold 4 for a heavily damaged life pod. No signs of life—" More lights and sounds activated as the in-depth scan completed. "Change that, Code S4, two souls on-board. Ceaver, grab yer' medical gear and meet me in Cargo Hold 4. Dock and Eddy, you're on standby." He let the mic go and it slinked back into its hole. "Shit."

Taking in a deep breath, the captain of the space junker flipped several switches and cast off from his seat, using the forward momentum of his bloated belly to continue his motion from the cockpit, oafing down the corridors to the cargo hold.

Within his dreamlike warbling, Darious could hear tinks echoing from somewhere off in the distance. He was lying on the beach with Zoe on her great-uncle's world. Everything had been so calm when the clouds started thundering. No, not thunder. It was more like the sound of arc welding, although somewhat muffled. Perhaps it was coming from under the water. No, that wasn't correct either. Where was it coming from? The sparking sounds echoed louder and closer. Something was approaching them. The small cognizant part of Darious uttered a short plea.

A loud metallic cracking shook the walls of Darious' unconsciousness. There was another loud thump and then silence reined through the land. Darkness was coming. It threatened to overwhelm the beach, the clouds, and Zoe.

A sudden white light filled the landscape. Its pure essence sent tears down Darious' face. He squinted and held his burned and bleeding arm out to it. He curled his fingers around the ineffable radiance. In his half-conscious state, he rambled—bargaining with the light to take his life and save the one next to him. She deserved to live. Through the piercing illumination, consciousness flickered brighter in his eyes. He became aware of the intense pain all around his body. It was so much, too much to bear. Darious could no longer hold up his arm and darkness began crawling inward from the periphery of his vision. Through his last glimpse of the pure light, a figure floated through it, reaching toward him with an outstretched hand. Darious' consciousness faded, and blackness consumed everything.

⇌⇌

Darious awoke with a sudden spasm.

"Zoe!"

He sat straight up with waxing alertness and stared at his new surroundings. He was within a small white room. Across from him were a mirror and a sink and to his left was a door. He was in a soft bed with white sheets. Darious inspected his hands and then his arms. The burns were very much faded, and his skin felt oily. Then he noticed his clothes. No longer was he wearing *his* clothes, but a pair of blue slacks and a grey shirt. *Where am I?* Darious moved his legs from the bed. He surveyed the room with a slower, keener eye. This was a minimal sleeping chamber and thus he was undoubtedly on a ship. Darious slowly got out of bed and stood up with careful movements. There were some vestiges of pain, but overall, he felt surprisingly well. He had evidently been taken care of and healed. Darious spotted his old shoes next to the bed and put them on.

With cautious steps, Darious made his way to the door and put an ear to it. There were no perceivable sounds on the other side. He knocked on it. After waiting for some time, he checked the handle and gave it a light pull. The door opened with ease, but it croaked unapologetically. An unpleasant odor wafted into the room. It smelt faintly of garbage and engine oil. Darious looked around his expanded surroundings. The door led into a broad corridor with ill-fitting panels over the walls. Between them he could see many working conduits. Darious looked up and down the hall and again listened. He was alone. He suddenly remembered the white light and the blackness. He had read about the afterlife; was this it? Then he remembered her.

"Zoe!"

Darious chose the hall direction that was better lit. He walked briskly, all the while assessing his surroundings. This seemed to be an old vessel—a poorly maintained vessel. Corrosion and rust were present everywhere. The slightly misshaped lattice floor reverberated loudly under each step. Upon the corridor's end, it split horizontally, heading off in both directions. Darious turned left and continued on. He spotted a small porthole and he ran up to it. Space lay just beyond. From this vantage point he could see more of the ship he was now a passenger of. It was bulbous and very clunky looking. Much of the outer paneling was mismatched and seemed to have been hand-welded.

"Interesting," he said to himself.

Continuing on, Darious every-so-often rapped his knuckles on the metal walls. Some parts were hollow while others resounded with stifled clanks. It was as if the ship was pieced together from the parts of many crafts. He passed by more portholes along the corridor, though all gave a similar view of outer-space.

After some minutes of walking, Darious reached another split. He paused, unsure of which path to take. He could continue along the current corridor, or turn left into the smaller one that seemed to end at a dark room. Darious called out.

"Zoe!"

Suddenly, there were sounds like the dropping of tools onto the metal floor from the shadowy room. He ran down the hall and paused at the entryway, scanning the darkness. The room seemed to be a small hub for docked spacecrafts.

"Zoe!" he called again.

A door to his left suddenly creaked open, causing him to jump back. Light flooded in from the aperture and there stood Zoe.

"Darious!" she happily chirped and ran to him, giving him a tight hug.

After she released her grasp, he looked over her. She had some bruising and cuts on her arms and face.

"Are you okay?" Darious asked.

"Yes sir."

She smiled at him and gave him another hug. He could feel many deep aches come to the surface, but he didn't care. Zoe was okay. She seemed to notice his pain and quickly let go.

"Oh sorry, sorry. How are you?"

"A little sore," said Darious. "Zoe, where are we?"

She looked around. "Onboard a salvage ship I presume. I tell you Darious, it's been one of those days."

He nodded in agreement. Zoe pulled out her lightcard and handed it to him. "Here, hold this for a moment, will ya?"

He took up the electronic instrument.

"How did we get here?"

"Rescued. By some nice folks."

"I have not met anyone yet."

"It's a big ship and they are a small crew."

"How do we know we are safe? If they are salvagers, we could be but scrap to them and be sold off, id est—to the CF."

"Oh, that's a bunch of baloney. I—"

"Baloney?" asked Darious, not sure if she was making a positive or negative reflection of his comment.

"Oh ermm, it's a congealed food paste from Earth. It's uniquely tasty. Anyhow, these are good people. No worries; we'll survive."

Zoe coughed. "Darious, would ya mind finding something for us to drink? It's been ages since I had a nice, cold pick-me-up."

"Certainly, Zoe. Though, I am somewhat lost."

"Down the hall and to the left. Or maybe two lefts. I'm not sure, but you'll find it."

He looked back, not wanting to go. Zoe stepped close to him and gave him another hug. She held him close and looked deep in his eyes.

"I will return shortly," he said. "If you're confident the people here are good people, then I am not worried."

He headed off, striding down the corridor. He was very much relieved to see that Zoe had not only survived their ordeal, but was back in good spirits. He replayed their escape from the Regency Station. They had almost died. *She* had almost died.

Darious took two lefts and indeed came upon a commissary. There were several sinks with dirty dishes. He opened up three refrigeration drawers before finding a couple of chilled bottles of water. He took them up and just as he turned around, a man entered in. Darious dropped one of the bottles and the man contracted in similar surprise.

"Oy, didn't think you'd be awake already," he said.

Darious looked him over, remembering what Zoe had said, but nevertheless remained circumspect. The man was wearing a white cloak blotted with small stains, a sweater and old pants underneath. He had a scraggily beard and was balding on top. He had kind eyes, like Zoe's.

"Awake already... how long was I asleep?" asked Darious.

"Oh, just a day. Pleased to meet you." The man held out a hand. "I'm Ceaver, the Chief Medical Doctor onboard."

Darious slowly shook his hand. "I am Darious."

"Well, Darious, it's a pleasure to meet you. I've been taking care of you since your arrival. You were lucky; we had some

Excelerar on hand along with a UV-R regenerator for your burns. You had a few broken bones too, but those were easily taken care of. There was also some internal bleeding. I'd say minimal. All-in-all, I believe you'll make a one hundred percent recovery in no time at all."

Darious lowered his guard a bit. "Thank you Mr. Ceaver. Thank you."

"My pleasure."

"How was Zoe?"

"Oh, the girl!" Doing just fine! Follow me," said Ceaver, picking up the bottle from the floor and handing it to Darious.

They left the commissary and headed down the corridor. "The Captain found you two floating in space onboard an escape pod. Life systems were nearly gone, and we weren't expecting much, but you two made it through." Ceaver opened both arms as if presenting a work of art. "You're onboard the Harriet Narne, a reclamation craft." He smirked. "We find the little treasures others leave behind."

"I see," said Darious.

"Come, come."

They rounded a corner and entered into a brightly illuminated rectangular room with doors on both sides. Ceaver led the way to the nearest one and opened it, ushering Darious in. Zoe was sitting on a similar bed that Darious had found himself in. When she spotted him, she smiled and coughed. He quickly brought her one of the waters.

"Thank you," she said and took large gulps from it.

Darious sat with her on the bed.

"I'll let you two be. Call me if ya need anything," said Ceaver, pointing to a push button speaker on the wall and left.

Zoe put down the bottle and turned toward Darious. "Oh, Darious!" She wrapped her arms around him. A shot of pain from his back made him wince.

"Oh sorry, sorry! I'm still feeling achy myself, but compared to how we were, I'd say Ceaver is pretty good at what he does."

Darious looked over Zoe once more. They had come so close to destruction. She stared back at him and put an arm delicately on his shoulder and then felt across his chin.

"Oh, here I have this."

Darious pulled out the lightcard from his pocket.

Zoe took it up with a smile. "Thank you for looking after it."

She put it away and gave him a soft kiss on the forehead. She then rested her head on his shoulder. Though Darious knew their journey was far from over, for the moment he felt calm and relaxed. All that running, all those that may be chasing them, none of it mattered in this moment.

A few minutes later, a stout man entered into the room, prompting Darious to raise his head. He had the air of one who had spent a lifetime traveling amongst the stars. The whiskers on his face parted and a large smile showed through them.

"Ah, you two are awake. How do ya feel?"

"Quite well," said Zoe, looking at him from an angle over Darious' shoulder.

"I am Captain Robert," he stated and offered them a pudgy hand.

Darious was first to reach for it. "We owe you our lives, Captain."

The Captain heartily shook his hand. Darious immediately realized that the Captain hadn't been taken aback by the clone hand he had been offered. *Good people,* Darious thought.

"Thank you, Sir," said Zoe, likewise shaking his hand.

"No trouble whatsoever. Almost didn't see ya out there. You two are very lucky, ya know. Now understand, we don't ask many questions around here. We're just glad to see you two are okay."

Zoe sat straight. "Thank you. I am Zoe, and this is Darious."

"A pleasure," he replied.

"Captain," said Zoe, "you've done so much for us. Can I ask you for just one more favor?"

"What is it, ma'am?"

"Do you have a phone we may use?"

He thought for a moment and then pulled out an oval device from his trouser pocket.

"Here ye' are. I'll give ya some privacy and check back on you later."

Zoe and Darious again thanked him and they were once more alone.

"Darious, please close the door." He complied and sat back down with her. "We need to make contact with Kappa, but before we do, I have some apologizing to do." She held his hands in her own and solemnly looked at him. "Back on the Regency Station... I... I gave up. And in doing so, I put us in a worse situation then we already were. Darious, never again. I will never again give up, not as long as you're by my side." She then added lightheartedly, "it was sure looking grim."

Darious smiled and laughed. "It most certainly was."

Zoe turned her attention back to the Captain's communicator. She synced her lightcard to it and enabled the speakerphone. The device crackled in her hand.

"I've set it to pass through an encrypted signal. We can't be too careful."

The call rang with a distorted tone. Then a familiar voice picked up.

"Ah, I know of only one person who could send an encoded polyharmonic call like that!" exclaimed Kappa.

"Hello sir!" said Zoe.

"Hello, ma'am. How did ya'll fare? I hope you're okay. Is Darious alright?"

"We are fine. A little battered." Zoe lowered her voice. "Are you alone?"

"Yes, ma'am. Go ahead."

"The mission was a success," she said. "The program has been sent out and is charting the galaxy as we speak. We almost made it out of there, but things went awry. They found us out. Kappa, they self-destructed the entire station, with us still in it."

"Ah, so that's what happened" Kappa said. "I've been monitoring CF communications. The chatter has been a bit chaotic, but it sure sounded like there was one hell of a fireworks show out there. I knew ya'll were alive because they're still looking for you. You guys are numero uno on the CF's list."

"Damn," said Zoe turning to Darious.

"Well, despite that little glitch, I was able to sink the CF cruiser and hotfoot it out of there. I can see from your communication telemetry you're onboard a large ship."

"A junker picked us up," said Zoe. "I don't know how I'm going to get back to my ship, especially with the CF surely on our trail."

"No worries. I'm towing it right now. Tell ya what, I'll meet ya at Port Jidus. It looks like the junker is headed in that direction."

"Towing it?"

"Yup. I've got a gravity-line attached to it. I can be at Jidus in... twenty-five minutes."

"Kappa!" exclaimed Zoe. "Thank you!"

"Hey, what kind of captain would ya be without a ship?"

"Ah Kappa, thank you."

"Don't go counting your chickens just yet little lady."

"True. Okay, let's regroup at the Port Jidus. I'm sure the Captain here will be willing to accommodate a quick drop-off."

"Understood, ma'am."

Zoe was about to hang up but added, "Oh and Kappa?"

"Yes, ma'am?"

"Please don't scratch my ship."

"Roger that. Be careful out there."

The call ended, and Zoe put her lightcard away. She scooted next to Darious.

"We need to talk about that self-destruct command."

Darious nodded. "Yes, I was about to bring it up too."

"When we were found out, an order came from the Magistrate to have the entire station reduced to nothing. I've been thinking about it; there is no way the Magistrate is under Pantheon's thumb. The Magistrate is just too high of a ruling power. I mean, it's the highest of galactic powers. Thus, I've come to the conclusion that it must be the other way around; someone, or multiple someones, in the Magistrate is calling the shots and apparently, we've hit a nerve, a really big nerve." Zoe grinned. "And that makes me quite happy."

"The Magistrate," said Darious.

"Yup. I'm not saying that Pantheon isn't guilty. There's definitely a link between the two, but I'm willing to bet it's someone in the Magistrate that's pulling the strings."

Darious thought it over and could see the logic in Zoe's reasoning. As the conversation diffused away, they sat together for some time in silence. Zoe was soon leaning toward Darious, as if she were slowly falling into him. Oh, how he cared for her. Their fingers intertwined in his lap. He looked at her and warmth filled him. Darious had never felt like this. It was such happiness.

"Darious."

Her beautiful eyes were just inches from his.

"Zoe," he said back, completely dazzled by her.

She seemed to hold back for a moment.

"Thank you."

Darious brought his lips to hers. A long, gentle kiss united them. Darious felt a bond beyond the physical, beyond the metaphysical, and beyond comprehension. *Zoe.*

CHAPTER 43

BLOOD FROM A STONE

Zoe shook Captain Robert's hand as they exited from his docked craft at Port Jidus.

"Now, you two stay safe," he stated. "I don't want to be pullin' no bodies from space."

Zoe and Darious gave him many thanks and waved goodbye as he departed.

"I didn't see Kappa's ship on the way in, but I assume he's here somewhere," said Zoe.

"They were very nice," said Darious, watching the flare from the junker's rockets fade into the stars.

"They sure were."

Zoe held out her hand. The pair entered into the main corridors of the port. It was a small station, but nevertheless it remained densely packed with all sorts of humans. Zoe didn't spend time playing her usual little game, instead she focused on individuals that fit Kappa's profile.

"If everything goes smoothly," said Zoe, "We'll have earned a feather in our caps."

"Oh? Oh, I understand."

"I got it!" she proclaimed, pausing momentarily amongst the angst crowds.

"What is it?" Darious asked.

"We gotta get you a book on idioms and formulaic language." She continued walking with Darious trailing just behind her. "Unfortunately, I doubt they'll have a book store here. I understand how 206 must have felt."

As they made their way down the corridors, Zoe constantly pulled at Darious as he was incessantly shoved by the grating crowds. Their progress was slow and there wasn't much she could do about it. Zoe directed Darious to a small café. Entering in, they took seats next to a window facing the corridor.

"I think we'll have more luck this way," she said. Zoe looked around for an attendant but didn't spot any. "Hmmph."

She put her elbows on the table and balanced her head in her hands. She looked out at the hodgepodge of people and then over at Darious, who was absorbed in his own search through the many faces beyond the glass.

"Ma'am, care for a drink?" asked a voice from just behind Zoe.

She spun around and there was Kappa, standing with a giant grin. He wore his familiar cloak and hat. Zoe could see he had recently been in conflict. She gave him a hug and then he shook Darious' hand.

"How are ya lad?" Kappa asked.

"Just fine, sir. It is a pleasure to see you."

"You as well. We don't have much time." Kappa flashed a small device from under his coat. Zoe immediately recognized it as a CF communicator. Kappa whispered, "I swiped it during the charade with the boys from the Regency Station. I've been using it to monitor their communications. There are several fleets headed to this sector. They are doing broad sweeps and you can sure as hell bet they've got enough ships to find us here. We need to move."

Zoe nodded, and the trio set off into the corridors. It was much easier following behind Kappa, as his large stature cleaved through the crowds, leaving plenty of space for Zoe and Darious in his wake. They were soon upon a parking bay of Port Jidus. As the door closed behind them, the three stood alone in the sub-dock. Kappa pulled out the communicator and read over its screen.

"Alrighty folks, a bit of a snag here."

"What is it?" asked Darious.

"This station is now under the monitoring sphere of the fleet. We need to get our ships out—without a green light from the port's space traffic control and without making a scene."

"No problem," said Zoe, pulling out her lightcard.

Just then, the door opened behind them and a single traveler passed by. The individual began entering in the key codes to his own bay. They all looked over their shoulders at him. The man looked back and had a momentary look of surprise upon his face, then a disgusted look, and then focused back on the keypad, typing faster. The trio grouped in a tight circle around Zoe's lightcard. She was typing on it, circumnavigating the port's systems. Kappa bent in, getting a good look at the little device in her hands.

"That's a hacker card!" he nearly shouted in surprise.

Zoe paused and looked at him. "A hacker card?"

He stood straight and his face became quite serious. "Where did you get it? I have only ever seen one and it was at a hyper-security CF facility." He stared down at her.

The man working the door turned his head towards them.

Zoe jabbed Kappa in the ribs. "Keep your voice down."

She put a finger to her lips to emphasize the need for quiet-ness. After a nod from Kappa, she went back to concentrating on rerouting their bay controls, so the gates would open without indicating any changes to traffic control.

Kappa leaned in. "Zoe," he whispered close to her face.

"Yes?" she whispered back.

"That's a hacker card. Seriously, where did ya get it? It should be in a CF vault. I believe there are only a couple in existence; I wouldn't have believed any at all if I hadn't seen one with my own eyes. And now, here ya are with one of your own. Where did you get it?"

Zoe smacked her face with the palm of her hand.

She whispered, straining her voice, "I found it. In a dump-yard years ago."

The traveler, evidently finished with his key codes, entered his dock and the three were alone once more.

"Zoe," Kappa said. "A hacker card—any door, any place."

Just then, two men with heavy beards and jumpsuits entered the sub-dock and made their way to their bay.

"How do you think I got the passcode to enter into this dock room in the first place?" Zoe whispered.

Kappa looked down at her at her, making a sarcastic 'O' shape with his eyes.

"You mean you didn't gain special access through permit designations?"

She rolled her eyes.

"Zoe..." he began.

"Shhh!"

The space lumberjacks entered their bay just as Zoe finished the control modifications.

"All done."

"Good," said Kappa. "Let's mosey on outta' here."

He went over to their door and it wooshed open without any need for an access code. He waved a great arm for Zoe and Darious to follow him. Entering in, Zoe smiled upon seeing her parked vessel. Oh, she had missed it. Kappa's Drak-9 was right next to it. The front of his craft was dented inward and mangled bits of metal stuck out from it.

"How did—," started Darious.

"Don't ask," interrupted Zoe.

"Alrighty," said Kappa as they walked toward their crafts, "The CF has been spreading out from the blast of the Regency Station. We need to be heading in the opposite direction. Aim for Sector Gamod. There is a planetary system there that's good for laying low."

Zoe gave him a sardonic look.

"I might have used it once or twice before," he added. "It'll take a few hours to get to at near max capacity of your ship. Don't make any stops and keep an open mic. Once there, we can plan out our next steps."

"The timing should work out," said Zoe, "by then Wormy will have nearly completed mapping everything. It should be instrumental in steering our next step."

"Understood. Okay troops, safe journey and light speed."

Kappa dipped his brimmed hat to Zoe and Darious and left toward his ship. Zoe motioned for Darious and they made their way to her vessel.

Onboard, Zoe took a deep breath in. The familiar smell was of home.

"Ahh," she exhaled.

Zoe quickly made her way to the captain's seat and began flipping switches all around her. Darious stood behind her with a firm grip on the back of her chair. Zoe instructed the computer to close the gangway and pre-ignite the thrusters. She placed the lightcard, or 'hacker card,' as Kappa called it, on her console and pressed the 'Enter' button on it. The double bay door began to slowly open, revealing the vacuum of space. The traffic systems showed an 'all normal.' If everything went well, the port's traffic control would see none of the silent escape happening right under their noses.

"Now, to fulfill a promise," she said.

Zoe picked up the lightcard and brought up the folder containing Wormy. She deleted it and initiated a full scrub of her device. In a few seconds, her lightcard signaled that the task was complete; all data pertaining to the worm had been erased, the resulting blank space was scrambled, and routine operating data had filled in those chunks. Zoe typed into her virtual console and set her ship to auto-depart. She then got up and motioned for Darious to follow her to the main chamber.

"Here, hold this," she said, handing him the bulky, vintage computer which held that mescal worm.

Zoe fumbled though a drawer and pulled out two cylinders connected by a single wire. She held each on opposite sides of the computer. They shook momentarily in her hands and then a puff of smoke dissipated from the top of the computer.

"Fried it with electromagnets. Okay now dump it in there."

She pointed with one of the electromagnets to a pull-out dumpster. Managing with one hand, Darious opened the small hinged lid and placed the sautéed computer in it. He closed the lid and wiped the dust from his hands. Zoe replaced the electromagnets in the drawer and smiled at Darious.

"I think a proper burial is in order for that old beast." She winked and returned to the cockpit.

The two ships lifted up from the bay and slowly turned, both lining up their bows to outer-space. With the gates fully opened, the crafts glided out side-by-side.

"Throttle up," said Kappa through the speakers. "Sector Gamod, planetary system 12-12.2."

"Oh, it's so popular it doesn't even have a name," teased Zoe.

She flipped a switch, dumping the trash hold into space, and engaged the rocket drives. Her craft propelled forward, vaporizing the old computer within the billion-degree burst into a million, million specks.

Just as the two ships shot out from the space station, there came an incomprehensible yell from Kappa.

"What is it?!" called Darious.

"Fu—the CF has flagged us! They're intercepting! Fucking hell!"

Zoe immediately brought up long range scanners. She held her breath in trepidation. An entire fleet was descending upon them. Scanners indicated an enormous mass at its center.

"They have a brink-class dreadnought!" shouted Kappa. "A planet destroyer!"

Darious leapt to his post, aiding Zoe in the ignition of all thrusters for an over-clocked burst.

As all settings were primed, the entire CF fleet came to a screeching halt from superluminal speeds, surrounding them. Zoe cut her engines and saw Kappa had done the same. She knew there would be no and outrunning the fleet. CF ships, armed at every interstice, swarmed around them. Empty parts of space were filling in with CF ships halting from their floating-parsec leaps.

"Weapons arming!" yelled Darious.

They didn't even bother hailing us, thought Zoe.

"Evasive maneuvers!" yelled Kappa. Zoe instinctively flipped switches above her, imparting alzthumal thrusters with all the power her ship had to offer.

"Weapons fired!" yelled Darious.

Zoe saw onscreen that two dozen small CF ships had fired missiles. A blue string of text appeared at her right-hand side; Kappa had sent her a program of flight actions.

With swift keystrokes, Zoe commanded her ship to have its belly facing the underside of Kappa's ship and engaged his evasive protocols. Her ship synced with the motions of his and together their crafts began a spiraling ascent. Zoe quickly understood their doubled twirling mass might confuse the projectiles to the point where they could burst accelerate at the last moment and dodge them. She swiped to the end of Kappa's program and indeed that's what he had planned. The missiles accelerated, reaching for them like the fingers of a specter. Zoe kept a close eye on the proximity alerts; she knew Kappa was doing the same.

"Now!" he yelled through the speaker and the two vessels broke apart with a rush of speed, sending the missiles arcing wildly in a confused manner. Their two ships looped around many CF vessels, attempting to cause as much disarray as possible. The missiles relocked on, but had lost their propinquity and were now traveling clumsily between the thick veil of CF vessels.

A red alert flashed on Zoe's screen. One of the missiles had impacted a CF ship.

"More lock-ons!" called Darious. "Plasma systems powering up!"

Zoe looked out at the swarming fleet; there had to be over one hundred ships. Meanwhile, the giant menacing CF vessel floated idly amidst the commotion. Zoe completed a series of quick bursts, looping around ships as more alerts rang across her screen from the growing number of projectiles headed in her direction. Just then, Kappa curved right toward her, narrowly missing her bow.

"Kappa!" Zoe yelled.

His ship fell back, and Zoe saw him fire upon the missiles right behind her, reducing them to ash. One missile made it through and both ships narrowly managed to avoid it. The projectile quickly swerved back around and headed straight for Zoe's craft. Zoe thought quickly. She didn't want to fire upon the CF, for she couldn't be an aggressor or else certainly she could be charged with capitol crime. Instead, Zoe swung her ship rearward, allowing Kappa to pass her. He immediately fired upon the missile, obliterating it.

Suddenly, plasma blasts ignited from the CF ships. Zoe flipped her craft around and pivoted back and forth as fast as she could. Kappa flew parallel to her whilst completing similar maneuvers. Green and blue gunfire sizzled past them. One hit its mark, burning through one of her aft thrusters. Zoe could see Kappa's ship had been hit several times and smoke was trailing from both its wings.

She quickly sealed off the damaged thruster and throttled her ship to full power, evading another volley of plasma fire.

"Agghh!!" Kappa yelled.

Zoe looked out and saw his ship had sustained a direct hit and smoke was now pouring from it. An indicator prompt on her screen signaled another plasma torrent was about to rain upon them. She slid her ship around a large CF vessel, managing to avoid the bulk of the attack, but Kappa was less fortunate. Though his ship was hidden from view, Zoe saw onscreen his engines had gone offline and metal debris became present around him.

Then all gunfire ceased from the CF. Zoe quickly flew her ship to Kappa's craft and visually surveyed the damage. It looked bad, really bad.

"Why have they stopped?" asked Darious.

Zoe had no idea.

"Kappa. Kappa, are you okay?"

A heavy voice breathed through the speakers. "My life systems are crashing. Engines offline. Armaments offline."

Zoe saw a small explosion rip through the top of his hull. Loud crackling resonated through the speakers.

"Just lost navigations," said Kappa exasperated. "Oh Shit!"

Ahead of them, the CF fleet opened up, exposing a clear path from the dreadnought to the two battered crafts. A large alert popped up on Zoe's screen. The massive vessel was charging its primary cannon. Zoe sat frozen. The weapon's energy levels were off the chart. It would erase them from space, and then some.

"Zoe, you gotta get out of here!" yelled Kappa through the crackling speakers. "I will hold them off the best I can!"

"No!" Zoe shouted back. "We can think of something!"

"We're locked-on!" yelled Darious.

Just then Zoe's ship announced with a giant red warning that the enormous cannon had indeed locked onto them.

"Oh my..." Zoe whispered in disbelief.

"Verve, nerve, and adventure," spoke the calm voice of Kappa.

Zoe saw he had managed to restart his main thruster and was charging it up with all the power left in his craft. Then, with explosive force, he shot toward the mammoth ship.

"Kappa!" Zoe shouted.

"I'm makin' ya an opening. Power everythin' ya got on my mark!"

Kappa's ship rocketed onward, black smoke shadowing it and sparks flashing along its engine lines. Kappa shot at every CF ship along his vector, exploding each with hellish bursts of fire. He then let loose every rocket the Drak-9 held under its wings, scattering ships along another course and creating a clear path for Zoe to escape.

"Bend the throttle!" Kappa yelled.

Zoe punched it. With feverous fierceness, her ship shot through the gap, just as Kappa's ship collided headlong with the giant cannon of the dreadnought, igniting it in a brilliant flash of white light. His ship was instantly enveloped in the explosion and the front half of the giant CF craft exploded, sending a wave of slag outward and impacting the nearest unfortunate ships. Chaos erupted as CF ships reeled and tumbled away. Some were hit with metal chunks and peripheral explosions caused tremendous collateral damage. Zoe pushed her ship's thrusters as high as they could go, hurriedly distancing herself from the giant fiery CF swarm. She pulled up long range scanners. No ships were following them. They had escaped, but at the cost of the greatest gunslinger the galaxy had every known.

CHAPTER 44

DIVIDED

"Are we still clear of the CF?" asked Darious, as the ship came upon the planetary system denoted by '12-12.2.'

"I believe so," said Zoe, rechecking over scanner readings. She then shot over her work from the last half hour to Darious. "Check it out, it's an old trick I learned some time ago—with a couple tweaks."

Zoe had been busy masking their trail the best she could by having the ship suction expelled gases from the engine. She had accomplished this by ramping up one exhaust port while reversing another to create a vacuuming streamline across the engine and then directing the flow through internal filters. By doing so, she limited the radioactive particulates that sensitive equipment could potentially track them by. The work had been calming, helpful for both the ship and the mood within the craft.

"Ingenious," said Darious.

"Why thank you sir." Zoe diminished the screens and began scanning the solar system. "Man, look at this place. It's as barren as they come."

Internal scans of the solar system showed a few planets completely desolate and an old expectorate star. Zoe slowed the ship as they passed through the system's heliosphere and initiated in-depth scans of the planets; all were desert wastelands: a few shrubs, some caverns, null water, and zero humans.

"I gotta remember this place for my next summer get-away," she said. "Let's pick the big one off our port bow—with the moon. Scans show it has the most metal and the most mountains. It'll be a good cover spot for us."

"Aye captain," replied Darious.

Zoe's ship sailed to the inhospitable world, its silvery and red rock surface expanding into view.

"Zoe?" asked Darious from his seat. "Do you think Kappa survived the assault at Port Jidus?"

"No," Zoe said. She could sense he was waiting for something better than a one-word response. She turned and met his inquisitive eyes. "Kappa had reversed the polarity of his fuel cells, essentially turning himself into a flying bomb. The temperatures at the flash point were in excess of 500 billion degrees. He and his ship were completely vaporized. Kappa sacrificed himself to save us."

"I see," said Darious somberly. "I will not forget him."

"In the end, he was a good man. I will miss him too."

Zoe remained pensive while her ship wound its way down to the planet. As they rounded an enormous mountain crest, Zoe plotted a course to the bottom of a low cliff with jutting, jagged edges.

Just when they started this slow descent, the ship suddenly rang an alert that long-range scanners had spotted an inbound ship.

"Damnit!" shouted Zoe.

She abandoned the descent and quickly pulled the ship upward. They arced through the ionosphere and away from the planet. New alerts rang on Zoe's console. Scanners had identified the inbound craft as a small, brigantine vessel. It was heading directly for them.

"I'm heading for the moon," she said. "We will lie low there for the moment."

Her quicksilver ship flew to the dark side of the moon and hovered about a quarter-kilometer from its surface. The craft then came into view. Zoe had her fingers ready on the thruster controls.

"It is a CF vessel," said Darious. "No perceivable weapons."

The ship stopped a few kilometers short of them, bearing down directly from above. Zoe opened a broad assortment of scanning utilities.

"It's a scout," she said, elevating her ship to be at the same altitude as the craft. It was somewhat larger than her ship and had a much more linear profile—obviously meant for quick reconnaissance runs.

"The vessel is scanning us," said Darious.

"Not on my watch." Zoe quickly scrolled through a list of her programs and engaged a harmonic jamming wave pattern, forcibly denying the scout's scan of her vessel. "Ha! No soup for you."

The CF vessel began lifting up and away from her ship. "Oh, no you don't," said Zoe, following the craft upwards.

An alert appeared across the lower section of Zoe's projection screen, but she was too focused on loading another computer routine.

"Zoe!" called Darous.

She engaged the protocol, building up a compressed field of ions at the bow of her craft and then shot them to the scout, like a bolt of lightning. The shocked craft tumbled for a couple of revolutions and then sped away to the horizon of the moon. Zoe suddenly noticed the boundary of the moon seemed unusually oblong, as if it were being stretched outwards.

"What the...?" she began.

"Zoe! There is another ship! It is massive!"

A gigantic vessel rounded out from the far side of the moon, matching the satellite in size and shape. It split out from the moon as its equal. The ship was of epic proportions, certainly the largest Zoe had ever seen. The brigantine scout ran from Zoe's ship toward its mother, bidding the latter for vengeance against its bully.

"Zoe!"

She stared at the giant vessel in awe. It was so massive and so state-of-the art. Her ship hadn't even picked it up, even though it was right on the other side of the moon! Apparently, the CF was dead-set on having them dead. *Well not today*, thought Zoe. They had come too far.

She snapped up the controls and veered away from the doppelganger moon. "Darious, prep for max thrust! We're—"

Without any warning, the colossal vessel fired a single shot. It struck Zoe's ship, burrowing through the engine core, and threw Zoe and Darious to the floor. Zoe hit her head hard on the ground. She felt woozy as she staggered to her feet. Darious was quick to get up and was straightaway typing into his console.

"We have lost thruster controls. Life systems are stable." Red lights began flashing all around them. "Life systems are no longer stable!" he cried out.

Zoe sat in the captain's seat. "Reroute power to secondary life support. I'm getting us out of here, even if I have to get out and push myself!" She quickly worked to get as much of the thrusters back online as she could. Zoe could feel the air pressure pulsating around her. "Get it fixed Darious!" The damage to the engine lines was extensive. Auxiliary controls had also been burnt through. She hurriedly repaired segment after segment at a dizzying rate.

Zoe's ship suddenly jolted forward, nearly making her slam her head on the console and then everything became very rigid. It was as if the organic controls of her ship had turned into petrified rock. *Crap*, thought Zoe. She knew exactly what had just happened.

"Captain!?" called Darious.

"They have a tractor beam on us." Zoe battled with the virtual keyboard. "Not enough power for the engines." She looked out and saw they were being pulled toward the mighty craft. Soon they were within its shadow and being guided toward a large open bay. The aperture of the bay had a semi-transparent blue hue to it. *Damnit; a force field*, thought Zoe. They were consumed by the vessel, brought into its bowels through the blue barrier and placed on the floor of the bay.

Zoe was hurriedly typing into her console, locking down her ship's controls and the entryway.

Darious had leapt from his seat and was looking out of the cockpit window. Rows of troops were hustling toward them, rifles raised and poised toward the ship. There was a loud sound of latches clamping in the main chamber.

"I've bolted down the door and fried the relays to it," said Zoe.

"What should I do Captain?" asked Darious.

"Not sure yet; let me think." She looked over the controls; the ship was completely immobilized. The infantry crew rounded underneath her craft and disappeared from view. Loud metallic bangs reverberated from behind Zoe. She ran to the main chamber. *What to do?! What to do?! There has to be something!*

The door suddenly burst open with such force that it was nearly ripped from its tracks. A smoke grenade was tossed inward and went off at Zoe's feet. She dove away and wrapped her arms around her face. In the abrupt chaos, troops boarded the ship. They grabbed Zoe and Darious and dragged them from the ship. Zoe struggled in vein against the arms wrapped around her. She saw Darious attempt to kick himself free but received the blunt end of a rifle in the stomach and was hurled back in the ship. Zoe turned with burning eyes and saw him rush toward her, but was blocked by the armed men. They brutally beat him on the gangway. Once he stopped moving, they again picked him up and threw him back into the ship. Zoe madly swung her torso side to side, attempting to throw her captor off balance, but his steps were too sturdy, and his strength was too overbearing.

"Darious!" she called back, but he did not respond.

The squad stopped in front of a CF commander adorned with many gold pins. He eyed Zoe with disdain.

"Take her to the cell in G-4. Eject the craft with that worthless clone."

Zoe spit in his face and gnashed her teeth at him. The butt-end of a rifle swiftly struck her in the stomach, knocking the air from her and reducing her to a heaving mound.

The commander wiped his face. "Get that scrap metal off my vessel!"

He turned on his heel and left. The unit assigned to Zoe strong-armed her forward. Through gasping breaths and hazy vision, she looked back at her ship containing Darious within. It was lifted from the ground by tractor beams and pitched out from the bay like a piece of space trash. Zoe gasped as an explosion plumed from the side of her ship. Her captors forced her beyond the bay and deep into the moon-sized base. Zoe's mind and heart were in utter disarray.

CHAPTER 45

THE ONLY REAL PRISON IS FEAR

Zoe was thrown to a cell floor, catching herself with open palms just in time and in doing so was in instant pain from the hard landing. She got up as quick as she could and spun around, but the soldiers had already left, and the door was slammed shut. Zoe stood there, panting for a good minute, waiting to catch her breath. As oxygen slowly returned and she didn't have to work so hard to suck in air, she began assessing her surroundings.

She was in a large room, dimly lit with flickering lights as if by candles. The floor seemed to be some sort of black polished stone. Off to one side, long blocks were carved out from this marble like seating for a jury. Opposite was a single raised platform cornering off at the wall. Zoe sneered; all that was missing was the gallows.

The cell door opened, and Zoe instinctively raised her fists. Two soldiers came in, followed by the oddest man she had ever seen. He was plump with a flowing emerald robe that almost seemed to glow, though this wasn't what had captured Zoe's attention. Through the poor lighting, she could see his arms and face reflected with a slight, yet true smaragdine hue. Zoe's mind snapped. He was from the Epigod System, known galactically for its power-hungry people. A large gold pendant shined on his chest. Her mind snapped again. *A Magister.*

The soldiers guided the Magister forward and held their rifles with the business end toward Zoe.

"Leave us," said the Magister in an offhand tone. "I require privacy with this one."

"Sir?" asked a guard, turning to him. He was reprimanded with a reproachful look through the Magister's jade eyes. "Sir," he said, clicking his heels. The two soldiers turned and left, closing the door behind them.

Zoe got a good look at the fat man. His bald head was shouldered by several chins and a lavish chain. The green dress adorning him seemed almost translucent and almost luminescent, with multifaceted gems sown into gilded seams. He appeared ordained simply by his clothes; no doubt this was an individual not to be trifled with. The Magister turned his gaze to Zoe.

"My girl, please put down your hands. There is no need for violence. You are already in prison."

"What sort of prison is this?" asked Zoe, refusing to yield her guard.

The Magister opened his hefty arms, making a large, sweeping circle. "All around you—prison. Your entire life in *my* society—prison. This entire galaxy of apathy is your prison. My child, please, lay down your arms."

Zoe made a quick motion, reaching for her lightcard in her shirt, but the Magister was faster, pulling out a similarly shaped device from his robe. In that moment, Zoe saw it appeared to be *exactly* like her lightcard. He pressed a single finger to it. Instantly, her entire body felt as if it was on fire. She fell to the floor in agony. All her joints felt like they were popping backward, and her heart felt as though it was a hot coal searing through her chest. She wanted to scream, but her lungs had seized up. As soon as the extreme pain had begun, it ceased. She shuddered on the floor, wheezing.

"Please," said the Magister, coming closer to her, "there is no need for violence. Let me introduce myself. I am the—"

"The Grandeur," said Zoe through loathing lips.

He contemptuously cleared his throat. "I apologize. I am not accustomed to being interrupted. I am glad you know my name." He raised his hacker card. "And now you shall know what it means." He pressed the digital button, sending more terrible burning shocks throughout Zoe's body. She curled up and her mind cried out. The pain stopped a second and a lifetime later.

"Obedience—there is never enough. You may sit. But please, do so slowly."

Zoe groaned as she slowly pulled herself up into a sitting position. She looked up at him. It was as if the Magister's jeweled eyes too were on fire. He had such a malicious look upon his face.

"You have been quite the thorn, Miss Zoe Halloconst. I despise thorns; they are so useless as it remains so easy to pluck those pretty little petals." He made a plucking motion with one hand and then began circling Zoe. "I know what you know. I know you've been having these little ideas—these little concepts of what is right and what is wrong." The motions of his hands augmented the expressions upon his face as he talked. "But that's fine. People such as yourself are anticipated for. In probabilistic logic, there will always be a 'Zoe,' a little bitch." He paused in front of her, leaning in close. "So, there are safeguards in place." He abruptly straightened up. "No matter. You are simply fodder. From your labors, my control grows. You see, all you've done is hurt yourself and those future stargazers." He raised his hacker card toward her. "Any last words before I kill you?"

Zoe stared at him. "A question, Sir," she said feebly.

"A question? Now? My dear, you are a tenacious one. I am glad I made the journey myself to see your end through." He motioned with a fat hand for her to speak.

"Pantheon... Pantheon Industries, how does it fit into all this?"

He laughed, a funny high-pitched laugh. "Pantheon Industries. Undoubtedly from your late mercenary accomplice you learned of Mr. Achan?" Zoe slowly nodded. "He has been dismissed. He was a... disappointment. Do not worry, a replacement has been found and behind that replacement, a million more men are waiting in line for their turn, crawling up that ladder one rung at a time with the ass of the man in front of them and the head of the man behind goading them on. Haha! All for the chance to serve my purpose in *my* society. Oh, Pantheon's influence reaches far, as you know, from edge to edge of the galaxy." The Magister raised up his fists as if the energy of just speaking about Pantheon was too much to be contained. He settled and resumed his cool demeanor. "I will let you know a little something about the Magister standing before you." He smoothed his robes, fluffing his persona. His expression became truly unhallowed. "I am Pantheon Industries. It has been handed down by generation after generation of my family for millennia. I am the one charged with keeping it safe..." He eyed her. "Withholding its secrets. Did you know that? Ha! Surely not. Call it a closely guarded family secret. Though, unlike my predecessors who had to abide by the spinning wheel of galactic government, I found a way through. Democracy—such a thorn. To truly secure Pantheon Industries I had to rise further. I am now a Magister. I like to say, The Magister. Or as I am otherwise known, *The* Grandeur; quite the name." He smiled at Zoe.

"Quite the name." Zoe could feel anger rising in her chest. "Are you the one responsible for what happened to Captain Henry?"

The Grandeur seemed to search his thoughts for a moment. "Oh yes, he has been disposed of. I do say, it has been more work than usual to tie up all those loose ends you've frayed. No matter." He resumed his circular walk around Zoe.

"You're a monster," said Zoe, through tense breaths.

He stopped abruptly and planted a stern hand under her chin, forcing her face upward. She tried to twist away but the Grandeur clamped down tighter on her jaw. With his other hand, he reached back and slapped her with the full weight of his hefty arm. Blood spurted from Zoe's lip and she fell to the floor.

Darious coughed once and groaned. He slowly turned over and got to his hands and knees. *What happened?* Consciousness slowly rose as he picked himself up and looked around. The CF scout... That immense moon vessel... The tractor beam dragging them in... He suddenly became aware of a disturbing scent akin to melting solder. Darious coughed again. It was dark, but he had become familiar enough with Zoe's ship to know he was still within it. There was a buzzing coming from somewhere. With a wince, Darious recalled being beaten and thrown back into the ship. His head was pounding. He put a hand to his left ear and it revealed coagulating blood. The air was thick, reminding him of the smog from that factory planet. *Something is burning.* He stood up in pain and began toward the cockpit, but his right leg gave way and he fell to the floor. Darious grunted and stood back up, ignoring the damaged limb. He limped to Zoe's seat and accessed the virtual console. Looking out through the glass he could see he was in space. Looking back down, his eyes narrowed. The console was only able to partially boot up. After some workarounds, rudimentary diagnostic systems begrudgingly came online. Darious quickly scanned through them. There was a fire currently burning in engine line three and the ship's filters were offline. That explained the smoke and smell around him. He managed a fix from the computer by reversing an electrovalve's direction, creating vacuum suction from space to the broken line and thus quelling the fire. His felt his head again. It throbbed at his touch. He remembered receiving the blunt end of a rifle. He closed his eyes, trying to remember additional details, but his mind kept returning to the pain.

Darious focused back on the console. He attempted a deeper diagnostic scan. It took the computer several minutes to compile a limited list of errors. Darious could feel the distinct rippling of anger and alarm; his mind constantly oscillated between each emotion. The ship was currently unflyable. The engines were heavily damaged, life support was running on its last backup energy cell, and many internal circuits were severed, preventing further analysis of the ship. Utilizing what was still available of outbound scanning utilities, Darious managed a broad search of the space around him. Emptiness. No CF vessels of any sort were in the vicinity. He then attempted to reboot navigational and communication systems. It took him a couple tries, as it was hard to concentrate through the pain, and several times he missed keystrokes. When the systems finally began loading, Darious took a moment to examine his own body. He had several long gashes and many non-consequential cuts; all seemed to be clotting normally. Along his midsection, there were several deep-skinned bruises that stung at the slightest touch. He surmised there was a possibility of internal bleeding. Darious purposely saved his leg for last. With careful fingertip caresses, he felt around his right leg, zeroing in on the epicenter of where the pain was coming from. His tibia didn't feel broken, but the area was swelling badly.

A blue screen popped up, detailing that most of the navigational systems had been unable to properly reboot, however basic communications were still available. Darious quickly brought up the lightcard-sync algorithm that Zoe and he had used during the Pantheon Industries heist on Kratos. He breathed a sigh of relief. The ship immediately located Zoe's lightcard, though it was rapidly moving away from him at floating-parsec speeds.

Darious knew he had work to do, and to do quickly. He stood up, mindful of his bum leg, and surveyed the battered ship, starting first with the cockpit, which was in shambles, and then moved on to the main chamber. There were burns etched along the walls and metal debris throughout the small room. Darious again became aware of that half-forgotten buzzing sound, but he couldn't localize it. Then he saw the hatchway. It was not metallic grey as before, but a shiny russet. With his full perception on the new door, he realized the thrumming sound was coming from it. Darious quickly concluded that there must be a pin-sized puncture somewhere there, seeping precious air to outer-space. He stepped up to the odd door. It had no handles or bolts! He held out a hand and lightly pressed on its surface. To his surprise it flexed outward, causing him to quickly retract his hand. Darious stared at the elastic material and then he understood what was before him. He grinned from ear to ear.

"Zoe, you have saved my life once again."

Darious laughed. The ship apparently had a rubber-like space polymer around the entryway—an airbag in the event of ship depressurization. *Thank you!*

Upon further inspection, Darious could see that the actual metal door was still intact, though jammed in a retracted position. The pain around his body and fogginess in his mind began dissipating as the winds of resolve strengthened. He went over to one of the long drawers and pulled out several tools. Next to the entryway, he opened up a panel and began repairing the filaments to the door. Darious was clicking objectives into place as his work proceeded rapidly. *First things first,* he thought, *repair leaks, then life systems, then navigation, then thrusters. Then Zoe.*

"What is the secret?" asked Zoe, straining to sit up. "What is it that's worth so many lives?"

The Grandeur looked pitifully down at her. "Oh, come now." Then a glean of pleasure crossed his face. "It all began millennia ago, with the first generation of Pantheon, though in those days it went by a different name. Arrival of the final frontier; oh, they knew..." Blood was slowly dripping from Zoe's lip. She did not wipe it away. "They knew it was time..." He paused and glared disgustingly down at her huddled body. "Time for a higher form of control. Whether they had the foresight to see what came next, I do not know. Whether it was gallantry or luck, they found it. How extra-ordinary it must have seemed—how unnatural. They took it to the fire, forged a new galactic society from it, and then they wielded it. Now I continue to wield it."

Zoe slowly raised a hand to her chest, grimacing as if her lungs were in pain, which they were. In actuality, she had begun typing instructions into her lightcard, navigating through its programming from memory. The Grandeur seemed not to notice, nor care. He began again slowly orbiting Zoe.

"The galaxy, every single grain of salt, every particle in it, belongs to me. After years of toiling with that Earl, the galaxy's greatest resource will now finally be mine. Kapteyn belongs to me. No more impediments. Nothing will stand in my way. I will end this clandestine war. This galaxy—*my galaxy*—is under *my* rule and soon to be under *my* complete subjugation. They will remember me until the end of time!" He stopped in front of Zoe, facing away from her as if she were no longer worth his noble sight. "You may rely on this single fact: I am in control."

To this, Zoe began balling a fist.

"Hey mister," she retorted in a strained voice.

The Grandeur turned around, continuing to hold his head up high. Still half crouched from the pain all over her body, Zoe slowly brought up a hand and wiped the blood from her face. She lifted her head and locked eyes with him, matching his embellished complacency.

"Watch this."

She pointed a finger to her chest. "Aaand..."

The Grandeur glowered down at her, his fiery scorn seeking to consume the plebian below. Zoe stared up at him. To the contrary, his fire was not consuming her; it could not. The flames wriggled around her; they bent at unnatural angles and began warping into something new. His oppression became a fan to her smoldering will.

"...enter," said Zoe coldly. She tapped the final command hidden under her shirt, engaging the program. In the following moment, the room remained silent.

Then suddenly, all the lights flickered, breaking the Grandeur's cruel, sumptuous stance. Zoe continued to stare at him, managing a devious smile through swollen, bloody lips. This made the Grandeur evidently somewhat uneasy. He was in the process of raising his hacker card when the surrounding lights shuddered again and then completely went out, instantly being replaced by red emergency lights and alarms. As confusion overtook the Grandeur, Zoe sprang into action.

She leapt forward, landing next to the Grandeur and bent low, performing a low sweeping kick and knocked his feet out from under him. As he fell, Zoe spun and used her momentum to swing herself back to a standing position. He hit the ground with a loud thud and a painful groan. Zoe ran to the door, pausing for just a moment to look back at the Grandeur, who was now an opulent mess on the floor. His robes covered his body while he slowly wiggled underneath, stunned and under pain of his hedonism.

Scanning the edges of the prison door, Zoe pulled out her lightcard. The electronic locks didn't stand a chance. With a single click, Zoe opened the door just a hair and looked out. She didn't spot any awaiting personnel. Wasting no time, she rushed into the room and then bounded down the corridor, with rotating reds and wailing sirens above her.

⚊⟨⊢ ⊣⟩⚊

Darious was plugging away, decrying having only been fashioned with only two eyes and two arms. He never dared blink whilst swift finger movements picked up wires, tested connections, soldered ends, and continued on. He felt black spears of whiplash as his vision out-sped his hands to guide his work. He had to concentrate intensely to keep his eyes from rolling down his face and onto the floor, or they too would be picked up and soldered back in place. His mind constantly splintered off with thoughts of Zoe.

"Zoe," he whispered to himself.

For a moment, Darious could feel the cold and unfathomable loneliness of outer-space converging on his dark corner of infinity. Then, stirring sounds, like the waking grumblings of some hibernating creature hungry for its first meal of the year, began from under Darious' feet. The ship was coming back to life.

Darious' heartbeat quickened. *Yes!* He quickly placed a key connector into its electrical slot and looked on with anticipation. Nothing happened.

"Damn it!"

Darious pulled back an arm and punched the exposed circuitry. A loud hum started from the engines and the entire console lit up with blinking lights and readying interfaces. Excited hooves and snarls arose in the craft. Darious leapt to the control console and began feverishly typing away. The bright screen made his eyes water, as if he had been an eternal wanderer in an underground maze and had finally sighted his salvation.

"Aaand..." Darious waited, poised and ready. The beast within the ship was churning and amplifying. Darious urged the screen on. "Come on, come on." Internal systems were compiling errors and autonomously reworking connections a million times a second. He stared at the loading bar as it worked its way from one edge of the screen to the other. It stopped and started, stopped and started again, continuously in limbo. The clone looked out to the stars. It took several minutes for the bar to fill. Then a prompt appeared onscreen. All fixes had been completed. "... enter." Darious pressed the command and the ship roared with vitality. He managed a little smile through the sweat and stress. Lights on the exterior of the ship flicked on, the engines test fired, and the entire ship broke free from its stone tomb. The beast bellowed, rattling its wingtips, and with a burst of its thrusters bright enough to challenge the pulsars of Andromeda, rocketed on toward Zoe.

As pumping heart from artery to artery, the lift raised Zoe from the depths of the underworld and up toward the deliverance earned by her temperance. Under the dim lights, Zoe looked at the drying blood upon her clothes. She filled her lungs with air and with a quick exhalation, shot out a wad of mucus and blood from her nose. She wiped her face with her arm and looked over at the elevator's display panel, which spasmodically blinked with the red background 'Emergency' and a small smile formed at the corner of her lips. The passing floors ticked by. Twenty. Twenty-one. Twenty-two. Twenty-three.

The lift stopped with a slight rattle and the doors retracted. Zoe glanced out from behind the side divider and breathed a sigh of relief upon seeing that the corridor was empty. The large hallway was without normal illumination, having only red flashing lights to guide the way. Zoe began running down the hall, stopping only momentarily at a computer terminal to make sure she was still heading toward the outer sections of the mammoth vessel. Thankfully, she continued to be on course to the closest bay area. Zoe sure hoped there was a ship there, any ship.

Just as Zoe neared the end of the hallway, she heard voices from around the corner and dove into an adjacent room. She quickly looked around. It was a small commissary, lacking sufficient light and consequently full of shadows. She ducked behind a table and listened. The hustling voices hit their max and soon faded out. Suddenly, her lightcard began beeping. Zoe fully scrunched under the table and pulled it out. An incoming call! She stared at it wide eyed for a moment and then held the lightcard close to her face.

"Hello?"

"Zoe!" cried Darious from the other end. "Zoe!"

"Darious!" she nearly shouted but quieted herself. "Oh Darious, you have no idea how great it is to hear your voice."

"Yours as well. Zoe, I can see you are still in the CF vessel. What is going on?"

"I am. They had put me in a cell, but they should have known no cell could hold the great and powerful Zoe. Where are you? Are you okay?"

"I am fine, heading in your direction with your ship."

"My ship," choked Zoe, suddenly recalling her dire dread when Darious was tossed into certain oblivion. "After they threw you back in there I... I saw an explosion... I thought... Oh, I'm so glad you're okay."

"I am tracking you with your lightcard. I am set to rendezvous shortly. Why are all the smaller ships leaving from the vessel you are on?"

"The ships are leaving? I... I... just overloaded the lighting system. Why are the ships leaving?"

"I do not know," responded Darious. "I have scanned your location within the ship. The closest landing point near you is

Dock 103. I will be there in approximately seven minutes. Can you meet me there?"

"Yes sir," said Zoe. "Over and out. See you soon."

"See you soon," he replied. The call ended.

Zoe stood up and spotted a control panel. She flipped it on and looked up Dock 103. It wasn't far at all. She might just survive this.

A monitor above the entryway flickered and turned on. Zoe looked up at it. The picture smoothed out, revealing the Grandeur centered onscreen, sitting on the bridge of some luxurious private spacecraft. He wore a wicked grin.

"See where your brashness has led you? Stupid girl. Your prison will now be your grave." He typed on the keypad at the arm of his chair. "It's too bad. I quite liked that ship. I had it created just so I could saunter across the galaxy to indulge in my little pleasures." The Grandeur leaned forward, and his expression turned to harsh judgement. "I've sent an order for the ship to self-destruct. Good riddance." He looked beyond the screen. "Let's be off! I have a meeting in the Orion System at three." The monitor feed cut out.

Zoe stood in amazement. *No way. No way he would do it.* Then, from some far-off place, deep within the massive vessel, she heard the sounds of pressure building, of bending rivets and expanding metal, and then a low mechanical groaning began. A siren wailed, and an automated voice came over the ship's speakers, echoing throughout the vessel.

"Warning. Self-destruct sequence One Zero Niner activated. Warning. Self-destruct sequence activated."

Zoe vaulted over the table and began running, using both arms and legs to propel herself as fast as humanly possible towards Dock 103. With each step she swung her arms forward, cupping the air and flinging it behind her to gain to gain extra speed.

A distant blast echoed from behind Zoe and vibrated through her chest. Upon reaching the end of the hallway, she gripped its cornered edge, pivoting to the next hall while maintaining her forward momentum. She ran at top speed, flying from corridor to corridor. Through heavy breathing she could smell burning oil and metals. It smelled of death.

"Warning. Catastrophic failure. Warni—"

A nearby thunderous explosion disabled the intercom voice and impelled Zoe to run even faster. She sprinted through flanged hatchways as she reached the outer engineering sections of the ship, timing leaps over the lip of each one. She swung around a secondary corridor and almost lost her balance, though quickly compensating and continuing her headlong run.

Upon the next intersection, Zoe quickly chose left but slowed and stopped after several meters. She began to run again but paused, looking back and then forward again. *Don't second guess yourself. There's no time.* She stretched her brain trying to remember the correct route through the inconceivably large ship.

"Arrgh," she said aloud in desperation.

Another explosion resounded from far off followed by crumpling metal. Sweat poured down Zoe's brow. She made up her mind to keep heading in the direction she was facing despite her burning uncertainty. Her first step sent her much further than anticipated.

"Crap!"

The ship's internal gravity stabilizers were giving out. Each stride sent Zoe several meters forward. She began again, keeping her stance low as not come into contact with the ceiling as she picked up speed. The corridor was never-ending. It was as if the ship was mocking her racked mind by funneling onwards in an exponential cone. Zoe threw out her thoughts of impending doom and refocused her determination. She would make it. In her mind's eye, she faintly remembered the left end of the hallway opening up to a larger hallway, which would then dead-end at Dock 103—where Darious would be waiting for her.

Another shock reverberated through the ship. Zoe looked back and saw red flaring up from the end of the hallway she had just traversed. She again centered her attention on her target and ran as the artificial gravity continued to loosen its synthetic grip on her. Her sprint became elongated leaps from just her tip-toes, carrying her forward with barely any contact to the ground.

Ongoing detonations behind Zoe seemed to be ripping the vessel apart from the seams. With one loud boom, the gravitational systems abruptly went completely offline, sending Zoe into the ceiling from her last vault. She hit her head on the riveted metal and spun in weightlessness. Despite the instant and agonizing pain, Zoe quickly regained her bearings. She again bounded forward, though the hallway appeared to have attained a slight spin to it. With fleet steps, she leapt onwards while grabbing at anything she could use to keep on going, to keep on moving. Zoe strained to keep her eyes on the hallway's end as the fog of spiraling dizziness rolled in.

She reached the end of the corridor, but was unable to properly stop and crumpled into the wall. Zoe quickly up-righted herself and stood horizontally on the wall. Bruised and battered, she looked down sideways through the corridor. A great relief came over her as she spotted the hatchway to her ship at its end. Zoe looked upward at the hallway she had just navigated and went pale. The far end glowed bright red and was undulating from the extreme heat and pressure; the corridor was literally melting away.

Suddenly, a mighty rivet-snapping wave rolled through the hallway's end and it exploded. Zoe's body went into an automated run as though she had been trained to race at the sound of a gunshot. Her body, free from thought, moved impulsively with pumping arms and legs. She scampered through the corridor, ricocheting off all its sides toward the hatchway of Dock 103. Her mind was insulated from her being. Instinct was now the sole conductor of all ratiocinations. Explosions rocked the ship about Zoe. No longer were they just behind her, but from all around.

She reached the hatch, securing her hands on it, and looked back. Behind her flames were rushing through the corridor, rushing towards her. They almost seemed to form a devilish grin, much like the Grandeur's.

Zoe clawed at the hatchway. There was no intelligence, just feral muscles pulling at levers, scratching at rivets, and banging on the porthole. Moments later, a click sounded inside the door's mechanism, signaling the correct combination of bangs and clangs had opened the Byzantine gateway. Zoe scurried into the vacuum seal, the portal from hell to salvation, taking once last glance at her assailant. The inferno was coming directly at her, shooting sparks and hurling shrapnel with mechanical, maniacal laughter. She slammed the hatch closed and vaulted herself toward her ship's awaiting entryway.

As soon as Zoe was inside her craft, she dashed to the cockpit, scrunching Darious to the side of the captain's seat and took the helm. Thrusters were instantly at maximum. There was a loud pop as the vacuum seal was ripped from the Grandeur's vessel. Flames licked around the edges of Zoe's windshield. With the engines at full tilt, the ship's two occupants were instantly pressed flat against the seat. They shot out from the firestorm, just as the entirety of the enormous moon vessel ruptured and was consumed by explosions. After the initial vibrations of her craft, everything soon settled and became evident the immediate danger had passed.

Zoe shook her head as disbelieving consciousness returned to her.

"Wow."

She brought up the rear view on her projection display and saw the giant vessel had been torn apart and was now being besieged by rubicund clouds from ongoing tertiary explosions. As they reached a reasonable distance from the shattered moon, Zoe's mind relaxed into a composed quietude. She sighed, letting loose nearly all the air from her lungs.

She turned to Darious. "Now that was a close one."

CHAPTER 46

THE TORPOR TORPEDO

The pair wasted no time in fixing the remainder of glitches on the ship. Before long, it was running like a well-oiled machine. Zoe plotted a course away from all planetary systems to a silent, sanctified sector of space. She then put her ship on autopilot with long-range scanners set to announce any anomalies and met up with Darious in the main chamber.

He took her hand and guided her to a seat, setting a first aid kit on the table. As he began to dress her wounds, she looked at him, observing his eyes deeply focused on tending to her injuries. A couple times, Zoe winced from the pain, but she was always comforted by his gaze. Zoe put her hand to Darious' cheek and brushed his damp hair back. He had cuts upon his face and a nasty gash atop his ear. She reached out to take up a medical sowing needle from the kit but Darious put a hand over hers.

"In a moment," he said gently. "Allow me to take care of you first." He slowly and meticulously worked his way from her arms upward. "You have a cut along your lip," he said and gently wiped the drying blood from it with a cloth. Darious leaned in close and Zoe could feel herself falling toward him. She caressed her cheek against his. They shared a soft kiss. Zoe rested her head on his shoulder and he put his arms around her. Her pain melted away. All their hardships, everything that had happened since they had met, within this moment was all worth it.

After a bit, Zoe straightened up and considered their current situation while staring into Darious' profound eyes. "Darious, I met the Magister responsible for all this."

His expression darkened. "He is the one that did this to you, is he not?" Zoe nodded. "I shall kill him if I ever meet him."

Zoe pulled herself tight against Darious and closed her eyes. "He is a terrible man." She opened her eyes. "However, he admitted there *is* something behind all of this. I hope our impending higher-energy scan will shed some light on his secret." Zoe sat up and gave Darious another kiss. She looked him over and smirked. "Look at us; we're covered in tar, blood, and sweat. I bet we're the best smelling couple in the galaxy."

After they finished addressing each other's injuries, Zoe returned to the cockpit to check on the status of her craft. She could hear Darious collecting their war-torn rags and dumping them in the trash shoot. With a single, hollow thump, they were shot out to space and Zoe felt renewed, as if that unhallowed part of her had been purified. Darious joined her momentarily after.

"All clear on scanners," she said as he bent over her seat.

"That is good to hear."

"Yup. And just an hour or so until the results from Wormy reaches us. Oh, the anticipation is always the worst." Darious took a seat on the arm of her chair. She patted him on the knee. "Hey, how about I warm us up some—"

Suddenly a red alert flashed across the main screen. Zoe and Darious froze in place.

'*Incoming Armada*'

Darious stood with a jolt. "Incoming armada?!"

Zoe too was in disbelief. "Incoming armada!? An entire armada!? Darious, battle stations!"

He flung himself to his post and Zoe prepped her ship's systems. Azimuthal thrusters were pre-fired, the ship's small weapons array was brought online, backup systems were all charged with full redundancies, a set of Zoe's custom programs were placed at the ready on a quick-jump list to her left, and all exterior protocol ports were shut off to avoid the possibility of any hacking attempts—lest Zoe get a taste of her own medicine, without a spoon full of sugar in the vacuum of space.

Zoe turned to Darious. "Ready?"

He nodded. "Ready. T-minus thirty seconds until they are upon us."

Zoe spun back around and fiddled her fingers over her projection console. This was going to be the truest test of her ship to date. Even though an entire CF armada was bearing down on them, Zoe felt assured, more than she ever had, that with Darious and with her ship, there wasn't anything she couldn't accomplish.

"Incoming!" shouted Darious.

The first wave of the fleet slowed from their superluminal speeds, skidding to a halt around Zoe's craft. They were large destroyers. The ships formed a blockade at fifteen-degree separations from one another, preventing any hasty move from the tiny craft at their center.

Zoe initiated a routine and sent out a pulsed wave to the ships, the same communication overload harmonic she had used against Dr. Saknussemm and Kappa, but the effect was null, as she expected. *It was worth a shot.* While her ship was recharging its energy banks, Zoe scrolled through other alternatives. Against a CF fleet their options were limited, very limited. She activated another program, sending out a burst scan to look for weak points in the CF embattlement positioning. Her ship's computer crunched a million scenarios, tracing out thrust, agility, and the capabilities of the many bodies to search for possible escape routes. Results were also null. There was no escape possible. *Okay,* thought Zoe, *so that's out too.*

"Weapons locked!" called Darious.

"We're safe for now," said Zoe. "They are just making sure we stay put until the big guys show up."

Zoe swiped through more unscrupulous programs. Nothing here could help them. Her eyes then broadened at the thought of Dr. Saknussemm's Z-Pulser program. Oh, but that might end badly for them, really bad. The possibility of unknowns was too much to attempt it. Zoe rapped her fingers on the console. She decided that as counterintuitive as it might seem, their best option would be to wait for most of the CF ships to arrive and stir them up, creating as much chaos as possible, then they could have a chance at escape. Statistical probabilities be damned. The thought reminded her of Kappa, the undisputed champion of controlled chaos.

Zoe slowly throttled forward and wound her ship in a tight figure-eight, like a fish surrounded by sharks.

"Ships inbound!" called Darious.

Just then dozens more CF vessels entered the area, reducing the view of the stars beyond. Large dreadnaught-class ships formed strategic outer rings around Zoe with smaller frigates and corvettes strategically filling in gaps of the bulwark.

Zoe looked over her long-range scanners. About half of the fleet that her long-range scanners had detected had arrived. Just a few more and she could use the last incoming bit to her advantage. Zoe continued inputting minimal power into her engines.

"Weapons locked!" said Darious.

"None powering, correct?" asked Zoe.

"Correct. 1,242 individual weapon locks."

That's a lot of locks, thought Zoe.

More ships flooded onto the battlefield. Zoe's computer now counted upwards of two hundred ships surrounding them.

"Darious, in a moment I'm going to try something very, very stupid. Strap in." She heard the click of his belt as she placed her fingers at the ready on the projection console. "Here goes nothing." She plotted out a twisting course, per the computer's best simulation, and engaged the ship's controls. Zoe's ship rocketed toward the closest frigate.

Right before impact, she pivoted upwards, nearly dousing the CF ship in the trail of her thrusters and then completed a similar maneuver over the next three closest crafts. She could see the CF armada was already shifting positions, reacting and anticipating her possible machinations.

"Weapons powering!" shouted Darious. A red alert suddenly appeared on Zoe's screen. "Weapons fired!"

Plasma bolts from the nearest battle group shot towards Zoe's craft. She spiraled her ship, avoiding the brute of them. Only two shots grazed her hull. Zoe then began wrapping her ship about a large destroyer as if tying a bow around it whilst fighting the centrifugal forces that pushed her away. She completed loop after loop, confusing CF volleys, before soaring perpendicularly from the innermost CF globule. Zoe's computer chirped; they had managed to pierce through the interior CF barricade, leaving that central circle of certain destruction. It would take that task force time to regroup and thus for the moment, they were an afterthought.

Ahead of Zoe and Darious, outlying CF vessels were now tightening their formations and drawing inward. Zoe could see more warships arriving in the distance, rushing in so fast they appeared to materialize from nothingness. An alert onscreen refocused Zoe's attention. Another volley of plasma bolts was searing through space toward her ship. She wasted no time, powering toward a semicircle-shaped frigate and bringing her ship as close to it as she could. She pivoted hard-right, just as the underbelly of her craft skimmed its hull and then she shot off vertically. Zoe saw one of the blazing blue bolts strike the frigate and smirked at the CF's clumsiness. They were, after all, getting outmaneuvered by a small ship built from a junkyard.

Zoe's computer signaled a pair of CF cruisers pulling up alongside one another. A momentary advantage! Zoe swiftly navigated between them and matched their velocity, using them as cover and appreciating they couldn't risk shooting one another at such close range. The advantage was indeed fleeting, as the two vessels quickly split away from one another and their turrets turned toward her ship. The reprieve however, had allowed Zoe to stretch her fingers and prepare for the next round of cat and mouse.

"Missiles locked! Missiles fired!" yelled Darious.

A multitude of alerts flashed across Zoe's screen. Playtime was apparently over. She piloted her ship straight ahead, hoping she could reach the enormous warship she had in her sights and use it as a shield. The missiles rounded just behind Zoe's ship, madly clawing through space. Just as the closest of the projectiles was in arm's reach of her craft, Zoe spun her ship and arced it around the great vessel within a finger's caress of its exterior. A missile clipped one of the warship's antennas, exploding on impact and sending a fireball across a good portion of its hull. Zoe swooped downward, experiencing a hard G-force and strained to keep her hands on the console. She then leapt from one portly ship to another, glancing off each before turning away in a different direction to the next. All around her craft, constant torrents of missiles whizzed by, some inadvertently impacting CF ships while others spun madly off course, lost to space. Zoe could only imagine the yelling of CF commanders seeing the crisscrossing of deadly projectiles across their bows.

Zoe's computer signaled another safe gap and she immediately seized the opportunity, pushing thrusters to maximum and swirling around a CF frigate that had broken rank in the confusion and created that transitory opening. An explosion at Zoe's starboard nearly shook her from her seat. She quickly altered course to elevate the disorder around her. Her computer beeped with expanding possibilities of escape. *There!* From the projection console, Zoe picked out a proposed outbound route with a 'moderate' success rate. With rapid finger movements, she plotted the course, tweaked it, and looked outward. *Probabilities be damned.* They could make it. Zoe wiped all screens and put forth all power to the engines, speeding toward freedom.

"Watch out Zoe!" shouted Darious. "Ship inbound!"

Just then, an enormous CF worldshaker intercepted them from superluminous flight, covering the entirety of Zoe's bow window. She immediately cut power from forward thrusters and engaged a full reverse. The ship wrenched, nearly tossing Zoe from her command station as equipment from the main chamber clattered on the floor. She quickly managed to regain control and skirted her craft to a stop while tilting it upward in the process.

"Weapons fired!"

"Thrusters to full!" Zoe shouted. "We're goin' up!"

A volley of plasma bolts and projectiles erupted from the giant vessel toward them. Zoe ignited the main forward thruster and began winding her ship with the hope of making it a more difficult target to maintain a lock onto.

Zoe looked out at the massive ship waning below her field of vision. Alerts sounded. The rest of the CF fleet was now also firing upon them.

"No. They are launching everything! No!" she yelled at her console. Desperation was quickly setting in.

Zoe maneuvered her ship as fast as her reflexes would allow. Her mind was racing; her heart could not keep up pace. "Darious. Darious we're not going to make it." Her screen indicated that included in the massive bombardment, 1,211 Scalar-class torpedoes were whipping through space toward them.

"Captain!"

"Darious! I've got one thing left to try!" Zoe then whispered to herself, "one last try." She quickly brought up a new menu, navigated through her list of folders, zoned in on a particular subsection and initiated its contents.

Her ship fell to a dead stop. With all hell raining on them, Zoe rerouted all engine power to a single computer program.

"Captain?!"

"More power!"

"Aye Captain!"

As Zoe typed away, shutting down all subsystems and rerouting every microwatt of power, she could see Darious was virtually alongside her, deactivating bilateral systems and others she had missed. Her projection console signaled that the thousands of CF projectiles were now within mere kilometers. There were only seconds before impact. With one last breath, Zoe turned off the tracking sensor array, utilizing even its power for her singular purpose. She glanced down at the projection console. The Z-Pulsers had been successfully turned inwards, their focal point centered within her own craft, and Dr. Saknussemm's algorithm was fully prepped. Zoe pressed enter.

⊶⊰⊱⊷

The brightest light ever witnessed by mankind occurred on this day. Beyond the mind's corporeal comprehension, it momentarily blinded both sight and thought impartially. At the heart of this brilliant aurora was that bantam craft belonging to Zoe Halloconst. To any that could have perceived through such light in that instant, her ship would have appeared to suddenly fracture—cleft in half—then splinter into millions of ongoing creasing fractals and furthermore into an innumerable number of dimensionless fields. In that marked moment, the ship's two occupants would have screamed; they would have flailed their limbs and gone insane had they been able to glimpse the breadth and depth of dot-point reality expanded to infinity and back again.

Zoe had dared to use the higher-order algorithm turned in toward her own spaceship. She had dared and fired the Z-Pulsers with every bit of power her craft had. If Zoe could have stuffed her soul into it too, she would have. The amount of energy injected unto itself at staged resonance nodes bent classical space to degrees unfathomable. The light from the ignition point had instantly and completely engulfed Zoe's ship. It had engulfed the entire region and in that moment of doing so, had filled every shadow with pure, unheeding light.

Just as quickly as the light begun, it ceased. A single cough came from the smoky cabin.

<hr/>

"Agh. Uhh." Zoe slowly opened an eye, revealing a familiar metallic floor. She sat upright. "Darious?"

There was the sound of grating metal behind her chair. She rushed over and helped lift the debris from Darious. He coughed and sat up, looking at her.

"Zoe. What did you—? How are we—?"

She took Darious' arm and helped him to his feet. They stood with arms around each other's shoulders. The smoke was rapidly being filtered out and normal lighting had come back on in her ship. As Zoe looked around, she noted the low grumbling of her ship's engines, indicating they too were online and idling. Zoe and Darious looked out of the cockpit window. The sight was unbelievable.

They were still surrounded by CF ships, hundreds, if not thousands, of them. Zoe stared at the enormous vessel closest to them. All its navigation lights were off, and its many windows were darkened. She then realized the vessel wasn't even stationary; it was drifting! The entire ship had been powered down and was now simply floating along in space. She looked beyond it. All the CF ships had been disabled! The entire armada!

"Zoe, what did you do?" asked Darious in a mesmerized tone.

Just then, a projectile came into view and tranquilly glided by, only meters from their port bow. Zoe followed it with her eyes until it passed beyond her window's panorama. She looked at Darious and then sat in her chair. With steadied keystrokes, she analyzed the area around them.

"Darious, all of the Copper ships, everything... engines are offline, weapons are offline, navigational systems are offline, but their life systems are on—though they are being powered by their last remaining back-up cells. Everything has been shut off somehow."

"Everything except for us," said Darious.

Zoe did a quick scan of her own ship's systems. He was right. Minor damage was evident, but overall her ship was operational and quite capable of spaceflight. She wasted no time.

"Let's get the hell out of here."

Zoe eased her ship forward to make sure there were no more surprises and then they shot out from the sea of petrified driftwood.

CHAPTER 47

RISE

The pair had completed close to 5 floating-parsecs before Zoe turned off the afterburners and gave the red-hot engines a much-needed reprieve. She had spent the entire time at her console, staring with unflinching eyes at long-range scans. For the last hour, not even the blip of a passing semi had appeared. The mood had finally calmed within the ship.

Zoe kept replaying in her mind what had happened when she had launched the Z-Pulsers in on themselves. It was like for a moment she was lifeless, or like some nescient creature, but at the same time, she felt as if she had been spread across the cosmos. The sensation was odd; it was hard to pin down and her memory was just too fuzzy. What struck her as even more odd was the fact that she didn't feel shaken up by the experience. Somehow it had felt *natural* in a very raw sort of way.

"Zoe," said Darious from behind her. "If you do not mind, I would much like to take a hot shower."

"Oh, please do!" she said, turning in her chair and smiling at him. "They can smell you all the way from Gamma-9."

Darious smirked and held her hand.

"I have a question."

"Shoot," she said.

"How did you know Doctor Earl Saknussemm's algorithm would work?"

Zoe looked at him for several seconds before responding. "I had a gut feeling." She then shook her head. "It was a last resort. We got lucky." This didn't seem to satisfy Darious, so she continued. "I thought perhaps it would pull us out of phase from all the matter around us and we could just pass through everyone while giving them the finger." She smiled. "Well, I figured either that would happen, or we'd be turned to goop."

"But neither occurred."

"I know. I... I'm not sure what happened. But I do know we are alive. And I am sure thankful for that." She gave his hand a squeeze. Darious then gave her a brief kiss and headed for the shower.

As Zoe stared off into space, continuing to repeat that seemingly arcane event, a soft ding came from her computer. She sat straight up. The ship was beginning to receive the data from her subspace worm, Wormy. Zoe brought up the download screen. *40%. 65%. 85%. 95%.* She stared at it with silent anticipation. *Download complete.* Zoe's fingers shook as she opened the repository of information collected from the furthest reaches of the galaxy, all ready to be compiled into a great galactic map of her home viewed from an angle never before observed.

Zoe loaded a predefined atlas of the Milky Way. It projected outwards in front of her, expanding over her cockpit window. Zoe could feel her heart tremble as she steadied her breathing. In blues and brilliant whites, the galaxy lay before her. From the top-down view, each of its swirled arms displayed millions upon millions of star systems, many of which humans inhabited. Zoe looked at the Milky Way's dazzling center, where the central black hole kept the entire arrangement in celestial balance. She placed her hands on the projection console and prepared to overlay Wormy's data. Zoe dimmed the interactive map of the galaxy and removed its coloring so that only a ghostly image remained. Then she had her computer superimpose all the accumulated readings from that higher-energy form of space. Instantly, orange dots appeared across the Milky Way, millions of them, present in every sector. Her eyes moistened as she marveled at the site and her mouth stood agape.

Zoe quickly picked an outer region and used her fingers to zoom in on it until the view was narrowed to a dozen star systems. She picked out random orange points for inspection. Some were cigar shaped, others were nearly spherical. Some were massive—the size of stars—while others remained as tiny illuminated specks. Zoe swiped the digital map to a completely different region; a similar view presented itself. She shrunk the map and expanded it in another area and then another. The higher stable-state readings were present over the entirety of the Milky Way! Her mouth opened wider. What were they? *They couldn't all be—*

"Zoe!" called an odd voice from the central chamber. The utterance sounded so etiolated, it took Zoe a second to recognize it was Darious'. She got up at once and headed to him. He was standing, with his back to her, frozen in place and pointing to the table at the center of the main room. Zoe looked past him, out to where his limb was directing, and nearly jumped back. There, on the metal table was something that Zoe definitely did not have onboard before. Moreover, she had never even seen anything like it before.

A wondrous shining statue, about a meter tall, stood on the table. It was a thin tower-like structure composed of several knife-like spiraling curves intertwining with one another as they rose to a flowering top. The sculpture reflected with hues like that of Kapteyn, but with even more radiance, as if it were the substance in its purest form. The object was almost ethereal; Zoe could nearly see through some of the intertwined helices and on the whole, the entire statue seemed to glow by its own hidden illumination against the backdrop of her ship. A band of light contoured its silhouette, adding to the transcendental nature of the mysterious object. It was beautiful.

Inching toward it, Zoe spoke slowly. "Where did it come from?"

"I... I don't know," replied Darious in a low voice. "I was getting the antiseptic cleaner from the compartment there." His arm twitched toward the direction, but he was apparently too stunned to move beyond that. "When I... I turned back I saw it there."

Zoe cautiously edged right up to the table. The object seemed harmless enough. She bent low and peered in closer. It was more than otherworldly; the overlapping curves were blurred, as if somewhat out of phase.

"Out of phase!" Zoe turned and sprung to a drawer, pulling out a device with an antenna. A quick scan confirmed her suspicion. "Those spirals are vibrating at largely different ground frequencies at nodes coinciding with the algorithm from Dr. Saknussemm's work. They are all near enough to our norm, so they can be seen." As Zoe's curiosity peaked, she added, "I bet we could even feel them." She took in a deep breath and reached her hand out.

"Careful," said Darious.

Zoe put her fingertips to the strange object. If felt cold to the touch and produced a tingling sensation. She used the device in her other hand to complete a closer scan.

"Look at that," she said. "Each loop exists independently, slightly out of phase with the next. They aren't actually physically touching each other. This is amazing."

The tingling sensation began to extend beyond Zoe's fingers. She retracted her hand and stared at it. The feeling quickly traveled up her arms and spread through her body, infusing deeper and deeper until she felt it within the core of her being.

Complete understanding suddenly swelled through Zoe: those orange readings showing higher-energy stable-state bodies, the Kapteyn, the semi drivers with their sensor ghosts, the secrets inducing sacrificial blood offerings… all the mismatching evidence, all the data, all that had occurred, the Grandeur's words—it all fit perfectly together… there was *one* absolute truth here and Zoe now saw it clearly.

"Darious." Zoe slowly stood up straight and began backing away from the object. "Darious, we are not alone."

"Zoe, what do you mean?"

Her mind was a flurry of excitement as variables and unknowns were guided to their correct positions, finally clicking into place and interlocking. The one truth was this: Intelligent life existed independent of mankind. Moreover, these *aliens* inhabited the entirety of the galaxy alongside mankind. There was an entire civilization, hidden just beyond sight, and this artifact on her table was a token from them.

An abrupt outpouring of stimulated emotion flowed from Zoe.

"The Grandeur! This is what he was referring to! Pantheon knew about this!" She kicked her foot out. "Those bastards have been exploiting alien technology for their own gain. Ohhh I really, really like it when I'm right!" She began rapidly pacing around the table. "But Dr. Saknussemm… what were they trying to have him do? Oh my! Oh my! Recall the info from his data stick saying that they were trying to destroy natural Kapteyn? Natural occurring Kapteyn? No, it's manufactured by Pantheon Industries. But who obviously created it first? Not us. Oh my!" She stopped midstep. "Darious, I think Pantheon has been at war with an alien species. And the Grandeur was using Dr. Saknussemm to plan something big before he was able to get away."

"But why?" Darious asked.

"As the Grandeur said himself, 'control.'"

"And think about this," Zoe continued, "They must be peaceful. I mean, Pantheon has been exploiting them for who knows how long and they, with obviously superior technology, have done what? Well, I do suppose they have acted out a couple times, like hitting semis brandishing the corporation's logos." She then thought of the two punctures on Captain Henry's ship. "But even in those instances, they never killed anyone, they just disabled their ships. Oh, and then Pantheon comes and hushes it all up. Oh man."

Just then a beeping sounded from the cockpit. Zoe ran and pitched herself into her seat. Darious was close behind, though his stance was positioned to be on the defensive, lest the statue try anything funny.

"It's the Z-Pulsers?" Zoe said confused. She typed into the virtual console.

"Are they malfunctioning?" asked Darious.

"I don't think so. They are offline... energy isn't going out, it's coming in." Zoe stared at Darious wide eyed. "I think we are receiving a message from higher order space." She quickly keyed in more commands for her computer and a large screen popped up with a repeating numerical sequence.

"It's a set of spatial coordinates," said Darious awestruck.

Zoe typed in the location. "It's close to us." Her skin was still tingling all over. "Darious. This is it. We have reached the rise."

CHAPTER 48

INTERLUDE TO A SHOWDOWN

I n space, there cannot be sound for there is no medium by which to apply it, yet there are echoes—self-contained memories scribed to quanta and stone all through the corpus of the continuum. Such recordings are present in the Milky Way, each one dispersing its perspective, like a message in a bottle upon the sea, on the meaning of what is to be an island in the universe. Alas, in the vastness of the cosmos, a time-dependant inverse-square law applies to these memories, to history, and to knowledge.

Rotating from the memory of its last grazing influence with a foreign body nearly four thousand years ago, an asteroid glided through frictionless space. For over 200,000 years, since its creation from the passionate impact of its progenitors, this stone had drifted among the stars, among worlds so foreign to its own. The spacefaring rock showed evidence of wear along its oblique profile in the form of small craters. After all, it had spent hundreds of thousands of years in space. Once, it had even passed close to a space station endemic to the species of man.

The asteroid had recently become evoked by the gravitational field of a planet. This was not the first time this had happened, but now something was different. There was no turning back. Heat whipped at its russet and grey exterior. The asteroid was in complete freefell, heading toward the world. Internal pressures of expanding gases fractured the icy rock's outer layers. Speeding nearer and nearer to the celestial sphere, the red-hot meteor reached its physical breaking point and exploded into a billion burning fragments. In that final burst of glory, lasting mere seconds, the ancient stone had been grated to dust against the dense atmosphere. A new life had been given to it; a new knowledge.

CHAPTER 49

IN THE THICK OF IT

Zoe and Darious reached the specified location within the hour. During their travel, the repeating higher-order communication had continued nonstop. Zoe could not trace the signal or gain any insight as to its origin. What was discomforting was the fact that it seemed to be transmitting throughout the entire galaxy. More than that, during their hour of travel, the signal's resonant nodes had been continuously lowering, like someone was turning down a dial, and now it could easily be perceived by any communications device. Everyone in the galaxy was undoubtedly at this moment reading the same message. All eyes would be upon this spot in space.

Zoe completed a quick scan of the surrounding region. It was void of life and nearby planetary systems, though she suspected not for long—not with the Copper Force on their tail and a galactic wide communication pointing toward a singular location, which they were centered on.

"What do you think Darious?" she asked.

"I am unsure Captain."

Zoe anchored her ship on the exact coordinates. She went over to Darious, who was at his computer station, and put her arms around him.

"Soon the CF will be here. I'm not sure what will happen either. But I know in my heart, we are meant to be here."

"Zoe," he said turning and looking up at her. "I strongly agree."

Zoe walked to the entryway of the main chamber and stared at the marvelous artifact still on the table. It was absolutely radiant. A beeping sound suddenly started from Zoe's console. Long-range scanners had picked up the first signs of inbound CF vessels.

"Here we go," said Zoe taking a seat. "Strap in." Darious nodded and secured himself as Zoe reviewed the scanners' analysis. Her hands twitched upon reading it. "Oh my. The… the entire CF is heading this way."

Thousands upon thousands of ships were converging on them from all directions.

"Orders, Captain?"

Her ship was still in lockdown mode from their recent encounter with the CF, so there was little to do. Zoe took in a deep breath. "We wait, Darious. We wait."

Soon enough, CF ships began to arrive on scene. First to arrive were interstellar fighters—heavy artillery first-responders purposed to intervene during a military crisis, to keep the peace, naturally. Next came the destroyers and dreadnaughts. Hundreds, then thousands, of ships dotted the region. The nearest battalions immediately locked their weapons onto Zoe's craft, but none powered them up. The sheer size of the CF's army imprinted upon Zoe the true scale of a *galactic* force. The CF hailed twice, but Zoe didn't accept any messages from them, knowing full well the dirty tricks that could be accomplished through normal communications.

"There are so many crafts, Zoe," said Darious from his station.

"Never mind your console. Come over and take a look," she said. "There's no way we are going anywhere today." Darious sat next to her, staring out in awe. Just from their sample of space, beyond the cockpit window, thousands of ships with gleaming metal and blinking lights filled the night sky; the closest bearing their ammo teeth while the further, larger ones loomed as brown dwarfs in the shadows.

"Well, I don't know about you, but I've never been the center of so much attention." Zoe smirked, though internally she could feel small flickers of dread.

A high-pitched alert came from her computer. Zoe quickly centered it on her main screen. "The Z-Pulsers." The galactic-wide transmission had just been altered and a new communication sequence was now coming through. Zoe typed into her console, bringing up the message. It made no sense. The communication seemed scrambled; it was a bizarre string of letters and numbers. Suddenly alerts rang out. The CF fleets had begun powering their weapon banks and charging shields. Zoe brought up her various scanning utilities.

"What are they doing!?" exclaimed Darious. "It is not us; we have not moved a millimeter!"

"No, look," said Zoe, pointing to her projection console. Out in the space around them, something was starting to happen. Her sensors were barely picking up the change. It was like a whisper in the foggy night. Zoe had a flash of insight and booted up Dr. Saknussemm's program. She synced its resonance rhythms to the incoming Z-Pulser message. *Bingo.* It was a match.

"An attempt at contact?" she asked herself.

Zoe's thoughts were abruptly arrested as small dots of white light began to speckle cosmic space. In the gaps between CF vessels, small but brilliantly bright nodes of light ignited across the eternal night, illuminating the many ships in the area. From these light sources, Zoe could now see the true extent of the CF. Vessels shone as far as the eye could see to a horizon that never ended.

The light-points intensified, each a tiny pin-prick version of a star. Continuous alerts cropped up on Zoe's screen; every CF ship was powering up weapons, but she ignored them, instead remaining captivated by the sight around her. There was a sudden flash and all the lights simultaneously vanished. Blackness once more surrounded them and Zoe, realizing she had been starving herself of breath, gulped down several large lungfuls.

Suddenly, a proximity warning covered the entirety of her console, signaling an enormous mass was about to impact the bow of her ship. The alert disappeared, reappeared, and then disappeared again. Zoe was quick on the controls, ready to burst-fire her ship's thrusters, but she didn't see anything in front of her.

"What the hell?" she said. At that moment, a bright white light flared up right in front of the cockpit window. Zoe jumped in her seat and covered her eyes. The light pulsed several times, sending blinding flashes throughout her ship.

"Damnit!" she shouted. "What the hell is that?!"

Just as soon as the light began, it disappeared, along with the proximity sirens. As Zoe's vision returned, she dared to look out again. Suddenly, at quite a distance away, the same light reappeared, near a large CF vessel. It pulsated several times before disappearing again. Then the light appeared again, this time off to her portside. Then two appeared. Then three. Zoe's heartbeat quickened.

She overlapped all her scanning programs, synced them to the cadencies of Dr. Saknussemm's algorithm, and gasped at what was revealed onscreen. There were more than blinking lights emerging into existence.

"Darious, something is coming. A lot of somethings."

CHAPTER 50

THE WATCHERS

Another bright light ignited just off Zoe's starboard bow. The radiance lit up her cockpit with brilliant whites and blues. Zoe's muscles tensed, and she saw Darious grip the armrest tight. Then a new blinking light appeared to their portside. Right after, three more sparked into existence.

"Zoe."

She didn't respond. This was a lot to process and it was time to put the processing power of her computer to work. She had to understand more about what was happening around them. More intense surges popped into view. The metallic hulls of CF ships glinted and flashed as light-points continued appearing around them. Zoe squinted her eyes to properly see her projection console.

"Zoe."

"Darious, I'm tracing out hundreds, no thousands of..."

"Of what?" he asked.

"Oh shit," she said in a breathless voice.

"Zoe, Zoe what is it?"

"A node has begun here. It's centered right on us."

Zoe knew what she had to do.

"We must move away!" uttered Darious. He leapt out of Zoe's chair toward his station.

"No, Darious, it's all around us. I think I can enhance the Saknussemm Field. If they don't know we are here, they will soon."

An illuminating haze began to fill the cockpit. Zoe took a quick glance around them. It was like a creeping fog, expanding throughout the cabin and working its way toward the main chamber. As Zoe typed on her console, her virtual keyboard started to evidence a sort of halo effect, very much like the helical statue.

"Zoe."

"Thirty more seconds Darious." She chanced to look out and saw that space had filled with the flashing lights. She gasped. They were growing! The lights now looked like contained bubbles of radiance expanding into one another. Zoe continued typing as fast as she could. "Come on. Come on," she whispered to herself.

The illumination within the cockpit was becoming unbearable. Zoe could barely see her own hands. *Come on!* She was attempting to synchronize her Z-Pulsers with the foreign transmissions and send back a message of her own, simply stating 'Welcome to the galaxy.' Finishing just moments later, Zoe closed her burning eyes and pressed enter.

As every bit of surrounding outer-space was enveloped by the refulgence, as the white fog completely permeated Zoe's ship, as she and Darious both exhaled one last time, their reality exploded. In that moment, pure achromatic light completely overtook Zoe's spaceship, quenching every shadow with intensity beyond the fathomable. Just as soon as the extreme light began, it ended, and all illumination evaporated. Zoe was blinded.

"Darious, Darious where are you?"

"Here, Zoe."

She felt her way up the seat, finding his hand and firmly gasping it. Zoe's vision slowly returned, at first only granting a blurred view of her surroundings. She squinted her eyes and stared out from the cockpit. All the lights were gone. She could only make out the nearest ships from the CF fleet. She rubbed her eyes.

"Zoe, what happened?"

Still holding Darious' hand, Zoe stood up to face him, only to freeze as soon as she made eye contact.

"Zoe? Zoe what is it?"

'*It*' was inside the ship.

"Zoe?"

"Darious. Darious slowly, slowly turn around."

She let go of his hand and cautiously moved past him to the entryway of the central chamber. In the middle of the room there was a dark shadow in the form of a tall, slender figure. It had specks of light shining throughout it, like glinting diamonds strung up and turning in a breeze. Zoe took several quick glances around the room. She then entered inward, never blinking; her full attention focused on the curious umbra. Very carefully, she edged around it until she had completed a full circle. She could not spot the source of the shadow. What was more eerie than that, as she had turned around the object was that, it seemed to have a rigid three-dimensionality to it.

"Amazing," Zoe said.

It was a confined visual obscurity, like a nebula in a bottle, yet it remained contained without the bottle. Darious came into the main chamber, just past the entry but no further. Zoe lifted a finger to touch the shadow.

"What are you?"

She carefully felt it with her fingertip and quickly withdrew her hand. The digit felt as though it had pierced through a partition of cold mist. She examined her finger, but it did not look damp in the least. Zoe sharpened her eyes, staring at the mirage-like figure. Its shadowy presence imparted an ominous impression but its lack of motion eased Zoe's nervousness. Her mind was in full gear, going through every stored memory for a cue or a clue as to what it was. Nothing.

"Hmmph," she said, peering in closer at the enigma.

Zoe lifted the same finger to prod it once more. As she slowly raised her arm, the shadow began to branch out, perpendicularly lifting a limb from its middle section, exactly mirroring her motions. Zoe yelped and jumped back but was quick to step forward, keen on maintaining her standing rank, and stared intently at the specter. It had put back down its appendage and was once more still. Zoe repeated her same movements and again the shadow copied them. She then put her hand forward and closed all her fingers except her pointer finger, slowly extending it toward the ethereal mass. It continued to match her gestures. The end of shadow's limb lengthened, becoming a fine line, as if it were outstretching a finger of its own to meet hers.

Their digits connected at the tips. Zoe gulped. A thought suddenly sparked in her mind, outshining all others. The shadow was alive. That was *in fact* a finger touching hers. She remained still, her hair on edge. Though not human, the figure was shaped to similar, albeit taller and slimmer, proportions. There was a definite, distinct intelligence here on her craft. The thought sallied Zoe's consciousness, resounding in her mind. Non-human origin—*alien*. She suddenly felt light on her feet as if she would swoon and faint. Zoe shattered through her self-hypnosis and did her best to shake off the remaining pieces. She straightened her shoulders, placing her arms at her sides, ready to test her hypothesis.

Zoe sidestepped the figure and brought out her lightcard. She raised it up to the shadow, which once more had become motionless, yet now, she felt as though it was watching her. Zoe's lightcard lit up with the scan results and she smirked, still in a half-baked state of mind.

"It seems, my non-human friend, you are not wholly here." Zoe suddenly felt an epiphany dawn on her. "Shit! You're not wholly here!"

She scrambled past an awed Darious and was quickly at her main console typing. She returned to the main chamber momentarily, shoulder-to-shoulder with Darious. Staring at the shadow, Zoe spoke to Darious, "I've set the Z-Pulsers to fire a small energetic node at our guest." Zoe pressed enter on her lightcard.

The figure suddenly became very sporadic. Sections of it lightened while others deepened in tone. Within the shadow, it looked like a complex series of woven lines. Streaks of pointed light shot out across the room. Zoe held Darious' hand as Dr. Saknussemm's algorithm, fed into the Z-Pulsers, detangled the entity from its offset vibrations. The phantom began pulsating, flickering in and out of sight, though becoming darker each time it flashed back to reality. Zoe looked at her lightcard and cranked up the energy output of the Z-Pulsers. Energy arced across the shadow as if it were a Tesla coil. The figure began to solidify; the cloud surrounding it was fading and a definite hominid form was beginning to take shape. Zoe's jaw descended lower and lower. A lifeform was coming into existence before them.

Zoe turned the energy to max and a shockwave burst out from the entity, knocking both Darious and her to the ground. The main chamber was instantly filled with smoke. Zoe coughed as she stood back up. The haze was too thick to see anything. She slowly started to move forward with an outstretched arm, feeling her way. She stopped cold as her hand encountered something unidentifiable. It felt warm, strong with a dense, complex structure underneath yet soft to the touch. In her mind's eye the only thing she could picture was skin stretched over tightly interwoven muscles of an arm, but it was not Darious' arm. Zoe breathed heavily. She dared not move. The mysterious limb slowly retracted in the presence of her fingers. It was sliding backwards, becoming smaller and smaller until it was something different altogether at her fingertips. Zoe's hand was shaking. She could feel a profile of skin and bone slowly work its way into her hand. Once it was at her palm, it began blossoming with singular digits, opening her hand with it. Zoe could feel long, thin fingers unraveling opposite hers. Her whole body trembled. The fingers straightened, extending beyond Zoe's, and their fleshy palms connected. The entire hand felt warm to her, warmer than that of a human's.

The ship's filters worked rapidly. The hand—and the being connected to it—emerged from the fog. Before Zoe stood a tall figure, very thin with stringy limbs. Its skin was brown, a deep Earth-1 tone. She could not tell if the entity was wearing some sort of body suit or was simply nude. If it was the latter, it was completely hairless and without any semblance of sexual organs. Elongated ribs shown along the being's chest. Tightly wrapped around its neck were connected rods of celestial blues with a single pendant hanging down from them that looked like a dark planet with specks of silver. Zoe looked up at the face; it was humanoid, but also very much elongated. Her heart dithered as she gazed at the eyes. They were so large; they too looked like black worlds.

With a long graceful movement of its torso, the alien closed its hand around the ornament it wore and bowed to Zoe and Darious. Zoe was in complete amazement. It then stood straight, towering over the pair. In an odd tenor, elongated like its physical body, the being spoke.

"Welcomme to the galaxy."

Zoe marveled at the alien. All she could manage to say was, "ha."

The being turned in a smooth, flowing motion and picked up the halo statue from the table. With superlatively graceful movements, it bent to one knee and presented the offering to Zoe with its head bowed. Zoe gulped. She slowly stepped forward and carefully took the statue, bowing her head, and then looked at the alien.

"Thank you. I shall put it on my mantle." Zoe immediately wanted to smack her forehead. *Mantle? Really?*

The alien stood and in a single fluid stride, as if gliding on a cloud, stepped past Zoe to Darious and bowed to him. Darious, who hadn't moved a muscle the entire time, attempted to reciprocate with a bow of his own, though his body remained rigid and his arms were stuck at his sides, thus transforming his gesture into more of an awkward bending kink than a cordial courtesy.

"Friennd, welcomme to the galaxy," the alien spoke.

"Si-r," said Darious, nearly tripping over the single-syllable reply. He held out his hand to the alien. Zoe, still in a sidereal bewilderment, couldn't help but smirk at Darious' manners. However, to her surprise, the alien put forward its own long hand and grasped Darious', giving it a single oscillatory shake. The being then strode past the pair, making its way to the cockpit and coming to a stop before the window to space. Beyond lay the awaiting CF fleet. Zoe followed at a couple paces behind and too stared out at the view.

The being pointed an elongated finger to the armada of destroyers, cruisers, and warships.

"Welcomme themm to the galaxy," it said.

Zoe understood. She snuck under the arm of the tall individual and took to her captain's seat. She began typing on the projection console, swiveling the Z-Pulsers back out and loading them with the same settings which had brought their new friend onboard. She enlarged the field of dispersion to cover the entirety of space around them. Darious had carefully made his way past the alien and was at the back of Zoe's chair, looking over her shoulder. The Z-Pulser modifications were quickly set up and Zoe pressed enter, sending out Dr. Saknussemm's signal to the stars.

"Resonance for the masses," said Zoe.

Looking out, she could see a shift in the eternal darkness, like fleeting shadows in a moonless night, and then it was as if knots of space began trembling around them.

"Oh my...," breathed Darious.

Unseen vessels about the region started to register on the ship's sensors, fully becoming in sync with reality. They were everywhere. Twisting nodes of filamentary light became the first hints of physical structures and soon entire alien ships emerged. They gleamed with halo bands, illuminating space with a fuzzy, yet gentle glow.

An alert chimed from Zoe's computer. Though this time, it was not due from missiles being fired, or some other impending disaster.

"The CF—they are powering down their weapons," Zoe said. She typed into her console. "Information is being sent back and forth between CF ships and the alien ships."

Zoe opened her communication ports. Messages of peace and welcoming from both sides pervaded through the speakers of the small cockpit. Zoe looked over at the being standing next to her. It tilted its long head down in her direction. She couldn't tell if it was smiling or not, but she somehow got the feeling that everything was finally going to be okay. Zoe looked up at Darious and smiled.

CHAPTER 51

THE AGE OF
ENLIGHTENMENT V2.0

"Just this afternoon, the newly appointed ambassador for mankind signed the first draft of a galactic treaty with the Vasherasnew—which linguists tell us translates to the 'Watchers,'" said the female news anchor, standing on the steps of the massive building bearing the Copper Force logo. "This comes after the revelation, just two days ago, that mankind is not alone in the galaxy. It is now known, through initial diplomatic meetings with the newcomers, that they have been occupying a higher reality of our shared space—a previously unknown higher island-of-stability form of matter and energy. They are now ready to join in everlasting, mutual unionship with humanity. Renewed excitement is abounding throughout the galaxy as new concepts are being exchanged, new technologies are being pursued together, and new friendships are being cultivated. Undoubtedly, we are at the dawn of a new age for mankind.

"This comes alongside the exposure of government corruption at the highest levels. Earlier, the recently promoted Admiral Vere of the CF gave the following statement:"

The video feed cut to an earlier recorded press conference, where a distinguished Admiral Edward Vere was standing in front of a podium addressing the media.

His gaze was set past the reporters as he spoke, as if he was truly speaking to an audience beyond the horizon. "The CF has concluded its investigations into the violations of galactic rights by senior diplomats and has arrested those at fault. The Magistrate official, commonly known as the 'Grandeur,'" a photograph appeared on the screen of the large green man with his ostentatious gems, "took his own life when the arrest warrant was issued for his particular crimes. Charges against the Grandeur include: intimidation, bribery, murder, and gross abuse of granted powers. Additionally, the CF has discovered that the Grandeur had been a prior leading body of Pantheon Industries and used his diplomatic influence to aid the company by illicit means. Raids and supplementary arrests have been conducted at Pantheon Industries and investigations are currently underway as to the depth of corruption within the company.

"We now know that the common material, Kapteyn, exclusively sold by Pantheon Industries and its subsidiaries, was never actually manufactured by them. This space-faring technology has, in fact, been stolen from the Vasherasnew for possibly thousands of years.

"Immediately, conveyance of apologies and regret for the ongoings of Pantheon Industries were extended to our new allies. The Vasherasnew have been more than amenable to all that has happened and have agreed to bilateral trade and technology accommodations. Humanity will continue to flourish among the stars."

Admiral Vere paused for a moment and then continued.

"Pantheon Industries had undertaken a massive campaign to conceal its many illegal activates. Current charges against the company include: bribery, large-scale price collusion, blackmail, murder, and the systematic altering of records from galactic informational repositories, including government databases."

"The CF has uncovered evidence that the Grandeur and his past family lineage, under the banner of Pantheon Industries and its former headings, had been waging a secret war against the Vasherasnew." Admiral Vere now turned his attention directly to the cameras facing him. "I must apologize on behalf of the CF. We had been fooled. We have let down the galaxy and all its citizens which we are sworn to protect. We now know the Grandeur and company had concocted a scheme to eradicate an entire intelligent species for the sake of amassing Kapteyn unimpeded. This would have been xenocide on the grandest of scales. I must again offer our sincerest apologies to the Vasherasnew. They have shown supreme restraint throughout the entire ordeal. For many centuries, Pantheon Industries has been tracking and stealing Vasherasnew material property. The Vasherasnew had responded only by peaceful means—by redirecting their reserves and safely sabotaging the ongoing thievery. Their composure and strength of will is most commendable.

"In addition, during our investigations, we have obtained evidence which directly implicates an Enemy of the Galaxy, Dr. Earl Saknussemm, as an unwilling accomplice of the Grandeur's plans.

"Dr. Saknussemm, a brilliant physicist, had been selected by the Grandeur so that he could learn more about higher-resonant space and how to impress upon massive select media within it. Upon the Doctor's discovery of the Grandeur's impending course of action to utilize this information to distress intelligent life within it to the point of likely dissociation, he refused to continue research and was subsequently forced into hiding. He was hunted by proxies of the Grandeur and Pantheon Industries.

"For many years, Dr. Saknussemm has been categorized by the CF as an 'Enemy of the Galaxy.' Stories about his extremist ideals and terrorist actions are just that, 'stories,' invented by these parties and maliciously inserted into government archives. From deep-field probes, the CF has found no actual evidence of the Doctor's alleged treachery. Unfortunately, we are too late to protect Dr. Saknussemm.

"Dr. Saknussemm is henceforth innocent of all charges. In fact," Admiral Vere straightened his stance, "Dr. Saknussemm is a hero and I am here to announce that the CF formally awards him the Medal of Galactic Honor. A statue is to be erected in the Cassiopeian System in honor of the late Doctor." He saluted. "We, at the Copper Force, thank you, Dr. Saknussemm, for your efforts to which you have made the ultimate sacrifice.

"We must also thank Dr. Saknussemm for his work in reaching beyond what was once thought to be the limits of our existence to another. From his work, the Grandeur could have annihilated an entire species, yet it is also from this work that a deeper understanding of higher-resonant space has come to be. It is due to his efforts and the efforts of those two brave explorers that we have been introduced to our new galactic allies."

The news feed cut back to the reporter. "Admiral Vere went on to thank Ms. Zoe Halloconst and Mr. Darious Designate 1-Alpha-011-.2.2, who overcame great odds, and at the risk of their own lives, to expose the corruption and bring to light the Watchers. During an earlier interview with the two, when asked what prompted them to go on such a daring scientific journey, Ms. Zoe said, 'verve, nerve, and adventure.' Back to you Tom."

The camera flicked over to a genial man in a suit sitting behind a desk. "Thanks Stacie. Coming after the break: where and when can you meet our new neighbors; and later, does the Tune Squad have what it takes to win it all? Stay with us to find out."

CHAPTER 52

ENDLESS SKY

Zoe turned off the galactic report from her screen. Subtle music resumed in the background—a tranquil, bass-infused melody. Darious was lounging with her, hand in hand, in the captain's seat.

"Well," said Zoe stretching, "no longer just a 'clone,' eh *Mr.* Darious?" She smiled.

"Indeed. Out of many, I am now conveyed as an individual. An honor," stated Darious.

Zoe stared out at space. The stars gleamed, and the band of the Milky Way seemed to shine brighter than she had remembered. Zoe was glad the last few days of interviews and being paraded around the galaxy were over. Finally, she and Darious could just relax with one another. As she held his hand and settled back, her mind replayed all the recent happenings.

When she had sent out Dr. Saknussemm's signal, Vasheras-new—Watcher—ships had arisen not only within the region, but simultaneously all throughout the galaxy. It must have been quite the shock for everyone. For the most part, it was a peaceful emergence. She was glad for that. Now humans were not alone. As the news report had stated, already joint efforts were underway to expand each's understanding of the universe. For people everywhere, the discovery that the space they occupied contained another corporeal island of stability opened up the possibility of others, perhaps even more far flung; perhaps there was an infinity of overlapping realities. Fantasies of the unknown were once more at the forefront of mankind's thoughts. From here on out, the terms 'explorer,' 'adventurer,' and 'mad scientist' might not even be as rare as they once were. Zoe smiled at the thought.

"You know, Hot Sauce," she said, "turns out starry Vere wasn't so bad after all. The CF just took a bit longer than I would have liked to figure things out for themselves."

"Indeed," said Darious, staring lazily through the window. He held up her hand and gave it a soft kiss. "What is next for us, Captain?"

"Ha. Well, I'm not sure. Lunch on Ganymede? Or a tour of Earth-1? Oh! How about a delectable Carnegie Cosmo while we watch the sun set on Luna-9?"

"Yes, yes, and yes," said Darious.

Zoe sat up and began typing on her console. However, she stopped before engaging the thrusters. Taking Darious' hand in her own again, she leaned toward him and rested her head on his shoulder. Together, they silently gazed out at the endless sky.

CHAPTER 53

EPILOGUE: THE IMPERIAL BOWER

A streak of cosmic lightning arced across the bow, causing both Zoe and Darious to jump simultaneously. Instantly, alerts rang out and red text flashed across the projection screen. As Zoe scanned through the readout, her ship was suddenly jerked aside from its anchored position, as if it had just been struck by a shockwave. The computer indicated that an immense energy fluctuation had just occurred, the nature of which was unknown. Zoe diminished the data and pivoted her ship to re-align the cockpit with the unidentified celestial disturbance. To her complete amazement, a ship came into view. It was a small spacecraft with a sleek profile.

"Zoe," said Darious, likewise awestruck. "That vessel has a very similar appearance to your ship."

She continued to stare at it. The ship was *very* similar to hers, except for some obvious minor differences to the primary thruster array, some sort of antenna system atop it, and scarring along the starboard side, like it had recently come in close contact with another vessel.

"What the—," Zoe began.

Just then, they were hailed by the ship. Before answering, Zoe did a quick scan of the vessel. To her somewhat surprise, her ship's computer registered it as her own and looped the information back to her own ship's characteristics.

"Hmmph," she grumbled. "It seems to be blocking our scans."

They were hailed again and this time she picked up.

"Zoe?" a woman's voice crackled through a low-quality microphone.

"Yes, ma'am," said Zoe. "And to whom am I speaking to?"

"Allow me to come aboard your vessel."

Zoe looked over at Darious and he reciprocated her skeptical expression.

"T'sk t'sk. Introductions first."

"Zoe, I swear sometimes I am just the worst." The call abruptly ended.

"Curiouser and curiouser," said Zoe.

A sudden tinny popping sound came from behind Zoe and Darious. Startled, they spun around. Standing at the entryway to the cockpit was a woman in sable combat gear, approximately Zoe's height and with long dark hair covering half her face.

Darious was quick to place himself in front of Zoe and held up his fists. "Stay back!" he shouted.

"Darious. Oh Darious!" the woman chirped in a happy, longing tone. She took a step forward with arms out, as if to embrace him, but withdrew and instead stayed at the entryway with her hands fixed to either side of it. A serious expression grew upon her face as she looked past Darious to Zoe.

"Well, missy," the woman said in a condescending tone. "Here I am, invited or not."

Zoe stepped up next to Darious. "And just who are you?" she asked.

"The one person you would never expect to meet in the entire universe: yourself."

"Myself...," repeated Zoe, eyeing the woman. She could not yet guesstimate the amount of craziness of the militarized person standing before her, but obviously this woman did possess some sort of remarkable space-leaping technology to be able to teleport onboard ships. This was new technology, at least to Zoe's knowledge, and thus her 'guest' probably had some advanced know-how to go along with it. Zoe put a hand over Darious' raised fists. He lowered them, but kept a hard stance. "Please, go on."

"Thank you." The woman brushed her hair back and Zoe saw her cheek was scarred and her neck had deep-tissue bruising. "I am you, from the future." Zoe felt an unexpected eerie sensation arise within her. "You are to go there. The tools you require will be at the coordinates found on your 'lightcard'—as you call it—within subsection B, the tilting parameters of your False Gamma Routine. They should become available right about now."

Just then, Zoe's lightcard dinged. She pulled it out and a string of text appeared across the screen.

Time delayed FG module loading. Coordinates available. FG executable available.

Zoe reread the words in astonishment, gulping back down her nerves. "Okay. Okay. That was odd." She looked at the woman. "When and how did you put that in there? I always have my lightcard on me."

The woman smiled. It was somehow familiar to Zoe.

"Let's back up a bit by going forward."

"No, no," said Zoe. "No tricky jargon and no funny 'time travel' shenanigans." Zoe had put up air quotes to the term 'time travel.' Of all her years in college and all her subsequent education, time travel had always been, at most, an abstract idea used mostly by professors to teach students about metaphysics. Untestable, unverifiable, and unstable concepts were the best that had come about from the theoretical community. No realistic experiment had ever even been conceived to assess such notions. *But then again*, thought Zoe, *if you were from the future, you'd have time to fig-ure out those things.* She shook her head. "No."

"Your lightcard," said the woman, pointing to the device in Zoe's hands.

"What about it?" Zoe looked down at it.

"It's a piece of future tech, manufactured from the fiftieth century onward and utilized to operate ancient computer tech-nology—the technology of today. I gave it to you."

"You... what?" asked Zoe.

"I snuck it to you in a trash pile on Gamma-9 when you were first building your ship." That uncanny feeling within Zoe swirled in her stomach. "There have been others though—other aions from us—lost in time. I know this because the CF has acquired some, no doubt from those of us who have traveled far back and have unfortunately left theirs there. Smart for the Coppers to keep those devices locked away in vaults."

Zoe opened her mouth. "The Grandeur," she near whispered.

"Yes," said the woman. "He had taken one of our aions."

Zoe spoke slowly. "In what future would I have the need for such a program as he had—to be able to wirelessly torture a per-son with the touch of a button?"

The woman grimaced. "There are dark days ahead, Zoe, know that. However, also understand that you are intertwined with the universe's past, present, and future far more than you can imag-ine. Your influence upon it is of many intertwining paths, much like the artifact gifted to you from the Watchers."

Zoe thought of the halo statue which she had bestowed upon her old university just yesterday. "And why can't you just do it then, eh?" she asked dubiously.

"I cannot. I have been mortally wounded and cannot continue."

"You don't seem to be," said Zoe, again looking the woman up and down.

"I assure you I am, even though I do not appear to be. I have failed. I knew I would come here to tell you all this, to begin the circles. In 36 hours I will be dead. I also know this because I have already seen the outcome. There is nowhere for me to go, no time I can try. My path is at its end."

Zoe thought for a moment. "'Begin the circles?'"

"Yes. I am the first, but I know I am not the last. You will try many attempts... with many failures."

"How many?"

The woman took in a long breath. "I have recorded direct signatures of over 140."

Zoe nearly chocked on her own saliva. "You mean I am going to die 140 times?" She snickered. "You are positively insane!"

"No," said the woman in an austere tone. The air in the ship suddenly seemed to become quite cold and still. "I anticipate we will die many more. These are just the ones I have been able to identify and like I said, this is my first go at it. I do not know how many attempts have led to this moment now of our meeting—to you. There may be hundreds, even thousands of failed attempts by us. The problem is obviously not yet solved and even now we are continuously spreading amongst time; each new iteration of us thinking of new ways to stop that man, with new circles and new casualties. Our ashes are spread all across the galaxy; all throughout time."

"This is a lot to take in," said Zoe. "And I'm no time travel expert. Wouldn't all of this have already happened then? I don't get it."

"You certainly have much to learn about traveling through time, but in the end, it boils down to harmonic physics. And who better than me?" The woman gave a small, held-back smile. "Do I have your attention now?"

Zoe gave a half-hearted nod. She was taking in the information in strides. It was slowly being processed through her logical parts and from what had been articulated and witnessed in the last five minutes, Zoe could see a potential, albeit far-fetched, possibility of truth to what the mysterious woman was saying.

Her self-proclaimed future-self looked over at Darious and a sad smile came upon her lips. "You, however, will be sitting this one out. Oh, how I've missed you." She looked as though she wanted so badly to wrap her arms around him.

"What do you mean?" asked Zoe.

The woman turned to Zoe and nearly snarled. "One hundred and forty-three deaths," she said with such anger and such pain. "I would not wish that upon my worst enemy. You know what is right." Her expression eased as she turned back to Darious and her demeanor was once more soothed. The woman then stared straight at Zoe and all evidence of her cheerfulness vanished.

"In the future, specifically the 53rd century, an evil man, a truly evil man," the woman hissed the words, "cracks the longstanding hyperbole of time-dimensional travel. He is the Imperial Bower. He threatens to alter the entire galaxy to his twisted liking with this technology. Moreover, as you will see, connected to this threat further in the future, there are machine men—disengaged creatures which threaten all life. If they get their metallic claws on this technology, it will be all over for mankind. It will be over for everyone and everything in every corner of time. You must stop him before this happens and before further damage can be done. Right now, you are the only other one that unlocks this ability—the ability to time travel."

"How is this so?" Zoe asked.

That familiar smile edged upon the woman's face. "Oh, you know, a bit of your own resonance ingenuity and a bit of 'borrowing.'"

Zoe internally reflected on the information presented. "How about using the CF? I mean, I assume this is a job for them?"

"No," replied the woman. "There has been enough damage already. Can you imagine what the CF would do with the ability to time travel?"

"Good point," said Zoe.

"We must keep this particular circle small. The only people I trust are currently aboard this ship. Listen, Zoe, you must do this. Look to your aion; it will lead you where you need to go. You must save them all."

Before Zoe could think of a response, the woman pulled out a small rectangular device, much like her own lightcard, yet slightly modified and more impressive looking. The woman keyed a command and the sound of a bursting hollow canister immediately followed. In the moment Zoe had blinked, the woman was gone. She looked over at Darious and then ran to the cockpit. Zoe looked out; there was nothing there. She did a scan of the region; she and Darious were alone.

Sitting in her captain's seat, Zoe soon became mentally enthralled by the singular event. For many minutes, she was consumed by hypothetical what-ifs before regaining an awareness of her surroundings. She cleared her mind, taking in a deep breath and turned to Darious, who had appropriated a seat on the arm of her chair. Zoe smirked.

"That look," she said waving a finger at him. "I know that look."

"Then you already know what I am thinking," he said.

"Could be dangerous."

"Indeed," he replied.

"Well then, shall we?"

He gave her a single nod.

Zoe loaded the coordinates from the 'aion' and plotted their course. "Let's see what all this hubbub is about."

Zoe engaged thrusters and the bantam ship rocketed forward. She looked ahead with Darious, their journey etched in the stars.

ABOUT THE AUTHOR

Greg Remy is a physicist and science fiction enthusiast. He lives in New Mexico among the coyotes and radio interferometers. When he's not soaking in the desert sun or a local brew, he's busy providing technical services to clients nationwide. At night, Greg's mind often wanders, leading him to imagine absurd and extraordinary solutions for the unknowns all around us.

gr.endlesssky@gmail.com

www.ingramcontent.com/pod-product-compliance
Lightning Source LLC
Chambersburg PA
CBHW071149250626
47159CB00001B/36